CHANCE ENCOUNTERS

CHANCE ENCOUNTERS

Rosie Harris

This first world edition published 2016
in Great Britain and the USA by
SEVERN HOUSE PUBLISHERS LTD of
19 Cedar Road, Sutton, Surrey, England, SM2 5DA.
Trade paperback edition first published
in Great Britain and the USA 2016 by
SEVERN HOUSE PUBLISHERS LTD

British Library Cataloguing in Publication Data
A CIP catalogue record for this title is available from the British Library.

ISBN-13: 978-0-7278-8640-8 (cased)
ISBN-13: 978-1-84751-741-8 (trade paper)
ISBN-13: 978-1-78010-806-3 (e-book)

All Severn House titles are printed on acid-free paper.

Severn House Publishers support the Forest Stewardship Council™ [FSC™],
the leading international forest certification organisation.
All our titles that are printed on FSC certified paper carry the FSC logo.

Typeset by Palimpsest Book Production Ltd.,
Falkirk, Stirlingshire, Scotland.
Printed and bound in Great Britain by
TJ International, Padstow, Cornwall.

For my youngest son . . . Keith

ACKNOWLEDGEMENTS

With grateful thanks to Caroline and Megan at the Caroline Sheldon Literary Agency, and to Severn House for all their support and hard work.

ONE

Megan Lloyd was bored.

A tall, slim girl with long, sleek, dark hair caught back in a bow at the nape of her neck, she was dressed in dark blue slacks and a green cotton top that reached to her hipline. Her expressive face with its high cheekbones, small, square chin and bright, dark eyes under their well-shaped brows normally gave her an alert, intelligent look but at the moment she looked discontented and unhappy.

It was August 1942 and she had just completed a three-year degree course at Aberystwyth University and was undecided about her future.

What she wanted to do immediately was to join up in one of the services and help her country like so many of her fellow students were already doing, but her father refused to give his permission for her to go ahead with her plans.

Her father, Lewis Lloyd, was the owner of a slate quarry in North Wales. A tall, broad man in his early fifties with a shock of thick black hair and piercing dark eyes, he was both wealthy and powerful. His family had lived in the area since the Middle Ages and their imposing grey stone ten-bedroom mansion Yr Glaslyn had been built in the 1600s.

Although the war had been raging between Germany and Britain since 1939 it had made very little difference to his way of life. As the owner of one of the largest slate mines in North Wales, he was held in high regard by his employees and, since many of them had allotments or large gardens, the wartime shortages and food rationing had not made very much difference to him or his way of life.

Items such as eggs, chicken, joints of lamb and pork, and even milk as well as vegetables and fruit in season, which many people were unable to buy because they were in short supply, or rationed, were brought along to him as tokens of their loyalty by the men who worked for him.

He accepted all this as a matter of right and consequently his family never went short of anything. Occasionally his wife Bronwyn, a small, dark-haired woman five years younger than Lewis, weakly protested about them accepting these items, but he would brush her remarks aside.

'Speak sense, woman, if they needed the stuff for themselves they wouldn't be bringing it along here for us now, would they?'

'They only do it because they want to keep in your good books,' she told him.

Lewis gave a derisory laugh. 'If that's the case then believe me they're wasting their time. They won't be getting a penny more in their pay packets from me just because they bring some trifling thing along and hand it to me.'

'You do pay them, I hope, Lewis, for the produce they bring in surely,' Bronwyn admonished.

'Half the time I don't know which of them has brought what in,' he said irritably. 'I leave it to the foreman to attend to that side of things and no doubt he takes his pick of what's been brought in before it's handed to me.'

'You should thank them personally, Lewis; it is very, very kind of them to give up items of food and for the wives to give up their clothing coupons just so that we can have more.'

'The women probably can't afford to buy new clothes anyway and as for the food, most of the fruit and vegetables they bring in is what they've grown themselves.'

'All the more reason for thanking them then,' she insisted.

'Nonsense! They probably have a glut of it and they would have to throw it on the midden or dig it back into the ground if they didn't give it to us.'

'No, Lewis, you know you are speaking nonsense,' Bronwyn told him, her small mouth tightening into an uncompromising line. 'What you're saying might have been true at one time, but these days what with rationing and shortages, every scrap of food is precious.'

'They would far rather be digging in their own gardens than fighting a war over in France,' he told her derisively.

'I'm sure they would but that doesn't mean we shouldn't say thank you to them for the sacrifice they are making.'

'It's their way of saying thank you to me for giving them the opportunity of working here in safety, in a reserved occupation, rather than being sent over to France or some other place where they'd be risking their necks in the midst of all the mud and bullets.'

Although the Blitz had been raging since 1940 with German bombers attacking London on fifty-seven consecutive nights, the only disruption that Lewis Lloyd was aware of was the occasional difficulties in transporting slate to other parts of the country or other areas of the world. So many of the larger seaports both in Britain and abroad had been bombed either by the Germans or by the Allied Air Forces. In addition, shipping was constantly under attack from the air as well as at risk from submarines.

Nevertheless, Lewis Lloyd was determined that his life would continue as smoothly as possible. Megan's twenty-first birthday party that April had been the highlight of the year in Beddgelert. It had fallen in the middle of the Easter vacation and all her university friends as well as her many local friends had been invited. For almost a week the Lloyds' mansion Yr Glaslyn had been filled with her friends from Aberystwyth. Lewis Lloyd had gone out of his way to regale them with tales about the history of his ancestors.

He was proud of the fact that his family dated back to the days of Llewellyn the Great and claimed that one of his relations had been present when the famous Prince Llewellyn had returned from a hunting trip and found that Gelert his faithful dog which he had left to guard his son was covered in blood.

Prince Llewellyn had immediately thought that the dog had attacked his small son and killed it. But after the dog had died he found the body of a wolf nearby and realized that his faithful dog had, in fact, saved the life of his son. Prince Llewellyn was so overcome by grief that he began digging a grave for the dog with his own hands and, according to legend, was often to be seen at the graveside where he watered it with his own tears.

Although Megan had returned to university immediately after her birthday, it had been her final term there and in no time at all her course ended. Degree achieved, her future hung in the balance.

Now her student life was over, everything seemed to her to be dull and uneventful. Most of her friends of her own age were already serving in the forces; boys in the Army, Navy or Air Force while the girls had joined the ATS or the WAAF or the Wrens. Some had even become Land Army girls working on farms throughout Britain.

All through July and August Megan lazed around playing tennis, partying, swimming, dancing and generally enjoying herself with those who were still awaiting their call-up papers or who were home on their first leave after completing their basic training.

Megan found that it was sheer torment to listen to their exploits and adventures and it made her all the more keen to join them, but no matter how many times she brought the subject up her father adamantly refused to even discuss her joining up.

She would have loved to become a Waaf or a Wren, but her father was strongly against it. To him she was still just a 'little girl', someone to protect from the harsh realities of life. He wouldn't even allow her to work in the offices of his own slate quarry.

'What do you think the men would think if I brought my daughter into work?' he intoned furiously. 'They'd think I was mad, that's what they would think. Anyway, it's quite unthinkable to have a woman working in a slate quarry.'

'I wouldn't be in the slate quarry working alongside the men,' Megan protested. 'I would be working in the office.'

'I don't have any women working in the office. I have young men training to become office managers or accountants. They start as office boys running errands, making the tea and doing the filing. You wouldn't want to be doing work of that nature, would you?'

'Well, there is a war on, Father, and by rights those young men should be in the forces. If you prefer to employ them then perhaps I ought to take their place and join up. A lot of my friends have already joined up,' she added pointedly.

'That will do! I have heard enough from you. I've already

told you, you are not coming to work at the quarry nor are you going to join any of the forces. Help your mother around the house and in the village. She'll find plenty for you to do and think yourself lucky that you are safe and that you don't have to suffer any hardships. Now that is the end of the matter and I don't want to hear another word about it.'

'I have a university degree in Economics,' Megan protested. 'What do you think I should do with that?'

'Put the certificate up on your bedroom wall and shut up. I don't want to hear any more. I have enough problems to deal with without some petty domestic quarrel taking over my mind,' he told her angrily.

Megan would have continued the argument but her mother who was also in the room motioned to her by placing a finger over her own lips to be quiet. Afterwards Bronwyn Lloyd took her daughter aside and counselled her not to aggravate her father any further.

'He has a lot of problems to deal with down at the quarry,' she told her seriously. 'So many of the ships that he uses to transport slate to other countries have been involved in incidents of one kind or another while at sea; some have even been sunk with all their cargo on board.'

'I'm very sorry to hear that but it still makes no difference to what I want to do; in fact it makes it all the more urgent. I want to do something constructive; something to help in the war effort. I don't want to sit at home while all my friends are in the services and doing war work of some kind or the other. If he doesn't want me to join the forces then at least he could let me help in his office.'

'No, *cariad*, that wouldn't be at all appropriate. If you are so anxious to help in the war effort then why not write to our boys overseas and help others to send them parcels of food or books and magazines and cigarettes and anything else you can think of. I am sure that your father will be happy to provide funds for you to do that.'

'Mother, I'm twenty-one not an old dear of seventy. I wonder you haven't suggested that I knit socks or scarves or something for the soldiers.'

'Well, *cariad*, that might be no bad thing either. I'm sure they need those sorts of items now that the winter is coming on. I know that some of the ladies in the village are doing just that and they would certainly welcome a new recruit.'

'I was joking!' She put her arms around her mother and kissed her to try and take the sting out of her words. She could tell how worried her mother was by the fact she had used the endearment in Welsh.

When she had been a child, Megan recalled, they had always spoken in Welsh but never since she had been at university.

'Well, it would certainly keep your father happy if he knew that was what you were doing. Think carefully about it, Megan. Your father is very concerned about your future. You have a lovely home here and you can invite your friends to come and stay any time you wish. Your father is very good to you and gives you a generous monthly allowance; probably far more than you would be able to earn if you went out to work. Certainly more than you would get in the forces.'

Megan didn't bother to argue. She knew that all this was true but it made no difference to the way she felt about what she wanted to do at the moment. Later, when the war was over, she would comply with her father's wishes for her to become a schoolteacher or anything else he asked her to do. For the moment she wanted to play her part in helping to win the war.

Lewis Lloyd's determination to protect her from the grim realities of the war only made her all the more keen to leave home even if it meant using devious means to do so.

Early in October 1942 she made up her mind to do something positive. She told her parents that she was going to spend a few days with one of her friends from Aberystwyth University who was now a schoolteacher.

She deliberately did not tell them that the friend lived in Liverpool because she knew that her father would forbid her to go there because of all the bombing that had taken place there over the last few months.

Even so, her father was immediately suspicious of her intentions.

'How long are you planning to stay with this friend?' he asked.

'About a week; she has a week off because it's half term,' Megan explained.

Her father looked at her so quizzically she was afraid he had seen through her plan. Her heart was beating so fast and so loud that she thought he must be able to hear it.

Reluctantly he agreed to her going but only on the proviso that she would not take advantage of being away from home to join any of the services. Solemnly she gave her promise that she would not do so.

It was a promise she had no intention of keeping. She intended to discover some way that she could play a useful part in the war. Her conscience wouldn't allow her to sit around doing nothing for the rest of the war. She wanted to play an active part. She knew that joining the forces was impossible because her father would take steps to have her discharged, but she was sure there were other things that she could do apart from those her mother had suggested.

It was difficult to find out what these might be while living in such a remote spot as Beddgelert but in a large city like Liverpool there would be several places such as a Citizen's Advice Bureau or even the Unemployment Offices where she would be able to obtain the kind of information she needed.

TWO

M egan was shocked when she arrived at Lime Street station; she stared around her wondering if she really was at the right place. Liverpool looked so very different from when she last visited there.

Her friend Audrey Wilson was waiting for her on the platform. Although the same height as Megan, Audrey was much plumper and had dark blonde hair that hung straight to her shoulders. She was smiling broadly as she greeted Megan.

When Megan expressed surprise at her surroundings, Audrey shrugged her plump shoulders and reminded her that

Liverpool had suffered very badly from bombing raids during the past year.

As they left Lime Street station Megan was horrified at the sight of the devastation that had been wrought on the city by the German bombing raids. Stores where on her previous visits she and Audrey had spent happy hours browsing; cafés where they had stopped for coffee or a snack as well as offices of all kinds had either vanished or were so badly damaged that they looked like piles of rubble.

Even the people they met or passed seemed to be different from the last time she had been in Liverpool, Megan mused. Most of them looked weary, as though they hadn't had a good night's sleep for weeks. Their clothes seemed drab, wrinkled and uncared for, almost as if they'd been sleeping in them.

They probably had, she thought, and it sent shivers through her and made her all the more determined to become involved in the war effort.

'You seem to have been very fortunate, your house is still all right,' Megan commented when they turned into the street where Audrey lived.

'Yes, we've been very lucky in this part of Liverpool,' Audrey agreed. 'We're far enough away from the docks and not near enough to the industrial area for the bombers to bother about us. Mind you, we did have to spend many nights in our shelter for weeks at a time and we did have damage from bomb blast. Several times we lost our windows and tiles off the roof but that was nothing compared with what some folks had to contend with; sadly a great many of them didn't survive, especially when their homes received a direct hit.'

The two girls spent the next few hours catching up with news of what they had been doing since they had last seen each other. Then Megan explained to Audrey the underlying reason for her visit.

'Why don't you just get a job in one of the companies who are engaged in war work?' Audrey suggested.

'You mean in an office helping to do the accounts and keep the books or something of that sort?'

'Well, someone has to and those jobs are important to keep the wheels of commerce turning smoothly.'

'I know but it sounds very tame. I want to be involved in something more dynamic; something that really brings me in contact with what is actually going on.'

'You can always spend your free time as an air-raid warden or work in one of the canteens that serve the troops or something of that sort,' Audrey added helpfully.

Megan pulled a face. 'No, that's not for me. I want to either be in the forces or have some special project of my own. I want to feel that I'm not only pulling my weight but that I am doing something of special value.'

Audrey shook her head. 'I can't advise you. I haven't a clue how you go about solving that one,' she said with a laugh.

'No, but you can direct me to the Citizens Advice Bureau, or whatever it is called, in Liverpool. I am sure if I go to them they'll be able to tell me what is needed or what is of the greatest importance.'

'Let's sleep on it,' Audrey yawned. 'We've talked so much and I'm so tired that I can't think clearly.'

'Agreed! I feel pretty exhausted too. It's been great catching up on all the news, Audrey, and as you say we'll both feel fresher in the morning.'

The next morning Audrey took her to the nearest Citizens Advice Bureau and Megan felt shocked and angry at the same time when she saw more and more of the damage that the bombing had done to the centre of Liverpool.

Several times she stopped and stared, unable to believe what she was seeing. Whole buildings were reduced to a mass of rubble; others looked as if they had been torn apart by a giant hand that had ripped down the centre of them, leaving rooms partially exposed. Others had boarded-up windows and makeshift doors.

She found it a sickening sight and her heart went out to all the people who had suffered as a result of the desolation.

In her mind's eye she compared it with the peaceful countryside around Beddgelert and how relatively unaffected her life and that of her parents had been; the war had barely touched them. She wondered if, had her father witnessed some of this desecration, he might understand her need to do something positive and not simply idle around at home.

Megan joined the queue of people waiting to consult the advisors behind the counter. When it came to her turn the woman tried to be helpful but she obviously didn't understand Megan's predicament.

'You say your home has not been damaged?' She frowned. 'So what is your problem?'

Megan tried hard to explain about not being allowed to go into the forces but that she wanted to do some sort of work that would help the war effort, but the woman still couldn't understand what she meant.

'If you want to join the forces you can apply at any of the recruiting offices,' she told her. 'If it is some other form of war work you want to do then you must find out where their headquarters are and apply there.'

'Thank you.' Megan turned away realizing that it was hopeless. She would have to find some other way to pursue what was in her mind.

When they met up later in the day Audrey could see that Megan was cross and frustrated. She listened to what had happened but she didn't know what she could do to help. Instead she resolved to take Megan's mind off her immediate problem by suggesting they went dancing that evening.

'You mean they still hold dances when things here are in such a terrible state?' Megan exclaimed in surprise.

'Of course! We need something to take our minds off the stress and strain of being bombed out and all the shortages. Also, it's one of our ways of entertaining the troops. Soldiers, sailors and airmen are allowed in free.'

'Sounds a great idea . . .' Megan agreed, but her face clouded as she looked down at the black trousers and striped jumper she was wearing under her short coat. 'I haven't anything suitable to wear.'

'Don't worry about that. Simply come as you are. No one dresses up these days like we used to. Wear a dress, or a blouse and skirt, or even come in slacks and you won't be turned away.'

'Well, I have brought a summer dress with me in case we had a warmish day so I suppose I could wear that,' Megan murmured.

'There you are then. So you like the idea that we should go dancing?'

'Indeed I do, I'm looking forward to it.'

'Good. You might even find the answer to your problem there,' Audrey said with a laugh.

'I very much doubt that but it will be good to let our hair down. I haven't been to a dance since my twenty-first birthday party.'

'Well, I can't guarantee that the surroundings for this dance will be as opulent as they were at your party,' Audrey warned.

'Maybe not but I am sure I'll enjoy myself,' Megan enthused.

The dance was held in a local hall and it was already packed when Audrey and Megan arrived. The majority of the girls were in their teens or early twenties and most of them were wearing either dresses or a skirt and pretty top. Some of them were barelegged but they had painted a dark line down the back of their leg to represent a seam so that it looked as if they were wearing very sheer stockings.

Megan was surprised at how many service personnel were there as well. She recognized most of the uniforms but there were some that she was unable to identify. One man in particular stood out from all the others. He was tall, slim but broad-shouldered and he was wearing such a smartly tailored, khaki uniform that she asked Audrey what regiment he was from.

'He's one of the GIs,' Audrey told her. 'Judging by his uniform I would say he's an officer.'

'GIs? Whatever are they?' Megan frowned.

'Americans. Yanks! America has joined in the war and men from their army are over here to collaborate with our forces.'

Megan studied him with fresh interest. Even the material of his uniform seemed to be a better quality than that of the British army, she mused.

As if aware that he was being watched he suddenly looked across towards where she and Audrey were standing and caught Megan's eye. She felt her colour rising when he walked over to them and in a very courteous manner asked her to dance.

She hesitated for a moment before accepting. She had never met an American before and she wondered what they would talk about. There were so many prominent notices telling people to be careful what they said because careless talk cost lives so that as a rule it was better not to speak to strangers.

He might be a stranger but he was here in Liverpool because he wanted to help Britain's war effort, she reminded herself.

Even so, as they moved on to the dance floor she found herself asking him questions about why he was in Liverpool and what his Company were doing there.

'My name is Hank Jackson. I can't tell you too much of what I do because I am sworn to secrecy. When we join the army we sign a paper to say we will not disclose any information about what we are doing.'

Megan smiled. 'I believe that the members of our forces have to do the same,' she said awkwardly. 'Do you like it here in England?' she rushed on to try and cover up her mistake.

'Sure. It's a fine country and you are a great people and we are eager to help you to fight this war and keep your country and not have it taken from you by the enemy.'

'I'm glad to hear that you enjoy being here,' Megan told him. 'Is there anything you don't like about our country?'

He pursed his lips together and said nothing for a moment. Then he took a deep breath before answering. 'Well, ma'am, since you ask, I am very disconcerted by the number of very young girls who hang around our camp.'

Megan raised a quizzical eyebrow. 'I'm not sure I understand,' she said.

'Soldiers being soldiers our men are inclined to take advantage of their company, if you know what I mean.'

Megan still looked puzzled. 'No, I don't think I do know what you mean.'

'Well, these young girls hang around outside the camp waiting for our boys to come out. They have been warned not to give the girls nylons and chocolate or cigarettes. Most of them are so kind-hearted though that they cannot see any harm in doing so and of course the girls come back again and again, for more and more.'

'So what harm is there in that?'

He raised his eyebrows. 'Well, that would be all right, it's what it is that our boys are given in return as a thank you that causes the problem.'

Megan felt herself colouring but said nothing.

Hank went on. 'Far too many of these girls end up pregnant. Many of them have nowhere to go because their parents disown them the moment they discover what has happened as they consider that they have brought disgrace to the family.'

'Oh dear! So what happens to the girls, what do they do? I take it that your men don't intend to marry the girls, not even after they have got them pregnant.'

'That sure is the problem,' Hank agreed. 'Some of the boys already have sweethearts or wives back home in America; some even have young families.'

'So what do these girls do?' Megan repeated.

He shrugged. 'Have an abortion or else go on the game and become prostitutes. A few even take their own lives because disgracing their family distresses them so much.'

Megan looked horrified. 'Are you sure that's what happens to them?' she gasped, her cheeks red with embarrassment.

He nodded, his handsome face serious. 'It's of considerable concern to us because we came over here to help your country, not to bring misery or disgrace on British families.'

'Are you quite sure about all this?' Megan frowned, wondering if it could possibly be true.

'It's what I've been told by my men and I have heard it said by other people who come to our camp to talk to us about our welfare as well as to lecture our men about the girls who flock to entertain us.'

'Is there no way of stopping the girls coming to your camp?'

'We have taken all precautions possible; we've lectured the men and forbidden them to bring girls back to camp. What we've failed to do is prevent our men meeting up with these young girls outside camp or control what goes on when they do.'

'Yet you have come to the dance?'

'Our men are only permitted to do so if there are officers present as well.' He grinned. 'They know we can be trusted to behave ourselves.'

Megan smiled fleetingly; she didn't know what to say in response to his comment. It had however implanted an idea in her mind. The thought of young girls finding themselves pregnant and not knowing how to cope with the situation made her wonder if there wasn't something she could do to help them.

That, she told herself, would be one way of doing her bit to help solve some of the problems brought about by the war. Although she danced twice more with other people what Hank had said stayed in her thoughts and her mind was busy trying to formulate some sort of plan.

When she talked about it afterwards to Audrey, her friend confirmed that what he had said was very true.

'If the girls are Catholics then the nuns will take them into the sanctuary of their infirmary when the time comes for the baby to be born,' Audrey told her.

'And the baby? What happens to that?'

'They keep the baby afterwards and arrange for it to be adopted.'

Megan shuddered. 'I know they are helping the girls but what an awful fate for both the mother and the baby. She loses her child and never sees it again or knows what happens to it and the baby is placed with strangers.'

'It's probably better than the poor girl having to bring it up herself, especially if her family have turned her out. She would probably end up becoming a full-time prostitute in order to do so and heaven alone knows what sort of life the child would have.'

'I'm sure you're right,' Megan said, 'but I still find it heartbreaking.'

'I know but there's not a lot we can do about it,' Audrey stated philosophically.

'What happens if the girl isn't a Catholic?' Megan mused aloud.

'Well, she either goes to a backstreet abortionist or has the baby, I suppose,' Audrey told her.

'And afterwards?'

'I don't know. She either puts it in a home or an orphanage, or else struggles to bring it up herself.'

'Doesn't anyone in authority do anything about it?'

'Well, there's the Salvation Army or Dr Barnardo's and there are do-gooders who try and talk to the girls and warn them of what will happen if they go out with Yanks, but the girls tend to ignore them. Apart from that, what can anyone do?'

Megan didn't have an answer but it gave her plenty to think about before she went to sleep that night. She was quite determined to try and help in some way.

THREE

B efore Megan left Liverpool she asked Audrey to take her to the Scotland Road area.

'What on earth do you want to go there for?' Audrey asked. 'It's the slums of Liverpool; surely you'd rather go and visit the shops in Lord Street or even visit Bold Street where the really expensive shops are.'

'No, I want to see Scotland Road and the streets around there,' Megan said firmly, her lips clamped together in a tight line.

'Well, all right if you insist, but there has been a lot of bomb damage in that area because it's so near the docks,' Audrey warned.

The sight that met their eyes when they reached Scotland Road was not merely bomb damage but deprivation. Many of the tenement houses had had windows blown in by the bomb blasts and most of the roads were still littered with broken glass and rubble, as well as old newspapers, boxes, discarded vegetables and general muck. Dogs and cats rummaged amongst the debris and some of the half-starved dogs came sniffing around their heels looking for food.

Megan ignored them; it was the raggedy children, some of them barefoot, dirty and bedraggled, who caught her attention and touched her heart.

Women stood on their doorsteps gossiping to each other. She was aware that they were watching them and whenever she met the gaze of one of the women she was aware of the sharp alertness and suspicion in their eyes.

'Is this the area where most of the girls who visit the Yanks come from?' she asked Audrey.

'Not many of them! In general the girls from around here wouldn't be allowed into the camp because they wouldn't be dressed smartly enough. It's where a lot of the girls who have babies by the Yanks are likely to end up though. Most of the girls who go out with the Yanks come from good homes; often from Wallasey on the other side of the Mersey.'

'So that means that very often the parents of the girls who get into trouble could afford to pay for their daughters to go somewhere and have the baby; and even afford to bring it up afterwards,' Megan mused.

Audrey gave a short bitter laugh. 'You are forgetting the disgrace and the shame that the girl has brought on her family. A few of them do, of course. They send the girl away to a relative in some other part of the country to have the baby, and then have it adopted as soon as it is born. Afterwards the girl comes home again and picks up her life as though nothing has happened. Anyone who asks about her is told simply that she has "been on holiday" or "been away studying".'

'You seem to know an awful lot about it,' Megan murmured.

'Yes, I do, because there have even been girls from our school, girls as young as fourteen, who have been in this predicament.'

On the train on the way home to Beddgelert, Megan tried to think what she could do about the problem in Liverpool. She wondered whether to keep her ideas to herself or to take her family into her confidence.

Her mother might understand what was involved but she very much doubted if her father would have any sympathy for the girls in question. He would probably tell her that it was up to the local authorities to take care of the girls and to deal with the problem and that it was nothing to do with her.

In a way, Megan knew this was true but it didn't deter her from construing that something ought to be done about it and contemplating that perhaps it could be her own special war effort.

Ideally what she ought to do, she resolved, was to find a

house in Liverpool where the girls would be made welcome and where they could stay until after their baby was born.

What happened after that was up to them. If they could manage to get their families to accept the child then once it was born they could go back to their own home. If not, then she would help them to have the baby adopted; the last resort would be to put it into an orphanage.

She would also try to help the young mother build a new future for herself. She was sure that most of the girls would realize what a mistake they had made and be anxious to make amends and start afresh.

When she told her parents of her idea it was exactly as she had imagined: her mother understood what she wanted to do but her father dismissed it as foolishness.

'We are at war; cities and towns are still being bombed by the Germans night after night. Here you are safe, so let's hear no more about it. Anyway, what the devil do you think you are taking on? Why assume responsibility for the stupid young girls who know no better than to sleep around with soldiers?'

'I simply want to help them; half of them don't know where to turn for help,' Megan explained. 'In many instances their families have disowned them and don't want to know about the baby because they feel it will bring disgrace or else they can't afford having another mouth to feed.'

Lewis Lloyd grunted but made no reply.

'You really should see the state some of the very poor people in Liverpool live in. There's nothing at all like that here. I was completely shocked when I walked down Scotland Road and saw the terrible places where some of them have to live.'

Megan's voice was high as she tried to make her point and tears were running down her cheeks.

'Yes, and if you go ahead with your silly ideas then that's where you'll end up as well, my girl,' her father told her. 'If they had worked hard and saved and budgeted they wouldn't be in that mess. Most of the women there are sluts who hang around waiting for the pubs to open the same as their menfolk. As for the men, most of them drink their wages away on a Friday night before they even go home.'

Megan knew it was useless to argue with him but it made her all the more resolute to do something to help the girls, so she waited until she was alone with her mother before broaching the subject again.

'Forget about it, my dear,' Bronwyn Lloyd told her daughter. 'What do you think you can do that the local authorities haven't already tried?'

'I'm sure there must be something I can do,' Megan insisted. 'I thought that perhaps I could provide them with some sort of retreat, a house where they knew they would be safe until the baby arrived, something of that sort.'

'That would cost quite a lot of money. Remember, you would have to feed them as well as provide them with a midwife to help deliver the baby. Do you think any of them would be prepared to pay for that?'

'I don't know and I haven't any way of finding out. I simply thought of providing them with somewhere safe to live until they'd had their baby.'

'It's certainly a very commendable idea, my dear, but I don't think it's very practical. It would take a great deal of organizing as well as a lot of money.'

Megan retreated to her bedroom but she couldn't put the idea from her mind. She was determined to do something to help those girls and she was sure there was some way she could do so.

The answer came to her in the middle of the night; she awoke with a scheme already formed in her mind, one that she felt she would be able to put into practice.

Next morning over breakfast she once more broached the subject.

Angrily her father banged his fist on the table, making the dishes jump as well as Megan and her mother.

'I don't intend to sit here and listen to your babble about fallen girls while I have my breakfast,' her father thundered and again banged on the table with his fist. 'I told you yesterday to forget about it.'

'I simply can't do that, Father,' Megan protested. 'I want to do something to help these girls and I feel that if I did this I would then be playing a vital part in the war effort.'

'And I have said no! As long as you are living under my roof then you will do as I tell you.'

'Father, I am twenty-one now and old enough to make my own decisions and that is what I intend to do,' she told him rebelliously. 'I want to help these girls and I have an idea of how to go about it, so that is what I am going to do.'

'Not if you want to remain under my roof!'

'In that case I have no option but to move out.'

'Megan! Please don't speak to your father like that,' Bronwyn exclaimed, her face white with dismay.

Megan stared at her mother, willing her to give her support, but Bronwyn had no intention of going against her husband's wishes.

'In that case then I will have to leave,' Megan insisted stubbornly.

'If you defy me, then remember you cannot come back again. If you leave this house now then you leave it for good,' her father told her harshly.

Megan flicked back her long dark hair and tossed her head defiantly. 'I quite understand.'

'So where will you go? How will you live?' her mother asked in a shaky voice.

'I'll manage somehow.'

'You won't get a penny piece more from me,' her father told her. 'Your allowance will be stopped right from this moment so you will have no money at all. So how do you think you can live?'

'I have money of my own, remember,' Megan said quietly. 'I have the money which my godmother left me when she died two years ago.'

'You have no access to that; it was left under my jurisdiction and as far as I am concerned you can't touch a penny of it.'

'That is where you are wrong, Father,' Megan said smugly. 'I have access to that money when I come of age and as I have already pointed out to you I am now twenty-one and able to manage my own affairs.'

'You mean you are going to use that money to support girls who have fallen into disgrace!' he exclaimed in a shocked voice.

'Exactly! I am going to use it to provide shelter and help for some of the girls in Liverpool who have fallen victim to the Yanks and who are now expecting their babies.'

'You are completely out of your mind,' her father told her, shaking his head in despair. 'If you do that then you are no longer my daughter; you are no better than the girls themselves. If you join them then that is the end of our relationship; I no longer regard you as my daughter; I disown you! I never want to see you or hear from you ever again.'

Megan felt fresh tears pricking behind her eyes and knew that at any moment they would be running down her face. She bit her lip and held her head high, determined not to give way, and looked at her mother for support.

Her lip trembled when she realized she was not going to get a response from her mother. Bronwyn had moved across the room to the window and was looking out, completely ignoring what was going on in the room behind her. She was making it quite clear that she did not want to be involved in what was happening.

Suppressing a sob, Megan squared her shoulders and walked towards the door. 'So it's goodbye,' she said in a voice that she struggled to keep normal.

Neither of her parents made any response.

With tears streaming down her cheeks Megan went upstairs to her bedroom knowing that she had burned her boats. Now, unless she went back and apologized to them both, she had no option but to pack her belongings and leave the house which had been her home all her life.

She sat down on her bed and tried to think what she must do next. Then, sniffing back her tears, she went over to her wardrobe, took out two suitcases and began to haphazardly pack clothes into them.

The house was eerily silent as she went downstairs and carried her cases along to the garage to put them into the back of her car.

When she opened the garage doors she gaped in amazement. Her mother's Rover was there and so was her father's Rolls Royce but her Morris was missing.

Frowning, she stared at the empty space wondering where

it was, but in her heart she knew it had been driven somewhere where she would be unable to access it.

It had been a present from her parents for her twenty-first birthday and this was their way of letting her know that unless she agreed to do as they wanted, then she really had severed all connection with them.

She stood there for a moment contemplating what to do. Pride stopped her from going back to the house and asking where her car was.

If she intended to help the girls in Liverpool then this was her opportunity to stand on her own two feet and do just that, she told herself.

She would go to Liverpool and hope that Audrey Wilson would let her stay at her place for a few days while she sorted herself out. She would find a house she could rent and then put her idea into practice.

Tossing back her long hair, she squared her shoulders, and picked up her suitcases and after taking a long lingering look at Yr Glaslyn, she headed for the railway station.

FOUR

Megan felt exhausted when she arrived at Audrey Wilson's front door. The two suitcases had become heavier and heavier as she made her way from Lime Street station to the taxi rank. She knew that really she should take a bus and save what little money she had, but she felt so tired that all she want to do was reach her destination as soon as possible.

The taxi driver took her two suitcases from the boot of his car, dumped them on the pavement outside Audrey's house and held out his hand for his fare.

Megan carried the cases to the front door and pressed the bell. Then she waited apprehensively. She hadn't let Audrey know that she was coming and she wondered what sort of a reception she would get.

The door was opened by a tall, fair-haired young man wearing khaki trousers and a khaki shirt that was open at the neck. For a moment Megan wondered whether she had come to the wrong address.

'I . . . I wanted to speak to Audrey Wilson,' she said hesitantly.

The young man grinned as if he knew her. 'You must be her friend Megan Lloyd. You were staying with Audrey last week at half term?'

'Yes, that's right.' She smiled at him nervously. 'And you are?'

'I'm her cousin Martin Wilson,' he told her. 'I'm here on leave from the army. Actually I'm paying Audrey and her family a quick visit because I'm on embarkation leave. When I return to my regiment in two days' time I'll be off overseas. I can't tell you how much I'm looking forward to seeing some action,' he said with a broad smile.

He ran a hand through his shock of fair hair then turned and called out, 'Audrey, there's a visitor here for you.'

Megan heard the sound of footsteps as Audrey came through from the kitchen into the hallway. Then she heard the gasp of astonishment as Audrey saw her standing there and glanced down at the two suitcases at her feet.

'Good heavens, this is a surprise! I wasn't expecting you! Have you decided to come and live in Liverpool?'

'Yes,' Megan said hesitantly. 'I . . . I was wondering if I could stay here with you for a couple of days until I can find some sort of lodgings. Do you think your mother would mind?'

For a moment Audrey hesitated, looking from Megan to Martin and back again. Before she could speak, however, Martin had stepped into the breach.

'I can kip down on the settee tonight. I've only one more night left and I have to be up at the crack of dawn so it's much better if I do that, then I won't disturb anyone.'

'No, no, you can't do that,' Megan protested.

'I certainly can,' he assured her. He bent down and picked up her two cases and began walking towards the stairs with them. 'I'll put these in my room and clear my things out and then you can get settled in.'

'Go on through to the kitchen with Audrey,' he ordered when Megan again tried to protest. 'There's fresh tea in the pot; make sure you keep a cuppa for me.'

The moment they were on their own, Megan gave Audrey a brief outline of what had happened before she had left Beddgelert.

Audrey looked shocked. 'Surely they didn't mean it, when they said that they were going to disown you? Surely it's something that your father said in the heat of the moment because he was upset and angry?'

'Don't you believe it! My father meant every word. The only way I can get him to forgive me is for me to grovel and go down on my knees and apologize and then spend the rest of my life doing exactly as he wants me to do.' Megan tossed her head defiantly. 'Well, I am not prepared to do that.'

'So what are you going to do?'

'War work! My kind of war work.'

Audrey frowned looking puzzled. 'What do you mean?'

'When I was staying here, you know we talked about the girls in Liverpool who went out with soldiers, especially the Yanks and ended up having babies? Well, I'm going to do something to help them. I'm thinking of renting a house, somewhere where they can come and be looked after when they have the baby.'

'You can't do that on your own! It'll take an awful lot of money and you would definitely need to have people to help,' Audrey gasped. 'You'll need a midwife and possibly a doctor, as well as people to help nurse the young mothers and get them back on their feet after their babies are born. And what are you going to do with all the babies if the girls don't want to keep them?'

'I know there's going to be a lot of work and planning and organizing involved. I'm going to spend the inheritance left to me by my godmother to get it started,' Megan explained. 'I can't afford to buy a house, of course, but I'm sure I'll be able to find one to rent. As for the babies, well that very much depends on what the girls want to do. I realize that some of them will want to get rid of their babies by having them adopted or something but there may be others who'll want to try and bring them up single-handed and I'm hoping I'll be able to help them in some way.'

Audrey shook her head, her grey eyes doubtful. 'You're going to take an awful lot on your shoulders. Are you sure you can manage?'

'That's something I've got to find out but I'm quite sure I can. I really feel very strongly about these girls and their babies.'

'Well, you're more than welcome to stay here for a few days until you find a house.'

'Are you sure your mum and dad won't mind?'

'Of course they won't. I can help you to find a house, if you like. I know the area a lot better than you do.'

'I know you do and I'd be more than grateful if you would help me. It needs to be somewhere near Scotland Road.'

Audrey looked startled. 'Why do you want to live there?'

'I think these girls will feel more comfortable because in that sort of area they won't be shunned by so-called respectable people,' Megan explained.

'There's been an awful lot of bomb damage around there so it might not be easy to find a suitable house,' Audrey warned.

'I'm sure we'll find the sort of place I want if we look hard enough,' Megan said confidently.

Audrey looked sceptical but didn't argue with her about it. 'You'll probably have to get some sort of permission from the council or local authority or the health authority, to run that sort of place,' she warned.

They went on talking about it even after Martin had rejoined them. He seemed extremely interested.

'It's not only the Yanks who are responsible for what happens to these girls,' he said as he drank the cup of tea that Audrey had poured out for him. 'Sailors are just as bad. The minute they get into port they pick up a girl and by the time they finally leave she's usually pregnant and she never hears from him ever again.'

'How do you know that?' Audrey asked.

'Your father told me and he should know because he was a sailor.'

They all laughed at this but they soon became serious again, knowing that what Megan was planning to do was no laughing matter.

The three of them talked for another hour or more; each of them putting forward various ideas that seemed appropriate but none of them too sure of what exactly was involved, or what it would cost to put such ideas into practice.

Realizing that he had to be up at six the next morning to report back to barracks and rejoin his regiment, Martin started to make up a bed for himself on the settee.

'Sorry, we're keeping you up,' Audrey said apologetically. 'I forgot you have to leave early tomorrow morning and that you need to get some sleep.'

'That's fine, you carry on talking as long as you don't mind if I drop off and start to snore.'

'No, it's high time we were both in bed as well,' Audrey said as she stood up and picked up their dirty cups to take into the kitchen.

'Sleep well, Martin,' she said as she came back into the room. 'I don't suppose either of us will be up to say goodbye to you in the morning so we had better do it now. Goodbye and good luck.'

'Thank you; and good luck to you, Megan, with your new enterprise.'

'Thank you, I'm sure all the ideas you've given me will be of great help.'

It was a long time before Megan fell asleep. When she did she dreamed that she was in charge of a large rambling country mansion filled with happy smiling women who were nursing fat bonny babies.

If only that dream could come true, she thought, when she awoke just before eight o'clock the next morning. She lay there thinking back over all the plans and ideas that Audrey and Martin had put forward the night before. Then she hurriedly prepared for the day ahead, vowing that before nightfall she would have set something in motion.

Audrey had already finished her breakfast and was putting on her coat ready to leave for school when Megan came downstairs.

'I'll be home again about four o'clock this afternoon,' she

said as she greeted Megan. 'Perhaps then I could take you down to Scotland Road so that you can see it again and have a good look around and find out if there are any empty properties,' she added as she fastened her coat and picked up her handbag and a pile of books.

'In the meantime,' she suggested, 'why don't you make some enquiries to find out if you need to inform the local authorities or anyone else about what you are proposing to do.'

'Yes, I'll do that. I'm not too sure where to start but if I go along to the council offices then I'm sure they'll point me in the right direction.'

'Yes, that sounds the best idea and when I get home tonight you can tell me what you've discovered. I'm sure there must be some regulations that you'll have to conform to,' she added as she headed for the door.

After Audrey had left Megan helped Mrs Wilson to clear away the breakfast dishes and as they washed up she told her about her plan.

'Yes, I think you're doing the right thing by going to the council offices first,' Mrs Wilson agreed. 'If they can't help you then why not try the police. They always seem to know everything there is to know about those sorts of things. Or you could try the Salvation Army.'

'I'd sooner try the council office and the police,' Megan murmured. 'I feel that they are the right authorities to deal with this.'

The woman in the council office didn't seem to understand what Megan wanted. She seemed to think that it was Megan who was in some sort of trouble and told her there were various organizations and charities that helped expectant mothers but she was rather vague about exactly what was available.

The desk sergeant at the police station wasn't much more helpful.

'You mean that you are in some sort of trouble and need help,' he said.

'No, no not at all,' Megan said quickly.

'So what is your problem then?'

'I want to try and help some of the young girls who are expecting babies . . . Illegitimate babies.'

'Well, you'll find plenty of them in Liverpool,' he told her, shaking his head sadly. 'It's them Yanks I blame most of all.'

'I know,' Megan agreed. 'That's why I'm trying to do something to help these girls.'

'There are charities all over Liverpool trying to do just that. I'm sure any one of them would be glad of your help. Look in the street directory, you'll find all of them listed there.'

'I want to set up a charity of my own,' Megan explained. 'I want to find a house where they can stay and I will arrange for them to be looked after.'

'Whew!' The sergeant pursed his lips in a whistle. 'That's some undertaking, miss!'

'I know. What I am trying to find out is am I allowed to do it?'

'You mean do you need a licence or something of that sort?' He shook his head from side to side. 'I'm not sure about that. I think you would have to go to the City Hall and ask them for advice. You'd probably have to register it with them.'

Megan thanked him for his help and left. She didn't bother to tell him that she had already been there and they had been unable to advise her.

She felt frustrated as she came back out into the street. This was the sort of prevarication she would have received from her father to try and prevent her from doing what she wanted to do.

She had no intention of seeking any more advice. She would wait until Audrey came home and then together they could visit the area around Scotland Road and see if they could find a suitable house to rent.

Once she actually had a place where she could provide accommodation for the girls then perhaps the authorities would take her more seriously.

FIVE

Megan had her hat and coat on and was fastening her walking shoes when Audrey arrived home shortly after half past four.

'Are you going somewhere?' Audrey asked with a smile.

'Yes, out with you; you haven't forgotten that we agreed to go and look for a house in the Scotland Road area, have you?'

'Of course I haven't. Give me time to change my shoes because my feet are killing me,' Audrey said. 'I've been standing up most of the day writing on the blackboard and I'm wearing the wrong shoes.'

'If you're so tired do you want to stop and have a cup of tea first before we go out?' Megan asked.

'Would you mind very much? I really am in need of one,' Audrey admitted. 'It's been one of those days.'

Megan tried to be patient while she waited for the kettle to boil and for Audrey to change her shoes and then come downstairs and drink the tea. The moment Audrey replaced her empty cup in its saucer Megan was on her feet ready to go.

They walked to the tram stop nearest to Audrey's home in silence. Once they were on the tram, Megan told her what had happened when she had gone to the council offices and to the police earlier that day.

'So you don't really know what you ought to do or where to go for permission,' Audrey said with a frown.

'No, and I'm not going to waste any more time trying to find out. I'm sure that if I am breaking some law or other then someone will be quick to come and tell me.'

'You are taking rather a risk, you know,' Audrey warned.

'Maybe but I don't really care. All I want to do now is find a house and get on with what I have in mind.'

They had taken seats on the upper deck of the tram and as it took them down through the heart of Liverpool, Megan was once again shocked by the amount of destruction that had been caused by the bombing.

The streets were busy with people and were reasonably clean and tidy apart from the boarded-up windows of shops that had been bombed and not reopened afterwards. The real truth lay behind the schools and houses the nearer they came to the dock area. At the rear of most houses there were piles of debris, rubble and broken glass.

Where Audrey lived in Grasmere Drive in Everton, there had been some damage but it was nothing compared to the devastation Megan saw in the heart of Liverpool and which became increasingly severe the closer they came to the docks.

'Do you think there will be any more bombing in Liverpool?' she queried.

'Who knows! I certainly hope not. I'll never forget when night after night the bombers came over dropping their loads and the sound of explosions as factories and warehouses went up in flames.'

'It must have been enough to give you nightmares for life,' Megan said with a shudder.

They got off the tram at Exchange station and Audrey led the way through a maze of streets to Scotland Road. A wide variety of small shops, bookies and barbers stood on either side of the road. There were flats above most of them that appeared to be empty but Audrey told Megan she assumed they were all occupied by the owners of the shops.

'There's nothing here in Scotland Road that is remotely suitable,' Megan said in a disappointed voice.

'No, I didn't think there would be but I thought you would want to see Scotland Road again to get an idea of what sort of district it is. I think there might be something suitable in one of the roads leading off Scotland Road. Shall we look?'

'Of course; that's what we came here to do,' Megan reminded her.

'Come on then, let's turn down here.'

The road they entered was so shabby and squalid that for a moment Megan was taken aback. She drew in a sharp breath as she saw the grim tenement buildings that lined either side of the road. There were broken stone steps leading down to cellars and, in some cases, stone steps leading up to the front door. Most of them were covered in debris. She had never seen such dirty streets in her life and the thought of living in a house here made her squirm.

They walked the full length of the street then turned the corner and went into the street that stood adjacent. It was hardly any better. Miserable looking half-starved dogs were sniffing through boxes of rubbish that had been left out in front of some of the houses.

There was an air of listlessness; they were so dingy that even the daylight seemed to dim and turn grey as it came into the street.

Megan thought longingly of her mansion home in North Wales and compared it with the sordid scenes around her and for one moment wished she was back there. Perhaps her father had been right and she wasn't cut out for living in this sort of place.

She squared her shoulders and took a deep breath knowing that if she didn't go ahead with her plan then she would have to go back home and let him know that he had been right after all and she couldn't bring herself to do that.

They spent a long time walking up and down the streets that led from Scotland Road and crisscrossed to other streets and all the roads leading off until their feet were aching and still they hadn't found anything that they thought remotely suitable.

By mutual consent they headed back towards Exchange train station to pick up a tram to take them back to Everton. They were both feeling tired and disillusioned. As they were walking down one of the streets they met a youngish woman coming towards them.

She was tall with short fair hair and she was heavily pregnant. They noticed that she was swaying from side to side. Suddenly she stumbled and would have fallen had Megan not rushed forward and grabbed her arm, steadying her and holding her upright until Audrey came and did the same on the other side.

'Thank you,' the woman gasped. She tried to smile at them but she was still breathless and trembling too much to do so.

'Have you got very far to go?' Audrey asked.

'No, not very far,' the woman said breathing heavily. 'Only around the corner into the next street.'

'We'll walk along with you then,' Megan said, gently taking her arm.

'Good heavens, no! I'm sure you have better things to do than waste your time doing that. I'll be all right in a minute or two.'

'We're not in any hurry,' Audrey murmured. 'We were really looking for a house; somewhere to rent,' she explained.

'If it's lodgings you're looking for,' the woman said, her face brightening, 'I may be able to help you. I have a boarding house but it's completely empty at the moment.'

'Really! You're not thinking of renting it out, are you?' Megan asked eagerly.

'No, it's my family home, I wouldn't want to leave there. Anyway, I think you would find it rather too large. It has six bedrooms as well as two large reception rooms downstairs and a very big kitchen.'

'Really!' Megan's eyes lit up with interest. 'It sounds exactly the sort of place that I'm looking for,' she told the woman eagerly. 'Of course, it would depend where it's located.'

'That's probably one of the reasons why you wouldn't want it,' the young woman told them. 'My mother was left to bring me up single-handed after my father was killed in the First World War. She took this house near the docks with the idea of people staying there overnight while waiting to board a ship to continue to their destination. It served its purpose very well and provided her with both a home and an income while I was growing up. Unfortunately she died about a year ago but I have been trying to continue the business because I am now in more or less the same situation as she was.' She ran a hand over her extended stomach and smiled ruefully.

'Do you mean your husband has been killed in this war?' Audrey murmured sympathetically.

'Not exactly but my situation is very similar. We were planning on being married next week but unfortunately Hank has been sent overseas at a moment's notice and there is no chance now of us being married before our baby is born.'

'Hank? That's an unusual name.'

'Yes. Hank Jackson. He's an officer in the American army. One of the Yankee GIs who have come over to this country to help out.'

'I know him!' Megan said in astonishment. 'I met him at a dance about a week ago. Tall and slim and wearing a very smart uniform?'

'It certainly sounds like him,' the girl agreed. 'He was on duty at a dance about a week ago, shortly before they were sent abroad. The officers had to be there to make sure that none of the GIs got into any trouble. Although at the time none of them knew it, they were due to go overseas almost right away. Now I've no idea where he has been sent, only that he is no longer in this country.'

'It's terribly worrying, isn't it?' Audrey murmured, shaking her head. 'I know how you must feel because my cousin Martin has been visiting us and he was on embarkation leave so I know exactly what you mean.'

'They are not told where they are going and of course no one knows how long they will be away from home.'

'How very true and we all are left to wonder and worry about them,' the girl said ruefully.

'It must be very hard for you,' Megan said sympathetically. 'How are you going to manage?'

'I'm not sure. I don't think I'm going to be able to continue running the house as a boarding house, not for a few months anyway. That's one of the reasons why I've not booked anyone in for the next few weeks. I'm not interested in selling but if you want somewhere to live for a few weeks then I would be quite happy to accommodate you, providing you looked after yourself.'

'Perhaps I should tell you what I am proposing to do,' Megan told her. 'I am going to open up a shelter for girls who have become pregnant and then deserted by Yankee soldiers or sailors, and even our own soldiers. Girls who have been left destitute because their families have turned them out as they feel it is a disgrace that they are pregnant.'

'That sounds very commendable,' the girl murmured. 'It's going to take an awful lot of work and resources though.'

'I know. I do have some money but not enough to buy the sort of property I would like to have. It's going to be very much a question of make do with what I can afford to rent. I am hoping that perhaps some of the girls will be able to afford to pay while they are with me or at least to give something towards their keep and care.'

'It certainly sounds a worthwhile project,' the girl said admiringly. 'Perhaps you should take look at my house and then, if it was suitable, you might be able to make a start there and give yourself a chance to find out if it was feasible or not before you commit yourself to renting anything bigger. Perhaps we could reach an agreement that you use it for say, six months?'

Megan looked astonished.

'You'd be prepared to let me do that?' she said in amazement.

'Why not? I can't run the place as a boarding house until after the baby is born and I'll probably need a few months' respite after that to get used to looking after it. If you took over the house for that time then at least I would be able to go on living there. I would help you all I could, of course, but the main responsibility would be yours.'

'It sounds the perfect answer to my dreams,' Megan breathed. 'Where did you say your house was?'

'Chapel Gardens. It's not far from here.'

'It sounds perfect. By the way, I don't even know your name. I'm Megan Lloyd and this is Audrey Wilson. Audrey is a schoolteacher here in Liverpool and I come from Wales, from Beddgelert.'

'My name is Sandra Peterson and I hope that in the not too distant future it will be Sandra Jackson,' she told them with a smile.

SIX

Sandra Peterson took the turning off Scotland Road that led into Chapel Gardens. Although it still showed signs of bomb damage there was nowhere near as much devastation as there was in Scotland Road itself.

Sandra's house was midway along the street. The centre of a row of terraced houses, she had told them it was three storeys high. Half of the house on one side of it had been partly demolished but the rest of it had been shored up and most of the rubble swept away into an orderly pile in the back garden.

Most of the other houses in the street were partially boarded up or had strips of brown adhesive tape across the broken windows to secure them.

'Here we are,' Sandra said as she led them up the two stone steps and pushed open the paint-scarred dark green front door that had obviously been left on the latch because she didn't use a key.

As they entered the hallway a middle-aged woman appeared from the back of the house. She was stout, broad-shouldered and wearing a blue flannel blouse and a voluminous grey skirt. Her face was weather-beaten and wrinkled but her hard blue eyes were sharp and alert. When she spoke her accent was a mixture of Liverpudlian and Irish brogue.

'And where do you think you've been traipsing off to then and you in your condition and like as not to drop that babe at any moment?' she greeted Sandra.

Megan was sure that the woman was a servant of some sort and she felt taken aback at the way she addressed Sandra. She waited for Sandra to reprove her. She knew what would have happened if any of their servants back home in Beddgelert had spoken to her mother like that.

To her astonishment Sandra only laughed.

'Shush! Nelly, don't make such a fuss. I've brought some

friends home with me and they're simply dying for a cup of tea and some of your special scones.'

'Are they now, me darlin' girl. Then in that case I'll go back in my kitchen and see to it. Take yourselves into the sitting room and make yourselves comfortable,' she added, addressing Megan and Audrey. 'You go and sit down as well,' she ordered, looking at Sandra, 'and put your feet up or you'll have ankles like balloons before tonight.'

It was a large pleasant room with a bay window overlooking the street they had just come along. It was comfortably furnished with two sofas upholstered in dark red velvet and three matching armchairs. There was a coffee table in the centre of the room, bookshelves down one wall and a writing bureau in one corner by the big window.

'Do sit down and make yourselves comfortable,' Sandra invited as she sat down on one of the sofas and put her feet up. 'While we have a cup of tea we can go into more detail of what you are proposing to do and you can tell me how I can help.'

'You live here all on your own?' Megan asked in amazement.

'Yes, I do now since my mother died, apart from Nelly Flynn. She has lived with us ever since I was a small child and she cleans and cooks and bullies me as you probably noticed. She has been with us for so many years that she now thinks of it as her home and I certainly wouldn't dream of turning her out.'

'She sounds something of a treasure,' Megan said with a smile.

'She is; in fact I don't know how I would manage without her. She could certainly be a great asset to us if we go ahead with your idea about taking in pregnant girls.

'While we are waiting for her to bring in the tea perhaps you would like to see the rest of the house,' Sandra suggested, getting up off the sofa and walking towards the door. 'That will give you some idea of the amount of space there is here.'

As well as the large sitting room there was a spacious dining room and at the rear of the house there was a very big working kitchen with another room almost as large that seemed to be used as a utility and junk room. On the first floor there were four bedrooms; two in the front of the house, both of them large and airy, and two smaller ones at the back. On the same floor there was a family bathroom and a separate toilet.

Sandra was puffing with the exertion of climbing the narrow stairs that led up to the top floor where there were two more bedrooms. They were much smaller and had very tiny windows. There was also a small bathroom and lavatory combined.

'Nelly has one of these as her bedroom,' Sandra told them. 'It's the one that runs across the front of the house and it's almost as large as the front bedrooms downstairs, only it has a sloping ceiling. Nelly loves it; she says that it reminds her of the room she had at her home back in Ireland when she was a child.'

To Megan the entire set up of the house in Chapel Gardens seemed absolutely perfect for the purpose she intended. She could hardly believe her luck that they had met Sandra and that she was willing to cooperate and allow her to offer shelter to young mothers there. She couldn't wait for them to discuss all the details and see how they could formulate plans to do this.

By the time they arrived back in the sitting room Nelly Flynn had brought in a tray of tea things and set them down on the low table. She poured out the tea for them and then disappeared again back into the kitchen, leaving them to help themselves to the home-made scones and free to discuss the matter in hand.

Audrey said very little, leaving Megan to do all the talking. Sandra listened intently, nodding in agreement from time to time.

'Did you have all this in mind when you came here to Liverpool?' Sandra asked, her intelligent green eyes alive with interest.

'No, I simply wanted to do war work of some kind and I thought there was more possibility of finding the right role here in Liverpool than there was in the remote part of Wales where I was living.'

'Well, I think it's a wonderful idea,' said Sandra.

Megan let out an audible sigh of relief.

'It's going to cost quite a lot of money though to set up and run such an establishment,' Sandra mused.

'I have some money that was left to me and I am prepared to use it,' Megan told her. 'It will save me considerable outlay if I don't have to rent a house and furnish it so that means that what money I have will go a great deal further.'

Sandra nodded. 'Well, as you know, most of the rooms already have a bed and furniture in them so there will be no expense involved there. Our initial expense will be feeding the girls and paying someone to help look after them. Nelly will do what she can but I think we'll also need other help.'

'There will also be fees to pay for midwives or if you need to call out a doctor and possibly for medicines. You will also probably have to supply nappies and clothes for the babies and even shawls to wrap them in,' Audrey reminded them.

'Surely the young mothers will have prepared clothes themselves for the coming babies?'

'Some of them might have done but certainly not all of them will have thought about it. They mightn't even have the money to do so.'

Sandra nodded. 'It's really very challenging, isn't it! I was beginning to feel that I wasn't going to be able to do anything to help the war effort once my baby arrived, but if I'm helping you to run things then I will certainly be doing my bit.'

'Nelly might object to you taking on a venture of this sort,' Audrey warned her.

Sandra shook her head. 'No, she tries to make sure I take care of myself, especially at the moment, but she knows better than to interfere in anything I decide to do.'

'I will take great care to see that you don't overdo it,' Megan promised. 'You will have your baby to take care of as well and that will take up a great deal of your time anyway,' she pointed out.

'I can't wait to write and tell Hank what we're planning to do. I'm sure he'll be delighted when he hears about it, especially when I tell him how it all started from a conversation he had with you.'

'Yes, it's amazing what a chance remark can lead to. I'm

sure he never thought for one moment that someone would act on what he said,' Megan agreed.

While they drank their tea and tucked into the delicious home-made scones that Nelly Flynn had brought in they finalized some more of the details.

'It will all be so much easier once you move in,' Sandra said thoughtfully.

'When can I move in?' Megan asked.

'As soon as you like,' Sandra answered with a smile. 'I take it that you will have to go back to your home in Wales to explain to your family what you are doing and to collect your clothes and so on.'

'No, that won't be necessary. I've already left home and I'm staying at Audrey's house.'

'So you could move in immediately?'

'Yes, right away if that's all right with you. '

'Today?'

'Yes, today!' Megan answered with a laugh. She looked across at Audrey. 'That's OK with you, isn't it?'

'Of course. We'll go back to my place and collect your belongings and come straight back if Sandra's in agreement.'

Sandra stood up and went across the room to her writing bureau, opened the drawer and took out a door key. 'Here,' she said, holding it out to Megan. 'Welcome to Chapel Gardens.'

'Thank you.' Megan took the key from her and turned it over and over in her hand.

'Would you like to see your room? I suggest you have the one on the first floor next to mine; it's quite large and the door has a lock on it so all your belongings will be safe in there.'

'I think that's important,' she went on when she saw Megan raise her eyebrows in surprise, 'because we have no idea of the type of girls we will be taking in; we are here to help them have their baby in comfort and not to concern ourselves with their morals or their background, aren't we?'

'She's right, Megan.' Audrey nodded her head in agreement with Sandra's words.

Sandra took them both back upstairs and opened the

bedroom door next to hers. As she had told them it was a large room furnished with a double bed and oak bedroom furniture consisting of a double wardrobe, dressing table, and a chest of drawers. There was a bedside cabinet beside the bed. It was so light and airy and had such a welcoming feel to it that Megan immediately felt at home.

'This is lovely,' Megan breathed as she looked round the room. She went over to the window and peeked through the lace curtains at the street below and then turned back to Sandra with a broad smile.

'Right. Go and collect your belongings. I'll tell Nelly that you are moving in and that you will be back here in time for supper,' Sandra said enthusiastically.

'I should be back in about an hour if that's all right.'

'Don't rush,' Sandra told her. 'Let's say an hour and a half. It will give Nelly time to make sure that dinner is waiting for you when you get here.'

SEVEN

'You've been gone so long that I thought you had changed your mind,' Sandra greeted them when Megan knocked on the door some two hours later.

'I know, I know,' Megan said. 'It took us far longer to put all my stuff together than we expected and then we had to wait for a taxi. Audrey's in a hurry because she has to be somewhere in half an hour so can I just dump everything in the hallway and take it up to my room later?'

'Of course you can; I'll help,' Sandra told her.

They formed a human chain from the taxi to the hall and in less than fifteen minutes the car was unloaded and Audrey heading on her way home in the cab, waves and good wishes ringing in their ears.

Nelly served supper almost immediately, grumbling that it was their fault not hers if it had dried up through being kept waiting.

'Take no notice of her,' Sandra said with a laugh. 'Enjoy your meal.'

The food was good and Megan commented on what a good cook Nelly was.

'Good plain wholesome food is her speciality. Nothing fancy, I'm afraid,' Sandra told her.

Left on their own after Nelly had cleared away the dishes Megan began to carry the various cases and bundles upstairs to the bedroom Sandra had told her was to be hers. Sandra tried to help with some of the lighter items but after two trips up the stairs she was breathless and had to give up.

'Could you go and ask Nelly to bring us a cup of tea,' Sandra gasped as she puffed her way into the sitting room and collapsed into a chair.

'Of course.'

Nelly looked quite annoyed when Megan made the request and explained what had happened.

'You shouldn't have let her help you to do something like that, not in her condition,' she scolded.

'She offered and I never thought any more about it,' Megan stated defensively. 'I thought she was feeling OK.'

'She struggled to help, that's the way she is,' Nelly retorted. 'Go back and stay with her and I'll bring the tea in as soon as it's brewed.'

Feeling rather like a naughty schoolgirl Megan went back to the sitting room. She found Sandra curled up in a heap and moaning softly. She had one hand held to the side of her bulging stomach and was obviously in pain.

Not waiting to ask her for details, Megan turned and rushed back into the kitchen to call Nelly.

'Out of my way, out of my way.' Nelly pushed Megan roughly to one side as she bustled out of the kitchen and hurried to the sitting room. Megan followed as fast as she could. When they reached the sitting room Nelly immediately took charge.

'You go and ring the doctor – the number is on the pad by the side of the phone,' she told Megan. 'When you've done that, come back and give me a hand to get her upstairs to her bed.'

'What do you want me to tell the doctor?' Megan asked.

'Tell him? What the divil do you think you ought to tell him? Tell him that Miss Sandra has gone into labour, of course, that's what you tell him.'

With a feeling of alarm Megan rushed to do as she had been told. A woman answered the phone and Megan explained what had happened, repeating her story over again to make sure the woman understood the urgency of the call.

'Dr Stott isn't here at the moment but you can assure Miss Peterson that I will put out a call to him and inform him that it is an emergency,' the woman told her.

'I hope you told her how serious it was and that he must come as soon as he can,' Nelly tut-tutted when Megan reported back to her.

'Of course I did,' Megan insisted, annoyed by Nelly's querulous manner.

'Well, let's hope that woman at the other end of the phone understands it is urgent,' Nelly muttered. 'Come on, we'd best try and get her upstairs.'

'Perhaps it would be best if we left her where she was until the doctor gets here,' Megan said uncertainly.

'Her bed is the best place for her,' Nelly countered firmly. 'Take an arm and I'll take the other and be as gentle as you can.'

It was quite a struggle but between them, moving very slowly, they managed to get Sandra up to her bedroom and on to her bed where she collapsed in a heap. Lying on her side with her knees drawn up she began groaning in pain and became so breathless that she was unable to speak.

'You'd best go back downstairs and let the doctor in when he arrives,' Nelly ordered as she mopped at Sandra's brow with a wet face flannel.

Dr Stott had obviously realized the seriousness of the situation and was there within ten minutes. As she opened the door to let him in, Megan was surprised at how young he seemed. Tall, with a shock of short fair hair, a clean-shaven chiselled face and piercing blue eyes, he looked extremely stern and authoritative.

His arrival calmed Sandra and she managed to tell him how

bad the pains were and how frequently the contractions were coming.

An hour and a half later, the baby, a little girl, was born. There was a feeling of relief all round and Megan in particular felt that a weight had been taken off her shoulders because she was quite sure that if anything had gone wrong then Nelly would have blamed her.

Before Dr Stott arrived Nelly had been full of dire warnings about what might happen. Sandra, she claimed, had gone into premature labour because she had been helping Megan to bring her belongings upstairs and that it was more than likely that there would be complications with the birth as a result.

When Megan went into the room, however, she found Sandra propped up in bed, her new baby cradled in her arms. Her fair hair had been combed back from her face and she was wearing a pretty blue nightdress and matching silk bed jacket and she looked radiant; a picture of happiness.

'Now, more than ever, I understand why you are so eager to do something for the young unmarried mothers, especially if the baby's father is not with them when the child is born,' she told Megan.

'I'm sure you do,' Megan agreed.

'Why don't you fetch a notebook and we'll start planning right away,' Sandra suggested.

'No, you must rest now and for the remainder of the week,' Megan told her firmly. 'I'm sure Dr Stott wouldn't approve if he came back and found you working.'

'Perhaps you're right and I must say I feel extremely tired, even though I'm sure I'm too excited to sleep,' Sandra admitted.

'Time enough for us to start drawing up plans when you are feeling strong again; when you are back on your feet and into your new routine.'

'Yes, I think that would be best,' Sandra said smothering a yawn. 'I do feel tired, I must admit. When you have made yourself comfortable in your room then perhaps you would like to put down some ideas on paper. As soon as I am feeling a little bit stronger we can go through them together and I can see if I can add anything of value to what you have suggested.'

'That sounds like a sensible idea,' Megan agreed. She bent over the bed, kissed Sandra on the brow and smiled down at the sleeping bundle in Sandra's arms before she left the room.

It was well over a week before Sandra felt strong enough to start talking about the plans Megan had drawn up for converting the house into rooms for the girls they planned to help.

Dr Stott called each day to check on Sandra's progress and to make sure the baby was settling in as well as it should. He was extremely interested when Sandra told him what she and Megan were proposing to do.

'Let me know as soon as you are ready to take someone in because I know of a young girl who is living under great duress in her parents' home and she would certainly like to avail herself of such an opportunity. Her boyfriend, an American GI, has been sent overseas just like Hank Jackson. They wanted to marry but her parents objected so much that they kept putting it off. Finally when they discovered that she was expecting a baby they decided to marry without telling her parents until afterwards and then they planned to announce that they were not only married but that she was expecting a baby.

'Before they could do that he was sent overseas. Now that her parents have discovered she's pregnant they are horrified and at the moment her father is refusing to even speak to her. She tells me that if it had not been for her mother's intervention then her father would have turned her out on to the street.

'The atmosphere in the house is so bad that she is desperately unhappy and feels that she cannot go on living there very much longer. She would be more than happy to move into your house. At the moment she is quite fit and I am sure she'd be willing to help you organize things.'

'She certainly sounds an ideal candidate.' Megan smiled when Sandra related the conversation to her.

'Shall we say that she can come to us then?' Sandra asked.

'Why not! With Nelly's help I can get one of the back bedrooms ready for her in a matter of a day or two.'

'From the way Dr Stott spoke she is not hard up so possibly

she will be able to help contribute something towards her keep,' Sandra said hopefully.

'At the moment it doesn't really matter because I have enough money to cover all our expenses.'

'Yes, I know that, Megan, but the sooner we can get money in the better. I would like to think we could keep some of your money in reserve for emergencies.'

'Yes, that would be a great advantage,' Megan agreed. 'We certainly don't know what expenses lie ahead.'

'No, but I have been promised by Dr Stott that he will come any time we send for him even if the girl in labour is not on his patient list or even if she comes from outside the area.'

'That is very reassuring,' Megan agreed.

'Yes it is and of course we always have Nelly here to act as midwife if for some reason he is unable to get here.'

'Is Nelly qualified to do that?' Megan asked in surprise.

'Not officially, but she does know what she's doing and has assisted at so many births in the past that she probably knows more about what to do than the doctor, only don't tell Harvey Stott that I said that.'

'Is he quite happy about Nelly assisting?'

'Well, he didn't object to her helping me just now, did he?' Sandra smiled. 'I think perhaps it's better to simply take it for granted that he does approve rather than make an issue of the matter.'

The next couple of weeks were very busy ones for Megan. Although Sandra was now up and about she still tired easily and Nelly was insistent that she rested every afternoon. Megan could fully understand this and didn't argue about it.

The girl Harvey Stott had suggested should come there had already arrived and was installed in one of the back bedrooms on the first floor.

Jennifer White was in her late teens. She was a very delicate looking girl with dark hair, hazel eyes and a thin-lipped mouth. She was bright and helpful and willing to do almost anything Megan asked of her.

When she said that she had clerical experience Megan asked her to compile a record of the names of the girls they took in and any other information she could find out about them. She also asked her if she would like her to keep a record of all costs incurred each week in the running of the place.

Jennifer accepted the task with alacrity. She didn't need Megan to explain how she was to go about it; she knew instinctively what to do. Within a week she had produced record books and charts that were simple to follow yet packed with information.

Sandra was thrilled when Megan told her what had happened and immediately reported back to Harvey Stott and told him how delighted they were that he had recommended Jennifer White to come and stay with them.

'You do know that her father is one of the partners in a shipping line so she can well afford to pay her way,' he reminded them.

'I think we should be the ones paying her,' Sandra said with a laugh. 'She seems to have produced a set of books that will save us hours of trying to devise them ourselves.'

'So you are now up and ready for business,' Harvey laughed. 'I'm on permanent standby remember; you will have Nelly on full-time duty and now you have a resident bookkeeper. So what are you and Megan going to be doing?' he joked.

'We'll have plenty to do organizing everything else once it becomes busy. I'm sure that as soon as word gets round that shelter can be found here we will be inundated with young girls, especially now that most of the Yanks have been sent overseas and many of the girls they've left behind here are pregnant.'

'Yes, you are probably right,' Harvey Stott agreed. 'There are also many young girls left behind by our own boys who are in the forces and who have been sent overseas. Don't forget about them.'

'We won't,' Megan assured him. 'Any young girl who is pregnant is welcome to come here if we have room for her. We won't ask about their religion, or their politics or comment about their nationality or their colour or that of their child. We won't even ask them their reason for coming to us unless they wish to tell us. All we want to do is provide a haven for girls who are in trouble.'

EIGHT

It didn't take long for news of what was happening at Sandra Peterson's house in Chapel Gardens to spread by word of mouth.

Every time Megan saw a pregnant woman pause outside and stare up at the house she felt tempted to rush down and see if she could help her. Common sense told her that this would be foolish; it was up to the girls to make the first move and approach them, not for them to invite the girls in.

They already had almost a houseful anyway. Since Dr Stott had introduced Jennifer White, they had taken in Lulu Banks, a black girl whose baby was due at any moment, if the dates she had given them were correct.

There was also Mavis Jenkins, a short, dark-haired, Welsh girl in her early twenties from Cardiff. Her father, a miner, was a strict chapel-going man who had refused to acknowledge that Mavis was pregnant when she refused to tell him who the father was.

He had turned her out and for several months she had been living in Cardiff's Tiger Bay, eking out a living by cleaning and any other menial work she could find.

When the man friend she was sharing a room with said he was moving to Liverpool, Mavis had decided to come with him hoping that perhaps they could both start a new life there. However, as the train pulled into Lime Street station her friend had said that he was going into the Gents and then he had disappeared. Although she waited on Lime Street station for several hours in the hope he would come back, he never did.

By chance Mavis had found her way to Chapel Gardens and obtained refuge with Sandra and Megan.

The latest to join then was Betsy Hagan from Ireland, a very innocent young girl who didn't seem to understand what had happened to her, only that she was getting fatter and fatter. She had come to Liverpool with a young man she'd known all her life who told her he was going to become a sailor and when he left her at the dockside he promised he would come back again for her one day.

Nelly Flynn immediately took Betsy under her wing and even insisted on letting the young girl share her bedroom. It turned out that they both came from the same village in Ireland – although, of course, Nelly hadn't been back there for years, since a young woman, but it was an important link back to home for both of them.

'She's just a child, so she is,' she defended when Megan advised her not to do that. 'I'll be telling her what it's all about, this business of having a baby, so I will, and show her how to care for it when it's born.'

Megan said no more although she didn't approve. She felt it would be better to leave it until Nelly had suffered a few sleepless nights after the baby arrived and then she might be able to make her see sense, she reasoned.

It was several weeks before Megan contacted Audrey Wilson to let her know all that was happening.

'I thought it might take you a little while to settle in and of course if Sandra has had her baby that must have also put an extra strain on things.'

'Everything is fine,' Megan assured her. 'You must come round some time and see Sandra's baby.'

'Thank you, I'd like to do that, but something awful has happened. You remember my cousin Martin, who you met the night you left home and came to our house? Well, I'm afraid he's been killed in action.'

'I'm so sorry to hear that, I thought he was extremely nice,' Megan said softly.

'He was and it has upset both my parents very much. He was Dad's sister's only child and she has been quite ill ever since the news arrived. She's a widow and lives in Rochdale. We're thinking of moving up that way. Dad wants be near her so I've applied for a transfer to a school in the area.'

'Wouldn't it be easier if she moved down to Liverpool?'

'Yes, but she doesn't want to do that. Her husband died in Rochdale and is buried there and she visits his grave every week.'

Megan didn't know what to say. She thought it was crazy of Audrey to give up a school where she was happy and settled and move away somewhere else.

'Well, keep in touch and let me know what happens. Good luck for the future if you do decide to move and please let's not lose contact with each other . . .' Megan felt sad that her one link with home and her new life in Liverpool was leaving, but she needed to learn to stand on her own two feet, especially now that she'd met Sandra and embarked on their new adventure together.

All the young mothers-to-be were fascinated by Sandra's baby. She had named her Hope and they took an avid interest in her daily routine and progress. They were always eager to help Sandra when it came to bathing her, although most of them squirmed at the thought of changing her dirty nappies.

'You'll have to get used to doing it when your own baby is born,' Sandra told them. 'It's not as bad as you think.'

Sandra herself was back into taking part in all that was going on and anxious to help Megan in every way she could. With Jennifer White undertaking all the clerical work it left both Sandra and Megan free to organize newcomers as they arrived and make them comfortable.

A timetable for the forthcoming births was drawn up and although they all knew that no one could be one hundred percent sure of when each new baby would arrive, it forecast a busy future ahead.

The war was still at its height and even though there were no American servicemen left in Liverpool, the area around the Pier Head was packed with men in uniform. Some of them were on their way overseas, others were sailors on short stays in Liverpool while their boats were repaired or reloaded with provisions and troops.

Fortunately the bombing in and around Liverpool had abated but the devastation visible in every road and street was depressing and a constant reminder that the war was still going on.

Sandra and Megan were worried for quite another reason. They had no idea what they would do with the babies when they arrived if the girls didn't want to keep them.

So far no one had said that they were willing to bring up their baby when it was born. The main reason for this appeared to be because none of them had a home they could go to. Because they were well advanced into their pregnancies they were not working and they had no savings so they had no money to keep the baby or themselves.

It was a problem that Megan and Sandra talked over and over without finding any solution.

'Why don't you ask Dr Stott if he has any ideas?' Megan suggested.

The next time that Harvey Stott called, Sandra did just that.

'This is surely something you should have thought about before you set up a home for these girls,' he said brusquely.

'Actually we were hoping that the girls would want to keep their babies once they arrived. I don't know how they can bring themselves to part with them once they have held them in their arms,' Sandra said, a doting smile on her face as she looked down at the little bundle she was cradling in her own arms.

'Your case is completely different from theirs,' Harvey Stott pointed out. 'You have a house, warmth and food, a comfortable bed and friends to help you.'

'Yes, you are right, Harvey. I know that I am very fortunate. Furthermore I have no one to reprimand me for being an unmarried mother. In addition, of course, I do know that Hank is coming back to marry me once this wretched war ends.'

'That still leaves the question of what do we do with any unwanted babies?' Megan repeated.

'Exactly, and we were wondering if you could help us, Harvey?' Sandra explained, giving him a hopeful smile.

'I can't help you myself but I can put you in touch with someone who can probably do so,' he told them.

'We don't want the babies to go to nuns or Dr Barnardo's or any other sort of institution like that,' Sandra told him quickly.

'No, this is a lady who acts independently. Her name is Angela Burton. She is middle-aged, well-to-do and a tremendous organizer. She has a great many contacts and will be able to advise you on the best way of dealing with unwanted babies. Would you like me to ask her to call and see you?'

Sandra and Megan exchanged glances.

'I suppose she could be the answer to our problem. Is she some kind of do-gooder?' Sandra asked.

'I don't think she would like to be referred to as such,' Harvey said with a brief smile. 'As I said, she is very well connected and she will certainly know how it would be possible to get the babies adopted privately. They would go to good homes, I can assure you.'

Both Megan and Sandra agreed that it sounded as though Angela Burton could be a valuable contact and that Harvey should ask her to come and see them.

When Angela Burton did come to see them a few days later they were both immensely impressed by her appearance.

As Harvey had said she was middle-aged and very organized. She was carrying a monogrammed brown leather briefcase in one hand and a black leather handbag on her arm. Under her black fur coat she was wearing a smartly tailored pale grey suit with a blue cashmere jumper. At the neckline was a double row of pearls complemented by matching pearl earrings.

For the first time since she had been at Chapel Gardens Megan felt dowdy. She was always so busy that she rarely thought about what she was wearing. Now, as she compared her serviceable tweed skirt and grey jumper with Angela Burton's fashionable attire, she felt drab. She thought wistfully of all the clothes she had left behind when she'd left home. Then, with a brief sigh, she brought her mind back to the present, to Angela Burton.

Her manner was brisk but friendly and she listened in attentive silence as between them Sandra and Megan outlined their concern about the forthcoming babies.

'You have certainly taken a lot on your shoulders providing lodgings for these young expectant mothers,' she said admiringly.

'Yes, but the problem is most of these young girls are not in a position to keep their babies even if they wanted to. Finding a good home for the baby is of paramount importance both to the girls themselves and to us,' Megan said firmly.

'We won't feel we have done our duty by them if we simply

hand the new baby over to some institution or other. What we would like to do is find a good home and know that the baby will be loved and cared for and brought up as if it was one of their own,' Sandra added.

'Do you think we are being overprotective, or overambitious?' Megan asked.

'You are doing only what I would expect you to do and what I would want to do if I was in your shoes,' Angela Burton told them.

She picked up the briefcase that she had placed on the floor beside her and put it on the table, opened it and took out a file.

'You do realize, of course, that once I have placed a child for adoption then the natural mother must not be told where the child has gone and certainly will not be able to see it ever again.'

'That will be very hard for some of the girls but a great relief for many of them,' Megan said wryly.

'Yes, some of the girls will be heartbroken at the thought of never seeing their baby again but I am sure they will understand that it is for the child's best interest,' Sandra said with a sigh.

'It's a sacrifice they have to make,' Angela Burton pointed out. 'Furthermore you must make it abundantly clear to them that that is the situation. Once they have handed over their baby and signed the appropriate forms then that is the last contact they will have with the child,' she concluded, her voice hard and businesslike.

Opening the file in front of her she poised her pen ready to write. 'How many babies do you have waiting for adoption at the moment? I thought I heard one crying as I came in.'

'You probably did but it is mine and it is not up for adoption,' Sandra said with a laugh.

'We'll probably have one or possibly two within the next couple of weeks,' Megan told her. 'We will let you know as soon as they are born.'

'Yes, do that. I will need to know the sex and weight of the baby and any other details you may feel are necessary. I should point out that black babies or those of another nationality are sometimes difficult to place. The demand is for full-term healthy white babies of either sex although many people do prefer boys.'

'What about if there are twins?' Megan frowned. 'Do you separate them?'

'Not if I can find someone willing to take both babies. If that is not possible then yes it is necessary to separate them, but since they will never know that they were one of a twin it doesn't really cause any problems.'

By the time Angela Burton left, both Megan and Sandra felt dazed by all the information they had been given and all the questions they had been asked.

'There's no doubt about it, we'll have to devise forms for our own use before we part with any of the babies,' Megan stated, pushing her dark hair back from her brow.

'Yes, and the form will have to be very detailed. I had thought a simple form that merely stated the name of the baby and date it was handed over for adoption would do but now, after listening to all Angela Burton has told us, I think it needs a great deal more details.'

'Yes, I agree and I think we are going to have to look into how we register the babies in our permanent records so that we have every possibility noted. We need to include details about the father where these are known in case the girl ever needs proof that her baby has gone for adoption.'

'This is equally important if the girl has decided to keep the baby and is struggling to bring it up single-handed. If the father has been serving overseas then the child may be as much as two years old when they return and they may find it hard to accept that it is theirs,' Sandra said with a sigh.

'That's all going to take a great deal of time. Will you do it or shall I? Or shall we do it together?' Megan asked, pulling a pad of blank paper towards her.

'I have a much better idea,' Sandra said with a triumphant smile. 'Why don't we let Jennifer White draw up the relevant forms, then we can check that they contain everything we feel is necessary and amend them if we find any points have been overlooked. She has a very good brain and is excellent for this sort of job and I am sure she will do it better than we would.'

'Great idea!' Megan agreed. 'It's a pity she didn't sit in on our meeting with Angela Burton, then we wouldn't even have to brief her.'

'That won't be much of a problem because she has a very analytical approach to such issues,' Sandra pointed out. 'Fortunately we have already taken down the details of the girls who have been admitted so far, so that will be a good starting point.'

'We could always get Angela Burton to check over our forms and see if they comply with the regulations as she knows them,' Megan said thoughtfully.

'We could, but I'd rather not do that. I'd like to think that we are capable of running our own show in our own way. We don't want any more outside intervention than we have to,' Sandra said firmly.

NINE

The first of the girls to go into labour was Mavis Jenkins early in December and it stirred the entire household into a bustle of activity. The only person who appeared to be calm and unflustered was Nelly Flynn.

'It was to be expected if the dates she gave us were the right ones; she was due before any of you others,' Nelly muttered as she prepared Mavis's bed in readiness.

'Will a couple of you help Mavis upstairs as quickly as you can and get her into bed,' Megan asked, 'and I'll phone for Dr Stott.'

'Tell him there's no great hurry but to come as soon as he can,' Nelly told her philosophically.

Lulu and Betsy offered to do as Megan had requested. Mavis was gasping and moaning as they shepherded her up to her bedroom and then tried to help her undress.

At first Mavis refused to lie down on her bed but walked

round and round the room, complaining bitterly that no one was helping her.

Nelly, wearing a big white apron over her dark skirt, came bustling in and took charge, issuing orders like a sergeant major.

'You get yourself into that bed, my darlin' girl, and do what we say. It will all be over in a couple of hours, so it will and then you'll be holding a lovely little baby in your arms.'

'A couple of hours!' Mavis's protest ended in a sharp scream as another searing pain seized her body, making her catch her breath and double over.

'Come on, me darlin' girl. Stop making so much fuss. Things will be easier if you do what I tell you. Now lie down on that bed and let's be having no more nonsense,' Nelly said in a firm but cajoling voice as she bustled around the room getting things in order.

'Lulu, you come and stand at this side of the bed and let Mavis hold on to your hand. Betsy, you come and stand on the other side of the bed and use this damp face flannel to wipe her brow and keep her cool,' Nelly instructed. 'Stay by her side and talk to her; try and comfort her.'

She then sent Jennifer White, who had heard the commotion and came to find out what was happening, to fetch towels from the kitchen and, at the same time, tell Megan and Sandra that Mavis was progressing well.

Megan, looking rather dishevelled, came rushing upstairs, anxious to make sure that Mavis was being well looked after.

'Sandra is feeding her baby and said she would come as soon as she has finished and can put little Hope down to sleep,' she explained when Nelly met her on the landing.

'Mavis is doing fine, so she is,' Nelly told her. 'There's nothing for you to worry about at all. Everything is going as it should do and I have everything in hand.' She laid a reassuring hand on Megan's arm as screams of agony came from the bedroom.

'Lulu and Betsy are in there with her, there's nothing else we can do; nature has to take its course. I'll call you if we need you.'

By the time Harvey Stott arrived half an hour later, the room was full of women, all trying to help but unable to do anything to calm the hysterical cries of pain coming from Mavis as she twisted and writhed in anguish.

Harvey Stott immediately took over responsibility and ordered Betsy and Lulu out of the room.

'I'm sure you both find it upsetting witnessing something like this, in your condition,' he told them brusquely. 'Wait outside and I'll call you if I need any further assistance,' he ordered.

The screams, protests and groans that Mavis was making had completely unleveraged both Lulu and Betsy. They were both anxious to leave the room the moment he said they could make their escape.

They huddled together on the landing outside the bedroom door, clutching each other, breathing heavily, their eyes wide with fear every time they heard Mavis scream.

'Do you think we will be in terrible pain like that when our time comes?' Lulu asked.

'I hope not. Anyway, I'll make sure that I won't be screaming like she is,' Betsy said indignantly.

'I suppose we should go back in there and see if we can do anything to help,' Lulu murmured. 'Nelly told me to hold Mavis's hand but she held on to mine so tightly that I thought she was going to break every bone there is in it and I made her let go. I suppose that was a bit mean of me, wasn't it?' she added guiltily.

'Come on,' Betsy took her by the shoulder and propelled her towards the door. 'We'll both go back in there whatever Dr Stott says and take it in turns to hold her hand and do anything else we are asked to do. Remember, we will be wanting people to do the same for us when our time comes so it's only fair that we do our bit for poor Mavis.'

Lulu hesitated, her eyes wide. 'Dr Stott told us to leave the room; in fact he ordered us to do so,' she pointed out.

'Only because he could see that we were upset,' Betsy said dismissively.

The scene inside the bedroom had changed very little. In between her screams Mavis was still moaning and groaning and bewailing the situation she found herself in. Then suddenly

she let out a long ear-shattering scream that had Betsy and
Lulu clinging to each other in alarm.

'Push, now, me darlin' girl. For sure, it is the right time for
you to push,' Nelly urged Mavis. 'One more big push, me
darlin' girl, and it will all be over and your lovely little baby
will be born.'

'You've said that before, you silly old woman,' Mavis yelled
back at Nelly. 'Can't one of you just cut me open and get it
out? I can't stand this pain any longer. If I ever meet up with
the bugger who did this to me I'll cut his bloody throat.'

'Mavis, Mavis, please try and control yourself,' Sandra
begged in a shocked tone of voice as she heard the bitterness
in Mavis's voice.

The painful process had advanced so much by now that all
Mavis could do was gasp exhaustedly. Then, with a huge effort,
she gave a final violent push as the baby made its entry into
the world.

For a moment there was a stunned silence and then it was
quickly followed by gasps and exclamations of astonishment.
The baby was black; a boy who not merely had a mop of tight
black curly hair but every inch of his skin was black as well.

Even Harvey Stott looked slightly taken aback and held up
a hand to delay Nelly passing the child to its mother until
after she had cleaned it up and wrapped it in a soft white
blanket.

'You have a little boy, Mavis,' he said in a low voice. Then,
after a brief pause he added, 'Your baby is black. Does that
come as a surprise to you?'

'It would be an even bigger surprise if it was any other
colour,' Mavis groaned, passing a hand over her flushed face.

The women around the bed exchanged looks with each
other. Sandra shook her head as though completely dismayed
by the turn of events.

'Nelly, perhaps you would go and make us a pot of tea to
celebrate the baby's safe arrival,' she instructed. 'I'm sure
Mavis would like one after all she's been through.'

'I'd love a cuppa but not to celebrate his arrival,' Mavis
told them as she pushed the baby to one side and sat up
straighter in the bed. 'I'm celebrating it's all over and now I

can get rid of the little bastard and get on with my own life once again.'

'Don't you want to keep him now you've seen him and held him in your arms?' Betsy asked in astonishment. 'I dream all the time about the day when I will be holding my baby in my arms.'

'Keep him!' Mavis laughed derisively and pushed her thick, sweat-drenched hair away from her face. 'Of course I don't. I'd never be able to go back home again if I was carrying a black baby in my arms. My father would slam the door in my face and then denounce me from the pulpit.'

'If he is a religious man as you imply, then surely he would take pity on the child and forgive you even if he thinks you have sinned,' Sandra murmured.

'Not him! A Bible basher of the worst kind but all the same he is still my dad and I want to go back home again as soon as I can. I can't leave here soon enough. I'm grateful to you for taking me in because I had nowhere to go, but now I've had the baby I want to get rid of it as soon as possible so that I can go back to Cardiff. I want to live my own life again and forget all this ever happened. It's been like one of those nightmares; the ones where you are running and running to get away from something evil and can't. Well, now I have.'

'What about your baby?' Megan interposed gently. 'You can't simply abandon it, *cariad*.'

'You told me that you'd arrange to have it adopted,' Mavis reminded her.

'Well . . . yes, I agree we did say that but then we didn't know—'

'That it would be black,' Mavis interrupted contemptuously. 'No one wants to adore a black baby, is that it?'

'Well, I don't know about that,' Megan parried. 'I am sure there are people who will, but it may be more difficult . . .'

It was something she would have to discuss with Angela Burton and somehow she knew they wouldn't find it easy, certainly not as simple as finding a home for a white child.

'You shouldn't have let him live, should you?' Mavis said, turning to face Harvey Stott.

'What are you talking about?' he frowned. 'What do you mean by that?'

'You didn't have to slap him and make him breathe,' Mavis said bitterly. 'You could have let him die and thrown him out with the trash. You didn't, so now it's up to you lot to get rid of him the best way you can. I want nothing at all to do with him.'

'What about his father?' Megan asked. 'Shouldn't he have a say in what happens to the child, *cariad*?' she persisted.

'That black bugger! A one-night stand! I never saw him again; I don't even know his name. I know, it was my own fault but I was drunk. That's what happens when you are brought up strictly teetotal; you have no head for drink. I had two port and lemons and then I was up for anything. He was an American GI, a smooth talker and as black as the night. That's all I can tell you about him.'

'Perhaps if your parents, especially your mother, saw your dear little baby, he would touch their hearts and they would accept him,' Sandra said softly. 'After all, Mavis, he is their grandchild.'

'They would still be horrified and refuse to let me go back home. They wouldn't welcome a grandchild unless I was married and they'd be mortified by a black one.'

'They might feel differently once they saw him so why not give it a chance, *cariad*,' Megan urged.

'Even though they know that there's every nationality under the sun living in Cardiff's Tiger Bay, they won't,' Mavis assured them. She laughed derisively. 'There's Whites, Chinks, Negroes and Indians and no one takes any notice but for a white girl like me to turn up with a black baby now that would bring disgrace on my family. I have two younger sisters and they would be shunned as well as me. No, I am not going to take that baby home. If you don't want him then I'll dump him somewhere on my way to the train station when I leave here or throw him into the Mersey.'

'Shush, shush, *cariad*,' Megan soothed. 'That's a terrible thing to say. You are overwrought; a good night's sleep and you may feel differently about things.'

'No, I won't,' Mavis shouted. 'And stop calling me *cariad*.

I know we're both Welsh and that it's a term of endearment, but I don't want sympathy from you or anyone else. I've had the baby and as I keep telling you I simply want to go back home and get on with my life and forget that any of this ever happened.'

'We all feel like that when we make a mistake but we've got to face up to the fact that it has happened and take responsibility for the result,' Jennifer White said quietly.

'We're not all as perfect as you,' Mavis told her bitterly.

'Come girls, there's no need for us all to quarrel,' Megan interposed as she saw a bright red flush flare up on Jennifer's cheeks. 'I think we should leave Mavis to drink her tea and then settle down for a sleep. We'll take our tea downstairs.'

'Good idea,' Mavis muttered. She picked up the baby which was lying on the bed beside her. 'Here –' she held him out to Megan – 'take this squalling brat with you and don't ever bring him back, I never want to see him again.'

TEN

The pitiful crying of Mavis's baby roused Megan very early the next morning. She slipped out of bed, put on her dressing gown and went to see if she could help in any way.

The door to Mavis's room was ajar and with a feeling of apprehension Megan pushed it open. The room was empty except for the baby which was lying in the middle of the unmade bed screaming lustily. There was no sign of Mavis.

Megan sighed. She knew that tracing her would be impossible. She suspected that the address Mavis had given them was a false one and to try and find her in Cardiff's Tiger Bay would be virtually impossible.

Megan picked up the screaming baby, cradling it in her arms and trying to soothe it as she made her way to the bathroom in case Mavis might be in there.

On her way downstairs she met Nelly who had also heard

the child crying and was on her way up to see what was the matter.

'Is Mavis having trouble getting it to feed?' Nelly asked, pushing back her straggling grey hair and smothering a yawn.

'Mavis has gone. Her room is empty,' Megan told her.

'You sure? That girl was in no fit state to leave. Perhaps she's in the bathroom,' Nelly persisted.

'No, she's not. I've already checked in there. All her clothes and belongings are gone as well, but she's left her baby,' Megan said sadly.

'Her family will never take her back,' Nelly said worriedly. 'She's told me all about them and I know the sort of man her father is. A bigoted man who always knows what is right. He's very religious and he regards Mavis as a "fallen woman".'

'Then let's hope she has friends in Tiger Bay or wherever she's gone who will give her a home and help her to get back on her feet,' Megan said shaking her head sadly. 'Now, if you will take this baby and see if you can get him to feed from a bottle, Nelly, I will see what arrangements I can make about finding him a home.'

'You won't find that easy to do,' Nelly murmured as Megan put the baby into her arms.

'Until he is taken away for adoption, do you think you will be able to look after him, Nelly? I'm sure that Lulu and probably Betsy will be willing to help you.'

Megan's phone call to Angela Burton later that morning did not go as smoothly as it might have done. Angela was on the point of going out for lunch but she said she would call round afterwards.

She instructed Megan to have the baby ready for collection and that she would have her own special carrycot in the car to take him away.

When she did arrive matters became even more complicated. She was delighted that they had a baby for her; that was until she saw it.

'You never mentioned that it was black,' she said caustically. 'Black babies are not easy to place; there are very few black families in need of a baby and white families don't want them as a general rule. I think he will have to go into a home if I can find one willing to take him. I'm afraid you will have to keep him here until I've managed to find one.'

Megan felt taken aback. This wasn't the arrangement as she recalled it, but she merely murmured her thanks and said no more. She didn't mind the baby staying with them for a few more days but she was concerned about what its eventual fate was going to be.

Nelly seemed to accept the news without question. 'Poor little mite,' she muttered. 'Sure and I'd keep him myself if I was a few years younger. We'd better give him a name though.'

'Perhaps Lulu should be the one to do that because she seems to be the one who cares about him the most,' Megan suggested.

Lulu was delighted at the idea. 'I think we should call him Moses,' she stated.

'Moses?' Megan thought about it but could find no reason why the baby shouldn't be called that and anyway, she told herself, he would probably be given a quite different name once he was adopted, so it might as well be Moses as anything else.

Having been the one to name him, Lulu immediately took over the responsibility for looking after Moses. She had plenty of help from the others. There was always someone ready to mix his feed and sit in the armchair nursing him while he took his bottle.

He was a contented baby and usually slept right through the night provided that his last feed was around ten o'clock. Lulu seemed to be happy enough to undertake to do this and to settle him for the night in the small cot that had been moved into her room.

Sandra left all this organizing to Megan. Most of her own time was now taken up with looking after her own baby; Hope was not nearly as placid as Moses.

Little Hope was a fretful baby, demanding a great deal of attention. Megan felt the child would have been better if she had not been fussed over quite so much but she was too tactful to say anything.

After all, she told herself, it was Sandra's house and although they were more or less partners, it was not up to her to interfere over what Sandra wanted to do when it came to looking after Hope. If Sandra wanted to take advice from Nelly then that was a different matter altogether since she seemed to regard Nelly almost like a surrogate mother.

They all had other things on their minds anyway. Christmas was less than a week away and they were trying hard to find extra food to make it as special an occasion as possible.

Nelly had quite a few contacts and she was also well known in Paddy's Market at the top end of Scotland Road. The stall-holders there often saved things for her and she made a point of reminding them how many she was going to have to feed over Christmas.

Megan and Sandra made up stockings for each of the girls almost as if they were still children. A few shiny coins, a small bar of chocolate, a pair of lisle stockings, a lipstick, a tablet of scented soap and a cheap magazine went into each one.

For Nelly, knowing how much she felt the cold when she went shopping, they decided on a thick woollen scarf and matching gloves.

The menu for Christmas Day included a capon that the butcher had kept for Nelly and a Christmas pudding to be served with custard.

The girls were delighted by their presents and by the festive feast. They sang carols and chattered happily about the Christmases they had known in the past.

Megan felt homesick remembering the Christmas festivities she had enjoyed at Yr Glaslyn. She wondered if her parents were missing her as much as she was missing them. Once or twice during the day she was tempted to phone them but managed to put the thought from her mind, afraid it might show a sense of weakness on her part.

She had made her decision to stand on her own feet and she had made a new life for herself here in Liverpool. She felt she was doing something worthwhile; her own special war work.

The war was still being fiercely fought in Europe and had now been extended to North Africa where the British had captured Tobruk, as well as to Burma and many of the troops had been sent there. It was where Sandra feared Hank might be fighting.

Shortly before Christmas they had heard that the British had bombed Eindhoven in the Netherlands and the Americans had bombed Naples, and the Allies had clashed with the Japanese. It seemed to Megan as she read the headlines that the whole world was at war and casualties mounting daily. It all seemed so senseless.

As the year came to an end, however, things looked brighter for the Allies: Rommel was trapped in Tunisia and the Germans were encircled at Stalingrad.

Early in 1943 two other girls moved in. Hilda Heath who was a big strapping twenty-year-old with red hair and a broad freckled face and Sally Ainsworth who was small and childlike and who laughed nervously or giggled at everything that was said to her.

They both came from Birmingham and when Megan asked them what they were doing in Liverpool they were very evasive. Hilda muttered something about being given a lift by a lorry driver bringing stuff down to the Liverpool docks. Sally merely giggled. She appeared to be dominated by Hilda and looked at her for guidance before answering any questions or speaking at all.

Neither of them had any luggage and neither of them had their ration books or clothing coupons; nothing, in fact, but the clothes they stood up in and no money at all.

It was going to be an extra drain on their already meagre rations and as Megan had feared there was a great deal of grumbling from Nelly when it came to planning their meals for the coming week.

Nevertheless, Megan felt she couldn't turn them away. From their appearance, Megan judged that their babies were due within a few weeks but they both still seemed fit and well and assured her that they were willing to help in whatever way they could.

When Megan warned Nelly not to allow them to do any really heavy work, Nelly merely laughed at her.

'Them two,' she scoffed. 'They could lift a three-ton lorry and think nothing of it. Still, if that's your orders, then I'll try and remember.'

Their arrival meant that the house was now so packed that Betsy would need to be in Nelly's room permanently, so that the two newcomers could each have a room of their own.

'Are you sure you'll both be happy about that?' Megan asked Betsy.

'Oh, Nelly won't mind. We're both from the same part of Ireland, sure we are, and we'll get on like a house on fire.'

When Megan tentatively spoke to Nelly about it she found that Nelly was in complete agreement.

'There's just one thing; a bit of a change I'd like to make if it's all right with you. I would sooner have the room next door to the kitchen as my bedroom.'

Megan frowned. 'You mean the utility room that we use as a storeroom or lumber room?'

'That's right,' Nelly said forcefully. 'It's bigger and it would be far more convenient. I'm that tired when I finish at night that having to drag myself up the stairs puts years on me. Now if I could just walk the few yards and be in me own quarters then that sure would be fine. It would free up another room for the girls, too, sure it would. Put those two Brumbies up on the top floor; they'll be less trouble up there and it's my opinion that they could be a rowdy pair and cause disruption amongst the other girls.'

'Well, Nelly, if you're quite sure,' Megan said hesitantly.

'Of course I'm sure; I've said so, haven't I! There'll be more room, too, for Betsy especially when she has the baby and that's in with us as well.'

It sounded almost too good to be true to have solved their problem so easily and, as it turned out, it was. Two days later a hatchet-faced, middle-aged man from Liverpool Council called to ask if he could inspect the place because it had been reported to them that they were living in an overcrowded situation.

Megan felt angry. She was doing her bit to help the war effort and she didn't want interference from any officials.

When she demurred about letting him in, he glowered at her and threatened to get a court order.

'Then I'll be back with a policeman and you'll have to let me in so you may as do it quietly now,' he told her.

Reluctantly she let him in and took him through the house, apologizing to each of the girls when she was forced to tap on their door and ask if they minded if he looked into their room.

When the inspection was over the official said he was sorry for disturbing them all.

'From information we received concerning all the girls who come and go here at all hours of the day someone had the impression that it was a brothel,' he explained. 'As it hadn't been registered as such, we were forced to check what was going on and assure ourselves that it wasn't overcrowded.'

'I wouldn't have thought you'd be so particular about over-crowding when half the homes in this city have been bombed and families made homeless so that they have to move in with relatives for shelter,' Megan said frostily.

'It's nothing to do with me, miss, I'm just the man they send out to check on these things.'

'Well, I hope you're satisfied and that they accept your report.'

'They will, there's nothing amiss here.' He smiled awkwardly. 'I am a bit confused however by all the very pregnant young ladies all living under one roof. Is it some sort of commune you've set up here?'

Briefly Megan explained what she was doing.

He gave her a look of respect. 'That's wonderful work, miss. Dreadful the way these Yanks came here, made so many of our girls pregnant and have now vanished completely.'

'You don't think that they will return as soon as they can and claim the girls they have promised to marry and be delighted to meet their children?'

'Not them Yanks! They're like the sailors; a fresh girl in every port, and if the girl gets pregnant then it is up to her to sort things out,' he said.

'You sound very bitter,' Megan murmured.

'My own daughter was trapped like that and now me and my wife have to help our girl to bring up the child. Lovely little lad but we are far too old for that sort of lark, I can tell you.'

'Well, I'm glad you didn't disown her or throw her out into the street to fend for herself,' Megan murmured.

'No,' he shook his head. 'I was tempted to do so when she first told us about it but she's our own flesh and blood and we should have protected her more.' He sighed lugubriously, 'Hindsight is a wonderful thing. You do what you think is best at the time.'

ELEVEN

Megan was roused the next morning by a loud banging on the front door. She peered at her bedside clock and saw that it was only twenty past six. As the knocking was repeated, she pulled on her dressing gown and went downstairs to see what was going on.

As she reached the hall Nelly came stumbling out of the room she had taken over as her bedroom. She was wearing an old coat over her nightdress and her grey hair hung around her shoulders like a dingy grey curtain.

'What on God's earth is going on? Who's hammering on the door at this time of the morning?'

'I don't know,' Megan told her. 'Wait here and I'll see who it is.'

As she undid the locks and opened the door a few inches, a stout middle-aged man hastily put his foot over the threshold so that she couldn't close it again.

'Is she here?' he demanded hoarsely, trying to push past Megan. 'My daughter, is she here?'

'I don't know, what is your daughter's name?' Megan said, trying to block his way even though she knew it was impossible because he was far more heavily built than she was.

'She's only a child,' he said accusingly as he pushed his way into the hall. 'I'll have the law on you,' he went on, ignoring Megan's question.

'Tell me her name,' Megan persisted.

'Sally. Sally Ainsworth and she's only a child, I'm telling you, and she doesn't know what she's doing.'

'And she's pregnant,' Megan said dryly.

'So she is here. You have her. You're planning to sell her baby when it's born.'

Megan drew herself up and clutched tightly at her dressing gown. 'I must warn you to watch what you are saying, Mr Ainsworth, or I will be the one having the law on you,' she said angrily.

'Your daughter is here,' Megan went on more calmly. 'She arrived a few days ago accompanied by an older girl called Hilda Heath. You probably know her as well.'

'Know her, I'll say I know her! She's the one who led my little Sally astray and got her into trouble. She's been a bad influence on Sally ever since the first day they met. Time and again I've told my missus to do something about it and stop our Sally seeing that Hilda Heath. I even told young Sally that I'd throw her out if she didn't stop going round with Hilda.'

'Well now, it seems she has taken you at your word and left home,' Megan told him.

Suddenly all the fight seemed to go out of Sally's father. He mopped at his brow and his shoulders sagged. He looked so beaten that Megan felt sorry for him and suggested he had better come and sit down so that they could discuss the matter in a more civil manner.

Turning to where Nelly was lurking in the shadows and listening to all that was going on, Megan said, 'Why don't you make us a pot of tea, Nelly, while I have a chat with Mr Ainsworth.'

Megan wished she could go and get dressed because she felt at a disadvantage in her dressing gown but, deciding that was impossible, she tried to behave in as dignified a manner as she could.

Instead of inviting him into the sitting room to sit down in one of the comfortable armchairs she took him into the dining room. 'We'll both sit here at the dining table, Mr Ainsworth,' she said in an authoritative manner.

He complied without question and as Megan took a seat facing him Nelly appeared with their tea.

'Milk and sugar?' Megan asked as she picked up the teapot.

'Yes please. Three sugars if you can spare them, I've a very sweet tooth.'

Megan gave a tight smile and said nothing as she complied with his request. Mentally she was thinking how this would deplete their meagre rations, especially since Sally hadn't brought her ration book with her.

As they sipped their tea Mr Ainsworth told Megan a harrowing story of how Sally had been led astray by Hilda Heath from the very first day she had gone to work and the two girls had met.

'Hilda Heath was a charge hand at the factory and she dominated our Sally from day one,' he said bitterly. 'I'd heard her name mentioned long before Sally met her because she'd dabbled in the black market and drugs from the day the war started.'

He took a gulp of tea and then wiped his mouth with the back of his hand. 'Led our Sally on to do the same. Then the pair of them started going out with the soldiers who were billeted nearby. Traded themselves for what they could get; nylon stockings, chocolate and, in Hilda's case, for cigarettes. Sally doesn't smoke, but that Hilda has smoked like a trooper ever since she was about ten years old or so I understand.'

'You tried to stop Sally seeing the soldiers, of course,' Megan murmured.

'Aye! We did everything we could. We even locked her in her room but she climbed out through the window, helped, of course, by that Hilda Heath,' he said bitterly.

'The wife and me were at our wits' end and then when she fell pregnant . . .' He paused and mopped at his brow with a red handkerchief that he pulled out of the top pocket of his jacket. 'I thought it would be the death of my wife. Took to her bed for three days crying non-stop, said it was all her fault for not watching over the girl more than she did.'

He took another mouthful of tea. 'Seeing as how she did everything any mortal person could do to protect our Sally it was ridiculous for her to take on like that. In the end I had strong words with her and told her that she needed to pull herself together, we needed all our strength to deal with the situation. I reminded her that Sally had no husband, nor was likely to have one now, so it would be up to us to bring the child up.'

'Your wife accepted this?'

'Aye, she's a sensible woman, I'll say that much for her. She knew what I was saying was true.'

'So why did Sally run away? Why did she come here to Liverpool?'

'She was persuaded to do so by that Hilda, I suppose. She was pregnant too only she knew that her family wouldn't do anything to help her when the baby arrived and it was probably her idea to get away from Birmingham. What with one thing and another the place was getting too hot for her and she wanted to go somewhere where she weren't known.'

'Why involve Sally? Why persuade your daughter to go with her, Mr Ainsworth?' Megan asked frowning.

'Probably hadn't the guts to do it on her own,' he said angrily.

'You think they intended to start a new life after they'd had their babies?'

'That's right. She'd have our Sally look after the kids and she'd be off doing her own thing. You can bet your boots it would be somewhere where there were plenty of soldiers,' he said bitterly. 'Hilda was always telling Sally that the Yanks were the ones to go for because they were well paid and generous and furthermore they supplied things like nylon stockings and cigarettes.'

'So why did they come to Liverpool and to our house here in Chapel Gardens?' Megan asked with a frown.

'Can't say, don't know why they did that. Are there any Yanks stationed nearby?'

'There were but as far as I know they've all gone overseas which is one of the reasons why Sandra Peterson and I have set up this house as a refuge for unmarried girls expecting babies.'

'They talk about coming over here to help us and all they do is give us a load of trouble,' Mr Ainsworth said angrily.

'Yes, the Yanks are responsible for a great many of the girls who now find themselves in trouble and deserted, not knowing which way to turn. Many of them are hoping that when the war is over the men they knew will come back and marry them as they have promised to do and accept their ready-made family. In a great many instances, however, we know that the girls will never see or hear from them again. Some of the girls we help are planning to keep their babies; others are offering them for adoption.

'I suppose it shows how caring and responsible Hilda and Sally are if they are planning to find lodgings together and bring up their babies,' Megan added thoughtfully.

Mr Ainsworth ran a hand through his thinning grey hair, pushing it back from his furrowed brow in a gesture of frustration and despair.

'No,' he said in an angry voice, 'from what a neighbour told my wife, Hilda had said that they intended to abandon them; leave them on a doorstep or something.'

'That's scandalous,' Megan gasped. 'Have you told the police?'

Mr Ainsworth shook his head. 'No! There's enough nasty business without getting involved with the law over it. It doesn't matter one way or the other anyway,' he stated. 'I'm here to take Sally back home. There's no need for her to abandon her baby, it will have a good home with us and so will she once she sees the error of her ways. Now, can I see her?' he asked forcefully.

'Of course. I'll ask Nelly to call her.'

'Don't tell her that I'm here,' Mr Ainsworth cautioned.

'Very well, I won't say why I need her,' Megan agreed.

As they waited for Sally to join them Megan wondered what would happen. She hoped there would not be any unpleasant scene. She understood Mr Ainsworth's concern for his young daughter. She could well see that Hilda could be a dominating influence and obviously not one for the best.

Sally's gasp of surprise when she came into the room and saw her father sitting there was followed by a burst of joy as she flung herself into his arms, wrapping her own arms around his neck as she hugged and kissed him.

The warmth in her voice as she asked anxiously, 'How is Mum?' confirmed Megan's suspicions that Sally was homesick.

'Missing you very much,' her father told her. 'I've come to take you home.'

Sally pulled away from him. 'I can't come home,' she said in a whisper. 'It would make Mum so unhappy when the neighbours and her friends find out I'm having a baby.'

'What utter rubbish,' her father said dismissively. 'Most of them know anyway and wonder where you are. We told them you were gone on a little holiday and most of them said we shouldn't have let you go gallivanting off in your condition. Come on now, don't waste time, get your things together and we'll be on the next train back to Birmingham.'

Sally hesitated, looking at Megan for support. 'Will that be all right, Miss Lloyd?' she asked.

'Of course it will, Sally. I am more than pleased to know that you will be back with your family and that they will be taking care of you.'

'Go and get your things then,' her father urged.

'I haven't anything to collect. I only have what I stand up in,' Sally said shamefacedly, tears filling her large blue eyes.

'Then we'll be off,' her father stated, standing up and holding out his hand to Megan. 'Thank you for taking care of my daughter.'

Sally still seemed to be reluctant. 'What about Hilda?' she blurted out. 'I ought to tell her I'm going home.'

'You'll do nothing of the sort,' her father told her in a severe voice. 'One word with her and she'll be trying to get you to stay here and go ahead with her madcap plan for a so-called new life.'

'No,' Sally said with a sweet smile. 'I've had enough of trying to have a new life. I really do want to come home again, Dad.'

'That's good to hear,' he said, putting an arm around her shoulder and squeezing it affectionately.

'Don't worry about Hilda, I'll tell her what you have decided to do,' Megan promised with a smile.

'Right then, now we really will be off,' Mr Ainsworth said. He pulled out his wallet and extracted a five-pound note. 'It's all I can spare at the moment but I'll send another when I get back home,' he said in a rather embarrassed voice.

Megan hesitated to take it, then remembering all the bills that were mounting up, held out her hand. 'Thank you, Mr Ainsworth, that is very kind of you.'

Hilda Heath was extremely angry when Megan broke the news that Sally had gone home with her father. She stormed and raved and grabbed Megan by the shoulders, threatening what she would do and shaking her until Megan's teeth chattered.

Hearing the commotion Nelly came out of the kitchen to find out what was going on. Grabbing hold of Hilda's shock of red hair, she dragged her backwards off Megan and then bundled her towards the door, pushing her out into the street and telling her to clear off and to go back to Birmingham herself before slamming the door shut.

'Are you all right?' Nelly asked anxiously, turning her attention to Megan who was breathing heavily and holding both hands to her head as if in pain. 'Shall I send for Dr Stott?'

'No, no, of course not! I'll be all right in a minute,' Megan gasped. She ran a hand over her hair and straightened her dressing gown. 'I wouldn't like to run into her on a dark night,' she said in a shaky voice.

'Nor at any other time,' Nelly agreed. 'I told you the moment I set eyes on her that she was going to be trouble. Has the other one gone home with her dad?'

'Yes, Mr Ainsworth has taken Sally home; we needn't worry about her any more. He and his wife will take care of her and the baby,' Megan murmured. 'I thought he was being over protective when he said that Sally was bullied by Hilda Heath but now I can see that he had every reason to be worried by their friendship.'

For the next ten minutes Hilda Heath banged on the front door, calling them every imaginable name. Then all was quiet and from where they were watching from the sitting-room window, Megan and Nelly saw Hilda thumbing a lift.

Megan gave a sigh of relief when she saw a car stop and a man lean out. After speaking to Hilda, he opened the passenger door.

As Hilda climbed inside, Megan momentarily felt concern.

'We really shouldn't let her go off like that with a perfect stranger, anything could happen to her,' she said contritely as she rushed to the door to try and stop her.

'No, perhaps not, but she's gone now and so there's nothing we can do about it, is there?' Nelly said complacently. 'Let's hope we never hear from her again,' she added, a look of relief on her lined face.

TWELVE

I t was an eventful day. As soon as Mr Ainsworth and Sally had left and Hilda Heath had been driven away, Megan started to go upstairs to get dressed.

'Don't wait for me, I want to take a shower and wash my hair,' she called to Nelly who had gone back into the kitchen to prepare breakfast.

She was halfway up the stairs when Nelly came bustling out into the hallway, wiping her hands on a towel.

'Why don't you sit down for a few minutes and get your breath back,' Nelly said. 'You still look shaken up by that attack from Hilda Heath.'

'I do feel shaken up,' Megan admitted. 'What's more my head really hurts. She had a really tight grip on my hair and when she started shaking me it felt as though a mad dog was savaging me.'

'Nasty piece of work that one, I thought so the first time I set eyes on her,' Nelly said again. 'Never mind, I gave her a touch of her own medicine. If your head hurts then hers must be hurting three times as much,' she added consolingly.

'What I would really like is a strong cup of coffee, if you can spare the coffee. Something to settle my nerves.'

'You go on into the sitting room and I'll bring it in to you with a slice of freshly made toast,' Nelly promised.

Within a few minutes Sandra joined her, wanting to know what all the noise and disruption had been about.

'Well, I for one am not sorry to see the back of those two

girls. I sensed they'd be trouble from the moment they crossed the doorstep.'

'Hilda Heath yes, but not little Sally Ainsworth. She was so childlike.'

'Yes, and vulnerable too, and that Hilda would have used her as a tool to demand all sorts of things if they had stayed on here. No, this is good news, so stop worrying about it. Sally has gone back home and from what I have heard from you of her father it's a warm and loving home and they'll keep the baby and help Sally to bring it up. Pity there aren't a few more families like that. Now,' Sandra said with a smile, 'I must go and give my little Hope her bath and feed her. Being a mother is a full-time job, I can tell you.'

Megan smiled understandingly. She felt a little worried because Sandra certainly did seem to be spending more and more time with the baby to the exclusion of everything else. Her whole life seemed to be centred around Hope and lately she had discouraged any of the girls doing anything at all to help her with the child.

Megan sat for quite some time after Sandra had left the room. She knew that she ought to go and have her shower and wash her hair and then get on with her daily tasks. She should be getting the accounts up to date and checking with Nelly that everything was running smoothly. After the upheaval of the early morning though, she was enjoying the peace and quiet of having the sitting room to herself.

She felt a trifle guilty at more or less turning Hilda Heath out but she knew that Nelly and Sandra were right and it had been the best thing to do. Hilda had all the hallmarks of a troublemaker and might well have caused upsets in the future.

She wondered if she ought to record the details about the two girls and their brief stay with them in case they were questioned by the authorities at some later date. She would have liked to forget all about them but she decided that perhaps it was the sensible thing to do.

At the moment everything was crystal clear in her mind but in a few months' time she was quite sure the details would be blurred. It wouldn't take her long because there was very little to record apart from their names and the dates they arrived and left.

They still had a fairly full house and she was particularly concerned about baby Moses. There had still been no word from Angela Burton about any adoption plans for him and she was fearful that it meant little Moses would have to go into a home.

She had just risen from her comfortable chair and walked across to the bureau that stood in the far corner of the room to make a note about Hilda Heath and Sally Ainsworth when Nelly burst into the room looking very agitated and flustered.

'You'd better come as quick as you can, Miss Megan,' she stated. 'Young Lulu has had a fall and she's bleeding badly. To make matters worse I think she's started her labour.'

'Where is she?'

'She's lying on the landing floor right outside the door of her room. I left her there because I was afraid to move her. I didn't want to disturb Miss Sandra because I know she's attending to little Hope so I've asked one of the girls to let Dr Stott know what has happened.'

Megan felt apprehensive as she accompanied Nelly to where Lulu was lying. As Nelly had said she was haemorrhaging badly and groaning in between crying out with pain.

'We can't let her lie there,' Megan said worriedly. 'Perhaps with Jennifer and Betsy to help we could manage to get her on to her bed. I'm sure she's not very heavy.'

Nelly shook her head. 'I don't think we should risk moving her, not with her in that state. I think we ought to wait until Dr Stott gets here,' she insisted.

'He may not be able to get here for ages,' Megan demurred.

Nelly's mouth tightened into a firm line. 'I'd still sooner leave her where she is,' she said firmly. 'We can make her comfortable; put a pillow under her head and a blanket over her if she's feeling cold.'

Megan decided it was pointless arguing. Nelly had been present at far more births than she had and if Nelly thought it was dangerous to move Lulu then it probably was.

'Whatever you think is best,' she agreed. 'I'm off to quickly get dressed. I won't have a shower now, so I'll only be a couple of minutes.'

THIRTEEN

The rest of the morning passed in a series of comings and goings. As soon as she was dressed Megan stayed with Lulu most of the time but she was very relieved when Harvey Stott finally arrived and took charge.

He agreed that Nelly had done the best thing in leaving Lulu where she was and he confirmed that the birth was imminent. Because of where Lulu was lying it was not easy for any of them to administer help and Lulu did not have the strength to push.

'I think we'll have to get her on to her bed,' he said at last. 'I've examined her pretty thoroughly and she doesn't seem to have broken any bones so I don't think it will hurt to move her as long as it is done carefully. Have you a board or something similar that we can slip underneath her?'

Nelly searched the kitchen diligently but there was nothing they could use. Then she had the bright idea of using the ironing board.

'If we keep it folded up flat it should serve the purpose,' Dr Stott agreed. 'Find some string, Nelly, so that we can tie it so that it doesn't start to open up when we lift it up with Lulu on it.'

It was a very ungainly contraption but it served the purpose. With the help of a couple of the girls they gently rolled Lulu on to her side, slipped the board underneath and then rolled her back so that she was lying on it.

With Nelly lifting at one end, Dr Stott at the other and a girl on each side to make sure Lulu didn't slip off, they carried her from the landing into her bedroom and gently transferred her on to the bed.

Although, as Dr Stott had said, Lulu wasn't hurt apart from bruising, she was very weak and exhausted. She had great difficulty in managing to push down when the contractions came. Her delivery was long and arduous and it was almost evening before her baby was born.

It was very small and despite all Dr Stott and Nelly's efforts it would not breathe. Eventually, with a deep sigh, Harvey Stott pronounced that it was stillborn.

At first Lulu cried uncontrollably, refusing to be comforted; crying until she was so completely exhausted that she fell into a sleep that was so deep that Megan began to worry in case she, too, never woke up.

Lulu's state of depression lasted for almost a week. Megan and Nelly did their best to rouse her out of it, making sure that someone stayed with her night and day.

The girls shared a good deal of this watchfulness. They sat there, talking to Lulu or trying to get her to eat and drink. For most of the time though she simply lay there, her eyes closed and her breathing so slow and shallow that sometimes they were afraid that she had stopped breathing altogether.

It was Betsy who hit on the idea of taking Moses in to Lulu and seeing if that might rouse her and bring her back to normality. At first Megan was against the idea, she felt it would only make losing her own baby even more harrowing for Lulu.

Secretly, against Megan's wishes, Betsy took Moses to see Lulu.

At first Lulu clapped her hands over her ears and buried her head under the quilt. Then, very slowly, she pulled the quilt back and stared at Moses. Finally, she held out her arms to him.

Gently Betsy settled the fat little black baby into the crook of Lulu's arms and then stood back leaving her to stare down at the enchanting little face and the big dark eyes that stared up at her.

Betsy left them together for about ten minutes and then went to take Moses away.

'No, leave him here with me,' Lulu begged.

'I can't. It's time for his feed and I have to put him to bed.'

'Bring him back again tomorrow morning then.'

When triumphantly Betsy told Megan what she had done

and that she had promised Lulu she would take Moses back to her the next day Megan felt uneasy.

'You might have made things much worse for Lulu,' she told her rather crossly.

'How have I done that? It's the first time she's shown any interest in anything.'

'I know, Betsy, but remember I'm already making arrangements for Moses to be adopted. If Mrs Burton turns up today or tomorrow to collect him then poor Lulu will feel more bereft than ever.'

Megan need not have worried. When Angela Burton did turn up a couple of days later it was to say that she had not managed to find anyone willing to adopt Moses and that she was making enquiries to see if there was a home where they would consider taking him.

'Meanwhile, I'm afraid you will have to keep Moses at Chapel Gardens for a little while longer,' she told Megan.

When the news of what had transpired reached Lulu she was most indignant.

'It's because he's black, isn't it? Well, if no one wants to adopt him then I will,' she declared. 'What's more I'll not merely look after him but I'll think of him as mine. Mavis left him and went back to Cardiff as if her baby had never existed. I'll be a better mother to him than anyone else!'

'Do you really mean you will actually adopt him, Lulu?' Megan said in astonishment.

'As far as I'm concerned he is my baby,' Lulu said, stroking the baby's face and kissing him on the brow. 'No one outside these four walls need know anything different. I've just given birth and this is *my* baby. Who's to know that he isn't mine? Who's going to concern themselves anyway?'

Megan and Sandra discussed the matter in detail and then took Harvey Stott into their confidence.

He looked rather grave. 'I'm not quite sure what is involved here?' he said frowning. 'Are you asking me to say that Moses is Lulu's baby?'

'Mavis abandoned him to us here at The Haven so she has no hold over him and it is certainly what Lulu wants,' Megan told him. 'Angela Burton can't find a home for Moses and it does solve the problem of what is to happen to him,' she added.

Harvey Stott pursed his lips in a silent whistle. 'Maybe it does and it is certainly a solution to your problem over adoption but I'm afraid that would be very irregular; it might even be considered a criminal offence.'

'Lulu claims that her family wants her back and they are prepared to overlook what has happened and they want to give a home to her baby,' Megan said.

'Unless we tell them they are not to know that Moses isn't her baby. They never met the father and she doesn't think that he will ever come back to Liverpool again, so what harm is there in it?' Sandra persisted.

'If Lulu doesn't take Moses then Angela Burton says he will have to go into a home,' Megan pointed out. 'What sort of life is a little black child going to have in one of those places?'

They argued about the matter for a long time. Eventually Harvey Stott shook his head, still unconvinced that it was the right thing to do although he could see that their reasons were excellent.

'What about when eventually Angela Burton comes back to collect him? What are you going to tell her?'

There was an uneasy silence then Megan said slowly, 'We'll tell her that the mother has decided to keep Moses.'

'When you start telling lies they only lead to more and more lies,' Harvey Stott warned with a sigh.

'Do you have a better story?' Sandra asked.

He shook his head. 'No, I'm afraid I haven't.'

'Well then, as Megan has pointed out, poor little Moses would have a far better life with Lulu and her family than in a home.'

'So why not agree to let us treat him as Lulu's baby?' Megan pressed.

Later that day when Megan spoke to Angela Burton and said that the mother of the black baby had decided to keep him, Mrs Burton was obviously relieved.

'Far the best outcome,' she said lightly. 'Let's hope you don't have any more problems like that for me. Now, when is the next baby due?'

'Probably any day now,' Megan told her.

'Good, I have quite a waiting list so I do hope they are all going to be white babies because that is what people want. I hope I shall be hearing from you very soon, very soon indeed,' she added cheerfully.

FOURTEEN

Three other babies were born over the next few weeks and were promptly given up and taken away by Angela Burton for adoption, but their mothers were still at Chapel Gardens.

Brenda Sutter, a Lancashire girl in her late twenties, had been relieved to know that her guilty secret had been dealt with so discreetly and was determined to forget it had ever happened.

Claire Parker, a pretty eighteen-year-old from a nearby road off Scotland Road, also vowed she would never forget the experience and she would never let another man touch her as long as she lived. She, too, had been completely uninterested in what happened to her baby once it had been born.

Angela Burton had been quite shocked by Claire's attitude when she had told her that she must not try and trace the baby's whereabouts once it was put up for adoption and that she must sign a paper to that effect.

'Don't you worry your head about that, luv,' Claire laughed. 'I can't wait to get rid of it; I didn't even want to know if it was a boy or a girl when it was born. As long as you take it away you can do whatever you like with it and I'll sign whatever I have to.'

The other young mother, Janet Williams, a soft-spoken, fair-haired girl with a round baby face, was full of tears and remorse at having to part with her baby.

'I wish I could keep him,' she said wistfully, 'but my mother is a widow and there are still six children at home and she's finding it a real struggle. I couldn't ask her to bring him up and I must go back to work to help her; she counts on my wages,' she explained.

'I ought to go home right away but I feel I need a bit of time away from them to pull myself together,' she added tearfully.

Since it was so bitterly cold, both Megan and Sandra felt that it would be heartless to send the girls away when they had only just had their babies.

'You can stay on for another week as long as you are prepared to share a room if any new girls arrive,' Megan told them.

The girls seemed to welcome the arrangement.

Betsy Hagan's baby, a little girl she called Mary, was born early in the spring while gales raged outside.

Angela Burton said there was nothing she could do about placing it for adoption until the weather calmed down, so Megan had no option but to let Betsy stay on.

They already shared a room, but now that the baby had been born Megan fully expected Nelly to complain about the baby keeping her awake at nights with its crying which was loud and persistent. To Megan's surprise Nelly made no comment at all and actually seemed to be enjoying both Betsy's company and that of the baby.

Relieved, Megan turned her attention to another problem that was very much more important. She had thought that she was running the house in Chapel Gardens in a very efficient way but at the end of the month her bank statement showed that the money she had inherited was rapidly dwindling away.

There had, of course, been several major outlays in the first few weeks for cots and bedding in order to make sure that all the bedrooms were adequately equipped.

Sandra had pointed out right from the start that she was willing to pay her share of the general running costs but that she couldn't afford to buy anything else, because she was no longer working and earning money.

At the time Megan had felt confident that she could afford to meet any extras that might be needed. She had, however, found that everything seemed to be far more expensive than she had thought they would be. Even though most of their cots and bedding had been bought either from pawnbrokers or from Paddy's Market and were either 'seconds' or second-hand, the outlay had been considerable.

Megan had quickly realized that their budget was limited. They also shopped for their food at Paddy's Market, buying the very cheapest they could find. Again, because they had no ration cards for any of the girls, they were forced into buying what she knew was Black Market produce, for which they had to pay high prices.

There were times when Megan felt quite guilty about this but then she salved her conscience by telling herself that it was justified because she was helping girls who were in trouble.

None of the girls had offered any kind of contribution towards their keep. Except for the five-pound note that Mr Ainsworth had given, there had been no other donation.

Angela Burton hadn't mentioned any payment either although Megan was quite sure that those people who took babies from her were asked to pay a fee for her services.

It was all very worrying but Megan hesitated to mention it to Sandra because she felt so indebted to her for her coopera-tion. Sandra had kindly given up the privacy of her home, they were living there rent-free and Sandra was paying the rates and so far she had not asked for any contribution towards the heating, lighting and general running costs of the house.

No, Megan decided, it was a problem she had to solve herself. She tried to think what her father would have done in such a situation. He was an astute businessman who had been running the slate mine and their estate in North Wales for countless years and she had never once heard him complain that he was short of money. He did have good returns from the slate quarry, of course, but he had to find the wages for all the men he employed there.

The upkeep of Yr Glaslyn, their large country mansion, must have been a drain on his resources, yet neither her father nor her mother ever seemed to be short of money and were always very generous whenever money was needed for local affairs.

She stood up and walked over to the window and stared

out, not seeing the dereliction, but instead remembering the peace and beauty of her home in North Wales.

Then she pulled herself together; that was all in the past and there was no way she could ask her father for advice or help, she reminded herself.

So whom could she ask? At once her thoughts flew to Harvey Stott. He was always so clear-thinking and sensible whenever she approached him on medical matters concerning the girls but could she trouble him with her own personal problems?

Finally, in desperation Megan did ask Harvey Stott for advice. He was the only person, she thought, who might be able to make suggestions as to how to solve the dilemma she found herself in.

His handsome face became extremely grave when he heard how things were organized.

'You can't possibly carry on funding everything out of your own pocket,' he told her firmly.

'I know,' she agreed ruefully, 'I'm at my wits' end because my money is almost exhausted. Yet how can I earn any money?'

'Well, for a start you must register this place as a charity.'

Megan looked at him in astonishment, her dark eyes wide with apprehension. 'What do you mean? It already is a charity. The girls can't afford to pay anything, most of them are destitute when they arrive at our door,' she pointed out. 'Half of them have only the clothes they stand up in.'

'All the more reason for you to register it as a charity immediately and then you'll be able to raise funds.'

'That sounds like begging,' Megan said scornfully, her mouth tightening into a thin line as she looked at him reproachfully.

'No, it's not! If it's a fully registered charity then you are legally entitled to organize events and raise money. No,' he said, holding up a hand to silence her when she was about to protest. 'I know what you are going to say but it is not begging, most definitely not. While the girls are with you awaiting the birth of their babies, why don't you set them to work to make things and then from time to time have a craft sale and make a profit from their endeavours.'

'What sort of things?' Megan frowned.

'I'm sure you'll find that they all have skills of some kind. They can probably all knit or sew and some may even be competent at other things like painting pictures, making gift cards, rug making or cane work.'

Megan's dubious expression changed to one of interest and she looked at him admiringly. 'That's certainly a possible idea,' she admitted.

'You make the most of their talents and then organize a craft fair and plough back the takings into the funds for running the place.'

'You make it sound easy,' Megan said thoughtfully, 'but would they be prepared to cooperate?'

'They'd probably enjoy it and since they will have different skills they'll egg each other on and then you will have a variety of items to sell.'

'It's certainly something to think about,' Megan agreed.

'Also, it will bring this place and what you are doing here to the attention of the general public. When you have a sale of the work the girls have produced, always make sure that you invite along a reporter from the local Liverpool newspaper to give you a write-up. There'll always be people who attend or read about it and whose heartstrings will be touched and who will then make a contribution.'

Emboldened by all his suggestions, Megan said tentatively, 'I keep wondering if we ought to ask Angela Burton to make some sort of contribution each time she takes a baby for adoption.'

'You mean she's not paying you anything?' he said in surprise, his blue eyes narrowing.

'No, she has never mentioned money. I can understand there would be no money involved when the baby has to go into a home but when it is placed with couples who want to adopt . . .' Her voice trailed off and she found the colour rushing to her face. It all sounded so mercenary, as if she was trying to sell the babies.

'She should be making a contribution of some kind,' he said firmly. 'You should have come to some arrangement with her long before this.'

'Perhaps then I should make it a late New Year resolution to do so,' Megan agreed with a smile.

'You need to go further than that; you need to ask her for payments for the babies you have already handed over to her.'

He began listing them but Megan interrupted him to remind him that Lulu had taken Moses and that Betsy's baby was also still with them. If Megan was being honest, it seemed that Betsy and Nelly were so attached and fond of each other that Betsy and Mary might end up being permanent members of the household. In fact, Betsy was very helpful in settling in the new girls, and she shared Nelly's room, so it seemed to suit them all for the moment.

'Make those the exception but there have still been three or four others that Angela Burton has placed,' he reminded her.

'There's also the question of your fee for attending all the deliveries,' Megan pointed out. 'You've never presented us with a bill.'

Harvey Stott looked uncomfortable. 'Initially I did it because I was a friend of Sandra's,' he stated.

'And now?'

'Well, I'm still a friend of Sandra's but there is another reason why I am happy to come here whenever I am needed.' He looked directly at her. 'It means I have a chance to see you.'

'See me!' Megan flushed, the hot blood rushing to her cheeks and her dark eyes opening wide with a mixture of astonishment and pleasure.

'Does that surprise you, Megan?'

'Well, yes,' she murmured shyly, clenching her lower lip with her teeth as their eyes met. 'I have come to think of you as a very good friend,' she added hastily.

'Nothing more?'

'We barely know each other, apart from when you come to attend one of the girls,' she said awkwardly.

'True and that is something I think we should put right as soon as possible. Will you have dinner with me tonight?'

Megan's heart started beating faster. Was she dreaming, she wondered, or was Harvey Stott really asking her out on a date? She was about to accept then some inner caution warned her not to rush things.

'I can't manage tonight,' she said hesitantly.

'Tomorrow night then?'

'Yes, I'd like that,' she said with a warm smile.

'Good! I'll pick you up at seven o'clock.'

Without waiting for an answer he stood up ready to leave.

'Until tomorrow night then,' he said as he headed for the door.

Megan stayed where she was for several minutes, going over in her mind what had just taken place. She could hardly believe that Harvey Stott had asked her to go out with him. She admired him and liked him a great deal and as their friendship had grown she knew she could trust him, but she had always regarded him as Sandra's friend.

She also thought about the suggestions he had made concerning funding the running of the place. They were good but it would be some time before she could organize enough craft items to make a sale a feasible possibility.

Registering their place as a charity sounded sensible but it would mean they would have to give it a name of some sort. Sandra would have to be consulted about this and that meant she would have to explain to Sandra why it was necessary and so far she had tried not to worry her about their financial status.

They would need to make it sound like a worthwhile project, one that didn't carry any stigma about the unmarried mothers; perhaps they could call it Chapel Garden Homes? She rather liked the sound of that.

Since it had to be done then there was no time like the present, Megan decided. She looked at the clock; with any luck Sandra would have finished feeding little Hope and would have put her down to sleep. Now might be an admirable time. She'd ask Nelly to bring a tray of tea into the sitting room and make sure that they weren't disturbed for the next hour.

Sandra was alarmed when Megan related the financial situation they were now in.

'You shouldn't have borne all this worry on your own,' she told Megan reprovingly. 'When we decided to set up this place I thought it was in partnership and if there were any concerns of any kind then we would discuss them and try and solve them between us.'

She listened in silence as Megan related the advice she'd been given by Harvey Stott.

'It all sounds very sensible,' she agreed, 'but it will take quite some time to organize. We could put this on the agenda for the coming year. If we have enough items then we could have a sale in the summer; failing that, we could stockpile anything that is made and have a sale shortly before Christmas.'

'We're going to need money long before that,' Megan pointed out.

'Yes, I realize that,' Sandra agreed. 'I think registering ourselves as a charity is a good idea though and that we should do so as soon as possible. I'm sure what Harvey had in the back of his mind was that he could then approach some of his more well-off patients and see if they would make a donation.'

'You really think he would do that?' Megan asked in surprise.

'To impress you he most probably would,' Sandra said dryly.

'What do you mean?' Megan asked, the colour rushing to her cheeks.

'Oh, come, Megan, you must have noticed how attentive he always is when you speak to him.'

'He's certainly always ready to help,' Megan admitted.

'Harvey has a crush on you; anyone can see that! I would have thought you would have realized it long ago.'

Megan smiled, her eyes dancing with mischief as she said, 'Perhaps that's why he's taking me out for dinner tomorrow night.'

'Really!' Sandra gave a beaming smile. 'That's wonderful news. What a terrific start for the spring.'

'You don't mind?'

'Mind, why should I mind? I'm absolutely delighted for you. My two favourite people getting together is tremendous news,' Sandra told her happily.

Megan took a deep breath of relief. For the first time she felt light-hearted about the feelings that she was slowly developing for Harvey Stott. Until that moment she had not realized that in some ways she had been holding back because she felt he belonged to Sandra, even though she knew Sandra was desperately in love with Hank. Now that it was all out in the open and Sandra actually approved, it brought such a feeling of relief that she wanted to shout about it from the rooftops and let everyone know how happy she was.

FIFTEEN

I t took a load off Megan's mind knowing that Sandra was in agreement about them registering as a charity but, like Sandra, she had no idea how they should go about it.

'Now that I know you're as keen as I am then I'll try and find out what we have to do,' Megan told her.

'I believe that there is an association called the Charity Commission or something that governs all charities, so perhaps if you can get in touch with them they will be able to guide me along the right lines.'

When she started to make enquiries Megan found that there was a great deal more involved than she had expected. It took her some time to accumulate and collate all the information that appeared relevant. She then found that the forms that had to be filled in were not only intricate but extremely confusing so in the end she suggested to Sandra that they took Jennifer White into their confidence and told her what they were planning to do.

'Jennifer is brilliant when it comes to filling in forms,' Megan said as she handed one of the forms to Sandra so that she could see for herself how arduous it was.

'I agree, and yes, we should ask her to help,' Sandra agreed with a nod as she handed the forms back to Megan. 'They certainly look complicated and I'm sure it's important to fill them in correctly.'

'There is one problem,' Megan said hesitantly. 'Jennifer's baby is due any day now so do you think it's fair to trouble her with a task like this?'

'I don't see why not,' Sandra said. 'It will help to take her mind off what is ahead.'

'That sounds a bit harsh,' Megan laughed, 'but I know what you mean.'

Jennifer seemed pleased to be asked to deal with the forms. She spent an afternoon and evening going through the papers that Megan had obtained and told them that before they could start to do anything it would be necessary to give the place a name.

'I was thinking we could call it Chapel Gardens Home,' Megan said thoughtfully.

'Does Sandra agree with that?'

'I haven't asked her yet.'

'Then perhaps we should do that first.'

Sandra had several objections. 'In the first place,' she said, 'some of the people in Chapel Gardens might object. Also it sounds far too institutional and anyway I don't particularly like it as a name.'

'So what do you want to call it?' Megan asked.

'I really don't know but I think it should be something that identifies the actual house and I don't want it to be called a home. That sounds far too much like a charitable institution.'

'Well, isn't that what it is?' Megan said dryly.

'Yes, but what I mean is it sounds somehow wrong almost as if we are a charity home. I can't quite explain what I mean but it doesn't feel right.'

'Have you any ideas, Jennifer?' Megan asked, turning to look at the girl.

'I think it would be rather nice to call it The Haven.'

There was a moment's silence as Megan and Sandra exchanged looks. Jennifer coloured up and looked embarrassed. 'It's only my idea,' she explained, 'but it is a haven.'

Megan's face softened. 'Is that the way you look at it?' she asked.

'I do and so do most of the other girls here. Where else would you be able to find somewhere where you could spend the last few days or weeks before your baby was born and know that you would be safe and well looked after?'

There was a moment's silence as if no one knew what to say although Megan felt pleased by what Jennifer had said. It was good to know that she was obviously succeeding in doing what she had hoped to do.

'What is more important to many of the girls who come here is the fact that the baby will be adopted if you are unable to take it home or you know you are going to be unable to bring it up. That is a terrific bonus and one that really does turn this place into a haven.'

'That's a wonderful tribute to what we are trying to do,' Sandra said. 'Thank you, Jennifer.'

'I agree, a wonderful tribute,' Megan murmured. 'Very well, that's settled, so we will go ahead and see if we can register it as a charitable undertaking called The Haven.'

It took Megan and Jennifer White almost a week to fill in the relevant forms and make sure they provided an accurate description of what went on at The Haven.

Both of them breathed a sigh of relief after Megan finally sealed the bulky envelope containing all the information that seemed to be needed and took it to the post office so that she could register the package to make sure that it didn't go astray.

'All we can do now is sit back and wait for the results,' she said when she returned.

'Let's hope we have given them all the details they want and that it will be plain sailing from now on.'

'I hope it will,' Jennifer agreed. 'I don't know whether it's because I've been sitting at the desk for so long or whether it's that I am starting labour but my backache has turned into sharp pains.'

She broke off and gave a gasp as her whole body shook and she clenched her teeth to stop herself crying out.

'I think there's no doubt that you are in labour,' Megan agreed. 'Come on, let's see if we can get you upstairs to your room and then I'll send someone to fetch Nelly. She'll know whether or not we ought to phone Dr Stott and let him know what's happening.'

It was a long hard labour for Jennifer. Her baby, a little boy, was born in the early hours of the following morning.

Jennifer was utterly exhausted and slept for most of the day.

When Harvey Stott called back in the evening to check if she was all right he was so worried about her he ordered complete bed rest for a couple of days.

She was still spending most of her time in bed a week later when the letter arrived informing them that The Haven was now officially registered as a charity.

'Unfortunately we can't make a toast in the traditional way but we have brought a cup of milky cocoa to celebrate our victory,' Megan and Sandra told her as they came together to break the news to her.

Although she drank the cocoa with them Jennifer was still so pale and listless that Harvey Stott became more concerned than ever.

'Is she showing any interest at all in the baby?' he asked.

'That's one of the main problems; she won't let us take it out of the room.'

'Have you any idea why that is?' he asked with a frown.

'She's afraid we may send it for adoption. She doesn't want to have it adopted and she simply won't believe us when we tell her that we have no intention of doing anything without her consent.'

'You mean that she's going to try and bring it up herself, single-handed?' he asked, his jaw tightening and his bright blue eyes widening with astonishment.

'I think that's what she's hoping to do, but I really can't see how it will be possible. She has nowhere to go and she has no job. Having the baby adopted would be the best thing for both of them.'

'Would it, though? I think you may be wrong about that. I have known the family for a long time and I am dismayed that they have rejected her.'

'Well, there's not very much we can do about that now, is there!' Megan said resignedly.

'I'm not so sure,' Harvey Stott said thoughtfully. 'I'm wondering if perhaps I should let Joshua White know that he is now a grandfather.'

'Surely that would be going against Jennifer's wishes,' Megan said briskly.

'Again, I'm not so sure. You see, it was her mother who

was so adamant that Jennifer should leave the family home before anyone was aware of the fact that she was pregnant. Mrs White moves in a very grand circle of ladies and adverse gossip of any kind about Jennifer would mortify her.'

'In those sort of cases isn't it usual for the girl to be sent to stay with relatives in some obscure part of the country and when it is all over she returns home and says she has been on holiday?' Megan said.

'In some families, yes, but in this instance I understand that Jennifer wouldn't agree to such a subterfuge.'

'I see. In that case the decision of whether to inform her father or not must rest with you. I certainly couldn't break my promise to her,' Megan said stiffly.

'I'll think about it,' Harvey Stott said thoughtfully as he took his leave.

Megan wondered whether to mention it to Sandra but in the end decided to keep her own counsel. She felt confident that Harvey would handle the matter in the best possible way but nevertheless it worried her that it was betraying Jennifer's trust.

As it happened she had no need to be alarmed. Harvey Stott did phone Joshua White at his office only to find that he and his wife were both away on holiday.

'I understand they won't be back for at least a week,' he told Megan the next time he visited The Haven. 'I did leave a message to let him know that Jennifer had had her baby. I said nothing else so it's now a question of waiting to see what he does. Meanwhile, we must do all we can to get Jennifer back to full health. Can you try and get her involved again in this business of registering The Haven as a charity?'

'It's already been done and we have had a letter confirming this and allocating us with the number of our registration,' Megan told him with a beaming smile.

'Great news! I think that perhaps I ought to take you out to dinner tonight to celebrate. I would ask Sandra to come as well,' he said teasingly, 'but I doubt if she would leave her baby for an entire evening.'

He promised to pick her up at seven that evening and said he would book a table at the Adelphi.

'That's very grand,' she commented with a smile.

'It's a very special celebration,' he countered.

The Adelphi was like another world. Although there was a war on it had not stopped them from putting on a wonderful meal. As she tucked into delicious delicacies that were beyond most people's reach Megan felt relaxed and happy.

As she caught sight of their reflection in the mirrored walls she thought what a good-looking couple they made and wished that everything was normal so that she could take him home to meet her parents.

Pushing such thoughts to the back of her mind she began to tell him about how Jennifer had helped them with all the form filling entailed in registering their undertaking.

'Splendid! Now I can begin to mention the project to some of the organizations and businesses that I'm involved with and send them details about what you're doing. Have you done a press release or planned any fundraising events?'

'No, we've done nothing at all yet. I'm not too sure what you mean by a press release,' she said in a puzzled tone.

'I mean a detailed description of what you are doing and one or two case histories. Something to send out to individuals and companies to gain their support.'

'I see.' Megan concentrated on the food on her plate. She still wasn't too sure what Harvey meant.

'Now that's something that Jennifer White would be good at,' he went on. 'I'm sure she's had experience of PR work when she was working for her father. Why don't you have a word with her?'

'Do you think she's strong enough to undertake a commitment as arduous as that?'

'I think it may be the challenge she needs; something to take her mind off the hard time she's had and stop her worrying about the future of her baby.'

'Well, if you think so,' Megan said with a feeling of relief. 'It would certainly save me a headache; in fact I'm not too sure what is actually required in a press release.'

'Don't give it another thought; Jennifer will know exactly what to do so leave it to her. She'll probably be very pleased to be asked to do it.'

Harvey was right; Jennifer was delighted.

'Can you bring me up all the relevant paperwork,' she said, sitting upright in bed and pushing the pillows behind her back to support her. 'I'll read through them and then make notes of exactly what we want to say. When I've done that you and Sandra can read them through and see if you approve.'

It took Jennifer less than a day to give them a rough outline of what she proposed to say in the press release. Megan and Sandra looked at each other in astonishment as they read through the lucid details she produced.

'You've certainly made it sound like a worthwhile project, Jennifer,' Sandra said admiringly.

'Well, it is,' Jennifer said with a smile. 'I owe you both a great deal. I am more than grateful.'

'It was Dr Stott who drew my attention to our need for a press release. Do you think we should let him have a look at it before we have it printed off?' Megan asked.

'I do. It would be a very good idea to let someone else read it to make sure I've included everything and not gone over the top,' Jennifer agreed.

Harvey thought she had done an extremely good job and asked them to let him have about twenty copies as soon as they were printed. He even recommended the printer they should use.

'He's quite right,' Jennifer confirmed. 'They are the firms that our company uses when we are having contracts or business proposals printed.'

Writing the press release seemed to bring Jennifer back into the real world as Harvey had hoped it would. She still looked very pale but the listlessness had gone. She was still emphatic however about having the baby with her all the time. He was progressing satisfactorily, fed well, but nevertheless she watched over him every moment of the day.

Megan and Sandra were worried about her. At the same time, they found her extremely helpful and would have been more than happy to employ her full-time had they been able to afford to do so.

'It would be wonderful if she could stay on because she

could organize campaigns to raise funds for us,' Sandra pointed out.

'Yes, that's very true but until we have some money we can't afford to pay for help of that kind.'

'Yet, at the same time, we need expert promotion in order to interest the right people who will want to provide us with funds.'

It was a dilemma that neither of them knew how to resolve in a satisfactory way no matter how hard they tried. There had been some response from people to whom Harvey Stott had sent the press release. Mostly they were enquiries or letters of approval but so far there had been no monetary help.

'Early days yet,' Megan said a few days later when she had been sorting out the post and Sandra had come in to ask if anything specific had turned up.

'We must have patience, I suppose,' Sandra said with a deep sigh.

Suddenly a loud knocking on the front door disturbed them. They heard Nelly go along the hallway to answer it followed by the murmur of her voice mingled with that of a man. The next minute Nelly was tapping on the door of the sitting room and saying, 'There's a gentleman here asking for you, Miss Megan.'

Frowning, Megan went to see who it was. A very tall, broad-shouldered man with thick grey hair and a neatly trimmed grey beard was standing there. He was very well dressed in a navy blue striped suit, white shirt with a stiff collar and dark blue tie and with a black alpaca overcoat and black trilby.

'Are you Megan Lloyd?' he demanded.

He looked so authoritative that Megan's pulse raced. She was afraid that he was some sort of official come to interrogate them about what went on at The Haven.

'Yes I am, how can I help you?' she asked, squaring her shoulders.

'Am I right in thinking that you have my daughter here?'

'Your daughter?' Megan took a deep breath. 'What is her name?' she asked, playing for time.

'Jennifer. Jennifer White.'

'There is a girl of that name here but—'

Before she could finish he interrupted. 'Good! I am her father Joshua White. My friend, Dr Harvey Stott, informed me that she is here and, what is more, that I am a grandfather. Is this correct?'

'Jennifer White has had her baby,' Megan admitted.

'Then can I see it? Jennifer as well, of course.'

Megan hesitated. She was unsure what to do. Jennifer had told her how her parents had turned her out and told her never to come back. She also recalled that Harvey had told her that it was Mrs White who had been so adamant that Jennifer could not remain at home in her condition.

Megan was anxious not to upset Jennifer by doing the wrong thing. But she knew Jennifer wanted to keep her baby and if her father was here asking to see them both then surely that meant he had forgiven her. It also possibly meant that he would be prepared to provide some sort of home for them both, Megan reasoned. Even if he and his wife didn't want her to go back to her home he might be prepared to provide her with a flat or house where she could bring up the baby.

'Come on, come on, what's the problem?' he asked impatiently.

'If you will step in here, Mr White,' Megan invited, backing into the sitting room, 'and take a seat I will ask someone to bring you a cup of coffee while I go and ask Jennifer if she is willing to see you.'

'Willing to see me! What utter nonsense! Of course she'll see me, she's my daughter!'

'Yes, Mr White, I hope she will see you but she has been under my care for quite some time now so I must warn you I have no intention of going against her wishes.'

SIXTEEN

J ennifer looked shocked when Megan told her that her father was downstairs and asking to see her and the baby.

'You mean he's come here?' she gasped, the colour draining from her face, making her look as scared as a naughty child. Megan felt sorry for her and wished she'd sent him on his way or even told him that Jennifer was no longer there.

'Yes, he's in the sitting room waiting to see you.'

Jennifer hesitated for a moment then threw back the bedclothes and stood up. 'I'd better see him, I suppose,' she said with a deep sigh. She picked up the baby sleeping in the crib alongside her bed and wrapped him carefully in the blanket that had been covering him. 'I'm ready!'

'You can't go down like that in your nightgown,' Megan said gently. 'Shall I hold the baby while you get dressed?'

Again Jennifer hesitated, then without a word she held the shawl-wrapped bundle out to Megan, picked up her clothes from the chair beside her bed and began to put them on.

She looked so young and vulnerable that Megan's heart ached for her.

As they went out on to the landing Jennifer was shaking so much that Megan insisted on carrying the baby down the stairs.

'I'll hand him over to you outside the sitting room door,' she promised when Jennifer started to protest.

In the hallway outside the sitting room Megan carefully handed the baby back to Jennifer. 'I'll go in and tell him that you're here,' she whispered.

Jennifer took a deep breath and again squared her thin shoulders. 'Nothing else, mind!'

'Very well.'

'I've had a shock, now it's time for him to have one,' Jennifer said, trying to smile but failing to do so.

'Sorry to have kept you waiting,' Megan said as she went

into the room. 'Jennifer is waiting outside the door, Mr White, if you would like to see her.'

'She is?' He looked perplexed for a moment. 'Then why doesn't she come in?' he asked curtly.

There was no need for Megan to reply. Jennifer had heard what he had said, pushed open the door and came into the room.

There was a moment of uneasy silence as they stared at each other almost like two strangers meeting for the first time. Then Joshua White strode across the room, arms outstretched, ready to embrace her.

Jennifer pulled back quickly, one hand held up as if warding him off.

Her father stiffened as if afraid that she was rejecting him. Then he saw what she was holding in her arms and instead placed his hands on her shoulders.

The frozen look on his face softened as he stared down at the miniature replica of himself that she was carrying in her arms. Murmuring softly he stroked the baby's cheek with his forefinger. Then he reached out to take the child from his daughter and hold it in his own arms.

For a brief second Jennifer hesitated. Then very gently she passed her precious bundle into his care.

Megan felt a lump rising in her throat and tears pricking her own eyes as she saw the joyous look on the girl's face and the proud look on her father's face as he nursed the baby.

'My grandson,' he exclaimed possessively. 'Another Joshua to carry on the family business.' He looked up questioningly at Jennifer. 'You have called him Joshua?'

'I've called him Joe,' she said quietly.

'Well, from this moment on he is Joshua, Joshua White,' her father stated firmly.

Megan felt relieved that the meeting between the two of them was so amenable because she was sure that it meant that Jennifer's problems, for the moment at least, were at an end. If she went home to her family then her future and that of the baby would be settled and safe.

She would miss Jennifer but this wonderful reconciliation

she had witnessed was more than she had ever dreamed could happen.

'So how did you find me?' Jennifer asked as her father handed the baby back to her.

'Harvey Stott left a message for me at the office, letting me know that you'd had a baby boy and that I could locate you at this address.'

'I see.'

'I couldn't believe it was the right address so I thought I ought to check it out and make sure that you really were here before I mentioned it to your mother.'

'I see,' Jennifer repeated in a noncommittal voice.

'I didn't want to raise her hopes until I had made sure that it was you.' He gave a beaming smile. 'She'll be so relieved when I take you back home with me.'

'Hold on!' Jennifer exclaimed. 'I'm not prepared to do that.'

Her father stared at her in surprise, his mouth tightening. 'Of course you must come home; I want you to come back with me right now,' he said forcefully.

She shook her head defiantly. 'I desperately want to come home but I'm not prepared to do so until I am quite certain that Mother wants me to be there.'

'Please, Jennifer, don't let the altercation we had all those months ago stand in the way of our being reunited as a family.'

'Not until I am quite sure that it's what Mother wants.'

'Of course she does,' he stated irritably. 'She's been terribly worried about you.'

'In that case why didn't she come here with you today?'

'Apart from the fact that I didn't tell her anything about Harvey Stott's message, your mother is not well, Jennifer. She's suffering from some sort of heart problem. I want her to visit a specialist but she refuses to do so. Maybe you will be able to persuade her how important it is that she does.'

'I'm sorry she's not well but I am not coming home until she has spoken to me and told me she has forgiven me,' Jennifer said stubbornly. 'If she isn't well enough to come over here to see me then tell her to telephone, and Miss Lloyd will let me speak to her.'

Joshua White stood up, pulled himself up to his full height, shaking his head in dismay.

'I tell you what I'll do, Jennifer, I will go home and tell her I have seen you and the baby and then I will ask her to invite you to dinner so that the two of you can discuss the matter and you can be sure that she has forgiven you. Will that do?'

Jennifer nodded cautiously. 'Can I bring Miss Lloyd with me?'

'Excellent idea! We'll invite Harvey Stott as well since it is thanks to him that I have found you again.'

Two days later Megan received a very formal letter inviting her to the Whites' home in Warren Drive, Wallasey and requesting that Miss Jennifer White should accompany her.

Megan read it through several times; each time she did so she thought how cold and impersonal it was. She knew that there had been a letter for Jennifer with a Wallasey postmark and she hoped that Jennifer's invitation was couched in a warmer manner than hers.

Later in the day Megan received a telephone call from Harvey Stott asking her if she had received the invitation and promising that he would pick them up in his car at six thirty the following evening.

Jennifer merely shrugged when Megan told her this.

'Would you like to see if there is anything in my wardrobe that you would like to wear for the occasion?' Megan asked, knowing how limited Jennifer's choice of clothes was.

'No thank you. I shall wear my skirt and I'll wash and iron my blouse so that I look clean and tidy,' she stated.

'What about a warm coat then? It has turned chilly again over the last few days.'

'The coat I came here in will do. We'll be in Dr Stott's car so I won't feel cold,' Jennifer insisted.

Megan sat in front alongside Harvey, Jennifer in the back, nursing the baby in her arms. Harvey tried to make conversation with them both but Jennifer didn't respond. She sat rocking the baby and crooning to it even though it was sound asleep.

Megan was on edge wondering what sort of a reception

they would get. She longed to ask Harvey details about Mrs White but she wasn't sure if Jennifer could overhear what they were saying or not so she kept quiet.

The Whites' house was very large and imposing. It was a double-fronted red brick edifice with a gabled roof and high bay windows both upstairs and down. They parked in the wide gravel drive and the front door was opened before they were out of the car.

Joshua White hurried forward to take the baby from Jennifer but as soon as she was out of the car she reached out and took it back from him. He greeted both Megan and Harvey with a handshake and then led the way into the house.

Mrs White, a short, plump, dark-haired woman was waiting in the hallway. She was wearing a black velvet dress and an exquisite gold and pearl necklace was her only jewellery. She greeted Megan and Harvey very effusively and invited them into a lavishly furnished sitting room where a log fire was burning brightly.

Megan was aware that Jennifer had hung back and she suspected that Jennifer wanted the rest of them out of the way before she greeted her mother.

As she sat next to Harvey on the green velvet settee in the sitting room Megan waited anxiously for Jennifer and her parents to join them. She could hear the murmur of their voices; Jennifer's sounded petulant, her mother's forceful and the deeper voice of Joshua White sounded as if he was acting as mediator between Jennifer and her mother.

After several minutes Joshua White came into the sitting room and offered them a glass of sherry. He talked of mundane matters but like Megan and Harvey he seemed to be half listening to what was happening on the other side of the door.

When, about five minutes later, Jennifer and her mother came into the room Megan noticed with relief that it was Margaret White who was carrying the baby.

Megan exchanged looks with Harvey and he gave a slight nod as if he agreed with her that it surely indicated that peace had been restored between Jennifer and her mother.

The rest of the evening passed very pleasantly. Their

meal was excellent. Delicious food and wine and the conversation was kept to general subjects.

Afterwards, though, when they were preparing to take their leave problems arose. Joshua White brought in their coats and helped Megan into hers. Mrs White looked astonished when Jennifer began wrapping the baby up in its blanket and then asked for her coat.

'Surely you're not leaving, are you, Jennifer? You can't! We've made our peace. I thought you were back home for good.'

Jennifer took a deep breath. 'All I want to do is come back home, Mother; you have no idea how homesick I've been. It's simply that I can't do so right away. Now that The Haven is registered as a charity I must finish the fundraising work that I've undertaken to do for Megan.'

Joshua White frowned deeply. He looked across at Megan but before he could speak Megan said quickly, 'No, no, Jennifer. You don't have to do that. Stay home, now. You must think of your own future and that of your baby, not of helping us.'

'You can carry on helping them from here, from home,' her father intervened. 'In fact, there will be far better facilities for you to do it here than there. You can call on the fully trained staff at my office to help you. They can send out your press releases and requests for donations and deal with all the correspondence that comes in. I am sure Miss Lloyd will agree to them doing that.'

He turned to face Megan. 'Please, let my company take over the administration for you and deal with all the correspondence that organizing a charity entails.'

'It is extremely kind of you, Mr White, but are you sure you want to take on so much extra work?'

'It will be a pleasure.' He smiled. 'That is the least I can do in gratitude for all the help and care you have given my daughter and baby grandson.'

Joshua White turned to his daughter and held out his arms again for the baby. 'I'll send someone from the office to pick up any papers and documents relating to this charity work. We'll sort them all out in the next few days,' he promised Megan.

'My offices are in Old Hall Street, which is not so very far away from you, so call in any time you or Miss Peterson have anything to pass on to Jennifer and they will see I get it and I'll bring it back home for her to attend to.'

Megan nodded understandingly. She was going to miss Jennifer but at the same time she was delighted that the girl was reunited with her own family.

As Joshua White, his wife and Jennifer said goodbye Megan was sad that Jennifer was leaving them but happy about the outcome for her.

'All in all, this arrangement with the Whites should work out very well,' Harvey commented as they drove away. 'Let's hope they're as successful when it comes to interesting people in what you are doing here and in raising adequate funds for you to carry on at The Haven as they are in running their shipping business.'

'Yes, 1943 has turned out even better than we thought possible. Let's hope the rest of the year will be as good.'

'I have a feeling it will,' Harvey said. 'Joshua is already talking about a write-up in the *Liverpool Echo*.'

'Well, I hope that turns out to be good publicity, we don't want people protesting about what we are doing or turning up on our doorstep and causing trouble,' Megan murmured.

'No, they won't,' Harvey said confidently. '1943 is going to continue to be a good year for all of us; it might even prove to be a very special year,' he said with a smile.

'Now,' he added, 'since we're not far from the promenades, what about a drive along there?'

'We won't be able to see very much in the dark,' she protested.

'True but it'll be nice and secluded and you say that you have never been there before,' he said with a low laugh, giving Megan a meaningful look that brought the colour rushing to her face.

'I'd certainly like to but it is very late,' she demurred, 'perhaps some other time.'

'Very well, what about Sunday afternoon?'

'I'd like that very much!'

'Good!'

'Tell me something about New Brighton,' Megan said as they headed back to Liverpool.

'In winter it's pretty deserted,' Harvey replied. 'In summer it's so packed that it is a place to avoid. Trippers come from the Midlands and of course from Liverpool. For them it is a ride on the ferry boat which only takes about twenty minutes.'

'So what else is there at New Brighton?' Megan questioned.

'The Tower Ballroom, which is quite famous and a favourite with dancers worldwide. There are also swings and round-abouts and sideshows of all kind. There's a variety theatre that has shows running all through the summer season. There used to be a menagerie in the Tower grounds but I'm not sure if they've managed to keep it going. Finding food for some of the animals became difficult once the war started.'

'And hotels?'

'A few; but mostly the accommodation for visitors is in boarding houses. There's also an excellent open-air swimming pool and a long wide promenade with a sea wall to protect you from the Mersey.'

'Oh!' Megan tried to envisage the scene but failed.

'The comings and goings on the Mersey are also very entertaining since there is everything from small craft like the ferry boats that travel constantly back and forth to Liverpool throughout the day, up to huge cargo boats and big ocean-going liners. Sometimes you see these waiting out at the bar at the mouth of the Mersey until the tide is safe for them to enter or leave on their way to and from all parts of the world,' Harvey went on.

'Have you always lived by the Mersey?' Megan asked, regarding him with renewed interest.

'Yes. My parents lived over here in Wallasey. You could see the Mersey from our house in Warren Drive. My father was part-owner of a major shipping line.'

'Is that why you know the Whites so well?'

'My father and Joshua White were very well acquainted and attended a lot of functions together. I used to stand for hours at my bedroom window watching for the liners carrying a flag bearing the emblem of his company up the Mersey.'

'Is he retired now?' Megan questioned.

There was a moment's silence and she saw the sadness come into Harvey's eyes and his jaw stiffen. She suspected a trauma of some kind and wished she had not asked.

'Like countless others on Merseyside both my parents were killed when our house received a direct hit a couple of years ago,' he said in a clipped voice.

'Oh, I'm so sorry.' Megan reached out and touched his arm. One of Harvey's hands covered hers briefly but he said nothing; it was as though he couldn't bear to talk about it.

'So I'll see you on Sunday,' he said as they reached The Haven and he got out of the car and walked to the door with her.

'I'll be over here about half past ten or is that too early for you?' he asked teasingly.

'I'll be ready on time so don't be late,' she told him.

'Good! Wear something warm and sensible shoes because I intend to make you walk from Seacombe to Leasowe; that's the entire length of the promenade,' he warned her.

'How far is that?'

'Wait and see, but make sure you wear comfortable shoes,' he advised.

'Will we have to walk all the way back or can we catch a bus or a train?'

'We walk both ways,' he told her firmly.

'What happens if I can't walk all that way, will you carry me?' she teased.

'No,' he told her gravely, 'I will help you to the nearest shelter and leave you there. Until Sunday then,' he murmured as he gave her a hug and a kiss that seemed to go on forever. 'I love you, Megan Lloyd,' he whispered, his voice husky, as finally they broke apart.

It was a long time before Megan dropped off to sleep. She went over every detail of their evening together after they had left the Whites' house. And the prospect of going to New Brighton with Harvey on Sunday was very exciting.

It was quite true she had never been to any seaside resort before. Her father didn't feel there was any need for them to go on holiday since they lived in a beautiful mountain area. The sea was not far from them but for some reason they never went there. Now she found it exhilarating and she looked forward to her walk with Harvey.

It was a long promenade and although she was blissfully happy walking along hand-in-hand with Harvey, by the time they reached Leasowe she was very tired. Far too tired to resist when he suggested a rest in one of the shelters dotted along the promenade.

For a few moments they sat there in silence, enjoying the sounds of the sea and the tranquillity that enshrouded them. She made no resistance when his arm went around her waist, pulling her closer. The warmth from his body enveloped her like a warm cloak and when he pulled her even closer into his arms she melted into his embrace, raising her face so that their lips met.

An hour later when they broke apart and Harvey said it was time they were getting back, her tiredness seemed to have vanished. This time however he didn't walk very far along the promenade before turning up a side street that led them directly to Wallasey village and back home.

SEVENTEEN

News that there was a new enterprise called The Haven in Chapel Gardens and that it was for unmarried mothers spread rapidly and brought mixed reactions. Some people sent them donations, others wrote requesting more details or asking if they could visit.

They were also visited by local clergy of almost all denominations as well as a battery of do-gooders concerned about the moral status of the girls who came there and anxious to educate them and show them a better way of life.

When Megan suggested that if they were so interested in the welfare of these girls then why had they not set up a retreat for them themselves, a place where they could have their babies, she received frosty looks.

In some cases they explained that they had no facilities for providing accommodation for such people and looked angrily at Megan when she suggested that they could always have taken one or two girls into their own home.

Gradually visits from such callers diminished and they were left to run The Haven in peace.

They had so many applications from pregnant girls, however, that they were forced to introduce restrictions about which girls they ought to take in and which ones they reluctantly were forced to turn away.

'We really haven't room for girls who are only a few months pregnant and looking for somewhere where they can stay for three or four months,' Sandra pointed out. 'We really must confine ourselves in future to only taking in girls who are in the final stages of their pregnancy.'

Although Megan agreed with Sandra because she knew she was right she found it much harder to turn girls away when they came to the door pleading for shelter than Sandra did.

'I hate to think how many homeless people you will take into our home when we have one,' Harvey teased when he heard about this.

'I won't want to have anyone there except you,' Megan assured him.

'Well, that's a relief,' he said with a smile. 'Now,' he went on, 'I have some very special news for you. Apparently Joshua White's wife, Margaret, has a heart problem and he has finally agreed to consult a specialist. She has asked me to persuade my uncle who is a leading heart specialist to come to see her.'

'I'm sorry to hear about Margaret but surely if she is seeing a specialist she will have to go to his consulting rooms,' Megan said with a frown.

'In the ordinary way she would.' Harvey smiled. 'In this instance, however, my uncle practises in Glasgow. She isn't well enough to travel there so I am arranging for to him come here to see her.'

'And he has agreed?'

'Yes. By lucky coincidence he is going on holiday next week to visit an old school friend in North Wales and he has agreed to come on here afterwards. He will be staying overnight so I hope you will be able to meet him.'

'Oh dear, that's going to be quite nerve wracking,' Megan said anxiously.

'Not at all.' Harvey assured her. 'You'll like him. He is in his early sixties but he has a very lively mind.'

'He might disapprove of me,' she countered with a nervous smile.

'Not a chance! He has an eye for the ladies and he is a widower so I will have to watch that he doesn't captivate your heart and take you from me.'

As he spoke, Harvey drew her into his arms, kissing her on the brow and then, placing a hand under her chin, raised her face so that his next kiss was full on her lips.

Megan sighed blissfully as she melted into his embrace and returned his kisses with equal passion.

Throughout the following week they were so busy installing two new girls into The Haven that Megan had no time to worry about her forthcoming meeting with Harvey's uncle.

The two newcomers, Susan Harris and Alice Fletcher, were both local girls. Susan Harris came from one of the better areas in Wallasey and it was obvious from her expression when she was shown into the small attic bedroom that she was horrified by what she had been reduced to accepting.

Too well brought up to make any comment she listened in silence as Megan told her the simple house rules and showed her where the bathroom and lavatory were situated.

The other girl Alice Fletcher came from Seacombe. She was not quite so well dressed as Susan Harris and it was obvious that the accommodation she was being offered did not in any way distress her.

Both girls were within days of having their babies and Megan was so busy making the necessary arrangements for this that she had no time to think about the coming meeting with Harvey's uncle and she was therefore taken by surprise when Harvey said his uncle had arrived in Liverpool.

'Joshua White has invited Uncle Marcus and his friend to dinner tonight and apparently he's told him that he was inviting us as well.'

'Oh, dear!' Megan hesitated.

'Come on, you've been over there before. It's an excellent opportunity to break the ice with Uncle Marcus, seeing that you are so nervous about meeting him.'

'Even more importantly it would be a chance to see Jennifer again and make sure she's settled in,' Megan ventured.

'Right, that's settled then. Be ready at six thirty.'

'Are you taking your uncle?'

'No, he and his friend will be making their own way there.'

Jennifer White came to the door to welcome them. She was wearing a pretty dress and looked well and happy, eager to take Megan to the nursery to see baby Joshua.

'My word he's grown,' Megan enthused. 'Is everything all right for you now, Jennifer?' she asked. 'You certainly look well.'

'Everything is great. Both Mother and Father adore Joshua and they . . . they . . .' She giggled. 'They seem to have grown up; they are so very much more understanding these days.'

'They might possibly think the same about you,' Megan said with a smile.

'Are you happy with the publicity we are getting for The Haven?' Jennifer said, changing the subject. 'We still have several ideas for new campaigns.'

'You've done wonders,' Megan assured her. 'If I don't get the opportunity to thank your father for all he has done to help us, will you tell him for me, please.'

'Of course! I suppose we should join him and his guests,' she murmured as she straightened the covers on Joshua's cot.

'You're right. Come on, lead the way.'

Once more Megan found herself in the Whites' luxurious sitting room and she felt happy for Jennifer that things had turned out so well and that she was back in the heart of her family.

'We were beginning to think you'd got lost,' Harvey said, coming over to them. Taking Megan by the arm, he led her over to where Joshua White was talking to two well-dressed older men.

'This is Megan Lloyd who is one of the founders of The Haven,' Harvey stated, pulling her forward. 'Megan, this is my uncle, Marcus Millward.'

Megan found her hand being shaken by a tall, distinguished man in his early sixties. His thatch of grey hair was brushed back revealing a high forehead and clean-shaven face with a strong jawline and a wide mouth. His eyes were a deep blue and his penetrating appraisal of her brought the colour to her cheeks.

'By heaven, that's a coincidence,' he exclaimed with a booming laugh. 'The friend I brought with me is also called Lloyd.'

For the first time Megan looked at the man who was standing beside Marcus Millward and drew in her breath sharply. She couldn't believe her eyes. The man standing there was her father.

She could hear Harvey speaking to her but she took no notice. She stared again, wondering if she was imagining things but there was no mistake at all. It was her father, Lewis Lloyd, who was standing there.

He looked slightly older than she remembered but as their eyes met and she saw the shock and hesitancy in them as he stared at her, it made her heart pound.

Overwhelmed by the unbearable homesickness that she had tried so hard to push to the back of her mind for the past few months and unable to stop herself, she flung herself into his arms.

'Dad, Dad!' she whispered, 'how wonderful to see you. I've missed you so much.'

He held her close, stroking her hair and murmuring his delight at seeing her again.

'Mother? How is she?' she asked, pulling back a little so that she could stare into his eyes.

He looked grave. 'I'm afraid that she is not very well at all. She misses you and worries about you a great deal. She'll be so relieved when I tell her I have found you. Will you come home, Megan?' he asked, his voice pleading.

'I'll come for a visit,' she agreed. 'My work is here though, there is so much to be done.'

'Marcus read about it in the paper and told us about it when he came to see us this weekend. When he said his nephew was involved and that he was coming to Liverpool to meet him I decided to come with him and find out if it really was you behind the scheme.' He squeezed her arm. 'I am so proud of you. It is a wonderful effort.'

'It's my war work,' she told him quietly.

He nodded. 'It's an extremely worthwhile project,' he said quietly. 'Can we come and look round The Haven?'

'Of course you can. I'd very much like you to see it.'

'Tomorrow? Before I go back to North Wales?'

'That would be wonderful. Will you be bringing Mr Millward with you?'

'Yes, we'll both come. I know he's extremely interested in what you are doing.'

'What time will you come?'

'That will be up to Marcus to decide. I'll go along with whatever he wants to do. Does it matter?'

'No, of course it doesn't. I want to make sure that Sandra Peterson, the woman who has let me use her house, is there to meet you as well, that's all.'

As it happened Lewis Lloyd arrived half an hour after Harvey with Megan's help had delivered Alice Fletcher's baby.

As Harvey and Megan came out of the room where Alice Fletcher was now resting, the baby in a crib at the side of her bed, Megan still in her bloodstained overall, her hair untidy and her face damp with sweat from her exertions, both of them were taken by surprise when they found Lewis Lloyd and Marcus Millward waiting for them on the landing.

'Heavens above, I didn't expect to meet you like this,' Harvey said in a startled voice as he passed a hand over his brow, pushing back his dampened hair.

'The housekeeper – Nelly, I think she said her name was – let us in and when I told her that I was a doctor she didn't ask any questions but sent us up here to find you,' his uncle told them.

Megan introduced her father and Marcus to Sandra and left them to enjoy a chat and a cup of coffee in the sitting room while she and Harvey went to get cleaned up. Then they took them on a tour of The Haven.

Both Marcus Millward and Lewis Lloyd were impressed by what they saw.

'So you've spent all your inheritance, have you?' Megan's father said with a smile. 'In that case then, I think I ought to reinstate your allowance, only make sure that you spend it on yourself, not on others.'

He held up a hand, as she was about to demur. 'You won't need it for The Haven,' he told her. 'I will make sure you get adequate funds for that when I get back to North Wales. There are a good many wealthy business people in the area, as you very well know, and they have no idea of the appalling conditions the people in and around Liverpool have suffered since this war started. They live in a different world but I shall make it my business to let them know what has been happening to so many young girls and I am confident that they will give generously.'

That evening they all went for dinner at the Adelphi Hotel where her father and Marcus Millward were staying. As their taxi took them through some of the poorer areas of Liverpool, Megan felt her father's hand tighten on her arm.

'It really is a different world,' he murmured with a deep sigh. 'I can't ever remember seeing so much poverty or people living in such squalid conditions. The Haven is like a beacon of hope for the young girls who find their way there.'

His words brought a smile to Megan's face. She felt that at last he understood her aims and would no longer oppose what she wanted to do. Knowing that, she loved him even more.

The splendid meal they enjoyed at the Adelphi made her realize how right he was and what a divide there was between those who lived in comfort and those who struggled to exist.

Before they left she promised her father that at the first opportunity she would come home on a visit.

'You are very welcome to bring Harvey Stott with you,' he told her solemnly. 'The poor boy looks as though he could do with a break. From what Marcus tells me, he is under great pressure and hasn't had a holiday since the war started.'

'Perhaps I will,' she agreed. 'Anyway I'll tell him what you said, but I think he probably has too many commitments to take a holiday.'

'Rubbish! He needs to recharge his batteries before he has a breakdown,' her father said crisply. 'What's more, I know his welfare matters to you every bit as much as the welfare of those poor girls you are trying to help. You make a first-class team,' he added proudly.

EIGHTEEN

It was six months and eight babies later before Harvey and Megan could manage to take a break and visit Megan's family in North Wales.

In the meantime Megan had kept in touch with them and it was her mother's repeated requests for her to come on a visit that finally Megan decided she ought to try and do so.

Harvey was in full agreement. 'Great idea! It will give me a chance to ask your father's permission,' he said.

'Permission? Permission for what?'

'Permission to marry you, of course.'

Megan stared at him in astonishment. 'You really ought to ask me first if I want to marry you,' she told him, trying hard not to smile as she said it.

Harvey pulled her into his arms. 'I know I don't need to do that. You've been waiting for me to propose for the last few months and I have always known what your answer would be.'

Megan wriggled free of his embrace. 'You really are very sure of yourself, Dr Harvey Stott,' she told him, tossing her head in assumed disdain.

'I know,' he replied with a confident grin. 'I want us to be married as much as you do and as soon as possible. I still think though that the correct thing to do is to ask your father for your hand.'

'What will you do if he refuses?' Megan teased.

'Marry you just the same,' he laughed. 'Now, have you any objections to that?'

'None at all,' she told him, 'and as you say the sooner we can get married the happier we will be.'

It was November before they were finally able to take a long weekend to spend with Megan's family in North Wales. They travelled by train and although it was lovely being together, the journey seemed to take them an awfully long time. Harvey kept looking out of the window and each time they drew into a station he would look enquiringly at Megan and ask, 'Are we there yet?'

When she shook her head he would frown and question whether she was right or not.

'I'll certainly know when we're there,' she told him laughing when he looked doubtful. 'It's my home we're going to, remember?'

'I know that but none of the stations are marked so how can you be so sure? This business of taking down all the nameplates is so confusing. I know it's been done because of the war so that the enemy won't be able to find their way around if we are invaded but I have no idea how far it is.'

'Don't worry, I'll recognize it when we get there,' she told him confidently.

Her father was waiting at the station for them. 'Come on, my car's outside; you must be weary after that journey. Ten minutes and we'll be home; there's a meal waiting and a glass of Madeira so that will put new life into both of you.'

Megan was amused by the look of amazement on Harvey's face as they drove up the gravel drive that led from the main road up to Yr Glaslyn.

'Here we are, home at last,' she said with a rapturous smile.

'This is some place you've got here,' Harvey said admiringly. 'It's almost like a mediaeval castle.'

'Yes, my ancestors were granted permission to have castellated walls,' Lewis Lloyd stated proudly.

'You also have a turret. Do you use it?'

'Not to watch out for the enemy approaching, but I have my study in there and Megan used to have the top room as her playroom when she was a child.'

'The view is outstanding,' Megan said. 'I'll show you tomorrow when I take you on a tour of the whole place.'

Bronwyn Lloyd, Megan's mother, was waiting at the door for them. Megan was dismayed to see how frail she looked. Surely six months couldn't have made all that difference to her, Megan thought worriedly.

As they embraced Megan was even more concerned when she felt how thin and birdlike her mother was when she put her arms around her. It seemed as though she had wasted away. Surely worrying about me hasn't done this to her? Megan thought guiltily.

Over their delicious meal of lamb with mint sauce, croquette potatoes, roast parsnips, carrots and peas, Megan tried to explain to her mother the sort of work she was doing in Liverpool.

'It sounds very fulfilling but couldn't you come back home and do something similar here?' Mrs Lloyd asked in a pleading tone.

'No, Mother, I'm afraid not,' Megan said gently. 'Many of the girls who come to us for help are from very squalid backgrounds; they are very poor and a great many of them have been bombed out of their homes.'

'All of them?' Her mother exclaimed in surprise.

'Well, no, not quite all of them,' Megan admitted.

'Most of them have been turned out by their parents because they are pregnant,' Harvey explained.

'Oh, my goodness, what a terrible thing to happen!' Bronwyn Lloyd exclaimed, her hand flying up to her mouth in horror. 'Why do they do that?'

'Because they feel the girls have brought shame on their families. None of these girls are married, you see, Mother. In fact, most of them are planning to get rid of their babies the moment they are born. They know they won't be able to support them since they have no jobs and no homes or anything so they either abandon their babies, give them up for adoption, or put them into a charitable institution of some sort.'

'I've only known of one young girl around here who got herself into such a predicament and she committed suicide before the baby was born,' Mrs Lloyd said, shaking her head sadly.

'I am afraid there are a great many more than that in Liverpool,' Harvey told her. 'Of course it is a seaport and visiting sailors . . .'

Bronwyn Lloyd clapped her hands to her ears and shook her head. 'Please, young man, don't tell me any more, it is far too harrowing.' She turned and looked directly at Megan. 'Are these the sort of girls you are trying to help?'

'Yes, Mother. Girls who have been left pregnant by the Yanks or the sailors who have been in Liverpool because of the war.'

'That is such a shocking state of affairs,' Bronwyn Lloyd said and shuddered. 'I really do think it is a dangerous environment for you to be in.'

Megan, knowing that it was pointless to argue with her mother, decided to change the subject.

For the rest of the evening they talked about local affairs and her mother related all she knew about what was happening in the village of Beddgelert.

After a stroll round the garden just before dusk, accompanied by her parents and Harvey, Megan said she was going to bed.

'It's been a long day and tomorrow I am going to take Harvey up Moel Hebog.'

'You do pick the most unsuitable places to go,' her mother scolded. 'I'm quite sure he doesn't want to climb up a mountain, do you?' she asked, directing her question at Harvey.

'Well, I have never climbed one yet so it could be quite a challenge,' he countered.

'We'll only be gone for a couple of hours, and we'll be back again before lunchtime,' Megan told her mother.

The walk up Moel Hebog was, as Harvey had predicted, something of a challenge.

'I take it that this is the mountain that dominates the skyline from here,' Harvey said as they set out.

'Yes, it's 2,750 feet high, not quite as high as Snowdon. The name Moel Hebog means the Hill of the Hawk and it is where Owen Glendower is said to have hidden from the English,' Megan told him.

She made short work of the climb but Harvey was breathing

heavily. To give him a chance to get his breath back, Megan paused on a patch of rocky ground.

'Do we have to go much further?' Harvey gasped, straining his neck to look up at the summit.

'No, it's not far now,' Megan assured him.

'I should hope not; we're already in low cloud.'

'Mist not cloud,' Megan laughed.

'Perhaps we should turn back,' he said cautiously. 'I've heard about people finding themselves caught out by the mist coming down when they are on a mountain and losing all sense of where they are. We don't want that to happen to us, do we?'

'Don't worry, I know my way to the top and back down again blindfold,' Megan replied with a laugh. 'I've been climbing Moel Hebog ever since I was ten years old. The mountain is an old friend to me and I couldn't get lost up here even if I wanted to.'

By the time they reached the summit the mist had cleared and the sun was out. From their vantage point they could see not only the rest of the Snowdon range but also right across to the Irish Sea.

'It's absolutely breathtaking,' Harvey exclaimed.

The journey back down Moel Hebog was less strenuous but they had to be careful because the ground, especially the grass, was extremely slippery.

By the time they arrived back at Yr Glaslyn, Harvey was exhausted and he readily welcomed the invitation to have a glass of sherry before they started lunch.

'I've been thinking over what you told me about life in Liverpool and I really do think that Megan should pack up working down there and come back home,' Megan's mother stated as she handed him a dry sherry.

'There's simply no knowing what she might pick up,' she went on. 'These girls are probably diseased and at best they will be full of lice and fleas. We didn't send her to university to end up spending her time amongst those sorts of people,' she murmured as they took their places at the table. 'I would like her to come back up here where things are far more civilized and where she has well-mannered, well-brought-up friends. If she really wants to work then let her father find her a job in his office.'

'Are you talking about me?' Megan asked as she came into the room and slipped into her place at the table.

'Yes, dear, I was explaining to Dr Stott how I would prefer you to be back here not down in Liverpool and that if you wanted to work then your father would find you something to do, wouldn't you, Lloyd?'

'I'm sure he would,' Megan said stiffly, 'but it is not the sort of work I want to do. Harvey will tell you that what I am doing is very important. I would have thought that you realized that after what we've told you about The Haven.'

'Your mother does know; she read the report in the newspaper I brought home after I came to visit you in Liverpool.'

'Yes, of course I did, but no one believes what they read in the newspaper,' her mother said forcefully.

The atmosphere became tense. To Megan's relief, Harvey changed the subject.

'Mr Lloyd,' he said in a firm but polite tone, 'I want to ask you something. It is one of the reasons why I came to see you this weekend. I want to ask if I can marry your daughter Megan.'

A hush descended over the room and for several minutes no one spoke. Then Lewis Lloyd cleared his throat. 'She is very young to be thinking of marriage,' he prevaricated.

'Young in years maybe but not in experience,' Harvey said with a smile.

'True!' Lewis Lloyd agreed. 'There is the question, however, of whether she is willing to marry you?' he went on in a speculative tone. 'I assume you've asked her?'

'I have and she has said yes but I still feel that I need your approval and permission.'

'Quite right, my boy, quite right,' Lewis Lloyd said approvingly. He looked directly at his wife. 'I have no objection. What about you, my dear?'

Bronwyn Lewis said nothing but delicately mopped at her eyes with a lace-trimmed handkerchief. Her husband picked up his glass and raised it in the air. 'A toast then to welcome Harvey into our family and to say how much I approve of the fact that he and Megan are getting married.'

'Have you decided when it is to be and where?' he asked as he set his empty glass down on the table.

'It will be here, of course; Megan must be married in our local church and it must be officiated at by our own vicar,' Bronwyn Lewis said tremulously.

'Are you sure that's what you want, Mother?' Megan asked. 'If we do that then there will be an awful lot of people attending and you know you hate all that sort of thing.'

'You are our only child and it is only right that you should be married from the family home,' Bronwyn Lloyd said firmly. 'I couldn't bear it if you had one of those awful register office weddings with none of us present.'

Megan bit her lip. She had been on the point of telling them that it would be at a register office and that the wedding would take place in Liverpool but now, as she caught a quick nod of approval from Harvey, she knew it was best to go along with her mother's wishes.

'I do hope, though, that you are going to wait until the war is over,' Bronwyn Lloyd said firmly.

'Good heavens, no! None of us have any idea when that could be. We might have to wait years before we could get married if that is one of the conditions.'

'No, of course it isn't,' her father said decisively. 'I have given my approval and you can get married any time you like and wherever you like.'

He looked directly at his wife as he spoke. 'This is wartime and we have to adjust accordingly. If these two want to get married in Liverpool then we must accept that and if it means it has to be a register office, I quite understand.'

He frowned across at his wife as if defying her to contradict him. Bronwyn merely gave a slight shrug, knowing that he was the master and in control and if he was willing for their only daughter to marry without them being present then so be it. She knew there was nothing she could do to change it.

As they travelled back to Liverpool the next day, Harvey raised the subject with Megan.

'Well, what is the answer? Have you given any thought as to whether we get married at your parents' home or in Liverpool?'

'You heard what my father said; he is prepared for us to make our own minds up about it.'

'I know, that's why I'm asking you what you want to do.'

'I'm not at all sure,' Megan said thoughtfully. 'But I would very much like Jennifer White and Sandra to be at our wedding if it's at all possible and I don't think they could travel to North Wales, not at the moment.'

'Then that makes it Liverpool,' Harvey said in a tone of relief. 'I'm sure your parents will come, so it's now up to us to set the date and let them know.'

'I rather think we'll have to consult Sandra and Jennifer to find out what's most convenient for them. We'll also have to check when our next babies are due before we can set a date,' Megan laughed.

'No, we'll make sure that Sandra and Jennifer are free but as far as the girls are concerned we are not going to let any of them interfere with our plans,' Harvey told her firmly as he gathered her into his arms and kissed her.

'We might have to postpone the idea of going on honeymoon until after the war is over but we'll still be able to move in together once we have signed the register and I know that you really are my wife,' he murmured as his kisses became more fervent.

NINETEEN

Sandra was delighted when Megan and Harvey told her that they were getting married.

'I was beginning to think that you two would never get around to it,' she laughed. 'It's certainly about time; Harvey has been running after you ever since the first day you met!'

'Rubbish! He thought I was a complete and utter idiot because I was so helpless and so inexperienced when it came to helping him to deliver a baby,' Megan said and grinned.

'You've proven to be a very apt pupil,' he told her,

placing an arm around her and squeezing her shoulders affectionately.

'I've certainly had plenty of practice,' she agreed.

'So when and where is the wedding to be?' Sandra asked.

'There's a slight problem over that,' Harvey told her. 'We want both you and Jennifer White to come and perhaps her father as well since he has been so very generous in helping us make The Haven a viable concern.'

'Well, in that case it will have to be in Liverpool, won't it?' Sandra said. 'How do your family feel about that, Megan?'

'My father is happy enough for us to get married wherever we think is most suitable, but my mother wants us to have a traditional wedding from my home with all the trimmings.'

'Surely that's out of the question? There is a war on! Think of all the problems about catering and all the clothing coupons you would need for a wedding dress.'

'True, and I think that's why she would like us to wait until the war is over and then we can do the whole thing in style. She is very much a traditionalist and she would like the entire village as well as all the employees from the slate mines to be part of the celebrations.'

'Everybody!' Sandra exclaimed in astonishment.

'You see, my father is held in high regard in Beddgelert and that's why she feels everyone must be invited.'

Sandra pursed her mouth in a silent whistle. 'The end of the war might be years ahead. At the moment we seem to be doing all right in Europe but who can tell? The war has taken so many twists and turns since it started and although at the moment we appear to be making headway there's no guarantee that things won't change again and we'll all be back to square one.'

'Now don't say that,' Harvey said sternly. 'Things are looking up and they look brighter than they have done for years. Anyway, we don't want to wait until the war is over. I'd get married tomorrow if it was possible.'

'Well, it's certainly taken you both long enough to come to a decision,' Sandra said in a scolding tone, 'so don't delay things for too long.'

Harvey shrugged. 'You know how it is, you have to be certain about these things,' he said in a mocking tone.

'The man who never makes any mistakes never makes anything,' Sandra rejoined. 'Seriously though, when are you two planning to get married?'

'As soon as possible and preferably here in Liverpool,' Harvey confirmed. He looked at Megan questioningly. 'You are in agreement with that too, aren't you?'

'Anything you say,' Megan replied and smiled happily.

'That's not the way to deal with it, you should always make sure that it is your wishes that are paramount not his, otherwise you will become a slave,' Sandra told her.

'I bet you wish you had the chance to be a slave,' Harvey joked. 'Have you heard from Hank lately?'

'No!' Sandra's face clouded over. 'I wish I had; it would be such a relief to know that he was safe and well.'

'No news is good news, or so they say,' Megan said quickly, sensing how worried Sandra was. 'You'll hear from him any day now and with any luck he'll be back in time for our wedding.'

'Stop raising my hopes,' Sandra retorted with a sad little smile.

Megan's prediction came true quicker than any of them expected. A few days later Sandra did hear from Hank. It was disturbing news. He was back in England but in hospital in Southport.

'Southport? Where's that?' Megan asked.

'A little bit further along the coast, not very far from here.'

'I see. Do you know what's wrong with him? Or the reason why he's been sent back to England? Has he been seriously injured?'

Sandra shook her head. 'I only know that he's back in England and in hospital in Southport.'

'You have no idea though what's wrong?'

'No, I'm going to ask Harvey to phone the hospital and find out.'

'Will they tell him? He's not a relation.'

'No, but he is a doctor and I'm sure he'll be able to get far more information from them than I will.'

Sandra was right. Harvey was successful in finding out what was wrong with Hank and why he had been sent back to England.

'It's nothing too bad,' he assured them when he came off the phone. 'He has broken his leg and it has not healed well; in fact it sounds as though he has an infection in it. They've sent him back to England for specialized treatment at the military hospital in Southport.'

'So can I go and visit him?' Sandra asked.

'Yes, provided you have identification to prove who you are and that you are related to him.'

'That's impossible. We're not married or anything so how can I prove who I am?'

'Perhaps you'd like me to take you over there?' Harvey offered. 'I'm sure that as a doctor it would be fairly easy for me to cut through any red tape.'

'That would be wonderful!' Sandra clapped her hands together in delight. 'When can we go?'

'Tomorrow, as soon as I've finished morning surgery.'

'Oh, I had hoped it would be today,' Sandra said in a disappointed voice.

Harvey frowned. 'Look, leave it with me. I'll phone again in a couple of hours' time and check if you can visit this evening,' he promised. 'It'll have to be after my evening surgery finishes so that means it won't be until about eight o'clock.'

'That'd be fine!'

'That will be rather late for you to be taking Hope out and I suppose you will want to take her with you,' Megan mused.

'Of course I must take her. Hank hasn't even seen her yet!' Sandra exclaimed.

'It will be rather late but I don't suppose that upsetting her routine just for once is going to matter very much,' Megan agreed.

'It's not nearly so important as Hope meeting her father for the very first time and for Hank to see his little daughter.'

'Very well, unless you hear from me to the contrary I will be here to collect you at eight o'clock tonight, providing the hospital will allow such a late visit,' Harvey promised. He looked at Megan and asked, 'Are you coming with us?'

Megan looked questioningly at Sandra. 'Would you like me to look after Hope for you?'

'I've already said that I'm taking Hope with me,' Sandra said quickly.

'Do you think that's a good idea? For your first meeting, I mean?' Harvey said with a frown. 'Hank may not be feeling well enough.'

'Of course I must take her! Hank must be dying to see her. I can't wait to show her to him, he's going to be over the moon with excitement.'

'He may not be,' Harvey warned. 'I really think it would be a good idea for you to see him on your own first. What about Megan coming with us and staying outside in the corridor or in the waiting room with the baby until you've had a chance to be reunited with Hank? Once you've done that, then you could tell him that the baby is outside and if he's well enough to see Hope then you can collect her from Megan.'

'I think that would be a good idea,' Megan agreed.

Sandra thought about it for a moment before she consented. 'Yes, very well then, although I think you're being rather overprotective, Harvey. I'm quite sure that Hank will want to see Hope the moment we get there.'

As it turned out, Sandra was right. Hank's broken leg was heavily bandaged and he was unable to put any weight on it, but he was sitting in an armchair by the side of his bed with his leg supported on a stool.

Harvey gave them a few moments alone while he went back outside into the corridor where Megan was waiting with the baby and told her there was no reason why she shouldn't take Hope in to see Hank.

Hank's attention was focused on Hope and he barely glanced at Megan. She didn't recognize him immediately either; he looked much thinner than the soldier she had seen at the dance and not nearly so imposing out of his uniform.

As she placed the child in his arms and he looked down and saw his little daughter for the very first time it was as if he couldn't believe his eyes. The expression of wonderment on his face brought a lump to Megan's throat.

He kept looking from the baby to Sandra and then back

again to the baby, his face wreathed in smiles. 'She is so beautiful,' he exclaimed huskily, 'so small and petite, I'm frightened I might crush her.'

'She'll soon let you know if you do that,' Sandra told him with a light laugh. 'She has a good pair of lungs on her.'

Harvey and Megan went for a walk around the hospital grounds so that Hank, Sandra and Hope could have time on their own. When they went back into the ward a nurse was already at the bedside admiring the little girl but telling Sandra it was time for her to leave.

'I'll be back tomorrow,' Sandra promised Hank as she kissed him goodbye.

'Are Megan and Harvey coming as well?' Hank asked.

'I'm not sure that we'll be able to spare the time,' Harvey explained. 'I have my patients to attend to and Megan has The Haven to run.'

'Yes, Sandra has been telling me all about it. I can't imagine how a chance comment from me could have inspired Megan to take on such a commitment. It sounds a fantastic undertaking.'

'I certainly wouldn't have been able to do it had it not been for Sandra's generosity in letting me have the use of her house,' Megan pointed out.

'That again was an incredible chance for both of you; I mean, meeting up in the street like you did.'

'Yes, it most certainly was,' Sandra agreed. 'I could hardly believe it when Megan said she had been talking to an American soldier called Hank and from her description I realized that it must be you,' she added with a smile.

'Incredible! To think that a chance remark that I made should have been the start of so much,' he repeated, shaking his head in bewilderment. 'I do hope you can both come tomorrow because I am eager to hear the full story.'

'We'll try,' Harvey promised.

'I also want to hear all about how you two met. I understand you're planning to be married in the very near future. As soon as they let me out of here I'll be doing the same thing. I want to marry Sandra as soon as I possibly can and make our darling little girl legal.'

'Perhaps we could make it a double event,' Megan said hopefully.

'Only if you make it very soon.'

'And in Liverpool,' Sandra said quickly. 'We can't wait until the war is over so that we can stage a grand event at your home.'

'Will you have to wait for the army to give you permission?' Harvey asked.

'I'm afraid so and of course that may take quite some time,' Hank warned.

'Not all that long, surely?' Sandra exclaimed. 'I don't want Hope to be there as a bridesmaid walking down the aisle behind us,' she quipped.

'I'm quite sure they'll make me wait until I can get out of here before I can even apply for permission,' Hank answered with a sigh.

'Have you any idea when that will be?' Sandra asked.

'No idea at all. Once the infection has cleared up it may take a little time for me to regain my mobility. I will have to do that and also meet all the other regulations to ensure that I am fighting fit. And when I am fit enough to go back to my unit that might mean a posting overseas again,' he warned.

'Oh, no! Don't say that,' Sandra wailed. 'I want you home with me where I can be with you every day.'

'I want to be home as well,' Hank told her. 'By that I mean really at home, back in America. This war can't end soon enough for me. I want to be able to take you and my little daughter back home to America to meet my folks.'

'Well, that's certainly out of the question for the moment,' Megan told him. 'Even if you were discharged from the army I doubt if you would be able to get back to America. You probably stand more chance of that happening if you are still in the army.'

'Yes, I'm caught between the devil and a hard place.' Hank sighed. 'If they think I am no longer suitable for active service then they will probably ship me back to America and I won't be able to see Sandra or Hope for heaven knows how long. If I am passed as fit for active service then I can be sent anywhere, even to the Far East.'

TWENTY

943 had been a very traumatic year, Megan reflected as she made the final entries for the year in the logbook-style account she kept of what was happening at The Haven and in her own life.

All through 1943 there had been conflicting stories about the progress of the war. The Luftwaffe had recommenced their bombing of Britain at the beginning of the year and Megan had lived in dread that they would start coming to Liverpool again. This time, however, the Germans had concentrated on the more historic towns of York, Norwich, Exeter and Canterbury.

Towards the end of the year there had also been a small Blitz when Hitler had once again ordered the mass bombing of southern England and as a result, the Luftwaffe gathered some 500 aircraft to carry out this order. But the raids were not of the same scale or intensity as before, mainly because most of the experienced bomber crews had been lost over Russia and in other campaigns.

Britain had, of course, retaliated. The bombing of German cities, spearheaded by Bomber Harris and the men from Bomber Command, brought utter destruction. Regardless of the effect on the Germans, it did a great deal to hearten people in Britain who had seen London, Liverpool, Cardiff, Coventry and many other cities attacked and bombed and remembered the terrible resulting casualties.

In 1943, though, Megan reflected, many people in Germany still believed that they were going to be victorious in the war – primarily because of the propaganda they were fed and the punishments handed out to those labeled 'defeatist'.

Britain's '1000 Bomber' raid on Cologne had shown that mass bombing was inaccurate and not totally fruitful in terms of strategic gains. However, Harris, supported by Winston Churchill, still believed that a devastating attack on a symbolic target would push the Nazis into seeking a peace deal. Cologne,

Dortmund and Dusseldorf had all been bombed. The most obvious other target of any symbolic importance to the Germans was Hamburg.

The first attack had been carried out in the early hours of a Sunday morning. It was reported that 1,000 tons of bombs were dropped which included 350,000 incendiary bombs. Some 15,000 people were killed and many more wounded.

In previous bombing raids, the RAF had sent in pathfinder planes to illuminate the target by dropping incendiary bombs. The main bulk of the attack followed on to what was now a burning target. For the attack on Hamburg, the RAF combined the use of high-explosive bombs and incendiary bombs, which were dropped together. The result made all but useless any form of firefighting.

The Americans had attacked on Monday 26th July and sustained heavy losses as a result of Luftwaffe attacks. An American attack on the Tuesday was called off due to poor weather.

The raid was resumed on the Wednesday. The 722 bombers were loaded with an extra 240 tons of incendiary bombs and dropped a total of 2,313 tons of bombs in just fifty minutes. The impact of this attack led to a firestorm with temperatures estimated to have reached 1,000 degrees centigrade. Bomber crews reported smoke reaching 20,000 feet. Winds on the ground reached 120 miles per hour.

While not exclusively a wooden city, Hamburg did have many old wooden houses and after a dry summer they easily burned. Even the tarmac on roads melted and anyone who had the chance of escape found they were stuck in the sticky mess that remained.

Megan recalled how Hank had told them that while he was in hospital wounded airmen had been brought in who told them that time and again they had seen burning people suddenly start to run and soon after, to fall. There was no way to save them. Some 30,000 died in this raid; the smoke blotted out the sunlight. It was 'the greatest crisis of the war for Germany'. Hamburg was cordoned off for the remainder of the war; such was the unnerving impact the raids had on the Nazi hierarchy.

Did the raids have any value? Megan wondered. There was

little doubt that the reported impact of the raids did a great deal to lift morale in Britain. Many of the girls admitted to The Haven around that time were confident that it meant the war would be over any day. They saw it, together with the birth of their baby and the baby being placed for adoption, as the start of a new life for them.

The raids clearly had an impact on the Nazi government. Hitler refused to visit the city, possibly not wanting to see what his war had resulted in. Hamburg was the major port of the north and the work done by the port was disrupted.

Now, with 1943 coming to an end, the war was still raging, Megan thought sadly. Italy had declared war on Germany; the Americans had invaded the Solomon Islands; less than a month ago Churchill, Roosevelt and Stalin had met at Tehran to discuss policy and strategy; when and where would it all end?

With a sigh she turned back to check the register of babies. Fourteen had been born at The Haven in 1943. Two had died at birth but the remainder had either been adopted or kept by their mothers. Megan wondered what 1944 held for the babies; would they be loved and cherished or would they always bear the stigma of being unwanted?

What of her own life; what would 1944 bring her? Megan wondered. She and Harvey were still not married, nor, for that matter, were Hank and Sandra.

Their plans for a spring wedding had been postponed and she was uncertain about a new date. When they finally did get married, would it be here in Liverpool in a register office or would they be able to hold the sort of wedding her mother hankered after in the church in Beddgelert? That would be a white wedding with the organ playing, a marquee for the guests and all the villagers and men from the slate works in attendance.

Time alone would tell, she told herself. She no more knew if that was going to be possible than she knew how many pregnant girls would turn up on their doorstep seeking refuge and expecting her to take control of the future of the babies after they were born so that they could start a new life.

Hank had been allowed out of hospital very briefly over Christmas but he was now back in there and things were not good. His wound had turned out to be far more serious than he had led them to believe and the infection difficult to control. He had come to them for Christmas Day but it was obvious that as the day went on he was becoming increasingly uncomfortable and in considerable pain.

Sandra had wanted Harvey to give him something to control the pain but Harvey refused.

'I can't do that, it would be dangerous as well as unethical, seeing that he's already having medication from the hospital,' he explained.

'In that case will you drive him back to Southport,' Sandra requested. 'I can't bear to see him in so much torment. I had no idea he was injured so badly.'

Two days later, when the three of them as well as little Hope had gone up to see him they found that he was back in bed, not even allowed to sit in an armchair.

'I don't know what he got up to while he was with you,' the nurse scolded Sandra. 'Did you take him dancing or something? His leg is very swollen, the infection has flared up and he's in a lot of pain.'

'I think his leg must have been far worse than any of us thought,' Sandra told her.

The nurse raised a speculative eyebrow. 'If it doesn't respond to further treatment, he may have to have it amputated,' she warned.

Megan finished getting the records for The Haven completed and looked at the clock. She was utterly weary. Within a few minutes it would be the start of 1944. She looked out of the window at the heavy dark sky. There was no moon, no stars, only a black space. At one time, before the war had started, there would have been a cacophony of sound at this time on New Year's Eve. Church bells would be ringing and here, in Liverpool, there would have been ships' hooters and klaxons sounding to welcome in the New Year.

She felt so alone; after spending most of the day with Hank at the hospital in Southport, Sandra had said she was too tired even to eat. When Megan had insisted that she must have something because they couldn't afford for her to be ill, Sandra had managed a bowl of soup. It was thick and packed with vegetables, one of Nelly's special recipes. After she'd finished it, Sandra said she was going to feed Hope, give her a bath and put her to bed and then she was going to bed herself.

Which leaves me all on my own, Megan sighed. Even the three babies and their mothers in The Haven were sleeping. She wished Harvey was there to celebrate with her but he was at the bedside of a dying man.

She went to the sideboard and brought out the bottle of Bristol Cream Sherry that she had bought for Christmas and poured herself a glassful. She knew that traditionally it should have been scotch but she didn't really like the taste of whisky.

As she raised the glass to her lips she thought about her family at Yr Glaslyn and friends in Beddgelert and wondered if they were all celebrating the start of 1944 and when she would manage to see them again.

She took another sip of the sweet sherry and wondered what the New Year would bring for her. Would she and Harvey finally manage to get married or would circumstances dictate that they would have to wait until the war was over? When would that be? If only Hitler would capitulate and all the men come back home. Even then it would probably take a long time for everything to return to normal, but at least the fear of bombings or of British and American soldiers being killed or injured would be at an end.

She drained her glass and decided that since it was now past midnight she might as well go to bed. She was halfway up the stairs when there was a knock on the front door. It sounded loud in the silence of the house and she felt so tired that she was on the point of ignoring it but her conscience got the better of her.

Suppose it is a girl in trouble, she thought and then reluctantly turned back down the stairs.

The girl on the doorstep was young, bedraggled and in tears. As Megan opened the door the girl tried to speak but a spasm of pain sieved through her and she doubled over gasping and tearful.

Without a word Megan helped her inside. It was obvious that the girl was in an advanced stage of labour.

Megan helped her into the only vacant bedroom they had and then on to the bed. Very gently she removed the threadbare coat the girl was wearing and the down-at-heel shoes.

The girl tried to protest and garbled an explanation about where she had come from but Megan hushed her to silence.

She knew enough now about childbirth to know the birth was imminent and that it was pointless sending for Harvey, even if he could leave the hospital he wouldn't arrive in time.

She was reluctant to disturb either Sandra or Nelly who by now would both be sound asleep, so there was only one thing she could do, Megan decided, and that was to roll up her sleeves and act as midwife and deliver the baby herself.

TWENTY-ONE

It was almost mid-morning before Harvey came to The Haven. Megan was still having breakfast. She felt utterly exhausted after the events of the night before.

'What's all this?' Harvey asked as he looked at her in surprise. 'Did you have a late night? Were you and Sandra up late celebrating?'

Megan shook her head. 'Not a chance! Sandra went to bed early and—'

'You stayed up and celebrated on your own and now you have a first-class hangover,' Harvey said, giving her a critical look.

'If you sit down I'll pour you a cup of tea and then I'll tell you exactly what happened,' Megan muttered.

'Right, whatever you wish. Do you want me to talk in whispers?' he asked with a wicked grin as he pulled out a chair and sat down. He stirred the cup of tea that Megan passed to him and waited patiently for her to tell him about what had happened the night before.

'I was on my own so at midnight I decided I would go to bed. Yes, I did have a drink, a sweet sherry, but only the one.

My mind was on what 1944 might bring for us and for The Haven.

'I was halfway up the stairs when I heard someone knocking on the front door. I thought about ignoring it but I couldn't. I went back down and there was a young girl so obviously in the final stages of labour that I simply hadn't the heart to turn her away.'

'Good heavens! Where is she?' He half rose from his chair but Megan laid a restraining hand on his arm.

'Sit down and finish your tea, she is quite all right and so is the baby.'

'The baby was born last night? Who delivered it?'

'I did, of course; I was the only one up.'

'Why the devil didn't you send for me?' Harvey said crossly.

'If I remember correctly you were unable to come round to see the New Year in with me because you were sitting at the bedside of a dying man,' Megan reminded him.

'I was. Even so, in an emergency like that I would have come immediately. The man was dying, there was nothing I could do for him except to be with him, to give him some feeling of comfort. He was my very first patient when I started in practice in Liverpool and he lost his wife and two daughters when their home received a direct hit.

'At the time he was working in a munitions factory and knew nothing about it until his shift finished and he came home. He was never the same again after that and I felt I owed it to him to be with him in his final hours. Even so, I would have come straight here if I had known what was going on.'

'Well, we can't turn the clock back and fortunately everything went quite smoothly.'

'Did Nelly help you?'

'No, like Sandra, Nelly was fast asleep and I thought it was better not to wake her since I felt quite sure I could cope on my own.'

'You mean you dealt with everything single-handed?' he said in amazement.

'That's right!'

'Good heavens! You say everything went smoothly? The baby is all right?'

'I've already told you so,' Megan said in an exasperated voice. 'I had a good teacher, remember,' she added with a smile.

Harvey stood up. 'I think I ought to see this girl right away. I'm quite sure you did your best but just to be on the safe side.'

'Of course.' She knew her voice was sharp but she was stung by his obvious doubt that she had been able to cope with the situation and she sensed his underlying disapproval that she had done so. 'I'll come with you.'

As they went up the stairs Harvey asked, 'Did you get her name?'

'No, I'm afraid I didn't. There was so much to do that I didn't even think to ask her and she didn't volunteer it. I haven't seen her this morning. I told Nelly about what had happened and asked her to look in on the girl and see if she wanted breakfast and asked her to let me know if everything was all right. When she reported that it was I decided to have my own breakfast before I went in to find out her history.'

'Perhaps you'd better go in first, since she knows you,' Harvey suggested when they reached the bedroom door.

'Very well.' Megan pushed open the door and as she did so the girl turned to smile at her. Then she saw Harvey standing behind Megan and slid back down under the bedclothes, pulling them up as high as she could, almost as if she wished to hide.

'Good Lord!' Harvey stared at the girl in the bed who was clenching her bottom lip between her teeth and trying to avoid his eyes.

'Josie Porter,' he said steamily, 'what on earth are you doing here? Does your mother know where you are?'

The girl made no reply, merely shook her head and turned her face away.

'You know her?' Megan said in astonishment.

'Oh yes; her mother is a patient of mine and so is Josie.'

'You knew she was pregnant?'

Before Harvey could answer Nelly came rushing into the room looking very flustered. 'Sorry to disturb you but there's a woman downstairs asking if we have her daughter here. She's in a terrible rage; I thought she was going to hit me.'

The next moment Nelly, who was standing in the doorway, was pushed to one side and a very stout woman in her early forties, wearing a bright red coat and with her shoulder-length, dark brown hair pinned back behind her ears, pushed her way into the bedroom.

'What the devil are you playing at running away from home and coming here?' she shouted angrily at the young girl in the bed. 'You're only fifteen, you're still a school kid.'

'I've heard all about you and what goes on here from Hilda Heath,' she continued in a loud belligerent voice, turning round to stare accusingly at Megan. 'She told me how you take in young girls and then snatch their babies from them the moment they're born and sell them. Well, you're not doing that with my kid's baby, so don't for one moment think that you are.'

As she stopped to draw breath she suddenly caught sight of Harvey Stott.

'What are you doing here then, Dr Stott? Surely you're not the doctor that Hilda Heath told me about. She said there was a doctor helping out at this place. I never dreamed it was you, of course. I can't believe that you're involved in baby farming like her,' she said scornfully, nodding her head in Megan's direction.

'I think it might be a good idea if you stopped talking for a moment, took a deep breath and calmed down, Mrs Porter,' Harvey said calmly. 'When you've done that and stopped making spurious accusations against Miss Lloyd you should be thanking her for not only taking your daughter in last night but for delivering her baby.'

'You mean my Josie's already had it?'

For a moment Mrs Porter stood mouth agape in surprise. 'Where is it? Let me see it or have you already sold it?' she demanded angrily

'Don't go on, Mam.' Josie Porter stretched out a hand towards her mother. 'I've had the baby, but I'm not coming home. You said you were going to get rid of it but I want to keep her, she's so sweet.'

'Ever so sweet,' Mrs Porter said in a mocking voice.

'You're going to keep her! Who's going to keep you, I'd like to know? That cocky young GI who got you pregnant isn't likely to come back here and take care of you now, is he!' she ranted.

'I don't care whether he does or doesn't, I'm keeping her,' Josie repeated stubbornly.

'Kids cost money; they don't live on fresh air, you know. Once she's off the titty then you'll have to buy real food for her and where are you going to get the money to do that?'

Josie was crying too much to answer. Megan bent down and picked up the baby from the crib at the side of Josie's bed and held her out so that Mrs Porter could see her.

'This is your granddaughter, Mrs Porter. I suggested to Josie that she should be called Dawn because she was born so very early this morning that the dawn had not yet broken.'

Mrs Porter turned to look at the baby and then drew in her breath sharply as she gazed at the tiny face and perfectly formed little hand that lay outside the shawl that Megan had wrapped her in.

'She's lovely, Mam, she's so sweet I can't give her away, I really can't,' Josie wept.

'So what do you want me to do? Bring her up as me own?'

'Well now, she very well could be yours, Mrs Porter,' Harvey Stott said quietly. 'She certainly looks like a miniature of Josie. She has the same dark hair and eyes and even her nose and chin look similar.'

'Bring her up as my own?' Mrs Porter stared at him in utter astonishment, then slowly the frown eased from her face leaving her looking thoughtful.

'Who's to know except you?' Harvey murmured.

Mrs Porter gave him a crafty look. 'Are you going to help me to do it?'

'What do you mean?'

'Well, you would have to keep your mouth shut for a start. I wouldn't want the neighbours to know what sort of game I was playing – it would give rise to too much gossip. I think I could do it though, that's if Josie wants me to.'

'I don't really know what you mean,' Josie said in a puzzled voice.

'What the doctor is saying, luv, is that I tell folks that little Dawn here is my baby and I bring her up as if she was your sister.'

'What about Dad? He'll know that's a lie!'

'No need for him to know the truth,' her mother defended. 'He's been away with the army in the desert for the past six months so he isn't to know whether it's the truth or not.'

'He'll wonder why you never told him in any of your letters that you were expecting a baby,' Josie reasoned.

'Keeping it as a big surprise for him, wasn't I?' her mother told her with cynical laugh. 'As for the neighbours, well, the size I am these days they don't know if I'm pregnant or not.'

'You mean you're going through with the idea?' Megan asked in amazement.

'What I'll do,' Mrs Porter went on, ignoring Megan and speaking directly to Harvey Stott, 'I'll go away for two or three weeks and then when I come back I'll be carrying the baby in my arms and no one need know the truth. She's tiny so folks won't know whether she's three weeks or a month old now, will they?'

'It all sounds very plausible,' Harvey agreed. 'What do you think, Josie?'

'I suppose it's a good idea. I'll be able to see her grow up; I'll even be able to look after her.'

'Oh, you'll be looking after her all right, make no mistake about that,' her mother said with a hearty belly laugh. 'I'm too old and too set in my ways to be bothered getting up in the night when she cries or running round the park playing ball with her when she gets a couple of years older. No, you'll be the one looking after her all right but she'll be at our house and as long as you keep your mouth shut no one need know the truth, that she's your kid not mine.'

'Well, Megan, that seems to be settled in a very satisfactory manner,' Harvey Stott said, smiling at her smugly.

'Not quite so fast, you two,' Mrs Porter said. 'If I'm to go along with this plan then you've got to help; you've got to keep our Josie and the baby here until it's time for me to take them home. I want a bit of a holiday, a bit of time to enjoy myself, before I take on the burden of a young baby. Three weeks. Is that all right?'

Harvey and Megan exchanged glances and when Megan nodded her head in acceptance of the idea, Harvey nodded too and turned back to Mrs Porter.

'Very well, we'll keep Josie and the baby here while you take a holiday. Two weeks though and no longer.'

'Yes, yes, whatever you say,' Mrs Porter agreed impatiently. 'You stay here and find out how to look after the baby,' she added as she reached the door and turned and waved a hand to Josie.

Harvey looked apologetically at Megan. 'It is an answer, I suppose,' he murmured.

'They're your patients so it will be up to you to make sure it works,' she pointed out. 'I hope you realize that it is going to put an extra strain on us keeping Josie and Dawn for another few weeks.'

'Sorry about that,' Harvey said contritely. 'I promise I'll make it up to you . . . as well as for not being here last night when you needed me.'

TWENTY-TWO

'Do you think my mam really is going to keep her promise to let me take my baby home?' Josie Porter asked wistfully the morning her mother was due back from her holiday.

'Well, she said she would,' Megan reassured her as she helped Josie to pack up her few meagre belongings, a face flannel and a couple of spare nappies for Dawn and some baby formula, into a carrier bag to take home with her.

'She should be here any time soon so then we'll know for certain,' she added as she looked at the clock.

Mrs Porter was already half an hour late and there had been no word from her all the time she had been on holiday, not even a postcard for Josie.

As the day wore on and there was still no sign of Mrs Porter, Josie seemed to be looking more and more miserable. Megan, too, was extremely worried because it certainly did look as though Mrs Porter didn't intend to keep her promise.

Megan wondered what the future would be like for Josie. She hadn't the stamina to bring up the baby single-handed and, as her mother had said, there was very little possibility of the baby's father ever showing up again in Liverpool. Also, Josie was still only fifteen, still a schoolgirl.

It was after eight o' clock in the evening when Mrs Porter finally came to collect Josie and baby Dawn. By then Harvey had finished at his surgery and was there with them. Like them he was dubious about whether Mrs Porter was going to keep her promise.

'I know I'm late, luv, but don't start moaning at me,' she gasped when Megan opened the door to her. 'I know I look a mess; as if I'd been pulled through a hedge backwards. I've run all the way up Water Street from the Pier Head lugging this damn suitcase because I knew our Josie would probably be bawling her eyes out and thinking that I wasn't coming,' she puffed as she put a brown fibre case down on the floor.

'The boat coming back from the Isle of Man was late leaving Douglas and the delay meant that it had to wait out at the Bar for over an hour before they could get into the usual berth here in Liverpool because there was already a liner there using it,' she explained breathlessly. 'Anyway, I'm here now. All's well that ends well as they say. Is our Josie all packed and ready to go home?'

'Yes she is,' Megan assured her.

'Don't you want to take a peep at the baby before we go?' Josie asked.

'I'll see all I want to see of your kid when we get home. I'm gasping for a cuppa so get a move on, girl,' her mother said sharply.

'No, come and sit down for a minute, Mrs Porter, and I'll ask Nelly to make us a cup of tea and then we can talk things through,' Megan said, taking her arm and propelling her towards the sitting room. 'You come as well, Josie,' she said over her shoulder as Josie hung back.

'Talk things through! What is there to talk through? I've brought up one bloody kid so I don't need advice on how to bring up another. Anyway, it's Josie you should have been telling what there is to do because she's the one who's going to be looking after it, not me!'

'Are you still going to say that Dawn is your baby and that she's my sister?' Josie asked in a querulous tone of voice.

'Of course I bloody well am! I told you that from the start, before I went on holiday.'

'I know that's what you said then, Mam, but I've been thinking about it ever since and I don't understand why we can't say that she's mine?' Josie persisted.

'Because you are only fifteen and if we say it's your baby then we'll have the authorities poking their noses in on our affairs and all sorts of inspectors calling. What's more, some busybody or do-gooder will try and take it away from you and you don't want that now, do you?' Mrs Porter paused as Nelly brought in a tray loaded with cups and saucers, a teapot and a jug of milk and put them down on the coffee table.

'What's more,' she went on when Nelly had left the room, 'because you're still only fifteen the rozzers will probably turn up, say it's a bloody crime or something and take the kid away. Say it's mine and they can't do a damn thing. Now do you understand?'

'I suppose so,' Josie admitted reluctantly.

'Then get that tea down you and shut up. Let's get out of here and on our way,' she added as she drained her cup and put it back on the table.

'I'm not at all sure that we're doing the right thing, Harvey,' Megan said worriedly after they had helped the Porters into a taxi, and Harvey had paid the cabby, and they were waving them goodbye.

'What do you mean?' he asked, putting his arm around her shoulders and squeezing her tight. 'I thought you would be relieved that Mrs Porter kept her promise and finally turned up?'

'Oh, I am pleased about that,' Megan assured him. 'I mean about this business of pretending that Dawn is Mrs Porter's child instead of Josie's.'

'No, I agree it's a ruse that I don't like but it is the best thing to do for the sake of Josie and the baby. As her mother says, Josie is breaking the law because she is still at school, or she was until Christmas. I don't suppose she will ever go back again. She'll be too busy looking after little Dawn.'

'Don't you think Mrs Porter will take over once they get home?'

'I very much doubt it. She's very lazy at the best of times. She might sit and nurse the baby while Josie does the housework, I suppose. Even then she'll either be eating, smoking or drinking and it probably won't be tea or coffee!'

'You never told me that she drank,' Megan said in alarm. 'That's terrible. Are you sure she's fit to bring up a young baby?'

'Don't worry yourself about them,' Harvey told her, kissing the top of her head affectionately. 'You've done all you can and I'll keep an eye on them. In any case, I'll certainly get a call from them if they have any problems, I don't doubt that for one moment,' he added with a laugh.

Nevertheless, Megan did worry about Josie. Over the next couple of weeks she regularly asked Harvey if he had seen them or had any news of them but he always assured her that they were fine and not to worry about them.

Megan's mind was finally set at rest when one day when she was shopping at Paddy's Market she met Josie, who was pushing an old but well-polished pram.

Josie greeted her enthusiastically and insisted she must stop and look at the baby and Megan was very impressed. Not only was the bedding spotlessly clean but also little Dawn had put on weight and looked the picture of health.

'She is lovely, isn't she?' Josie said, smiling happily as she pulled back the little blanket to display how plump and healthy the baby was.

'She certainly seems to be thriving,' Megan agreed. 'Are you finding that things are working out all right between you and your mother?'

'Oh yes,' Josie answered with a smile. 'We never mention whose baby it is any more. It was so kind of you and Dr Stott to buy this pram for me, it means that I can take Dawn out every day and it's lovely and safe for her to sleep in.'

Her mind set at rest that all was going well, Megan told
Harvey that she had seen Josie and baby Dawn and that Josie
seemed very pleased with the pram that they had given her.
'That was news to me, of course,' she added with a grin. 'You
might have told me.'

'It must have slipped my mind.' He smiled back. 'Anyway,
now you've seen her and the baby and you know that all is
well perhaps you'll stop worrying about them. I'm sure there
are plenty of other things happening at The Haven to merit
your attention.'

Harvey was quite right. To start with, Hank had been given
weekend leave. Sandra was highly elated because it meant that
they had cleared up the infection and that once again he was
back on the road to full health.

'Do we have a spare room?' she asked Megan.

'No, we don't have a spare room. Anyway, why do you
need a spare room?'

'For Hank, of course! I was hoping he'd be able to stay
here at The Haven but if there isn't a room free then he will
have to book into a hotel,' Sandra said in a disappointed voice.

'Why will he have to do that? He can sleep in your room,
can't he?'

'I suppose he could but he really needs to be in a bed, not
making do on the sofa. I suppose I could sleep on the sofa
and let him have my bed,' she said thoughtfully.

'What on earth do you want to do that for?' Megan said
with a broad smile. 'What's wrong with you both sleeping in
your bed?'

Sandra looked taken aback. 'You mean sleep together?
Here?' she said in astonishment.

'Yes, sleep together! That is precisely what I mean. You
already have a child and you are planning to be married as
soon as possible, aren't you?'

'Of course we are, you know that perfectly well.'

'Then what's wrong with you sleeping together?'

Sandra looked at her wide-eyed, shaking her head slowly
from side to side. 'Haven't you any morals at all, Megan
Lloyd?' she said with mock severity. 'Yes, you're quite right,
there's no reason at all why we shouldn't sleep together.'

'So that problem's solved, now can we move on to the next one?' Megan asked, trying not to laugh.

When Hank eventually turned up for the weekend he had other news to give them. Following his most recent medical, he had been told that he was no longer fit for active service. As a result of that, he was being sent back to America where in due course he would be employed in a clerical position at a recruiting centre.

'They think that I'll be a good ambassador because I've seen active service, been injured, and come out the other side more or less fine. Isn't that great!'

'It's certainly great that they think you are reasonably fit,' Sandra said, 'but where does that leave us? We'll be separated by the Atlantic Ocean. When will we see each other again?'

'Well, that's the other part of the good news; they say I can take my family with me.'

'They have!' Megan looked amazed.

'So many of our men have married English girls and this proviso is now standard,' Hank explained.

'You can take your family when you go back to America but you haven't any family,' Sandra said in a bemused voice.

'I have you, and Hope,' Hank said, pulling her into his arms and hugging her. 'I want you to come back to America with me but, of course, in order to do that you will have to be my wife so we need to be married. How soon can we do that? I only have about a week.'

'That's impossible, it takes months to arrange a wedding,' Sandra said with a groan.

'Not if you get married in a register office,' Megan pointed out.

'What about the grand wedding ceremony we were planning to have at your home in North Wales? We were counting on it being a double wedding, if you remember.'

'That was then, this is now,' Hank drawled with a shrug of his broad shoulders. 'It's still wartime so you have to live for the minute and take opportunities as they come.'

Sandra looked across at Megan helplessly. 'What do you think, Megan?'

'I agree with Hank and since it's February why don't we

settle for St Valentine's Day? That's only four days away.'

'You mean you'll get married on the same day?' Sandra gasped, her eyes wide with astonishment.

'Why not? We always said we would have a double wedding. Well, I'm sure we can do that at the register office.'

'What about your promise to your family?' Sandra asked uneasily.

'They'll understand and then sometime in the future you can come back from America on holiday and we'll arrange the grand affair at the church in Beddgelert that my mother dreams about, if you still want to do that.'

'Can you do that . . . get married twice, I mean?' Sandra asked.

'I'm sure we'll be able to have some sort of ceremony,' Megan said airily.

The next few days were so hectic as they made their plans for their weddings that neither of them had time for anything else. They even turned away two girls because they were so caught up in their own affairs.

'I feel awful about that,' Sandra admitted, 'but we really can't take on anything else at the moment. I still have to pack what I want to take to America with me and there are all Hope's things to be sorted out as well.'

'Why don't you ask Nelly to help you? She'll see to all Hope's things and then you can concentrate on what you want to take,' Megan advised.

'Nelly is a treasure, isn't she?' Sandra sighed. 'I don't know how I'm going to manage without her. At least I won't have to worry about her future though, will I, because she'll be here with you. Are you going to be able to cope here on your own with only Nelly to help out?' she asked worriedly.

'I won't be completely on my own,' Megan replied and smiled. 'Harvey will be here as well.'

'You mean he's going to move in and live here?'

'Of course! He's keeping the flat over the surgery for emergencies; if he's called out in the middle of the night then he can sleep there rather than come back here and disturb the entire household.'

'Lucky Devil! You mean he's got a bolthole for when married life becomes too much for him,' Hank teased.

'Are you going to tell your parents what you've decided to do?' Sandra asked Megan.

'No.' Megan shook her head. 'Not much point, is there? It's such short notice. I don't think my mother would come this far anyway and I don't think my father would want to come on his own. No, I'll tell them the next time we go up to see them.'

'They'll be terribly disappointed,' Sandra murmured.

'I'm not so sure. I think my mother may be relieved to know that Harvey has made an honest woman of me. She still has Victorian values, remember, and I'm sure she suspects we may be sleeping together.'

Although they had very little time to make any elaborate preparations, Megan and Sandra managed to dress up for the occasion. They both wore smart dresses with short matching coats over them and pretty hats. They looked radiant on what was a rather dull overcast February day.

Hank looked very smart in his American officer's uniform and Harvey chose a dark grey suit with a crisp white shirt and striped grey and red tie.

When the brief ceremony was over, they took a taxi to The Adelphi for a celebratory meal. They toasted each other in champagne and vowed a lifetime of friendship no matter what part of the world they eventually ended up in.

TWENTY-THREE

Sandra, Hank and little Hope were up early, their cases packed, ready to leave The Haven on the first stage of their journey to America. They had said their goodbyes to Nelly and were on the point of kissing Megan goodbye when a dispatch rider arrived with a message for Hank.

His face blanched as he read it.

'What's wrong?' Sandra demanded.

'It's not good, you're not going to like this,' he said, shaking his head.

'Why? What's the matter?'

'We're not travelling by boat; they're flying me back. I have to leave immediately.'

'We're flying with you, how thrilling!' Sandra exclaimed excitedly. Then her expression of animation faded. 'They are flying Hope and me out as well?'

'No, I'm afraid you'll have to stay on here in England and wait until they start to ship wives back to America sometime in the future. There are over 4,000 wives to be transported but they promise you will be on the very first ship.'

Sandra stared at him blankly. 'I don't want to wait for a ship, I want to come with you. It was a promise they made; they said that your family would be able to accompany you to America when they sent you back. We took it that they meant together.'

'I know, I know.' He ran a hand through his hair. 'It distresses me, sweetheart, just as much as it upsets you, but there is absolutely nothing we can do about it. I'm still a soldier and orders are orders and you simply have to jump-to and carry them out.' He looked at his watch. 'I must go right now, they're sending a car for me immediately. It's probably outside waiting for me now,' he added as he went to look out of the window.

'It is,' he affirmed. 'I'll have to go.'

He took Sandra in his arms and kissed her, wiping away her tears with the ball of his thumb. Then he picked up little Hope and kissed her. 'Look after your mummy,' he told the tiny tot, 'I'll miss you both but I hope to see you again very soon.'

He passed Hope over to Megan. 'Take great care of them both for me,' he said solemnly as he kissed her on the cheek.

Then he picked up his army holdall and he was gone, leaving both women in tears and little Hope crying because that was what everyone else was doing.

Nelly came to see what all the commotion was about and

when she heard the news she expressed astonishment that the army could do a thing like that.

'Heartless, that's what it is,' she said shaking her head dolefully.

She whisked Hope off to the kitchen to give her a glass of milk and a biscuit, leaving Megan and Sandra alone.

Megan put an arm around Sandra to try and comfort her but Sandra was so distraught that she wasn't listening to anything Megan said.

'If I have to go by boat then it will take fourteen days to cross the Atlantic,' Sandra snuffled. 'Fourteen days with Hope fretful and no one on board that I know.'

'There will be other wives in the same position,' Megan pointed out.

'If that's supposed to make me feel any better then it doesn't,' Sandra replied with a scowl as she dried her eyes. 'Shut up on a ship for fourteen days with a gaggle of women I don't know and don't wish to know. They'll probably all have screaming kids and it will be sheer hell.'

'Yes, but remember Hank will be waiting for you at the other end,' Megan reminded her.

'Knowing how the army acts, they'll probably send him back to England the day I arrive and then I'll be in a strange country where I know no one.'

'You have the address of Hank's family so you can go direct to them,' Megan said consolingly.

'I don't know them though, do I? They're complete strangers. I might not like them! They may not like me. They may resent me taking Hank away from them. They may not like Hope.'

'Hush, for goodness' sake. You make it sound like a trip to Hell,' Megan said. 'I'll go and ask Nelly to make a pot of tea and see if that will make you feel any better.'

Nelly forestalled her. She had hardly finished speaking when the door opened and Nelly came in with a tray carrying not only tea but a couple of rounds of freshly made toast.

'Here, have something to eat and drink and you'll feel better,' she told Sandra. 'Little Hope is in the kitchen eating a biscuit along with Mary. Betsy is keeping an eye on them.

Hope's quite happy as can be so don't worry about her. I'll keep her with me in the kitchen until you're feeling calmer.'

'Have you brought in a cup for me, Nelly?'

'Of course I have, Miss Megan. I know you two will want to have a quiet natter about what happens next. Shame to have all your plans turned up and down like this. Have you told Dr Stott yet about the change of plans?'

'Not yet, Nelly, but we will do so as soon as we have talked things through.'

There was a moment's silence after Nelly had left and it was Sandra who spoke first. 'I'm so sorry about this, Megan, Harvey was planning to move in and now this will change everything.'

'I don't see why it has to,' Megan said quickly. 'He's moving into my room so how will it affect things except that he'll be here for our evening meal which of course we will all have together.'

'How's he going to feel about that?' Sandra said with a worried frown.

'I don't understand. It's not as though the two of you are strangers. You don't mind him coming to live here, do you?'

'Of course I don't. How will he feel about the new arrangement though? He was expecting to have you to himself when he's finished work at the end of the day.'

'Stop worrying, it will all work out, I know it will.'

'Even so, it's bound to make a difference,' Sandra insisted.

'The only difference you still being here will make is that I will have to reallocate some of the jobs,' Megan told her. 'I take it that you'll still want to play an active part in the running of The Haven?'

'I'd certainly like to. I can hardly sit back and twiddle my thumbs indefinitely and I have no idea when the first boatload of wives will be taken over to America. I really do think it's very bad that they have decided to fly Hank back and not let me go with him because they did promise that he could take his family with him.'

'Yes, but you thought you would be going back by ship and

I suppose it's quite another matter if they're flying him back on a military aircraft,' Megan said.

'Then why couldn't they have left him here until they were ready to transport us both back by sea?' Sandra argued.

'There is a war on, you know, and even though we are hoping that it's going to end very, very soon, we civilians don't really know what has been planned from a military point of view. They obviously have a special job waiting for Hank, one that they couldn't delay. Try and think of it as being so important that he had to return in order that you can go to America as soon as possible.'

'Yes, you're probably right. Draw up a new rota and make sure I have plenty to fill in my time, then I won't be able to think any more about what I'm missing.'

'You are quite happy about Harvey moving in here?' Megan asked anxiously.

'Of course; ignore me. Pretend I'm not here.'

'We might be able to do that as far as you're concerned but I hardly think we can tell little Hope to ignore her favourite uncle, now, can we?'

'She's probably quite happy to stay here instead of going to America,' Sandra said ruefully.

It was the beginning of June before they heard from Hank and then it was only a brief note to say he was in America and working so damned hard he hadn't time to sleep let alone write letters. He hoped she was well and that little Hope wasn't missing him too much. He went on to say there was so much happening but of course he couldn't comment on it and she would understand in time.

'Well, what do you make of that?' Sandra asked as she read the note aloud to Megan.

'It's what we thought, they need him for some very special job; something so important that he's unable to mention what it is he's doing.'

'That's what I took it to mean but I'm puzzled what he means when he says "I will understand in time"?'

Megan shrugged her shoulders. 'We'll just have to be patient,

I suppose, and hope he is right and that you will understand what's going on all in good time. We do know that they are contemplating invading Normandy so perhaps that's what he's talking about.'

Two days later and the news broke about D-Day.

'Do you think this is what Hank meant?' Sandra questioned.

'It seems to be a British enterprise but perhaps the Americans are involved in some way,' Megan said. 'Let's hope that whoever is behind the invasion, it will be a success and bring an end to this terrible war.'

'They've tried before but it didn't work,' Sandra reminded her. 'You surely haven't forgotten what a disaster it was when they attempted to invade France in 1940 and ended up with the soldiers having to be evacuated from the beaches of Dunkirk in May?'

'Yes, but the Americans joined us after that so this new offensive probably does have something to do with them. Don't forget that since January this year General Eisenhower has been in command of the Allies.'

Megan was right. Eisenhower was in command and on June 5th he gave the go-ahead for Operation Overlord. Later that day, they heard on the radio that more than 5,000 ships and landing craft carrying troops and supplies left England for the trip across the Channel to France, while more than 1,200 aircraft were mobilized to provide air cover and support for the invasion.

By dawn on June 6th, thousands of paratroopers and glider troops were already on the ground behind enemy lines, securing bridges and exit roads. The amphibious invasions began at six thirty a.m. The British and Canadians overcame light opposition to capture beaches codenamed Gold, Juno and Sword, as did the Americans at Utah Beach. The American forces faced heavy resistance at Omaha Beach, where there were over 2,000 casualties.

However, by the end of the day, approximately 156,000 Allied troops had been successful and had stormed the Normandy beaches.

Less than a week later, on June 11th, the beaches were fully secured and over 326,000 troops, more than 50,000 vehicles and some 100,000 tons of equipment had landed at Normandy.

For their part, the Germans suffered from confusion in the ranks and the absence of their celebrated commander Rommel, who was away on leave.

Megan and Sandra took it in turns to listen to the news bulletins put out on the wireless. They were anxious not to miss any details of the Allies' progress.

They rejoiced when they heard that Hitler, believing the invasion was merely designed to distract the Germans from an attack north of the Seine River, refused to release nearby divisions to join the counterattack.

'That means they'll have to call for reinforcements from further afield and that will cause considerable delay,' Harvey pointed out. 'I've also heard that Hitler hesitated in calling for armored divisions to help in the defence.'

The rumours were correct. Moreover, the Germans were hampered by effective Allied air support, which took out many key bridges and forced the Germans to take long detours. There was also efficient Allied naval support, which helped to protect the advancing Allied troops.

In the ensuing weeks, the Allies fought their way across the Normandy countryside in the face of determined German resistance, as well as a dense landscape of marshes and hedgerows. By the end of June, the Allies had seized the vital port of Cherbourg, landed approximately 850,000 men and 150,000 vehicles in Normandy, and were poised to continue their march across France.

Sandra worried constantly in case Hank was involved in some way although Megan kept reminding her that he had been told that he was no longer fit enough for active service.

By the end of August 1944, the Allies had reached the Seine River. Paris was liberated and the Germans had been removed from northwestern France, effectively concluding the Battle of Normandy. The Allied forces then prepared to enter Germany, where they would meet up with Soviet troops moving in from the east.

The Normandy invasion began to turn the tide against the

Nazis. Not only was it a significant psychological blow but it also prevented Hitler from sending troops from France to build up his Eastern Front against the advancing Soviet troops.

'Hank was right when he said that in time we would know what he meant,' Sandra said with a smile of relief. 'The Normandy landings really have been the beginning of the end of the war in Europe.'

From then on Sandra and Megan continued to spend every minute they could listening to the news bulletins and discussing them with each other afterwards. Sandra was thrilled to hear that the Americans were dropping bombs on targets in northern France.

Sandra also scoured the daily newspaper for any mention of the American troops and although she said nothing to Megan she began to cut out any references she found and collect them all up together.

The war was on everyone's mind and references about what was going on were everywhere to the exclusion of almost everything else. Prime Minister Winston Churchill spoke to the nation on the wireless and so too did King George VI.

The American President, Franklin D Roosevelt told a news conference the invasion did not mean the war was over. He said, 'You don't stop until you walk into Berlin, and the sooner this country realizes that the better.'

'Yes, and the sooner President Roosevelt realizes that there are several thousand GI brides in Britain who are waiting to be transported to America the better,' Sandra added cryptically when for the second time she and Megan listened to the broadcast.

It wasn't until the following spring, May 8, 1945, that the Allies formally accepted the unconditional surrender of Nazi Germany.

At the same time they heard that Hitler had committed suicide a week earlier.

'Evil man!' Sandra exclaimed. 'He's been the cause of all this trouble. It's a pity in one way that he's dead. He should have stood trial and been punished for causing so much misery in the world.'

'Never mind, it's all over now and it won't be long before you hear from the American army to tell you which ship you're going to be on,' Megan assured her.

'I'd like some proper news from Hank first,' Sandra told her. 'I still don't know if he is in America or somewhere else and I want him to be at the dockside to meet me when I do travel to America.'

'Let's hope that after waiting so long you like it when you get there and you're not homesick about leaving Liverpool,' Megan said with a smile.

TWENTY-FOUR

Megan had looked forward so much to Harvey moving into The Haven that she found it extremely disappointing when she realized that it wasn't working out as well as she had anticipated.

She blamed Sandra. She had thought that Sandra would respect their privacy but she didn't. When in the evening after they had finished dinner the two of them settled for a quiet chat in the sitting room, within minutes Sandra would join them and stay there, asking Harvey's opinion about the progress of the war and about things in general until it was time for bed.

Megan realized that Sandra and Harvey were very old friends and that they had known each other long before she'd come on the scene, but nevertheless she found it irksome.

She didn't say anything to Harvey because she thought it might make him feel uncomfortable and she couldn't bring herself to mention it to Sandra so there was nothing for it but to put up with it.

There were far bigger problems to contend with, she kept reminding herself. There had been so many girls arriving on the doorstep and asking for help that they had been exceptionally busy.

On average four babies a week had been born at The Haven

in the last few months. One of the big issues was that the girls arrived not only penniless and with nothing except the clothes they stood up in, but they had no ration books either. This meant that more and more often she had to send Nelly out foraging for food. They had even sent Nelly across to the Wirral to see if there were any blackberries to be found on Bidston Hill. She had come back with enough to make jam to last them for months, although it had meant a couple of weeks with very little sugar for anything else.

Nelly knew where to go for Black Market butter, margarine, sugar and even meat. Buying on the Black Market though was expensive and even though Nelly was a first-class haggler she had to pay far more than if they had bought the goods in a conventional way.

Late on Saturday nights, shortly before Paddy's Market was closing, Nelly would go there to see what she could acquire in the way of meat, vegetables and any other produce that wouldn't keep until the market reopened the following week.

Britain's rationing system ensured that no one starved. Indeed, most of the poor were better nourished than in peace time. But few found anything to enjoy about their fare because it was very basic and monotonous.

Housewives were using grated-up beetroots, apples, potatoes and carrots to eke out the flour and other ingredients when making cakes. Carrot and onion marmalade and rhubarb and onion chutney were some of the other combinations that people tried and relished because it was better than nothing on their bread.

People fantasized about large juicy steaks and longed for asparagus with lumps of golden butter as they chewed on omelettes made with dried egg powder. They longed to have a breakfast fry up instead of toast with a scrape of margarine.

A further problem Megan was experiencing at The Haven was that many of the regular donations had trailed off, especially since the official end of the war with Germany. People thought that because the war was over there was no need for them to help as much.

It didn't help matters that Sandra was so very disappointed by the continued delay about her being transported to America.

As Megan kept telling her, one million American GIs had been stationed in Britain in the two years preceding D-Day, and in all nearly 70,000 British girls had married their GI boyfriends.

'Remember, the GIs proved to be exceptionally popular in Liverpool because of their movie star accents, smart uniforms and money, as well as being generous with items like cigarettes, nylons and sweets.'

'The GIs weren't popular with everyone,' Sandra argued. 'I remember how the local men felt threatened by the Americans with their glamour and wealth.'

'Nevertheless more than 60,000 US servicemen married British women and they have been promised that their wives and babies will receive free passage to the US, so even though you thought you would be given special treatment, it looks as though you'll have to be patient and wait your turn.'

Although Sandra knew she had no real argument she continued to be discontented because she had to wait, but she did try to hide her resentment over Christmas, and as far as possible, they celebrated in traditional manner at The Haven.

'Here's hoping that 1946 will see us all back to normal,' Harvey said as the three of them drank a toast together on New Year's Eve.

'I'll second that,' Sandra declared gloomily. 'I haven't seen Hank now for so long that we won't know what each other looks like. Hope can't even remember her daddy.'

'She certainly recognizes his picture whenever she sees it,' Megan said quietly. 'Don't worry; you will be reunited some time in 1946.'

'Is that a prophecy or a promise?' Sandra asked mockingly.

Megan was right. In late January 1946 the first batch of war brides were transported to America.

Some 455 British war brides arrived in America on the 4th February; the same day as the first dedicated British war bride ship to leave from Liverpool for Canada arrived in Halifax.

When Sandra eventually received details and papers to enable her to go to America she suddenly became nervous and uncertain about the unknown life that now lay ahead of her.

She bombarded Harvey and Megan with questions about

what would she do if she arrived in America and Hank wasn't there to meet her. What would she do if she didn't like his family or they didn't like her? She worried about how much luggage she could take, about what the weather would be like and what they thought she ought to wear.

She was very concerned that Hope might not settle in a strange country, about the new life she would have to adjust to as well as strange people.

By the time her departure arrived both Harvey and Megan felt drained after they had finally waved her and Hope off.

'I feel like getting drunk but I'm too tired to do so,' Harvey groaned.

'I know exactly how you feel. I think we should go home and have a quiet night. Think how wonderful it's going to be to be on our own. Let's hope that things are good for Sandra and she settles,' Megan went on. 'I've heard some terrible stories about the first brides to get there and how disappointed they were. Sometimes the husband wasn't the man he had pretended to be, other times it was his family that objected to him having married a British girl.'

'None of those things are likely to happen with Sandra,' Harvey said confidently. 'Hank's a good guy, he wouldn't have been made an officer if he had a shady past.'

'I think the American army was very much like the British army, they were so desperately in need of men they were prepared to take anyone who was willing to sign up,' Megan commented.

'Perhaps, fingers crossed, Sandra will be blissfully happy. I think we should now agree not to mention her name until we get a letter from her telling us what a wonderful place it is and how plentiful everything is and assuring us that she has done the right thing and wouldn't dream of coming back to Britain again.'

'Let's hope she tells us the truth about the place,' Megan murmured, 'because we've promised to go out and see her sometime in the future and if we are going to take a holiday that is as expensive as that will be then I want a good time when we reach our destination.'

TWENTY-FIVE

I t took Megan some little time to adjust to not having Sandra there to talk over any problems that arose from running The Haven.

She quickly discovered, however, that in some ways Harvey was better than Sandra in this respect. He was positive, decisive and very logical. He saw right to the heart of the matter and dealt with it without quibbling.

Nelly accepted his authority without any trouble. In fact, she was always quick to say 'perhaps we ought to ask Dr Stott' whenever there was a problem, especially when it concerned one of the girls.

In next to no time the wheels were running as smoothly as ever and Megan found that there was an increasing under-standing between her and Harvey.

It was a couple of months before they heard from Sandra but when they did the news was good. She liked America and its people. In particular she was very enthusiastic about their plentiful selection of food.

'Our breakfast each day includes tomato juice, porridge or cereal, scrambled eggs, toast, marmalade and coffee,' she wrote. 'The stores here are full of food, clothes and toys of every description and the prices are even better than we knew in pre-war Britain. I'm looking forward to you paying us a visit as soon as you can so that you can see all these wonderful things for yourselves. Hank's parents are delightful; they have made me so welcome and they absolutely adore Hope. She has really taken to them and they never cease to lavish affection and goodies on her. I shall have to watch out or she will be thoroughly spoiled.'

'There, what did I tell you. Sandra is fine, better off than we are by the sound of it,' Harvey commented. 'We're still rationed for most things even though the war is now confined to Japan.'

'Why can't the Japanese admit defeat and let the rest of the world get back to normal,' Megan grumbled.

After that they rarely spoke about Sandra because there were so many changes on the home front to take their attention. One of these was the Labour Party members of the coalition government resigning an order to prepare for the upcoming general election. In the meantime Churchill had appointed a largely Conservative caretaker government.

In August, the Family Allowances Act came into force. In future mothers would receive a tax-free cash payment for each child in their care. This was the first time in Britain that a state payment was paid directly to a wife rather than her husband and it was headline news.

Megan thoroughly approved of it and wished it had come long before. 'If it had been sooner then half the girls we've had here would have kept their babies and not had them adopted,' she commented sadly.

'Possibly,' Harvey agreed. 'Let's hope that it will be spent on the children and not on cigarettes. They've certainly timed it well immediately before the general election. That should secure the votes from the women. It will be interesting to see the results.'

Although the election took place a few days later all ballots boxes were sealed immediately afterwards and they had to wait for three weeks before the results were announced to allow for the collection and counting of overseas service votes.

Then the announcement came that the Labour Party had proved successful. It was a historic landslide. Clement Atlee became Prime Minister and formed a new government.

'Will that make any difference to us?' Megan asked.

'Who knows?' Harvey said with a shrug. 'They'll probably bring in all sorts of reforms so we'll have to wait and see.'

Harvey was right; the end of the war brought a good many changes even at The Haven. They still had a few pregnant girls coming to them for help because they had nowhere else to go and had been turned out by their families but there were not nearly so many.

To start with, demobilization meant that soldiers went back to their homes; secondly, unmarried mothers were no longer the lepers they had once been. True, there were a few families who still felt that their unmarried pregnant daughter brought shame and disgrace on them, but the numbers were decreasing rapidly.

There were now so many single-parent families because the menfolk had been killed while on active service that unmarried mothers were no longer regarded as out of the ordinary. The number of girls who had been left stranded when their soldier boyfriend departed had diminished because men were no longer being sent overseas or being billeted in and around Liverpool.

As their numbers declined Megan had more time for her own life. Now that things were gradually getting back to normal she felt that it was time for her and Harvey to have their own family.

He agreed wholeheartedly but, as he sensibly pointed out, it was not feasible as long as she was running The Haven.

'It's not the sort of background I want my children to be brought up in,' he told her.

'Nor do I but what do we do?'

'We could employ someone to manage The Haven, I suppose, and then we could buy a house somewhere else, preferably in the Wirral.'

'I don't think I can do that, not without Sandra's permission.'

'Why not? She has her own life now, I can't see her coming back to run the place.'

'No, I know that, but it is her house, remember.'

For a moment Harvey looked taken aback. 'I'd forgotten about that!' he admitted. 'Well, we'll simply have to write to her and ask her what she wants us to do about it.'

Although she agreed with him, it took Megan several weeks before she could bring herself to take his advice. It was more than simply refusing to take in any more girls and then closing down The Haven; there was Nelly to be considered.

When she did finally write to Sandra and explain all this, it sounded so cold and callous that she tore the letter up and tried again. In the end she asked Harvey to read what she had written and see what he thought.

He made one or two minor changes but he more or less

agreed with everything she'd said. While they waited with trepidation for Sandra's reply Harvey insisted that they should consider taking their long-delayed holiday.

'Let's go and visit your family in North Wales,' he suggested. 'It's a long time since we saw them and your mother must be longing to see you.'

Megan agreed, and they decided that the moment the girls now at The Haven left they would go.

'Don't take any more girls in for the next couple of weeks, and remind Nelly so that she doesn't either,' Harvey instructed.

TWENTY-SIX

Megan took a deep breath as they reached Beddgelert. The grass seemed to be greener, the sky more blue and the mountains were like welcoming arms waiting to greet her.

Her parents were waiting to greet them and even Harvey seemed visibly to relax as he took in the mountain air and the glorious scenery.

'I can't wait to show you all the wonderful views and places there are around here,' Megan enthused.

'I thought you'd already shown me all the local sights when we came before,' Harvey said with a laugh.

'No, I really only took you to see Gelert's grave from which Beddgelert gets its name,' she told him.

'Let's see, was that the grave of the faithful dog that belonged to Llewellyn the Great? The dog that was covered in blood and his master thought the dog had killed his little son but in fact the dog had killed a wolf that had attacked his small son. Right?'

Megan looked at him in surprise. 'Wow! You remembered it.'

'Yes, of course, and also the fact that he watered the grave with his tears according to the poem by WR Spencer. "And now a gallant tomb they raise/ With costly sculpture decked/

And marbles covered with his praise/ Poor Gelert's bones protect.'"

'Very impressive,' Megan said admiringly.

'Well, you were so determined that I should pay attention that I was hardly likely to forget and when I got back home I checked it out to make sure you had the story correct,' he told her with a grin.

'Well, I'm glad you remembered but there are other things I want to show you. There are lakes, mountain passes and wonderful views that will all stay in your mind forever. As well as climbing Moel Hebog, like we did last time, you must visit Llyn Glaslyn, the lake in a cwm on the eastern slopes of Snowdon from which our ancestors took the name for our house Yr Glaslyn.'

Megan took Harvey there the very next day. As they reached the lake the aspect opened up and was so beautiful, especially on a sunny day with the lake sparkling in the sunshine, and the distant mountain as a backdrop, that Harvey agreed it was something he would never forget.

A brisk walk up the slopes of Mynydd Sygun gave them even better views of Llyn Glaslyn.

'Llyn Glaslyn translates to English as Blue Lake,' Megan told him.

Harvey nodded; he was gazing towards the summit of Snowdon, which loomed large to the north of where they were standing. The vista of purples and greens of the heather and bracken of summertime covered the surrounding hills.

When they reached the top of the hill close to the fingerposts that guided them on their way, Megan suggested they stop and have the picnic she had brought with them.

Feeling refreshed, they set off for Cwm Bleiddiaid afterwards and very soon were descending the cwm. Here, the landscape was softer, with grassland, bracken, and rushes interspersed with rocky outcrops.

Harvey stopped to admire the view of the Glaslyn Estuary.

'What's all this?' he asked as they came across metal stanchions and the cable terminus gear.

'That's all that remains of the Cwm Bychan copper mine, where mining for ore started in the early eighteenth century,'

Megan told him. 'We are walking among reminders of Wales's industrial heritage. Nearby are reminders of Wales' more recent pastoral heritage,' she added as she pointed out a number of sheepfolds that appeared to be part of the rock-strewn landscape.

They took a path that ran alongside a small stream which was forded by large stepping-stones. It made a pleasant place to stop for another break and enjoy the view of the valley below.

When they resumed their walk Megan took track leads through ancient woodlands before joining the trail that headed north through the Aberglaslyn Pass alongside the Afon Glaslyn River.

'Keep an eye open now for we are in the woodlands for Pen-y-Groes the eighteenth-century cottage that was the birthplace of Richard Owen, the Welsh bard known as Glaslyn who lived there in the nineteenth century,' Megan told him. 'Within the pass the trail is squeezed between the river and the track of the Welsh Highland Railway that runs from Caernarvon in the north to Porthmadog in the south.'

'Are you sure we're on the right road?' Harvey asked anxiously.

'I know it's not too easy to walk along here but it is worth it to see the clear waters of the Glaslyn tumbling over the boulder strewn river bed,' Megan explained.

On leaving the gorge Megan took a route that led across the river and entered a wide flat landscape leading them to back to Beddgelert.

'Tomorrow I want to take you to the village of Capel Curig which lies to the east of the Snowdonia,' she told Harvey.

'Hold on, I'll be on my knees if you walk me so far, tomorrow,' he grumbled.

'Today is only the start; there's half a dozen other mountain walks I want to show you as well as some spectacular waterfalls, but they are at their best after rain.'

'We're only here for a week,' Harvey protested. 'What are you trying to do? Walk me off my feet!'

'I'd also like to make you walk to the top of Snowdon,

although if you're very good we could go up on the train and walk down.'

'Why not take the train up and also come back by train?' he suggested with a grin.

Megan considered the idea for a moment. 'Well, maybe,' she agreed reluctantly.

When Lewis Lloyd heard of their plans, he frowned. 'If you do all that sightseeing then there'll be no time for me to show Harvey over the slate mine. I rather think it was something he said he would really like to do,' he added, looking questioningly from Megan to Harvey.

'Yes, yes, I would very much like to find time to visit the slate mine,' Harvey confirmed.

'I do understand,' Megan said, 'but there are so many places I want to show Harvey and I know we have very little time to pack it all in.'

'Then surely the answer is to stay here longer,' her father suggested.

'We'd really like to do that, but we're waiting for a letter from Sandra about The Haven.'

Her father frowned. 'Why? Is the place in trouble?'

Megan hesitated, then she said, 'Not really, but we are wondering about the future.'

'I don't understand what you mean?' Bronwyn said in a bewildered voice. 'You are still happy there, aren't you?'

'Yes, quite happy for the moment,' Megan said reassuringly.

'What do you mean by "for the moment"?' her father asked sharply.

'Well, we want to start a family, our own family and—'

'You can't do that living where you are,' her father said sternly. 'That's no place for my grandchildren to be brought up in. The war is over, you've done your bit, it's time now for you to pack up and move away from Liverpool's dockland area. Don't you agree, Harvey?'

'Yes, I do think that,' Harvey said quietly. 'I want for us to have a home on the Wirral, somewhere either near the sea or in pleasant countryside. It may not be as picturesque as Beddgelert but I can assure you there are some lovely places even in Wallasey that overlook both the Mersey and the sea and have a wonderful view of the Welsh mountains in the distance.'

'Yes, well, that certainly sounds more civilized,' Lewis Lloyd admitted. He turned to look at Megan. 'What about you then? Do you agree with what Harvey has in mind?'

'Yes, I'm in full agreement with that plan just as soon as we can make arrangements to leave The Haven.'

'What's the problem about leaving the place? I don't suppose it's the sort of business you can sell but you can sell the house and put whatever you get for it towards the house you want on the Wirral.'

'It's not quite as simple as that, Father,' Megan told him. 'You seem to have forgotten that it's not my house but Sandra's and she's now living in America.'

'I see. Is that proving to be something of a problem?'

'We have written to her explaining the situation and asking what she wants to do about the premises,' Harvey explained. 'At the moment we are waiting for a reply and until we get that we can't do anything.'

'So this business of walking from one mountain to the next is more or less to take your mind off the future.'

'Yes, in a way I suppose it is,' Megan admitted.

'We know what we want to do and we will do it eventually but we must take Sandra into consideration and find out what she wants us to do about the ownership of The Haven,' Harvey added.

'I think that's pretty obvious,' Lewis Lloyd said in a business-like voice. 'You must sell the property. She's hardly likely to want to keep it on when she's living so far away now, is she?'

'There is one problem over that,' Harvey explained. 'You see, it's also home to Nelly who at one time was housekeeper to Sandra's family and who has helped us in running the place ever since Megan and Sandra opened it up to pregnant girls.'

'Since Nelly has been with Sandra and her family all her life we can hardly turn her out when she has nowhere to go and no family of her own,' Megan added.

'Have you considered taking her with you? When you move you will need servants of some sort,' Lewis murmured.

Megan and Harvey exchanged glances. 'We aren't really sure,' Megan said slowly. 'You see, she is in her mid-sixties and I rather think if we are going to start a family we need someone much younger than that to help around the house and to assist in bringing up our children.'

'Of course you do,' her mother said firmly. 'Make a fresh start, Megan, put all that business behind you. If you have this old woman living with you, then she'll be forever reminding you of The Haven.'

'I think I'll leave you and your mother to talk about such matters, Megan. She knows more about the domestic side of life than I do,' Lewis Lloyd stated. He turned to Harvey, 'Come on, I'll show you around the slate mine while I still have the chance.'

TWENTY-SEVEN

Harvey found his tour of the slate mine a very interesting experience. On the way there Lewis related something of the history of the slate trade.

'Slate has been used as a building and roofing material since Roman times,' he told Harvey. 'Not long ago they found a Roman fort roofed with tiles; and they also claim that the Romans used slate for flooring as well.

'The first record of slate quarrying in this neighborhood was in 1413. Records show that in the sixteenth century the local house Plas Aberllefenni was roofed in slates from this very quarry,' he said proudly.

'I suppose transport problems would have meant that the slate was usually used fairly close to the quarry,' Harvey observed.

'True, but there was some transport by sea. Not so very long ago a wooden ship carrying finished slates was discovered in the Menai Straits and they thought it dated from the sixteenth century,' Lewis Lloyd told him.

'They'd transported the slate from the mine to the nearest port,' Harvey murmured.

'That's right!' Lewis Lloyd nodded. 'In the early days the slates were carried to the ports by packhorses, and later by carts. This was sometimes done by women, the only female involvement in what was otherwise an exclusively male industry,' he emphasized. 'Did you know, in 1898, a workforce of 17,000 men produced half a million tons of slate.'

'That sounds quite incredible!'

'I quite believe it to be true,' Lewis Lloyd told him. 'The first Monday of every month was "bargain letting day" when these agreements were made between men and management. The men had to pay for their ropes and chains, for tools and for services such as sharpening and repairing. Subs or advances were paid every week, everything being settled up on the "day of the big pay". If conditions had not been good, the men could end up owing the management money. There were other grievances too, including unfairness in setting bargains and disputes over days off.'

Lewis Lloyd paused and looked apologetically at Harvey. 'You must be fed up with listening to me but once I get on the subject of the quarry, I could go on forever.'

'It's all been very interesting,' Harvey assured him. 'What I don't understand is why is the slate trade now in the doldrums?'

'Well, the First World War saw a great reduction in the number of men employed in the industry. Now this war has had a similar effect,' Lewis Lloyd said, shaking his head. 'It has already led to the closure of many smaller quarries, and competition from other roofing materials, particularly tiles.'

'Is that because the industry hasn't kept up with the times and made use of modern technology?' Harvey asked.

Lewis shook his head. 'No, the use of electric saws and other machinery has reduced the hard manual labour involved in extracting the slate, but unfortunately it produces much more slate dust than the old manual methods.'

'Which has resulted in more men being affected by silicosis,' Harvey said thoughtfully.

'That's right. Also the work is dangerous in other ways, with the blasting operations responsible for many deaths. The number of men employed in the slate industry in North Wales has dropped by more than half since the war started and now there are fewer than twenty quarries still open compared with forty before the war. Demand for slate is dropping as tiles are increasingly used for roofing, and imports from countries such as Portugal, France and Italy are increasing.'

'Surely there's been some increase in demand for slates to repair bombed buildings,' Harvey commented.

'True, but once they've been repaired, what then?'

'We've been told by the government that there'll also be a lot of new homes built in the near future. Won't slates be needed for those?'

'No, it's more likely they'll use tiles rather than slates,' Lewis said in a contemptuous voice.

He stopped the car at the quarry entrance. 'Here we are. I'll show you round and you can form your own opinion about the future of the business,' he said as they got out of the car and walked towards the entrance.

'I haven't mentioned anything to my wife about the state of things in the industry so we won't discuss it when we get home,' he said in an authoritative voice. 'There's no need for her to worry about it. I shall be retiring quite soon. If I can sell the mine I will, otherwise if the mine has to close it will mean all the workforce will have to be stood down.'

TWENTY-EIGHT

Megan and Harvey arrived back at The Haven to find a letter from Sandra waiting for them. Megan read it while Harvey mixed a drink for them both. When he came back into the sitting room she took her glass from him and handed the letter to him without a word.

Megan watched his face as he placed his glass down on the table and read the letter. Taking a sip of her own drink she waited for his comment.

'Sandra doesn't seem to be very pleased at the idea of us all packing in the work we've been doing here at The Haven, does she?' Harvey said with a sigh as he put the letter to one side and picked up his drink.

'No, but we don't want to have our family here and by the sound of it my parents aren't in favour of us doing so either.'

Harvey took a long drink and then replaced his glass on the table. 'So what are we going to do?'

Megan shook her head. 'I really don't know.'

'I suppose we could suggest to Sandra that we simply move out and leave Nelly living here to take care of the place until she comes home? Nelly wouldn't be completely on her own because Betsy Hagan and her little girl are still here and likely to remain here as they have nowhere else to go.'

'That sounds fine,' Megan agreed, 'but what about the running costs of the place? There wouldn't be any rent to pay but there would be rates as well as heating and lighting and, of course, they would need money for food as well. Where are they going to get that from until Sandra makes other arrangements?'

'Do you think if Betsy could get a job they would be able to manage on her wages?' Harvey suggested.

'What about little Mary?' Megan asked.

'Well, Nelly could look after Betsy's little girl while Betsy was out at work.'

Megan passed a hand across her forehead pushing her hair away. 'It's a possibility, I suppose, but would Sandra agree to that?'

'I don't see why not. Anyway, Sandra will probably come home for a holiday at some time and then she could take a decision about the house and about Nelly's future depending on how well they were managing.'

'Yes, I suppose it is one solution,' Megan said thoughtfully.

'There's only one way to find out,' Harvey told her as he drained his glass, 'and that's to write to Sandra and ask her.'

It was nearly three weeks before they had an answer from Sandra. She didn't for one moment think that Betsy could earn enough to keep herself, her child and Nelly and anyway it wouldn't be fair on any of them.

'So what is the answer?' Harvey asked when Megan gave him the letter to read.

'I don't know but we've got to do something and do it pretty promptly. Now that we've decided to give up using The Haven as a shelter for girls in trouble we also have to let the Charities Commission know that we have done so.'

'That means we can no longer accept donations!'

'Exactly! They've been a life saver for us but once they stop coming in then we'll have to pay all the bills ourselves.'

'Well, I suppose we can afford to do that,' Harvey assured her.

'I know, but only if we stay on here. We want to get our own home and we don't want to stay in Liverpool.'

'What did Sandra live on before this place became The Haven?' Harvey pondered. 'I've been trying to remember but I can't.'

'Well, she told me that her mother had run this place for years as a sort of guest house for people waiting for a boat.'

'Of course! I remember now. It was a sort of high-class, halfway stopping place for people who had arrived in Liverpool from other parts of Britain and were waiting for a boat and either didn't like staying in hotels or couldn't afford them. A top-of-the-range, short-stay boarding house. Well, we can't go back to doing that again, can we!'

'It's not my idea of a future career,' Megan told him with a scathing laugh. 'Anyway, at the moment there aren't all that many people sailing away on liners for exotic holidays like there were before the war.'

'No, I agree. It might be the answer though.'

'What on earth do you mean?' Megan asked, raising her eyebrows.

'I was wondering if Nelly would be able to run it, with Betsy's help, of course. If that was possible then it would leave us free to find a house somewhere on the Wirral.'

'It is an idea,' Megan agreed, 'but I'm not at all sure that Nelly would be capable of running a place like that on her own?'

'I don't see why not,' Harvey argued. 'After all, she was living here with Sandra's mother so she was probably involved in all that was happening here long before Sandra took over. In all probability she knew more about how to run the place than

Sandra did. Anyway, there's only one way to find out and that is to ask her.'

'You mean ask Nelly?'

'That's right.'

Megan shrugged. 'Will you do it or shall I?'

'We'll do it together,' Harvey said firmly. 'We'll put the idea to Nelly and then if she's in agreement we'll also explain to Betsy what's happening and tell her that she can either stay on here and help Nelly or else find herself somewhere else to live.'

'That's rather harsh, isn't it?' Megan protested.

'No, not at all. She has a good home here and she knows it. She also knows that her little girl thinks of Nelly as her grandmother and that she will be heartbroken if they move away. Betsy has had it easy here for several years now and it's time she worked for her keep.'

'I think she does do her fair share of the chores and is a great help to Nelly as it is.'

'In that case then it will be no hardship at all for her to help out a bit more. The two of them should be able to run a bed-and-breakfast place without too much effort.'

'I don't know,' Megan said dubiously.

'You'll be here to advise and guide them at the beginning and they'll soon pick up the routine,' Harvey said confidently.

When they spoke to Nelly about it she stared from one to the other in silence, her hands plucking nervously at her skirt.

'I don't know what to say,' she said at last as all three of them sat there waiting for her to make a decision.

'Are you willing to give it a try?' Harvey asked impatiently.

'Well, is it what Miss Sandra wants me to do?' Nelly asked.

'She wants us to sort out some future for this place,' Harvey told her before Megan could speak. 'At the moment she doesn't want to sell it because that would leave you without a home. She would like to be able to keep a base here in England so that whenever she wants a holiday she has somewhere to stay. Now, if you say you will stay on and run this place like you used to do when she was here, before it was turned into The Haven, then we will write and tell her that and it will put her mind at rest.'

'If it's what you think she wants and it's going to keep her happy then yes, of course I'll do it,' Nelly said with a smile.

'Good! That's settled then.'

'Mind you, I'm not as young as I was back in those days,' Nelly warned them. 'I'm wondering if it's all going to be too much for me,' she added with a deep sigh.

'I am quite sure you will manage perfectly well,' Harvey assured her. 'Remember, you will have Betsy here to help you. We haven't said anything to her as yet but if you are in agreement then that's the very next thing we'll do. We'll put it to her that she can go on living here rent free and have all her meals and those for her little girl provided without having to pay a penny piece if she is prepared to help you to run the place. Now, how does that sound to you?'

'I'm sure she will be happy about that, except . . .' Nelly paused and looked worried. 'Except that her little girl keeps growing out of her clothes and shoes. I've been buying them but I've used up most of my savings.' She stopped again, her face troubled.

'Very well, we'll even agree to pay you both a small regular wage so that Betsy has money of her own to buy things for her little girl and to buy her own clothes and so on. Now does all that help you to make your mind up, Nelly?'

'It all sounds almost too good to be true. What worries me though is how do I go about getting people to come and stay here? Miss Sandra saw to all that side of things and also to keeping the records and the books. I wonder if Betsy could be trained to do that sort of thing?' she said thoughtfully.

'I am sure she could but don't let it worry you. At the start Megan will be here to do all that sort of thing and she will always be in the background ready with advice and guidance. All we want from you is an agreement that you will give it a trial. If, after the first three months, you really feel that it is all too much for you then we'll have to think of some other way of keeping the house and providing you with somewhere to live.'

'Yes, I suppose it is worth a try,' Nelly said rather reluctantly. 'I don't suppose it will be the same as it was in the old days but I'll give it a go. Yes, you can tell Miss Sandra that I'll do my best. Let me know what she says.'

'Of course we will, Nelly, and I can tell you now she'll be delighted. It will be a load off her mind to know that her home here in England is in good hands and that you are doing the very thing she wanted most.'

It took an exchange of several letters to convince Sandra that this would be a suitable future for The Haven. Both Megan and Harvey wrote very detailed letters about how they would go about setting up the change of direction and assuring Sandra that they would retain a full interest in how it was organized and run even after they had managed to find a separate home of their own.

As soon as they received the go-ahead from Sandra, they arranged to have The Haven redecorated throughout from top to bottom before they placed a single advert in one of the local papers.

'I was wondering if we should ask Jennifer White to handle this side of the organization?' Megan mused when, after two weeks, they had received only a trickle of applicants.

'That's a splendid idea!' Harvey agreed. 'Remember her father is connected with the shipping lines so she probably knows people she can contact personally at some of the shipping companies and they can recommend people to stay here.'

A month later and business was in full swing. Betsy took to it like a duck to water. She had always helped Nelly in a general sort of way but now she was the one who was taking control most of the time while Nelly looked after her little Mary.

'It's all working a treat,' Nelly reported when the trial period came to an end and once again the three of them had a meeting to decide about the future.

'Young Betsy is a real treasure. She's taken so much of the work off my hands that I've never had such an easy time.'

'Well, when she's doing the work you are looking after her little girl. Doesn't that tire you out?' Megan asked.

'Bless you no. That child is a little angel. She's as good as gold; in fact she behaves better when she's with me than she does when she's with her mother,' Nelly added with a proud smile.

'I suppose that in next to no time Mary will be off to school,' Megan said thoughtfully when she congratulated Betsy on how well things were going.

'Nelly will miss her when that happens,' Betsy said. 'Still it will give her more time to rest and walking Mary to school and picking her up again in the afternoon will give Nelly any exercise she might need.'

They had a fairly small number of bookings over Christmas and Megan sounded both Nelly and Betsy out to see if they thought they could manage on their own.

'I would like to go home,' Megan explained. 'I haven't spent Christmas with my family since I've been married. It means we would be away for about a week.'

'We would like you to be here to celebrate with us,' Nelly told her, 'but we understand. Of course you and Dr Stott must do what you think best. I'm sure your parents will be delighted to have you both there with them.'

'We'll leave you a telephone number and if anything goes wrong or you are concerned about anything you have only to ring this number and you can talk to us. Understand?'

'We'll all have dinner together before we go and that includes little Mary, I'm sure she'd love to stay up late for one night.'

'I'm sure she would,' Nelly chuckled.

Their meal the night before Megan and Harvey left for Beddgelert was a real celebratory one. There were presents for Nelly and Betsy from Megan and Harvey and three for little Mary. As well as a cuddly doll, and a little pram, Megan had bought her a beautiful little winter outfit. The little red coat had its own fur-trimmed hood, and to go with it matching red gloves and warm little red boots that were also trimmed with fur.

Mary insisted on putting them on right away and when it was time for her to go to bed she was in tears because it meant she would have to take her new little boots off.

TWENTY-NINE

They reached Beddgelert mid-afternoon and the surrounding countryside had never looked lovelier. Even Harvey gave a long low whistle of appreciation as they stood outside Yr Glaslyn looking round. The tops of the mountains in the Snowdon range glistened white with snow; Moel Hebog towered over them like a benign guardian. There were a few sheep huddled together, nibbling at the sparse grass on the lower slopes but most of the flocks had been taken inside, sheltered from the winter weather.

Yr Glaslyn stood grey and solid as a fortress as it had done for the past two hundred years. There was a silence; it was almost like standing in the middle of a picture, Harvey thought.

'I'll never understand how you gave up all this to come to Liverpool,' he remarked wryly.

'I wanted to do my bit for the war effort,' Megan said softly. 'And if I hadn't come to Liverpool then we would probably have never met,' she added after a moment's silence.

'True!' He pulled her into his arms and kissed her. 'Life wouldn't be the same for either of us, would it, if we hadn't met?'

She didn't answer, merely moved closer to him and surrendered her lips to his demanding kiss.

'Come on, let's get indoors before we freeze to death,' Harvey murmured as he released her.

Lewis and Bronwyn Lloyd were expecting them and the heavy oak door was opened the moment they touched the bell pull. Inside, it was warm and welcoming with a fire glowing in the wide entrance hall and another huge log fire in the spacious sitting room.

'Come in, come in,' Lewis boomed. He held out a hand to shake hands with Harvey and enfolded Megan in a bear hug.

Bronwyn came rushing forward to kiss her daughter and to

hold out her hand to Harvey who raised it to his lips and kissed it.

A hot mulled wine was waiting for them and Lewis pressed a glass into their hands even before they could take their coats off.

Megan gave a sigh of sheer happiness as she looked round the room. A huge Christmas tree, covered in tinsel and baubles that she remembered from her childhood stood in one corner of the room. On it hung numerous small ornamental decorations that she remembered making herself and which her mother had carefully stored away each year when the tree was dismantled.

'Now we're eager to hear all your news but not until after we've had dinner,' her mother told them. 'Everything is ready. I'm sure you are both starving so don't wait until you've finished your drinks, bring them into the dining room with you.'

Chicken soup was followed by lamb cutlets and roast vegetables. Megan felt almost too full to eat the delicious apple tart and cream that followed.

Dinner over, they returned to the sitting room and relaxed in front of the log fire to have their coffee. Lewis and Bronwyn sat in armchairs on either side of the fire and Megan and Harvey on the settee which had been drawn up to face the fire.

'Now, what's happening about The Haven?' Lewis Lloyd demanded as soon as the coffee was served. 'Have you decided to sell the place and get away from Liverpool?' he asked hopefully.

'Not exactly,' Megan told him. 'We did tell you that the house belongs to Sandra and we had to wait and see what she wanted us to do.'

'Surely she doesn't want to keep the place if she's living in America?' he said with a frown.

'You're forgetting there is the question of finding a home for Nelly, an old retainer who has been with the Peterson family all her life,' Harvey said.

'Ah, yes, I remember you mentioned her. So what is happening?'

Megan told him about their plan to turn it back into a

short-stay boarding house which was what it had been before it became The Haven.

'I see, and does your friend Sandra agree with this?'

'She seems to quite like the idea, doesn't she?' Megan said, looking at Harvey for confirmation.

'Yes,' he agreed, 'and so does Nelly.'

'That doesn't mean you are going to stay on there though, I hope?' Bronwyn said worriedly.

'For the moment we'll go on living there, until we find a place of our own in the Wirral,' Harvey stated. 'We are training Nelly to run it, though with help from a youngish girl called Betsy and with Jennifer White to take care of the books, records and promotion of the place.'

'Jennifer White? You mean Joshua's daughter?' Lewis said in surprise.

'Yes, she's married now and living on the Wirral but both her husband and her father have their offices in Old Hall Street which is only a stone's throw from Chapel Gardens. She says it's no problem because she's often at their offices so she can always come and collect the books or send someone for them.'

'Well, that certainly sounds sensible but we both want to see you away from the Scotland Road area, you know that. It's not the sort of district we want you living in, so hurry up and find that house in the Wirral,' Bronwyn urged.

'Have you any idea exactly where you want to live?' Lewis Lloyd asked. 'I believe there are some quite good properties around West Kirby, Hoylake and Heswall.'

'There are,' Harvey agreed, 'but that's rather a long way for me to travel each day to my surgery in Liverpool.'

'Perhaps you should move to another practice,' Lewis suggested.

Harvey didn't answer; he merely gave an almost imperceptible shrug.

'So where are you looking then?' Lewis persisted.

'Wallasey. My family lived in Warren Drive until their house was bombed. There are some very nice properties in that area. I've already been in touch with one or two estate agents and I have my name on their list in case anything comes up.'

Lewis Lloyd nodded but said nothing.

'I don't think I've ever been to Wallasey,' Bronwyn Lloyd murmured.

'I like it there,' Megan said quickly. 'There's a lovely promenade from New Brighton right up to Harrison Drive and as you walk along it you can look across the Mersey and see Liverpool on the other side and it's like a different world.'

'Well, most parts of Wallasey are certainly better than around Scotland Road,' her father stated. 'New Brighton is to be avoided. It's all right if you're young and want to spend your time on the sand, or paddling, or going on rides and roundabouts in the fairground. During the day it's so packed with trippers that you can't move. But at night, I'm told, Victoria Road and the Pier are full of drunks. Most of them travel over on the ferry from Liverpool and then the police bundle them back again on the last boat. Regardless of where they come from.'

'That is certainly not the area where I am looking,' Harvey said quietly. 'As I mentioned before, I am looking for a property in the Warren Drive, Harrison Drive area. It's very quiet there and nearby is a first-class golf links.'

The subject was dropped and Mrs Lloyd began to tell them about the party they had planned for Boxing Day evening.

'We've invited all your old friends,' she told Megan. 'It will give them a chance to meet Harvey and to catch up with all your news. I'll show you the list after breakfast so that you know who'll be coming. I've also invited some cousins you haven't seen since you were quite small and they will be staying here overnight.'

The next morning it was snowing and the world outside Yr Glaslyn looked even more picturesque than it had done the night before.

'Now don't go walking anywhere and certainly don't go up any of the mountains,' Lewis Lloyd warned them. 'In fact, it might be better if you didn't venture out at all today. The snow looks inviting but it's damn slippery underfoot.'

'I promise we won't do anything risky but I thought a Christmas Day walk as far as Beddgelert would be nice,' Megan told them. 'Harvey has never really seen the village, only passed through it when we've been coming here or when we've been setting off for a walk.'

Christmas Day passed off in a lovely haze of delicious food and happy companionship. They exchanged the small presents they'd brought with them and retired early that evening in preparation for the party the next day.

The Boxing Day evening event was well attended and a great success but by the end Megan found she had talked so much that she was quite hoarse.

When they were sitting quietly afterwards having a cup of hot chocolate before they went to bed, Harvey asked, 'Are you quite sure you want to move to Merseyside?'

'Of course I do! Whatever makes you ask that?"

'You have so many friends here that I wondered.'

'No, I have flown the nest and although I love coming back here, and I always will, I think it was time for me to spread my wings. Anyway,' she added in a teasing voice, 'that's where you are proposing to live so of course I want to be there.'

They planned to go back to Liverpool on New Year's Day and so they spent New Year's Eve quietly with Lewis and Bronwyn.

As midnight struck they raised their glasses in a toast to 1947 and wished each other a Happy New Year.

'I hope 1947 really will see you two settled in a home of your own,' Lewis said ponderously. 'It's time you settled down, Megan.'

'Yes, Father,' she answered primly. 'I don't know about settling down though; I rather think I will be embarking on a new career.'

He frowned. 'What do you mean by that?'

'Yes, my dear, what do you mean?' her mother echoed.

'I'm going to have a baby,' Megan said softly.

'You're what!'

The outburst came from Harvey. He grabbed her by the shoulders and stared at her in surprise. 'When?'

'Sometime in June so you'd better hurry up and find that house,' she told him smiling.

He pulled her into his arms, kissing her hair, hugging her close, staring at Lewis and Bronwyn with surprise written all over his face. 'I had no idea,' he said lamely to Lewis and Bronwyn.

'Well, I never thought I would be celebrating the coming of a grandchild,' Lewis murmured, shaking his head in disbelief.

'A baby,' Bronwyn repeated. 'Oh dear, what a calamity!'

'Calamity? Whatever do you mean, Mother? Don't you want to be a grandmother?'

'Yes, of course I do but you and Harvey aren't properly married.'

'Yes, we are; we married in a register office over two years ago.'

'That's not really being married; that's only a civil requirement to make it legal for you to live together,' her mother told her sharply. 'What about the wedding you said you would have at the church here in Beddgelert?'

'Well, we are married; we can hardly get married again, now, can we?' Megan laughed, trying to bring an end to the discussion.

'You could have a service there. I think it's called "a blessing" or something when you renew your vows to each other.'

'The important thing now is the baby,' Lewis boomed as he refilled their glasses. 'Come on, let's drink a toast to the new baby, to the new life ahead for all of us.'

'It will be so wonderful to have children running around Yr Glaslyn again,' Bronwyn sighed. 'The house sometimes seems to be dead, it's so very quiet here when we are on our own.'

'You won't be saying that when we come next Christmas,' Megan told her. 'There'll be a lusty six-month-old baby to keep you busy.'

'You kept that a secret,' Harvey told her later that night when they were alone. 'Why didn't you tell me?'

'I wanted to be quite sure. I thought at first I was imagining it, and that it was the result of all the stress because of all the changes we were making at The Haven.'

'Well, it's wonderful news,' he told her, 'and as you say I really will have to make sure that we have a house to move into before the baby is born. The spring is always a good time for buying a house because people are on the move. They've made their plans for the New Year and so often these include a change of job or home or both. We'll find something suitable for us, don't you worry.'

'I'm not worrying; I'm leaving all that to you,' Megan told him with a broad smile.

'This will affect the future of The Haven, of course,' Harvey pointed out a few minutes later. 'You really must let Sandra know that we are definitely moving out within the next month or so, and so she must let us know if she's happy for Nelly to carry on running it. Once you have the baby you won't have much time to do anything to help her run it and anyway I don't want you to be worried by it. Our child must come first.'

'Of course it will. Anyway, Jennifer White has already taken all the planning and responsibility for the accounts and records off my hands so I haven't really all that much involvement with the place.'

'No, except listen to Nelly's prattle every day and tell her what to do for the best when she has a problem.'

'Yes, but Betsy is taking over more and more. They'll cope so don't you worry about it either.'

Before they left Yr Glaslyn, Lewis Lloyd took Harvey to one side and reminded him how urgent it was that he found a house for Megan. 'The girl needs a proper home if she is to settle down and raise a family,' he said authoritatively. 'If you have any financial problems then let me know, I'll be only too willing to help.'

'I'm sure I can manage but thank you for the offer,' Harvey said courteously.

'When are we going to see you again? Do make it soon and do take care of yourself, Megan,' her mother implored as they finally took their leave. 'I'm so happy for you but I do wish you didn't have to travel so far to come and see us. And you know my health isn't as good as it once was.'

'Yes, I know, Mother, although you have seemed much better than last time we visited. Father says you're better, at least. I promise you, as soon as we are settled into a home of our own then you can come and visit us. I want you and Father to be our very first visitors,' Megan promised as she kissed her goodbye.

THIRTY

When they arrived back at The Haven, Megan and Harvey found a letter waiting for them from Sandra. Megan read it through quickly and then handed it to Harvey.

'Sandra is coming back to England early in the new year for a holiday,' she said. 'Isn't that great! We'll be able to settle on what is to happen to this place before we move.'

'It certainly means I must speed things up,' Harvey agreed. 'I'd definitely like to have a house in mind even if we haven't time to settle all the details before they arrive so that she knows we are serious about moving.'

'It would certainly help to clinch matters,' Megan agreed.

'I'll contact the estate agent first thing on Monday morning and tell him how important it is to speed things up and find out what he can do,' Harvey promised.

He picked up the letter and scanned though it again. 'I see she says they are planning to be here by the beginning of February. That gives us barely a month!' he exclaimed, pursing his lips in a silent whistle.

'Not very long at all,' Megan agreed.

'I hope you're feeling fit enough to come house viewing if I manage to find somewhere,' he said, drawing Megan into his arms and kissing her.

'Try and stop me. I can't wait to have a home of my very own,' she breathed as she returned his kiss.

Exactly two weeks later they made their first inspection.

'It's a dormer bungalow in St Hilary's Drive, in Wallasey.'

'What's a dormer bungalow?' Megan frowned.

'Well, a fancy name for a bungalow as far as I'm concerned,'

Harvey said, shrugging his shoulders. 'I've seen a picture of this one and it has a very spacious area downstairs and upstairs the three bedrooms have sloping roofs and the windows are in the eaves.'

'Where did you say it was in Wallasey?'

'Almost next door to St Hilary's church,' he told her. 'It's a very nice part of the town and high up on a promontory so it has great views, right across to the Welsh mountains. You can probably see your beloved Moel Hebog from there,' he teased.

'Is it near the shops?'

'Yes; you have the choice of Wallasey Village or Liscard. Both of them are good shopping centres with plenty of choice.'

'It certainly sounds all right.'

'It's only a few minutes' walk from Harrison Drive which has a golf course and access to the beach,' he added as he dodged the cushion she had thrown at him.

'Oh, and there's a very good school close by,' he went on as he read from the descriptive leaflet the estate agent had sent him.

'Stop, stop, I haven't had the baby yet,' Megan laughed, 'there's no need to worry about schools.'

'No, I know that, but it does mean that it's in a very good neighborhood and it's surprising how quickly time passes. It's not long before we'll have to think about schools.'

'Let's look at the house first,' Megan said. 'I might not like it.'

'I think you will.'

'We haven't seen any others yet though,' she protested.

'No, but wait until you see this and you'll know what I mean when I say it's the home for us.'

Harvey was quite right. The dormer bungalow had three bedrooms and a family bathroom upstairs, and downstairs a huge lounge with a picture window that had stunning views and an equally pleasant dining room. There was a morning room that could be used as a study as well as a downstairs cloakroom opening off the hall and a large kitchen and a utility room at the back of the house. Outside there was a manageable garden and a double garage. Even Megan had to agree that it was perfect for them.

'What about the price?' she asked.

'Leave all that side of things to me,' Harvey told her. 'Make sure you really like the house. Have another look round, check out the kitchen and make sure that it is big enough for you.'

'The house is perfect, the views are stunning and I love every inch of it. Is the garden the right size for you?'

'You mean I'm going to be the one who has to keep it in order?' he joked.

'Of course!'

'Actually, I couldn't ask for anything better. The lawn is in good shape and a decent size and the flowerbeds and shrubs have been well-planned and will be reasonably easy to keep in order. No, as you say, it's perfect. Shall I go ahead and tell the estate agent that we'll take it?'

'As long as you think we can afford it,' she agreed cautiously.

'Don't say anything to your parents until we've actually signed the deeds and completed the deal,' Harvey told her. 'I want to do this on our own. Your father has several times said he would help us out financially if necessary but I don't want to start our new life under an obligation to anyone.'

'Whatever you say, you're the boss,' Megan told him, squeezing his arm.

When they did write and tell her parents they had found a house in Wallasey that they both liked, they received an enthusiastic response. Both her parents were very relieved to know that soon she would be moving away from the Liverpool docks area.

Megan had also mentioned in her letter that Sandra was coming over to Liverpool for a holiday in February. When her mother wrote a second letter a couple of days later to say how relieved they were that they had found a suitable house, she also added, 'If your friend Sandra is going to be here in February then what about the two of you having a blessing or renewal of your vows or whatever it's called at our church here in Beddgelert? You both said that you would like to do that one day, so this would be a good opportunity to fulfill your promise.'

'Oh dear,' Harvey groaned, 'your mother never gives up, does she? To look at her she seems to be so meek and mild, yet she's like a terrier hanging on to a rabbit.'

'So you're saying I'm a rabbit now, are you?' Megan teased.

'No.' He pulled her into his arms and kissed her. 'Not a bit like a rabbit,' he said, cupping her chin with his hand and then kissing her again so that she was unable to answer him.

'Perhaps you should write and warn Sandra what your mother expects and see how she reacts?' he told Megan as he released her.

Sandra's letter came back by return to post to say it would be lovely to do that and could Hope be their bridesmaid.

'I know she's rather young for such an onerous task but I am confident she'll do it well,' Sandra wrote.

'This is gradually growing into a full-scale do,' Harvey commented. 'What's the betting that your mother doesn't invite half the village to attend as well?'

'Of course she will and my father will probably invite the men from his slate quarry.'

'You are joking!' Harvey frowned.

'No, not at all. My father is held in high regard because he's one of the largest employers in the area and on an occasion like this his workers as well as the villagers will all want to show their loyalty.'

'Talk about killing the fatted calf!'

'I don't think they'll do that but they'll probably roast a couple of sheep over a spit and the local band will play and a choir of male voices will regale us with traditional songs.'

Harvey clamped his hands over his ears. 'I don't want to hear any more. I suppose you expect me to be there as well?'

'I most certainly do, you'll be one of the star performers,' Megan told him. She narrowed her eyes and studied him. 'You should look quite good in morning dress complete with a shiny black top hat.'

Nelly was overjoyed at the news that Sandra was coming home for a holiday.

'We've got so much to talk about,' she said and beamed. 'I never like writing letters, it's not the same as sitting down over a cup of tea and talking.'

'Sandra will probably want to sort out what you want to do about this place,' Megan said.

Nelly's face clouded. 'I know and that bothers me. Things are going along well enough at the moment but I don't mind telling you, Miss Megan, that I'm not as young as I was and I do find it all a bit of a worry. Don't get me wrong,' she added hastily, 'Betsy works hard and manages things very well and that Jennifer, well, she's got magic in her touch the things she manages to achieve, but I still feel that I am the one responsible.'

'I know what you mean, Nelly,' Megan agreed.

'The place is doing well at the moment,' Nelly went on, 'but can we keep up the pace? That's what I ask myself every night before I go to sleep.'

'If you weren't here doing this, Nelly, then where would you like to be? What would you want to be doing?'

'That's the problem, I've nowhere to go and no family to take me in. I wish sometimes that Betsy was my daughter and that we could go and live somewhere quiet and bring up little Mary and not have to worry about anything.'

'That might suit you, Nelly, but don't you think Betsy might get restless with nothing to do all day?'

'Yes, I suppose you're right. Perhaps we ought to see if we could open a little sweet shop or tea place in some quiet village somewhere. Enough to earn us money to live on but somewhere where we could shut the door at five o'clock and not have to worry about other people. Here we are working until bedtime and every weekend as well. It's too much for an old body like me.'

'Perhaps you should tell Sandra all this and see what she thinks,' Megan said evasively.

THIRTY-ONE

The furnishing of the house that they had found in St Hilary's Drive went smoothly and they both enjoyed the experience.

They had very few items to take with them from The Haven

except a few personal belongings. The furniture at The Haven belonged to Sandra so they were able to enjoy a wonderful spending spree and furnish their new home with pieces of their own choice. The newly decorated house was a blank canvas and Megan was able to indulge her taste to the full.

They spent so much of their savings that she became alarmed. 'I think we should have made do with some orange boxes for a while until we are sure we can afford all this,' she said as she proudly surveyed the tastefully furnished sitting room.

'If you would prefer that, then we can always send this stuff back,' Harvey told her.

She shot a quick look at him and was relieved to see that he was laughing at her.

They didn't move into their new home immediately. They still felt responsible for The Haven and that, together with Harvey's work at the surgery, made it more convenient to go on living in Liverpool. They stayed either at The Haven or at the flat Harvey still owned above the surgery where he worked rather than travelling all the way across to Wallasey.

At first whenever they did go over to their new house Megan kept walking from room to room feasting her eyes on their new possessions. She couldn't stop admiring the new carpets and curtains or touching the new furniture as if to make sure it was real and not a figment of her imagination.

The room she took a special delight in was the smallest bedroom, which they had fitted out as a nursery. There was a small cot, a large toy cupboard and nursery rhyme pictures on the wall.

In due course, a single bed or even bunk beds would replace the cot. She wanted it to be a playroom; a retreat. Somewhere their child could call its own when he or she grew older, the same as her own bedroom back at Yr Glaslyn had been.

Although she was barely four months pregnant, Harvey was insistent that she must register with a doctor, preferably in Wallasey, and book into either a clinic or hospital as soon as possible.

'I don't need to do that, I'm living with a doctor,' she reminded him.

'Yes, I know that, but it's not ethical for me to act as your doctor. Leave it with me and I'll check and find out where the nearest one is. I know there's a cottage hospital in Wallasey but it's some distance away from where we'll be living so I'll see if we can find a private clinic or maternity home that's nearer to our house.'

In the end it was Megan who found both a doctor as well as a private clinic.

'I've registered with a Dr Parker in Penkett Road,' she told Harvey. 'He's recommended a private clinic not very far from his surgery and he has said he will arrange for me to go there to have the baby.'

'Fine, if you are happy with him. What did you say his name was?'

'Dr Parker.'

'Really! I went to medical school with a Richard Parker, it could be the same man, I suppose.'

'I very much doubt it. This Dr Parker is in his sixties and grey haired.'

'Well, as long as you're confident about him. I'll check out the clinic some time. No hurry about that, as long as you are registered with a doctor. I suppose the next thing we ought to do is ask your parents to come and stay so that they can see our new house and satisfy themselves that we are as far away from Scotland Road as we can possibly be and that you are not living in a shack.'

'I think they already know that from the glowing reports I've sent them. No, I think our first visitors will have to be Sandra and Hank. They are coming over in February, remember, and that's not very far away.'

'They won't want to stay with us surely?' Harvey frowned. 'What's wrong with The Haven?'

'Well, it might be fully booked,' Megan pointed out.

'Then you'd better tell Nelly and Betsy not to accept any bookings for the next couple of weeks. I'm sure that Sandra would prefer to stay there. She'll want to go over the place and decide what to do with it and she might find it easier if the place is empty. It'll also give her a chance to have time with Nelly.'

'Yes, that might be a very good idea,' Megan agreed.

'There's far more room at The Haven than we have at the house anyway,' Harvey said as if to clinch the discussion. 'We can hardly put all three of them into the spare bedroom and somehow I have a feeling that you won't want any of them sleeping in the nursery, not even little Hope.'

'She's probably too big to fit into a cot,' Megan said evasively.

'You wouldn't want her in there anyway, come on, admit it,' Harvey teased, laughing down at her.

'If there are no paying guests at The Haven then we can also stay there overnight if we have a late night out in Liverpool with Sandra and Hank,' he went on.

'True. You think of everything, don't you?' Megan retorted.

'Well, we haven't seen them for a long time and it may be years before we see them again so we'll want to make the most of their company while they are here.'

January whizzed past and almost before she knew it Megan found that February had arrived and with it Sandra, Hank and Hope.

The arrival of Sandra and her family came as something of a shock because Sandra seemed to have changed so much. She'd not only altered her hairstyle but she now spoke with a definite American twang. It took Megan a little while to get used to it. Hope was now a sturdy five year old and already she also spoke with a strong American accent. To Nelly's dismay, she didn't remember any of them but it only took her a matter of hours to not only know their names but also be able to find her way from Sandra's bedroom or the sitting room to Nelly's kitchen.

Nelly, of course, spoiled her with biscuits and sweets.

At first there was rivalry between Hope and Mary for attention but in next to no time they were good friends and leading each other into mischief.

Now that Hope and little Mary had become buddies, as Hope termed it, they never seemed to be apart for more than five minutes unless they were in bed and asleep. It was wonderful that they played together so well because they entertained each other.

Sandra and Hank were delighted to hear that Megan and Harvey were thinking of staying at The Haven while they were there.

'It will be just like old times,' Hank drawled with a broad smile.

'It means we'll get a lot more time together and we won't have to dash off in case we miss the last boat to Seacombe,' Harvey explained.

'Anyway, we haven't properly moved into our house over there yet,' Megan explained. 'It's now fully furnished and so on but because I'm still helping organize things at The Haven, most of the time I stay here or with Harvey at his flat over the surgery. I thought it was sensible to keep on my room here at The Haven in case I have to stay on in an emergency.'

Megan waited for Sandra to bring up the matter of the proposed church service at Beddgelert but when three or four days went by and she still hadn't mentioned it she wondered if this was because Sandra didn't want to go ahead with it.

After a phone call from her mother to find out if Sandra and her family had arrived safely, Megan decided it was time to bring the matter out into the open.

'Sure we want to go ahead with it,' Sandra said in surprise. 'Hank and I think it's the most romantic thing we've ever heard of.'

Megan and Harvey exchanged looks; Megan's was one of relief, Harvey's of resignation.

'The fourteenth is on a Saturday and since it's St Valentine's Day, Hank and I thought that would be the perfect day to hold it. What do you think?'

'Sounds great,' Megan agreed. 'If we have it then it won't interrupt the normal church services on the Sunday.'

'Sure, then we'd really like to do that,' Sandra agreed.

'We could travel to Beddgelert on the Thursday before, and that will give us Friday to get settled in and make any last-minute changes if we don't like what has been planned by my parents. Have you brought a dress?'

'Not a full bridal ensemble,' Sandra said. 'We didn't think

that was appropriate but I have packed a cream lace dress that will serve the purpose very well.'

'That sounds terrific,' Megan enthused. 'I have a white lace one that I was going to wear with a short white fur jacket over it because it might be very cold.'

'Gosh!' Sandra frowned. 'I hadn't thought of that. My heavy topcoat will look out of place. Do you think there's anywhere in town where I can buy or hire something suitable? If I remember, there are stores in Bold Street that before the war specialized in fur coats. I wonder if they're still in business?'

'I'm sure there's somewhere here in Liverpool but why don't you borrow something of mine? I have a cream velvet cape that's really warm and I'm sure it would look good over your dress.'

'Sounds great! Thanks, Megan. That means I only have to worry about Hope. It's so easy for the men, all they have to do is wear a smart suit and stick a flower in their buttonhole.'

'Yes indeed,' Megan agreed and tried to hide her smile as she saw the look of relief on Harvey's face. 'I'm sure we can find a shop in town that has something suitable for Hope. We'll take her with us and go and look tomorrow. We'll make it a girls' day out. You haven't been shopping in Liverpool for a long time but I'm sure you still know where all the best shops are. It'll also give you an opportunity to see how rejuvenated Liverpool is.'

'Sure thing, that's a great idea!' Sandra enthused. 'We'll have lunch out and that will give us a chance to talk. I must decide about the future of this place and I'm hesitant about talking about it here in case Nelly overhears.'

THIRTY-TWO

Their outing was a great success. They found an adorable little fur jacket and a pretty blue lace dress for Hope and she looked enchanting in them.

Their talk over lunch was very productive. Megan was able

to tell Sandra what Nelly had said about being too old for the responsibility of running the place as a guest house. She also mentioned that Nelly had said how she would like to semi retire and run a little shop or some kind of a tea room with Betsy.

'I think that would be a splendid idea but I've never liked to suggest anything like that to her,' Sandra confessed.

'I think Nelly will welcome the opportunity to do so,' Megan assured her.

'She's almost seventy, you know,' Sandra said with a fond smile, 'and she's worked all her life so it's no wonder she feels worn out. Poor dear.'

'Betsy is very fond of Nelly and I'm sure that if you put it to her she would be prepared to look after Nelly in her old age in return for a small house and some sort of income.'

'Yes,' Sandra replied and nodded thoughtfully. 'I wonder if they would both like to go back to Ireland?'

A couple of days later when Sandra mentioned this idea to Nelly the older woman broke down in tears. 'My darling girl, that is the stuff of my dreams, so it is, Miss Sandra. I never thought as I would ever see the old place again. To spend my last days there would indeed be heaven itself if it was possible.'

'Everything is possible, Nelly,' Sandra told her, placing her hand on Nelly's arm. 'We'll have to see what Betsy thinks of the idea.'

Betsy was equally enthusiastic. She too missed Ireland and longed to go back there but had never thought she'd be able to.

'Right, we'll see if we can sell The Haven and then set about finding something suitable in your home village or near enough to it so that you are both back where you belong,' Sandra promised. 'It may take a little time, remember,' she warned, 'and you'll have to put up with the estate agent sending people to view this place until it is actually sold.'

Both women agreed that this made no difference and they certainly didn't mind people having to be shown over The Haven because it was a means to an end and they were quite happy about it.

Sandra asked Harvey if he thought the estate agent he had

used to find his and Megan's new home in Wallasey would be able to help them.

'More than likely,' Harvey said. 'He's a splendid chap and seems to have links with other estate agents throughout the country. He probably has connections in Ireland too, so he'll be able to help with that idea as well as selling this place.'

'Sounds good! Give us a few days to mull it all over and then perhaps you'd introduce us to him,' Sandra said. She looked pleased. 'Then all we have to worry about now is this church do at your home, Megan, so let's enjoy that to the full.'

Over the next few days they all celebrated in style. They had dinner out at the Adelphi or at The Stork. They even took the ferryboat across to New Brighton and had dinner at The Grand. They walked along the promenade and took Hope for rides on the swings and roundabouts in The Tower fairground.

Hank took Hope down to the Pier Head to watch the ships come and go while Harvey was at work and Sandra and Megan went shopping. When they came home she couldn't stop talking about the great gilded bird that was perched at the very top of the Liver building.

'I think she was more impressed by that than by the ocean-going liners,' Hank laughed.

'It's so wonderful to see all the old familiar shops again,' Sandra said as they browsed in C&A, Lewis's, Marks and Spencer, Bon Marche, Woolworths and some of the exclusive shops in Bold Street.

'If only we had a fortune to spend,' Megan sighed.

'You're not broke, are you?' Sandra questioned anxiously.

'Nearly,' Megan said with a laugh. 'I've spent a fortune buying furniture and furnishing our new house in Wallasey.'

'That's where we must go next,' Sandra declared.

'I'll give you a tour tomorrow,' Megan promised. 'There is somewhere else we have to go as well, I'm a little hesitant about mentioning it again.'

Sandra looked puzzled. 'You've lost me, babe,' she said with a pronounced American drawl that made Megan smile.

When she reminded Sandra about their promise to her mother about the church wedding at Beddgelert, and that although they had decided on what they would wear they hadn't mentioned it since then, Sandra smiled apologetically.

'I know, I know, but so much else has been going on. Never mind, a promise is a promise.'

'Only if you and Hank really do want to do it?' Megan said quickly.

'We did say we would go up on the Thursday before so the answer is yes, we ought to go ahead with it,' Sandra said thoughtfully.

'Thank you,' Megan said quietly. It was such a relief that Sandra had consented without any argument that she was almost speechless.

'There's just one thing,' Sandra said. 'We can't stay up there for too long because I want to take Nelly and Betsy over to Ireland, back to the village they came from, to see if there is any property in the area that I can buy for them after I sell The Haven. There's no doubt about it that Nelly is ready to take life easier.'

'I couldn't agree with you more and I'm so happy that you've made up your mind to sell The Haven. Will you sell it as a business?'

'Yes, if I can find anyone to buy it on that basis, or I'd be equally happy to sell it as a private home. I'll take whichever offer comes in first. Hank and I would like to complete the deal while we're here in England. We'd also like to have something in sight in Ireland for Nelly and Betsy to move into.'

'You can't possibly achieve all that before you go home,' Megan protested.

'No, but we can put it all in motion and ask the estate agent that Harvey recommended to go ahead and then leave it to you to see it through to completion. I know you'll do that for us,' she said in a positive voice.

'Of course we will,' Megan agreed, 'I think it's a perfect solution and I hope things go smoothly.'

'Perhaps we should discuss it in more detail with Betsy just in case she objects to going back there.'

'I don't think she will especially if she is going to be with Nelly,' Megan said with a smile.

'Well, since we all agree on that then let's pay a visit to this new house of yours and see if I approve of what you've bought,' Sandra stated.

Sandra did like the house in St Hilary's Drive. She was almost as enthusiastic as Megan. She thought the rooms spacious, she adored the views and thought the garden 'cute'.

'So you'll be happy to stay here with us when you next come on a visit to England?'

'Sure! I don't see us coming for a few years though and long before that I shall expect a visit from you two.'

'That's right. You must come and inspect the old homestead before we pay you another visit,' Hank insisted.

Megan smiled and agreed but explained, 'It won't be for a couple of years, I'm afraid.'

'Why ever not?' Sandra demanded.

'I'm pregnant and I wouldn't want to travel all that way with a very young baby.'

'Pregnant!' Sandra shouted the word. 'How pregnant? You don't look pregnant!'

'Well, that's probably a good thing. My mother might feel embarrassed next week if I was obviously pregnant.'

'When is it due?'

'Not until June.'

'Well, well, well,' Sandra said with an enormous grin. 'Many congratulations,'

'Thank you! Harvey is delighted.'

'June! That's only four months ahead. You should be showing by now. You're still as slim as ever.'

Yes, I'm very lucky,' Megan agreed smugly.

'You know, I did wonder why you had furnished one of the bedrooms as a nursery but I didn't say anything because I thought it might be mere speculation or hopefulness on your part. Perhaps under the circumstances we will come back to see you in about twelve months' time in order to meet the new arrival. Don't forget to keep us posted every step of the way.'

THIRTY-THREE

They arrived at Yr Glaslyn late afternoon on the Thursday. Harvey and Megan took Betsy and little Mary in their car and Hank, Sandra, Hope and Nelly travelled in the other one.

Their cars drew up within minutes of each other. Nelly was stiff from sitting for such a long time but when she managed to get out of the car, she took a deep breath, looked around and exclaimed, 'Why, it's almost like being back in Ireland. All this fresh and lovely green grass is like heaven after those grey old streets of Liverpool. I'll never understand how you could bring yourself to leave a place like this, Miss Megan.'

The children had slept for most of the journey so they were now wide awake and alert. They had never seen mountains before and they could hardly believe their eyes when they saw Moel Hebog close up.

'It won't fall down on us, will it?' Mary said in a rather frightened little voice.

'No, it won't do that,' Megan assured her. 'It has been here for hundreds of years and it was here when I was a little girl. I used to say hello to it every morning when I went to school.'

'Did it say hello back to you?' Hope asked.

'No, it never said a word but I know it liked me to speak to it. I often talked to it on my way home from school as well and I told it what I'd been doing all day.'

Hope and Mary giggled and clutched hands as they said in unison, 'Hello Mountain.'

Inside Yr Glaslyn they all gasped in amazement at how lovely the house looked. Bronwyn had taken great pains to deck the hallway out in pristine white and the glowing fire contrasted to the stark white decorations.

Bronwyn ushered them all into the sitting room and insisted on them sitting down and enjoying a cup of tea and one of their cook's famous Welsh cakes before they took their cases upstairs to unpack.

'Joshua White and Jennifer and little Joshua will be arriving late tomorrow,' Bronwyn told them. 'Mr White has an important meeting first thing tomorrow morning so he can't leave until midday. They're looking forward to seeing you all again.'

The children were very excited and also tired so Bronwyn suggested that they should be given supper early and put to bed, leaving the grown-ups time to sit down to a leisurely dinner and discuss the plans for Saturday.

'All we need now is a fine day,' Megan remarked as they sat in the sitting room after dinner enjoying a nightcap before going to bed.

'It will be fine,' her father stated. It sounded almost as if he had arranged that as well as all the ceremony that was to take place before and after they went to church.

Saturday was fine, sunlight dappled the road as they drove in a convoy of cars to the church in Beddgelert. As Megan had anticipated, there were men from the slate works there as well as most of their tenants and all the villagers.

The miners, each of them carrying a well-polished sheet of blue slate, lined up on either side of the path that led up to the church with the slates held high and the edges touching to form an archway for the two couples to walk under.

The church itself was packed and people were standing in the aisles as well as at the back.

Lewis and Bronwyn Lloyd had seats in their own family pew and the Whites were also in the pew with them as well as Nelly, Betsy and Mary.

Megan and Sandra stood side by side; Harvey and Hank on either side of them. Little Hope stood immediately in front of Sandra clutching a tiny posy of white violets.

The renewal of their vows did not take very long and then the church choir sang as they left the church.

Outside a male voice choir made up of men from the slate quarry and men from the village rendered love songs that brought tears to Megan's eyes.

They did not go back to Yr Glaslyn immediately. First there

was a lavish spread to be enjoyed in the village hall. People crowded around the two couples to offer their best wishes for their future happiness.

They also asked Megan countless questions about where she would be living and they wanted to know all about America and if Sandra liked living there.

Nelly and Betsy spent a great deal of their time making sure that Hope, Joe and Mary behaved themselves and didn't cause any trouble.

Mary and Hope had been firm friends and good companions up until now but Joe being there seemed to upset this as both little girls wanted to be the one who held his hand and played with him. In order to avoid the grown-ups, they ran around the gravestones, dodging this way and that, running circles around Nelly and skipping out her way so it was left to Betsy to run after them and bring them to order.

It was late afternoon when, tired out but happy, they took their farewell from the people in the village hall and returned to Yr Glaslyn.

Bronwyn was beaming. 'Now you really are married,' she told Megan. 'I'm so pleased for you and for the baby you're expecting, I'd never thought it would ever happen,' she hesitated, then smiled and said, 'I am so much happier about things now that you're properly married.'

Megan held her close and kissed her cheek. 'Yes, Mother, I know what you mean and you are right. Now everything is perfect.'

'You haven't told me what's happening about The Haven now that you've moved into your new house in Wallasey?' she said, looking enquiringly at Megan and then back to Sandra.

Megan left it to Sandra to tell her mother that The Haven was being put up for sale and that if all went well then in a couple of months' time she hoped that Nelly and Betsy would be moving back to Ireland, to the village they both called home.

'We're planning to buy a little shop for them, a place large enough so that they can sell souvenirs and such like, or have it as a tea shop, whatever they think best,' Sandra told her.

'That sounds as though it will be ideal,' Bronwyn Lloyd said approvingly.

'Well, Nelly is too old now for anything too strenuous but Betsy needs an interest and an income and we hope that this will provide her with both. We'll be keeping in touch with them and probably coming back for a holiday every couple of years.'

'Oh, that is good,' Bronwyn breathed. 'Megan was so worried about them. She thinks the world of Nelly. She'll keep in touch with them as well,' she said, patting Sandra's arm.

'Next year when the baby is old enough for them to take on holiday, I'm sure that's where they'll go. So that she can see Nelly and Betsy and make sure they've settled in and are happy. It means that we can go back home to America without any worries. But I'm sure we'll come over again sometime in the near future to check out for ourselves that all is well.'

'When you do, you must come and stay a few days with us again,' Bronwyn told her. 'It's been such a pleasure having you here.'

THIRTY-FOUR

Sandra was determined that before she and her family returned to America she would take a trip over to Ireland, to the village where Nelly and Betsy had come from, to see if there was any suitable property she could buy.

'I'd like for them to know they had somewhere definite to go when The Haven is sold or Nelly will be worrying in case they find themselves homeless,' she told Megan.

'I was hoping you might come along as well,' she added, 'but I suppose it's out of the question now that you are pregnant.'

'I don't see why it should be,' Megan told her. 'I'm as fit as a fiddle. Are you planning on flying or taking a boat?'

'Whichever way you prefer. I don't suppose there's a great deal of difference time-wise. We'd have to drive out to the airport or we could simply walk down to the Pier Head. There's a boat once or twice a day still sailing to Ireland, isn't there?'

'I think I'd sooner fly,' Megan said. 'I do get seasick quite easily especially if it's at all rough.'

'Right, we'll fly. Will Harvey come as well, do you think?'

'I very much doubt it because they're short-staffed at his surgery.'

'OK. Now, do you think we could leave Hope with Betsy and Mary? It would be so much easier without her. She'll be bored and tired and start grizzling. Either that or we could take Mary with us.'

'No, leave her to play with little Mary. They're such good friends they'll be no trouble at all and Nelly and Betsy will keep an eye on her.'

'Yes, I know that and I agree that it would be for the best,' Sandra said and nodded. 'By the way,' she added, 'not a word to Nelly or Betsy about where we're going. I don't want to raise their hopes.'

'Very sensible and I do understand,' Megan agreed.

Megan had never been to Ireland and she was quite looking forward to the trip. When she mentioned it to Harvey he confirmed that he couldn't spare the time to go with them. He was rather worried about her going.

'Do you think you should be undertaking a journey like that?' he questioned.

'You mean in my state of health?' she retorted with a cheeky smile. 'I thought you were a doctor not a fussy old woman. Most doctors tell you to get on with things and carry on as normal. Being pregnant isn't an illness.'

'Hmm! They do, do they? You've forgotten, though, that I'm not your ordinary doctor, I'm a father-in-waiting and I am very well aware of it. I don't want you taking any chances whatsoever. Understand!'

She reached up and pulled his head closer and kissed him. 'I won't take any chances,' she promised. 'This baby means as much to me as it does to you.'

'Hank is going over to Ireland with you?'

'Yes he is, so you can ask him to make sure I don't do anything I shouldn't. We're not taking Hope, we are leaving her to play with Mary, and Betsy will keep an eye on them. We'll only be away for one night.'

'I'd sooner you came back the same day if at all possible,' Harvey told her. 'If you do stay overnight, then you must look after yourself and take care.'

'I will, I promise.'

'If you do stay overnight then where are you staying, do you know?'

'A hotel in Dublin. We're flying to Dublin and then Hank is hiring a car there. Do stop worrying, I'll be quite all right,' she added impatiently as she reached up and kissed him.

Harvey held her close, kissing her on the brow and then on the lips. The look of concern on his face touched her and for a moment she considered pulling out of the trip. But she knew Sandra was counting on her company, so in the end she returned Harvey's kiss and said no more.

The flight from Liverpool to Dublin was uneventful. Megan had been afraid that she might feel queasy. But she felt fine, even when they descended through the mist at Dublin airport.

By the time they were through customs and had picked up their hire car the sun was shining.

The village they went to that had been home for Nelly and Betsy was not far from the airport but so very small and rural that it was like being transported back into the Middle Ages.

'They'll never make a living here from a teashop,' Sandra said worriedly. 'It's far too remote and I shouldn't imagine they'd get more than half a dozen visitors a year.'

'We've plenty of time to look around, honey,' Hank told her. 'There must be other villages nearby that offer better prospects.'

'It's very picturesque here and similar to Wales,' Megan observed. 'I can understand why Nelly was so entranced by Beddgelert.'

'If only it was Beddgelert. Now that does attract tourists and the like,' Sandra sighed.

'We'll keep looking, honey,' Hank drawled, 'and if we haven't found anywhere by lunchtime then we'll go into the nearest hostelry and ask them to tell us the name of some of the larger villages or small towns.'

Sandra and Megan both agreed with this. Sandra spread out the map she had brought with her and suggested that they should start by circling Dublin and see if they could find something within a ten miles' radius.

'Why is it so important that you find a village so near to Dublin?' Megan asked.

'It'll make it so much easier for us when we want to visit. We can probably fly direct from America to Dublin,' Sandra pointed out when she saw that Hank was also looking rather puzzled. 'Also, it's an area that Nelly and Betsy know. Isn't that right, Hank?'

'Whatever you say, honey,' he agreed. 'So where do you want me to drive to next?'

Sandra reeled off a list of names. 'Hold it, hold it, you sound as though you're talking in another language and I can't take it all in,' Hank laughed. 'What with Bally this and Bally that and Kill something and Kin something, it's going round and round in my mind and confusing me.'

They drove round for over an hour, Sandra giving instructions of when to turn left or right. Now and again she would tell him to stop in one or another of the little towns they were passing through so that they could weigh up the possibilities of Nelly and Betsy making a living there.

Eventually they decided on three places; one was a large village, with a long main street with four shops but no tearooms, a church, two pubs and a school, and the other two were large enough to be called small towns.

'Any of these would be ideal,' Sandra confirmed as she made a note of their names in the notebook she'd brought with her. 'They're not too far from Dublin and near enough to the village where Nelly and Betsy came from for them to feel at home because they are bound to know the places all around here.'

'Do you think they would be able to make a living here though?' Megan asked dubiously.

'Yes, I do. They're quiet spots, I know, but they do get an awful lot of walkers and hikers around here and they all of them need somewhere to stop and have a cup of tea, a snack and a rest. I think any of them would be ideal.'

'So do we try and find out if there are any suitable properties available?'

Hank looked at his watch. 'You were thinking about getting home tonight, weren't you, Megan?' he chuckled.

'Well, yes, I would like to do so if it's at all possible. Harvey seemed to be worried at the thought of me staying in Dublin overnight.'

'There was no need for him to be concerned. I was planning to book us into the best hotel in town,' Hank assured her, 'but if you would prefer to fly back tonight then that's all right with me. How about you, honey?' he asked, looking at Sandra.

'I'd like to get back as well, to make sure that Hope is all right. I know Betsy will take great care of her but we've never been apart before and I'm sure she'll miss her daddy if he isn't there to read her a bedtime story.'

'Then in that case it has to be home. Do you want to have dinner here first?'

Sandra and Megan exchanged glances before saying in unison, 'No, we'd sooner get home.'

'Right then, that's what we'll do. Does this mean we'll have to come back again to see if we can find any vacant properties?'

'No,' Sandra told him, 'we have the names of the village and towns, so we'll leave it to the estate agent Harvey recommended. Let him do the searching. If he can't find a suitable property in any of the places we've given him, then I'm sure he can find something nearby.'

'He won't manage that before we go back to America,' Hank warned. 'We're booked to fly home in three days' time.'

'I know but it doesn't matter. I'm making arrangements for Megan and Harvey to sign any papers necessary to say that we will buy the property so we don't have to worry about that.'

'Are you making the same arrangements over selling your house, honey?' Hank asked.

'I am. I'm quite settled in my own mind that everything is taken care of, so don't worry.'

THIRTY-FIVE

Megan's baby was born in early June; a healthy boy weighing eight pounds. He had a mass of dark hair and a very lusty cry.

Harvey was delighted with his new son and immediately telephoned the Lloyds to give them the good news and to tell them that they had decided to call the baby David.

As he spoke to Lewis, he could hear Bronwyn's gasp of relief in the background as the news was relayed to her.

'When are you planning to come to Wallasey to see Megan and the baby?' Harvey asked.

There was a brief pause and then Lewis Lloyd said, 'Not at the moment. We'll let you know the date later.'

Later that day Harvey received a phone call from Lewis Lloyd to say that his wife was suffering from a summer cold and he thought it unwise for them to travel at the moment.

'You wouldn't want her around the baby either. I know at that tender age they are supposed to be immune from such germs but you never know. Perhaps we'll be able to come in a couple of weeks' time. Or, better still, perhaps you would like to come here for a break as soon as Megan feels fit enough to travel.'

Harvey didn't argue but accepted the invitation on the understanding that he would have to find out if he would be able to get the time off.

'We're a doctor down so we are rather busy at the surgery at the moment,' he explained.

'Not too busy to take care of our daughter and our new grandson, I hope,' Lewis boomed.

'No, they'll be taken great care of, I can assure you on that score,' Harvey promised.

Later that day when he went to the Maternity Home in Penkett Road the receptionist stopped him from going to

Megan's room. 'Dr Parker is with Mrs Stott at the moment,' she explained.

'Nothing wrong is there?' he asked.

'Oh no, a routine visit. Dr Parker always visits new patients twice a day for the first week.'

'I see. Well, I'll go up just the same,' he stated and headed for the stairs before she could stop him.

Dr Parker greeted him cordially but his attention was focused on Megan. He was grey-haired and probably in his sixties exactly as Megan had described him. When he stood up and turned round Harvey immediately recognized him.

'Are you Richard Parker's father?' he asked.

'Yes, that's right. Do you know my son?'

'We were at medical school together. I went into practice in Liverpool afterwards and I understand Richard was planning to join the forces so we haven't seen each other since.'

'Indeed!' Dr Parker held out a hand to Harvey. 'Richard has recently been demobbed and will be back home next week. He's been abroad for most of the war, first one place and then another. Fortunately he's come through unscathed. I'll tell him I've met you.'

'Yes, please do. I'd like to meet up with him again sometime.'

'I'll tell him. Your wife is doing very well indeed, Dr Stott. No worries at all and you have a very healthy baby.'

'So he is your friend's father,' Megan said in surprise after Dr Parker had left. 'What a coincidence!'

'Yes, isn't it. It would be great to see Richard again. You'll like him. Enough about that, how are you feeling?'

They spent the rest of Harvey's visit planning the future and when she would be likely to come home. He told her about his phone call to her parents and their relief at knowing she and the baby were both doing well.

'I've said we'll go and visit them as soon as you feel strong enough to do so. There's no immediate hurry as your mother has a summer cold and is scared that either you or the baby might catch it.'

'Oh, I'm sorry to hear that. Never mind, by the time we visit them we may be able to tell them that the sale of The

Haven has been finalized and that the place in Ireland is ready and waiting for Nelly and Betsy.'

'Make sure you don't go rushing around doing too much in trying to help them to pack up when they are ready to leave Liverpool,' Harley warned.

'Don't worry, I won't. For one thing Nelly wouldn't let me. She fusses even more than my mother if that's at all possible.'

Ten days later when Harvey arrived to take Megan and the baby home he had a pleasant surprise. Richard Parker was at the clinic talking to Megan and waiting to meet him.

Richard was tall and broad with short dark hair and grey eyes. He had a wide smile and Megan thought he must have looked very handsome in his uniform. Now he was wearing grey slacks, a plain blue open-necked shirt and a Harris tweed sports jacket.

Both men seemed delighted to see each other again and before they left the clinic Richard had promised to meet Harvey in a few days' time for a night out together.

'I'm not inviting you, Megan, because I'm sure you'll be far too busy,' he said with a grin as he looked down at the baby she was holding in her arms.

'I wouldn't want to come,' she told him. 'You two will be far too busy reminiscing to even notice if I am there or not.'

'You're quite right, we have three or four years to catch up on and to anyone else our chat will be extremely boring. We'll make it up to you at a later date,' he promised.

Harvey was so keyed up and excited when he came home a few nights' later after his evening out with Richard Parker that for one moment Megan thought he was drunk.

'Drunk with excitement,' he told her. 'You'd never guess, not in a hundred years, I couldn't believe it myself.'

'Will you calm down and tell me what I wouldn't believe! What is it that you're so excited about?'

'A partnership,' he told her, his eyes glowing. 'A partnership with Richard Parker and it will be right here in Wallasey. Can you believe it?'

Megan stared at him wide-eyed. 'What about your present job?'

'I'll tell them that I'm leaving. There won't be any problem.'

'You'll probably have to give a month's notice!'

He shrugged as if that was of no real importance.

'I'll be working right here, right on the spot. Isn't that wonderful! No more daily commuting on the bus and ferry boat to Liverpool, no more late nights being called out in an emergency. I'll be working right here on my own doorstep.'

He pulled her into his arms and waltzed round the room. 'A partner! Not just a salaried member of a team, but as a full-blown partner.'

'Hold on, hold on,' she said, pulling away and staring at him. 'Can you afford to buy into a partnership? We spent all our savings furnishing our new home.'

'That's the beauty of it all; I don't have to pay anything. Well, just a nominal sum of a few hundred pounds, but that's nothing. Old man Parker wants to retire but the practice has grown so much that he feels it's too much for Richard to handle on his own so he suggested to him that he should find himself a partner. Richard immediately thought of me and of course old man Parker has met me and he agreed without any argument.'

'When does all this start?' Megan asked in bewilderment.

'In August! From the first of August Richard's father will retire and Richard and I will be partners. Richard's father will stay on call for six months in case we should need his advice over any of the patients. After that, providing everything is going smoothly, we'll be on our own. Fantastic news, isn't it? Wait until I tell your parents.'

Lewis and Bronwyn were extremely pleased when they heard the news.

'Anything that means you are severing all connections with that rough area of Liverpool is wonderful news,' Bronwyn breathed with relief.

'Yes, it's a very good move and we're delighted for you, Harvey, and very relieved to know that both our daughter and our grandson are well away from the Scotland Road area. I know you've never had any trouble while you've been working and living there, but it is a very rough area so you are much better away from there.'

Harvey nodded but said nothing.

'And once you're settled into your new job and can take some time off,' said Lewis Lloyd, 'it mightn't be such a bad idea to take that proposed trip to America. I'm sure that little David is old enough now to travel and Megan fully recovered from his birth, so why not enjoy a holiday?'

He handed Harvey a cheque. 'This is a belated wedding present from us; it should cover the expense of your holiday.'

THIRTY-SIX

David was ten months old when Megan and Harvey took him to America to visit Sandra and her family. Megan had been wanting to make the trip to Bellingham which was on the borders of America and Canada for months but first of all they'd had to pay a visit to Yr Glaslyn at Christmas and Harvey had said it was no good going to the USA before that because November was the wettest month of the year in Bellingham.

'How on earth do you know that?' Megan asked in surprise.

'I've been doing my homework. I thought you'd want to see the place when it was at its best so I made enquiries from a travel agency.'

'I see!'

'The rainy period extends from October until April. November is typically the wettest month, with numerous frontal rainstorms arriving. At the height of the really cold spell, local ponds and smaller lakes freeze solidly enough to allow skating.'

'Doesn't the place ever have any decent sunshine?'

'Oh yes, but it does has the lowest average sunshine amount of any city in America.'

'Well, at least I suppose that means we won't get sunstroke,' Megan muttered.

'Despite this, Bellingham also has mild, pleasant summers and drought is rare. Although I must warn you, wells have been known to run dry in August and September.'

'OK, I get the picture,' Megan laughed. 'You don't want us to go there in winter or in the height of summer. In that case what about March or April?'

Harvey frowned. 'That might be all right. I'll have to check with Richard Parker to find out what his plans are, and if it's OK with him then I'll see if we can book in a locum to take my place while I'm away.'

'Since you seem to be giving me a lesson about Bellingham, what other things have you found out about the place?' Megan asked.

'Well, it's in the state of Washington and is about 90 miles north of Seattle, 21 miles south of the Canadian border and about 52 miles south of Vancouver.'

'Really!'

'"It started out as four separate towns on the shores of Bellingham Bay with Mount Baker as its backdrop, Bellingham is the last major city before the Washington coastline meets the Canadian border. The city of Bellingham, which serves as the county seat of Whatcom County, is at the centre of a uniquely picturesque area offering a rich variety of recreational, cultural, educational and economic activities",' Harvey read from the pamphlet he was holding.

'Is that something the travel agent gave you?' Megan asked.

'It is. Do you want to hear any more?'

'Go on.'

'"There is an arts and cultural district downtown and a very active waterfront hosts a range of marine activities. Housing ranges from regal Victorians, waterfront bungalows and country farmhouses to downtown condominiums.

'"Prior to white settlement, the Lummi, Nooksack and other Coast Salish tribes thrived there. An English captain called George Vancouver first explored the area in 1792 and named Bellingham Bay for Sir William Bellingham, Vancouver's British Navy provisioner. The city of Bellingham was incorporated in 1904 after the populations of four adjacent bayside towns voted to consolidate. Bellingham's historic character is remarkably well-preserved, with a large number of historic buildings downtown, in the Fairhaven District, and in adjacent neighborhoods".'

Megan clapped her hands over her ears. 'I feel I know the place already so don't tell me any more,' she begged, 'or I won't want to go there.'

'I told you I'd done my homework,' Harvey said with a broad grin.

'Yes, a bit too well. You're not thinking of getting a job as a guide when you get there, are you, Dr Stott?'

'No, but I found it interesting to read about it; I like to know where I'm going,' Harvey said. 'By the way, the flight takes about thirteen hours so be sure to pack whatever you think David is going to need en route into our hand luggage. They may have baby food on board but it might be wise to take whatever he is most used to.'

Megan tucked her hair back behind her ears as though exhausted. 'Right, I'll remember that. This trip is beginning to look more arduous the nearer it comes. I think there's a time difference as well, London is about five hours ahead of Washington and I suppose that could upset David's routine.'

'Not if we don't tell him,' Harvey said with a smile. 'He'll probably sleep most of the way.'

As it turned out their journey went very smoothly indeed and Hank, Sandra and Hope were waiting at Bellingham airport when their plane touched down. Almost before they knew what was happening they were at the Jacksons' spacious waterfront bungalow.

'This is quite stunning,' Megan said admiringly. 'I had no idea what sort of place Bellingham was or what your home was like. We never got round to talking about it when you came over on holiday.'

'We will have great pleasure in showing you round,' Hank assured her. 'Everything will be new for you.'

'I'm not too sure about that,' Megan said wryly. 'Harvey has discovered so many facts and details about Bellingham that he could work here as a guide.'

'Reading about it in a book or pamphlet is OK but it can't be compared with seeing things with your own eyes and forming your own opinion of them,' Hank told her.

'If that baby of yours is awake at last then can we have a

proper look at him?' Sandra asked. 'He's nine months old now, isn't he?'

'Almost ten months,' Megan corrected as she sat David up on her knee.

'Is he walking yet?'

'Almost. He's at the stage where he can pull himself up by holding on to seats and then move a few steps before he falls over again.'

'Hope has been looking forward to seeing him, haven't you, sweetie?' Sandra asked, turning to where her six-year-old daughter was staring at David, wide-eyed.

'I sure have,' Hope said and nodded. 'I've got some of my toys for him to play with. Can I get them, Mom?' she asked, looking at her mother.

'Of course you can! I'll put a rug down on the floor and then if Megan puts David down on to it you can look after him while we have a drink.'

In the days that followed Megan found that Hope was a great help. She was always ready to play with David and she was so gentle and protective that Megan had no qualms at all about leaving them together, not that she was ever more than a few yards away. The slightest cry from David, she was at his side to see what was the matter.

Sandra was keen to know what the news was about her house in Chapel Gardens and about Nelly and Betsy.

'They're both still there but the house has been sold and when we get back we'll be helping them move over to Ireland,' Harvey told them.

'Yes, we had a letter from the estate agent saying he had found a place for them and I was wondering if it was suitable.'

'Harvey has already been over to see it,' Megan assured her. 'It was a flying visit in every sense of the word, but he was there long enough to make sure that the property was sound and that it was suitable for them to run a tea shop or gift shop.'

'It's quite a big area downstairs and there's a very well-fitted kitchen which is ideal for their purpose. Upstairs there are four bedrooms so they can have a sitting room and a bedroom each if they want to do it that way. With Mary now starting school they might like to have separate living rooms so that she can do her homework in peace when the time comes. Or they can give her one of the large bedrooms and she can have it as a playroom and bedroom now, and then turn it into a combined bedroom and study later on. It will still leave them with one spare bedroom. There's a very nice bathroom and separate toilet up there as well.'

'What about the garden?'

'Well, that's on the small side and is at the back of the building. I suggested to them that if they simply had a big lawn out there Betsy would be able to cut it and they would have somewhere to sit in the summer.'

'I bet Nelly wanted to grow her own vegetables out there,' Sandra laughed.

'She did until I pointed out to her that would call for a lot of hard work and she agreed she wasn't up to it and if they were running a shop then Betsy would be busy enough.'

'What about the financial details? The estate agent hasn't finalized those yet, has he?'

'Yes, he has and I've brought all the papers with me. The figures are extremely satisfactory. The price he managed to get for your house, Sandra, not only covers the cost of the house in Ireland but leaves a very healthy balance.'

'Enough to pay for their moving expenses?' Sandra asked hopefully.

'Oh yes, more than enough. There'll be enough left for you to fit out the shop and provide them with some stock as well as set up a standing order to pay the rates and other charges for the next five years if you want to do that.'

'That's wonderful,' Sandra breathed. 'Thank you both for helping us in arranging all this. Now, we'll put it all to the back of our minds and enjoy your visit. Ten days isn't long and there's so much we want to show you and so many places we want to take you to see.'

Their visit to Bellingham passed all too swiftly. Before they knew it they were on the plane back to London.

'It's been a great holiday and I think Bellingham is lovely but it will be good to get back home again,' Megan admitted as the plane taxied down the runway.

'Yes, I agree,' Harvey said, taking her hand and squeezing it. 'Back to our own home and a chance to relax.'

'We still have to help Nelly and Betsy pack up and move to Ireland,' she warned him.

'That won't take up too much of our time,' he assured her.

'We also have to visit my parents at Yr Glaslyn. They'll be eager to know all about our American holiday.'

'We won't be able to do that for a while,' Harvey told her. 'I have to get back to work. Richard Parker is waiting to take his holiday, remember.'

'Yes, I know, but we don't want to leave it too long because you don't like me travelling when I'm pregnant,' Megan cautioned.

'Pregnant!' Harvey sat bolt upright in his seat and swiveled round and stared at her. 'Are you sure?'

'Quite sure, do you think I should see a doctor?' she asked with a roguish smile.

'That's absolutely wonderful,' Harvey told her, kissing her. 'When?'

'According to my calculations it should be early September.'

'September,' he murmured, shaking his head from side to side as if he couldn't believe the news. Then he put his arm around her shoulders, drawing her closer and kissed her again, a deep passionate kiss that told her how delighted he was and how much he loved her.

One Summer

David Baldacci is a worldwide bestselling novelist. With his books published in over 45 different languages and in more than 80 countries, and with over 110 million copies in print, he is one of the world's favourite storytellers. His family foundation, the Wish You Well Foundation, a non-profit organization, works to eliminate illiteracy across America. Still a resident of his native Virginia, he invites you to visit him at www.DavidBaldacci.com, and his foundation at www.WishYouWellFoundation.org, and to look into its programme to spread books across America at www.FeedingBodyandMind.com.

ALSO BY DAVID BALDACCI

DAVID BALDACCI

One Summer

PAN BOOKS

First published 2011 by Grand Central Publishing, USA

First published in Great Britain 2011 by Macmillan

This edition published 2012 by Pan Books
an imprint of Pan Macmillan, a division of Macmillan Publishers Limited
Pan Macmillan, 20 New Wharf Road, London N1 9RR
Basingstoke and Oxford
Associated companies throughout the world
www.panmacmillan.com

ISBN 978-0-330-53370-6

1 3 5 7 9 8 6 4 2

A CIP catalogue record for this book is available from
the British Library.

Typeset by CPI Typesetting
Printed and bound by CPI Group (UK) Ltd, Croydon, CR0 4YY

Visit www.panmacmillan.com to read more about all our books
and to buy them. You will also find features, author interviews and
news of any author events, and you can sign up for e-newsletters
so that you're always first to hear about our new releases.

To Spencer, my little girl all grown up.
And I couldn't be prouder of the
person you've become.

One Summer

1

Jack Armstrong sat up in the secondhand hospital bed that had been wedged into a corner of the den in his home in Cleveland. A father at nineteen, he and his wife, Lizzie, had conceived their second child when he'd been home on leave from the army. Jack had been in the military for five years when the war in the Middle East started. He'd survived his first tour in Afghanistan and earned a Purple Heart for taking one in the arm. After that he'd weathered several tours of duty in Iraq, one of which included the destruction of his Humvee while he was still inside. That injury had won him his second Purple. And he had a Bronze Star on top of that for rescuing three ambushed grunts from his unit and nearly getting killed in the process. After all that, here he was, dying fast in his cheaply paneled den in Ohio's Rust Belt.

His goal was simple: just hang on until Christmas. He sucked greedily on the oxygen coming from the line in his nose. The converter that stayed in the corner of the small room was on maximum production, and Jack knew that one day soon it would be turned off because he'd be dead.

Before Thanksgiving he was certain he could last another month. Now Jack was not sure he could make another day.

But he would.

I have to.

In high school the six-foot-two, good-looking Jack had varsity lettered in three sports, quarterbacked the football team, and had his pick of the ladies. But from the first time he'd seen Elizabeth "Lizzie" O'Toole, it was all over for him in the falling-in-love department. His heart had been won perhaps even before he quite realized it. His mouth curled into a smile at the memory of seeing her for the first time. Her family had come from South Carolina. Jack had often wondered why the O'Tooles had moved to Cleveland, where there was no ocean, a lot less sun, a lot more snow and ice, and not a palm tree in sight. Later, he'd learned it was because of a job change for Lizzie's father.

She'd come into class that first day, tall, with long auburn hair and vibrant green eyes, her face already mature and lovely. They had started going together in high school and had never been separated since, except long enough for Jack to fight in two wars.

"Jack; Jack honey?"

Lizzie was crouched down in front of him. In her hand was a syringe. She was still beautiful, though her looks had taken on a fragile edge. There were dark circles under her eyes and recently stamped worry lines on her face. The glow had gone from her skin, and her body was harder, less supple than it had been. Jack was the one dying, but in a way she was too.

"It's time for your pain meds."

He nodded, and she shot the drugs directly into an

access line cut right below his collarbone. That way the medicine flowed directly into his bloodstream and started working faster. Fast was good when the pain felt like every nerve in his body was being incinerated.

After she finished, Lizzie sat and hugged him. The doctors had a long name for what was wrong with him, one that Jack still could not pronounce or even spell. It was rare, they had said; one in a million. When he'd asked about his odds of survival, the docs had looked at each other before one finally answered.

"There's really nothing we can do. I'm sorry."

"Do the things you've always wanted to do," another had advised him, "but never had the chance."

"I have three kids and a mortgage," Jack had shot back, still reeling from this sudden death sentence. "I don't have the luxury of filling out some end-of-life bucket list."

"How long?" he'd finally asked, though part of him didn't really want to know.

"You're young and strong," said one. "And the disease is in its early stages."

Jack had survived the Taliban and Al-Qaeda. He could maybe hold on and see his oldest child graduate from college. "So how long?" he'd asked again.

The doctor said, "Six months. Maybe eight if you're lucky."

Jack did not feel very lucky.

He vividly remembered the morning he started feeling not quite right. It was an ache in his forearm and a stab of pain in his right leg. He was a building contractor by trade, so aches and pains were to be expected. But things soon carried to a new level. His limbs would grow tired from three hours of physical labor as opposed to ten. The stabs of pain became more frequent, and his balance began to deteriorate. His back finally couldn't make it up the ladder with the stacks of shingles. Then it hurt to carry his youngest son around after ten minutes. Then the fire in his nerves started, and his legs felt like an old man's. And one morning he woke up and his lungs were like balloons filled with water. Everything had accelerated after that, as though his body had simply given way to whatever was invading it.

His youngest child, Jack Jr., whom everyone called Jackie, toddled in and climbed on his dad's lap, resting his head against his father's sunken chest. Jackie's hair was long and inky black, curled up at the ends. His eyes were the color of toast; his thick eyebrows nearly met in the middle, like a burly woolen thread. Jackie had been their little surprise. Their other kids were much older.

Jack slowly slid his arm around his two-year-old son. Chubby fingers gripped his forearm, and warm breath touched his skin. It felt like the pierce of needles, but Jack simply gritted his teeth and didn't move his arm because there wouldn't be many more of these embraces. He slowly turned his head and looked out the window, where the snow was steadily falling. South Carolina and palm trees had nothing on Cleveland when it came to the holidays. It was truly beautiful.

He took his wife's hand.

"Christmas," Jack said in a wheezy voice. "I'll be there."

"Promise?" said Lizzie, her voice beginning to crack.

"Promise."

2

Jack awoke, looked around, and didn't know where he was. He could feel nothing, wasn't even sure if he was still breathing.

Am I dead? Was this it?

"Pop-pop," said Jackie as he slid next to his father on the bed. Jack turned and saw the chubby cheeks and light brown eyes.

Jack stroked his son's hair. Good, thick strands, like he used to have before the disease had stolen that too. Curious, Jackie tried to pull out the oxygen line from his father's nose, but he redirected his son's hand and cupped it with his own.

Lizzie walked in with his meds and shot them into the access line. An IV drip took care of Jack's nutrition and hydration needs. Solid foods were beyond him now.

"I just dropped the kids off at school," she told him.

"Mikki?" said Jack.

Lizzie made a face. Their daughter, Michelle, would be turning sixteen next summer, and her rebellious streak had been going strong since she'd become a teenager. She was into playing her guitar and working on her music, wearing junky clothes, sneaking out at night, and ignoring the books. "At least she showed up for the math test. I suppose actually passing it would've been asking too much. On the bright side, she received an A in music theory."

Jackie got down and ran into the other room, probably for a toy. Jack watched him go with an unwieldy mixture of pride and sorrow. He would never see his son as a man. He would never even see him start kindergarten. That cut against the natural order of things. But it was what it was.

Jack had experienced an exceptionally long phase of denial after being told he had little time left. That was partially because he had always been a survivor. A rocky childhood and two wars had not done him in, so he had initially felt confident that despite the doctors' fatal verdict, his disease was beatable. As time went by, however, and his body continued to fail, it had become clear that this battle was not winnable. It had reached a point where making the most of his time left was more important to him than trying to beat his head against an impenetrable wall. Most significantly, he wanted his kids' memories of his final days to be as positive as possible. Jack had concluded that if he had to die prematurely, that was about as good a way to do so as there was. It beat being depressed and making everyone else around him miserable, waiting for him to die.

Before he'd gotten sick, Jack had talked to his daughter many times about making good life choices, about the importance of school, but nothing seemed to make a difference to the young woman. There was a clear disconnect now between father and daughter. When she'd been a little girl, Mikki had unconditionally loved her dad, wanted to be around him all the time. Now he rarely saw her. To her, it seemed to Jack, he might as well have been already dead.

"Mikki seems lost around me," he said slowly.

Lizzie sat next to him, held his hand. "She's scared and confused, honey. Some of it has to do with her age. Most of it has to do with . . ."

"Me." Jack couldn't look at her when he made this admission.

"She and I have talked about it. Well, I talked and she didn't say much. She's a smart kid, but she really doesn't understand why this is happening, Jack. And her defense mechanism is to just detach herself from it. It's not the healthiest way to cope with things, though."

"I can understand," said Jack.

She looked at him. "Because of your dad?"

He nodded and rubbed her hand with his fingers, his eyes moistening as he remembered his father's painful death. He took several long pulls on the oxygen. "If I could change things, I would, Lizzie."

She rested her body next to his, wrapped her arms around his shoulders, and kissed him. When she spoke, her voice was husky and seemed right on the edge of failing. "Jack, this is hard on everyone. But it's hardest on you. You have been so brave; no one could have handled—" She couldn't continue. Lizzie laid her head next to his and wept softly. Jack held her with what little strength he had left.

"I love you, Lizzie. No matter what happens, nothing will ever change that."

He'd been sleeping in the hospital bed because he

couldn't make it up the stairs to their bedroom even with assistance. He'd fought against that the hardest because as his life dwindled away he had desperately wanted to feel Lizzie's warm body against his. It was another piece of his life taken from him, like he was being dismantled, brick by brick.

And I am, brick by brick.

After a few minutes, she composed herself and wiped her eyes. "Cory is playing the Grinch in the class play at the school on Christmas Eve, remember?"

Jack nodded. "I remember."

"I'll film it for you."

Cory was the middle child, twelve years old and the ham in the family.

Jack smiled and said, "Grinch!"

Lizzie smiled back, then said, "I've got a conference call in an hour, and then I'll be in the kitchen working after I give Jackie his breakfast."

She'd become a telecommuter when Jack had gotten ill. When she had to go out, a neighbor would come over or Lizzie's parents would stop by to help.

After Lizzie left, Jack sat up, slowly reached under the pillow, and pulled out the calendar and pen. He looked at the dates in December, all of which had been crossed out up to December twentieth. Over three decades of life, marriage, fatherhood, defending his country, and working hard, it had come down to him marking off the few days left. He looked out the window and to the street beyond. The snow had stopped, but he'd heard on the news that another wintry blast was expected, with more ice than snow.

There was a knock at the door, and a few moments later

Sammy Duvall appeared. He was in his early sixties, with longish salt-and-pepper hair and a trim beard. Sammy was as tall as Jack, but leaner, though his arms and shoulders bulged with muscles from all the manual labor he'd done. He was far stronger than most men half his age and tougher than anyone Jack had ever met. He'd spent twenty years in the military and fought in Vietnam and done some things after that around the world that he never talked about. A first-rate, self-taught carpenter and all-around handyman, Sammy was the reason Jack had joined the service. After Jack left the army, he and Sammy had started the contracting business. Lacking a family of his own, Sammy had adopted the Armstrongs.

The military vets shared a glance, and then Sammy looked over all the equipment helping to keep his friend alive. He shook his head slightly and his mouth twitched. This was as close as stoic Sammy ever came to showing emotion.

"How's work?" Jack asked, and then he took a long pull of oxygen.

"No worries. Stuff's getting done and the money's coming in."

Jack knew that Sammy had been completing all the jobs pretty much on his own and then bringing all the payments to Lizzie. "At least half of that money is yours, Sammy. You're doing all the work."

"I got my Uncle Sam pension, and it's more than I need. That changes, I'll let you know."

Sammy lived in a converted one-car garage with his enormous Bernese mountain dog, Sam Jr. His needs were simple, his wants apparently nonexistent.

Sammy combed Jack's hair and even gave him a shave. Then the friends talked for a while. At least Sammy said a few words and Jack listened. The rest of the time they sat in silence. Jack didn't mind; just being with Sammy made him feel better.

After Sammy left, Jack lifted the pen and crossed out December twenty-first. That was being optimistic, Jack knew, since the day had really just begun. He put the calendar and pen away.

And then it happened.

He couldn't breathe. He sat up, convulsing, but that just made it worse. He could feel his heart racing, his lungs squeezing, his face first growing red and then pale as the oxygen left his body and nothing replenished it.

December twenty-first, he thought, *my last day.*

"Pop-pop?"

Jack looked up to see his son holding the end of the oxygen line that attached to the converter. He held it up higher, as though he were giving it back to his dad.

"Jackie!"

A horrified Lizzie appeared in the doorway, snatched the line from her son's hand, and rushed to reattach the oxygen line to the converter. A few moments later, the oxygen started to flow into the line and Jack fell back on the bed, breathing hard, trying to fill his lungs.

Lizzie raced past her youngest son and was by Jack's side in an instant. "Oh my God, Jack, oh my God." Her whole body was trembling.

He held up his hand to show he was okay.

Lizzie whirled around and snapped, "That was bad, Jackie, bad."

Jackie's face crumbled, and he started to bawl.

She snatched up Jackie and carried him out. The little boy was struggling to free himself, staring at Jack over her shoulder, reaching his arms out to his father. His son's look was pleading.

"Pop-pop," wailed Jackie.

The tears trickled down Jack's face as his son's cries faded away. But then Jack heard Lizzie sobbing and pictured her crying her heart out and wondering what the hell she'd done to deserve all this.

Sometimes, Jack thought, living was far harder than dying.

3

Jack awoke from a nap late the next day in time to see his daughter opening the front door, guitar case in hand. He motioned to her to come see him. She closed the door and dutifully trudged to his room.

Mikki had auburn hair like her mother's. However, she had dyed it several different colors, and Jack had no idea what it would be called now. She was shooting up in height, her legs long and slender and her hips and bosom filling out. Though she acted like she was totally grown up now, her face was caught in that time thread that was firmly past the little-girl stage but not yet a woman. She would be a junior in high school next year. Where had the time gone?

"Yeah, Dad?" she said, not looking at him.

He thought about what to say. In truth, they didn't have much to talk about. Even when he'd been healthy, their lives lately had taken separate paths. *That was my fault,* he thought. *Not hers.*

"Your A." He took a long breath, tried to smile.

She smirked. "Right. Music theory. My only one. I'm sure Mom told you that too. Right?"

"Still an A."

"Thanks for mentioning it." She looked at the floor, an awkward expression on her features. "Look, Dad, I gotta go. People are waiting. We're rehearsing."

She was in a band, Jack knew, though he couldn't recall the name of it just now.

"Okay, be careful."

She turned to leave, and then hesitated. Her fingers fiddled with the guitar case handle. She glanced back but still didn't meet his gaze. "Just so you know, when you were asleep I duct taped your oxygen line onto the converter so it can't be pulled off again. Jackie didn't know what he was doing. Mom didn't have to give him such a hard time."

Jack gathered more oxygen and said, "Thanks."

A part of him wanted her to look at him, and another part of him didn't. He didn't want to see pity in her eyes. Her big, strong father reduced to this. He wondered whom she would marry. Where would they live? Would it be far from Cleveland?

Will she visit my grave?

"Mikki?"

"Dad, I really got to go. I'm already late."

"I hope you have a great . . . day, sweetie."

He thought he saw her lips quiver for a moment, but then she turned and left. A few moments later, the front door closed behind her. He peered out the window. She hopped across the snow and climbed into a car that one of her guy friends was driving. Jack had never felt more disconnected from life.

After dinner that night, Cory, in full costume, performed his Grinch role for his father. Cory was a chunky twelve-year-old, though his long feet and lanky limbs promised height later. His hair was a mop of brown cowlicks, the same look Jack had had at that age. Lizzie's parents had come over for dinner and to watch the show and had brought Lizzie's grandmother. Cecilia was a stylish lady in her eighties who used a walker and had her own portable oxygen tank. She'd grown up and lived most of her life in South Carolina. She'd come to live with her daughter in Cleveland after her husband died and her health started failing. Her laugh was infectious and her speech was mellifluous, like water trickling over smooth rocks.

Cecilia joked that Jack and she should start their own oxygen business since they had so much of the stuff. She was dying too, only not quite as fast as Jack. This probably would also be her last Christmas, but she had lived a good long life and had apparently made peace with her fate. She was uniformly upbeat, talking about her life in the South, the tea parties and the debutante balls, sneaking smokes and drinking hooch behind the local Baptist church at night. Yet every once in a while Jack would catch her staring at him, and he could sense the sadness the old lady held in her heart for his plight.

After Cory finished his performance, Cecilia leaned down and whispered into Jack's ear. "It's Christmas. The time of miracles." This was not the first time she'd said this. Yet for some reason Jack's spirits sparked for a moment.

But then the doctor's pronouncement sobered this feeling.

Six months, eight if you're lucky.

Science, it seemed, always trumped hope.

At eleven o'clock he heard the front door open, and Mikki slipped in. Jack thought he saw her glance his way, but she didn't come into the den. When Jack was healthy they had kept a strict watch over her comings and goings. And for months after he'd become ill, Lizzie had kept up that vigil. Now she barely had time to shower or snatch a meal, and Mikki had taken advantage of this lack of oversight to do as she pleased.

When everyone was asleep, Jack reached under his pillow and took out his pen. This time he wasn't crossing off dates on a calendar. He took out the piece of paper and carefully unfolded it. He spread it out on a book he kept next to the bed. Pen poised over the paper, he began to write. It took him a long time, at least an hour to write less than one page. His handwriting was poor because he was so weak, but his thoughts were clear. Eventually there would be seven of these letters. One for each day of the last week of his life, the date neatly printed at the top of the page—or as neatly as Jack's trembling hand could manage. Each letter began with "Dear Lizzie," and ended with "Love, Jack." In the body of the letter he did his best to convey to his wife all that he felt for her. That though he would no longer be alive, he would always be there for her.

These letters, he'd come to realize, were the most important thing he would ever do in his life. And he labored to make sure every word was the right one. Finished, he put the letter in an envelope, marked it with a number, and slipped it in the nightstand next to his bed.

He would write the seventh and last letter on Christmas Eve, after everyone had gone to bed.

Jack turned his head and looked out the window. Even in the darkness he could see the snow coming down hard.

He now knew how a condemned man felt though he had committed no crime. The time left to him was precious. But there was only so much he could do with it.

4

Jack marked off December twenty-fourth on his calendar. He had one letter left to write. It would go into the drawer with the number seven written on the envelope. After he was gone, Lizzie would read them, and Jack hoped they would provide some comfort to her. Actually, writing them had provided some comfort for Jack. It made him focus on what was really important in life.

Jack's mother-in-law, Bonnie, had stayed with him while the rest of the family went to see Cory in the school play. Lizzie had put her foot down and made Mikki go as well. Bonnie had made a cup of tea and had settled herself down with a book, while Jack was perched in a chair by the window waiting for the van to pull up with Lizzie and the others.

Sammy came by, stomping snow off his boots and tugging off his knit cap to let his long, shaggy hair fall out. He sat next to Jack and handed him a gift. When Jack opened it he looked up in surprise.

It was five passes to Disney World, good for the upcoming year.

Sammy gripped Jack by the shoulder. "I expect you and the family to get there."

Jack glanced over to see Bonnie shaking her head in mild reproach. Bonnie O'Toole was not a woman who believed in miracles. Yet Jack knew the man well enough to realize that Sammy fully believed he would use those tickets. He patted Sammy on the arm, smiled, and nodded.

After Sammy left, Jack glanced at the tickets. He appreciated his friend's confidence, but Jack was the only one who knew how close he was to the end. He had fought as hard as he could. He didn't want to die and leave his family, but he couldn't live like this either. His mind focused totally on the last letter he would ever compose. He knew when his pen had finished writing the words and the paper was safely in the envelope, he could go peacefully. It was a small yet obviously important benchmark. But he would wait until Christmas was over, when presents were opened and a new day had dawned. It was some comfort to know that he had a little control left over his fate, even if it was simply the specific timing of his passing.

He saw the headlights of the oncoming van flick across the window. Bonnie went to open the front door, and Jack watched anxiously from the window as the kids piled out of the vehicle. Lizzie's dad led them up the driveway, carrying Jackie because it was so slick out. The snow was still coming down, although the latest weather report had said that with the temperatures staying where they were, it was more ice than snow at this point, making driving treacherous.

His gaze held on Lizzie as she closed up the van, and

then turned, not toward the house, but away from it. Jack hadn't noticed the person approach her because his attention had been on his wife. The man came into focus; it was Bill Miller. They'd all gone to school together. Bill had blocked on the line for Jack the quarterback. He'd attended Jack and Lizzie's wedding. Bill was single, in the plumbing business, and doing well.

Jack pressed his face to the glass when he saw Bill draw close to his wife. Lizzie slipped her purse over her shoulder and swiped the hair out of her eyes. They were so close to one another, Jack couldn't find even a sliver of darkness between them. His breath was fogging the glass, he was so near it. He watched Bill lean in toward Lizzie. He saw his wife rise up on tiptoe. And then Bill staggered back as Lizzie slapped him across the face. Though he was weak, Jack reared up in his chair as though he wanted to go and defend his wife's honor. Yet there was no need. Bill Miller stumbled off into the darkness as Lizzie turned away and marched toward the house.

A minute later he heard Lizzie come in, knocking snow off her boots.

Lizzie strode into the den, first pulling off her scarf and then rubbing her hands together because of the cold. Her face was flushed, and she didn't look at him like she normally did. "Time for the presents; then Mom and Dad are going to take off. They'll be back tomorrow, okay, sweetie? It'll be a great day."

"How's your hand?"

She glanced at him. "What?"

He pointed to the window. "I think Bill's lucky he's still conscious."

"He was also drunk, or I don't think he would've tried that. Idiot."

Jack started to say something, but then stopped and looked away. Lizzie quickly picked up on this and sat next to him.

"Jack, you don't think that Bill and I—"

He gripped her hand. "Of course not. Don't be crazy." He kissed her cheek.

"So what then? Something's bothering you."

"You're young, and you have three kids."

"That I get." She attempted a smile that flickered out when she saw the earnest look on his face.

"You need somebody in your life."

"I don't want to talk about this." She tried to rise, but he held her back.

"Lizzie, look at me. Look at me."

She turned to face him, her eyes glimmering with tears.

"You will find someone else."

"No."

"You will."

"I've got a full life. I've got no room for—"

"Yes, you do."

"Do we have to talk about this now? It's Christmas Eve."

"I can't be picky about timing, Lizzie," he said, a little out of breath.

Her face flushed. "I didn't mean that. I . . . you look better tonight. Maybe . . . the doctors—"

"No, Lizzie. No," he said firmly. "That can't happen. We're past that stage, honey." He sucked on his air, his gaze resolutely on her.

She put a hand to her eyes. "If I think about things like that, then it means, I don't want to . . . You might . . ."

He held her. "Things will work out all right. Just take it slow. And be happy." He made her look at him, and he brushed the tears from her eyes. He took a long pull on his oxygen and managed a grin. "And for God's sake, don't pick Bill."

She laughed. And then it turned into a sob as he held her.

When they pulled away a few moments later, Lizzie wiped her nose with a tissue and said, "I was actually thinking about next summer. And I wanted to talk to you about it."

Jack's heart was buoyed by the fact that she still sought out his opinion. "What about it?"

"You'll probably think it's silly."

"Tell me."

"I was thinking I would take the kids to the Palace."

"The Palace? You haven't been back there since—"

"I know. I know. I just think it's time. It's in bad shape from what I heard. I know it needs a lot of work. But just for one summer it should be fine."

"I know how hard that was for you."

She reached in her pocket and pulled out a photo. She showed it to Jack. "Haven't looked at that in years. Do you remember me showing it to you?"

It was a photo of the O'Tooles when the kids were all little.

"That's Tillie next to you. Your twin sister."

"Mom said she never could tell us apart."

Jack had to sit back against his pillow and drew several long breaths on his line while Lizzie patiently waited.

Finally he said, "She was five when she died?"

"Almost six. Meningitis. Nothing the doctors could do." She glanced briefly at Jack, and then looked away. Her unspoken thought could have been, *Just like you.*

"I remember my parents telling me that Tillie had gone to Heaven." She smiled at the same time a couple of tears slid down her cheeks. "There's an old lighthouse on the property down there. It was so beautiful."

"I remember you telling me about it. Your grandmother . . . still owns the Palace, right?"

"Yes. I was going to ask her if it would be all right if we went down there this summer."

"The O'Tooles exchanging the sunny ocean for cold Cleveland?" He coughed several times, and Lizzie went to adjust his air level. When she did so he started breathing easier.

She said, "Well, I think leaving the Palace was because of me."

"What do you mean?"

"I never really told you about this before, and maybe I'd forgotten it myself. But I've been thinking about Tillie lately." She faltered.

"Lizzie, please tell me."

She turned to face him. "When my parents told me my sister had gone to Heaven, I . . . I wanted to find her. I didn't really understand that she was dead. I knew that Heaven was in the sky. So I started looking for, well, looking for Heaven to find Tillie."

"You were just a little kid."

"I would go up in the lighthouse. Back then it still worked. And I'd look for Heaven, for Tillie really, with the help of the light." She paused and let out a little sob. "Never found either one."

Jack held her. "It's okay, Lizzie; it's okay," he said softly.

She wiped her eyes on his shirt and said, "It became a sort of obsession, I guess. I don't know why. But every day that went by and I couldn't find her, it just hurt so bad. And when I got older, my parents told me that Tillie was dead. Well, it didn't help much." She paused. "I can't believe I never told you all this before. But I guess I was a little ashamed."

His wife's distress was taking a toll on Jack. He breathed deeply for several seconds before saying, "You lost your twin. You were just a little kid."

"By the time we moved to Ohio, I knew I would never find her by looking at the sky. I knew she was gone. And the lighthouse wasn't working anymore anyway. But I think my parents, my mom especially, wanted to get me away from the place. She didn't think it was good for me. But it was just . . . silly."

"It was what you were feeling, Lizzie." He touched his chest. "Here."

"I know. So I thought I'd go back there. See the place. Let the kids experience how I grew up." She looked at him.

"Great idea," Jack gasped.

She rubbed his shoulder. "You might enjoy it too. You could really fix the place up. Even make the lighthouse work again." It was so evident she desperately wanted to believe this could actually happen.

He attempted a smile. "Yeah."

The looks on both their faces were clear despite the hopeful words.

Jack would never see the Palace.

5

Later that night his father-in-law helped Jack into a wheelchair and rolled him into the living room, where their little tree stood. It was silver tinsel with blue and red ornaments. Jack usually got a real tree for Christmas, but not this year of course.

The kids had hot chocolate and some snacks. Mikki even played a few carols on her guitar, though she looked totally embarrassed doing so. Cory told his dad about the play, and Lizzie bustled around making sure everyone had everything they needed. Then she played the DVD for Jack so he could see the performance for himself. Finally his in-laws prepared to leave. The ice was getting worse and they wanted to get home, they said. Lizzie's father helped Jack into bed.

At the front door Lizzie gave them each a hug. Jack heard Bonnie tell her daughter to just hang in there. It was always darkest before the dawn.

"The kids are the most important thing," said her dad. "Afterward, we'll be right here for you."

Next, Jack heard Lizzie say, "I was thinking about talking to Cee," referring to her grandmother Cecilia.

"About what?" Bonnie said quickly, in a wary tone.

"Next summer I was thinking of taking the kids to the Palace, maybe for the entire summer break. I wanted to make sure Cee would be okay with that."

There were a few moments of silence; then Bonnie said, "The Palace! Lizzie, you know—"

"Mom, don't."

"This is not something you need, certainly not right now. It's too painful."

"That was a long time ago," Lizzie said quietly. "It's different now. It's okay. I'm okay. I have been for a long time, actually, if you'd ever taken the time to notice."

"It's never long enough," her mother shot back.

"Let's not discuss it tonight. Not tonight," said Lizzie.

After her parents left, Jack listened as his wife's footsteps came his way. Lizzie appeared in the doorway. "That was a nice Christmas Eve."

He nodded his head dumbly, his gaze never leaving her face. The tick of the clock next to his bed pounded fiercely in Jack's head.

"Don't let her talk you out of going to the Palace, Lizzie. Stick to your guns."

"My mother can be a little . . ."

"I know. But promise me you'll go?"

She nodded, smiled. "Okay, I promise. Do you need anything else?" she asked.

Jack looked at the clock and motioned to the access line below his collarbone, where his pain meds were administered.

"Oh my gosh. Your meds. Okay." She started to the

small cabinet in the corner where she kept his medications. But then Lizzie stopped, looking slightly panicked.

"I forgot to pick up your prescription today. The play and . . . I forgot to get them." She checked her watch. "They're still open. I'll go get them now."

"Don't go. I'm okay without the meds."

"It'll just take a few minutes. I'll be back in no time. And then it'll just be you and me. I want to talk to you some more about next summer."

"Lizzie, you don't have to—"

But she was already gone.

The front door slammed. The van started up and raced down the street.

Later Jack woke, confused. He turned slowly to find Mikki dozing in the chair next to his bed. She must have come downstairs while he was asleep. He looked out the window. There were streams of light whizzing past his house. For a moment he had the absurd notion that Santa Claus had just arrived. Then he tried to sit up because he heard it. Sounds on the roof.

Reindeer? What the hell was going on?

The sounds came again. Only now he realized they weren't on the roof. Someone was pounding on the front door.

"Mom? Dad?" It was Cory. His voice grew closer. His head poked in the den. He was dressed in boxer shorts and a T-shirt and looked nervous. "There's someone at the door."

By now Mikki had woken. She stretched and saw Cory standing there.

"Someone's at the front door," her brother said again.

Mikki looked at her dad. He was staring out at the swirl of lights. It was like a spaceship was landing on their front lawn. *In Cleveland?* Jack thought he was hallucinating. Yet when he looked at Mikki, it was clear that she saw the lights too. Jack raised a hand and pointed at the front door. He nodded to his daughter.

Looking scared, she hurried to the door and opened it. The man was big, dressed in a uniform, and had a gun on his belt. He looked cold, tired, and uncomfortable. Mostly uncomfortable.

"Is your dad home?" he asked Mikki. She backed away and pointed toward the den. The police officer stamped off his boots and stepped in. The squeak of his gun belt sounded like a scream in miniature. He walked where Mikki was pointing, saw Jack in the bed with the lines hooked to him, and muttered something under his breath. He looked at Mikki and Cory. "Can he understand? I mean, is he real sick?"

Mikki said, "He's sick, but he can understand."

The cop drew next to the bed. Jack lifted himself up on his elbows. He was gasping. In his anxiety, his withered lungs were demanding so much air the converter couldn't keep up.

The officer swallowed hard. "Mr. Armstrong?" He paused as Jack stared up at him. "I'm afraid there's been an accident involving your wife."

6

Jack sat strapped into a wheelchair staring up at his wife's coffin. Mikki and Cory sat next to him. Jackie had been deemed too young to attend his mother's funeral; he was being taken care of by a neighbor. The priest came down and gave Jack and his children holy communion. Jack nearly choked on the host but finally managed to swallow it. Ironically, it was the first solid food he'd had in months.

At my wife's funeral.

The weather was cold, the sky puffy with clouds. The wind cleaved the thickest coats. The roads were still iced and treacherous. They'd been driven to the cemetery in the funeral home sedan designated for family members. His father-in-law, Fred, rode up front, next to the driver, while he and the kids were squeezed in the back with Bonnie. She had barely uttered a word since learning her youngest daughter had been instantly killed when her van ran a red light and was broadsided by an oncoming snowplow.

The graveside service was mercifully brief; the priest

seemed to understand that if he didn't hustle things along, some of the older people might not survive the event.

Jack looked over at Mikki. She'd pinned her hair back and put on a black dress that hung below her knees; she sat staring vacantly at the coffin. Cory had not looked at the casket even once. As a final act, Jack was wheeled up to the coffin. He put his hand on top of it, mumbled a few words, and sat back, feeling totally disoriented. He had played this scene out in his head a hundred times. Only he was in the box and it was Lizzie out here saying good-bye. Nothing about this was right. He felt like he was staring at the world upside down.

"I'll be with you soon, Lizzie," he said in a halting voice. The words seemed hollow, forced, but he could think of nothing else to say.

As he started to collapse, a strong hand gripped him.

"It's okay, Jack. We'll get you back to the car now." He looked up into the face of Sammy Duvall.

Sammy proceeded to maneuver him to the sedan in record time. Before closing the door, he put a reassuring hand on Jack's shoulder. "I'll always be there for you, buddy."

They were driven home, the absence of Lizzie in their midst a festering wound that had no possible healing ointment. Jackie was brought home, and people stopped by with plates of food. An impromptu wake was held; devastated folks chatted in low tones. More than once Jack caught people gazing at him, no doubt thinking, *My God, what now?*

Jack was thinking the same thing. *What now?*

Two hours later the house was empty except for Jack, the kids, and his in-laws. The children instantly disappeared. Minutes later Jack could hear guitar strumming coming from Mikki's bedroom, the tunes melancholy and abbreviated. Cory and Jackie shared a bedroom, but no sound was coming from them. Jack could imagine Cory quietly sobbing, while a confused Jackie attempted to comfort him.

Bonnie and Fred O'Toole looked as disoriented as Jack felt. They had signed on to help their healthy daughter transition with her kids to being a widow and then getting on with her life. Without the buffer that Lizzie had been, Jack could focus now on the fact that his relationship with his in-laws had been largely superficial.

Fred was a big man with a waistline large enough to portend a host of health problems down the road. He tended to defer to his wife in all things other than sports and selling cars, which was the line of work that had brought him to Cleveland. He was a man who would prefer to look at the floor rather than in your eye, unless he was trying to sell you the latest Ford F-150. Then he could be animated enough, at least until you signed on the dotted line and the financing cleared.

Bonnie was shorter than her daughter. The mother of four grown children, she was now well into her sixties, and her figure had lost its shape. Her waist and hips had turned into a solid wall of flesh. Her hair was white, cut short and rather brutally, and her eyeglasses filled most of her square face. Fred kept sighing, rubbing his big hands over his pressed suit pants, as though attempting to rub some dirt off his fingers. Bonnie, who had kept on her black outfit, was sitting very still on the couch, her gaze aimed at a corner of the ceiling but apparently not actually registering on it.

Fred sighed again, and this seemed to rouse Bonnie.

"Well," she said. "Well," she said again. Fred eyed her, as did Jack.

She looked over and gave Jack a quick glance that was undecipherable.

Then came more silence.

Finally, a few minutes later Fred helped Jack get into bed, and then he and Bonnie went up to Jack and Lizzie's room. They would be staying here full-time until other arrangements were made.

Jack lay in the dark staring at the ceiling. The days after Lizzie had died had been far worse than when he'd received his own death sentence. His life ending he'd accepted. Hers he had not. Could not. Mikki and Cory had barely spoken since the police officer had come with the awful news. Jackie had wandered the house looking for his mother and crying when he couldn't find her.

Jack slid open the drawer of the nightstand and took out the six letters. He obviously had not written one on Christmas Eve. In these pages he had poured out his heart to the person he cherished above all others. As he looked down at the pages, wasted pages now, his spirits sank even lower.

Jack rarely cried. He'd seen fellow soldiers die horribly in the Middle East, watched his father perish from lung cancer, and attended the funeral of his wife. He had shed a few tears at each of these events, but not for long and always in a controlled way. Now, staring at the ceiling, thinking a thousand anguished thoughts, he did weep quietly as it finally struck him that Lizzie was really gone.

7

The next morning Bonnie took charge. She came to see Jack with Fred in tow. "This won't be easy, Jack," she cautioned, "but we really don't have much time." She squared her shoulders and seemed to attempt a sympathetic look. "The children of course come first. I've talked to Becky and also to Frances several times."

Frances and Becky were Lizzie's older sisters, who lived on the West Coast. The only brother, Fred Jr., was on active military duty, stationed in Korea. He had not been able to make it to the funeral.

"Becky can take Jack Jr., and Frances has agreed to take Cory. That just leaves Michelle." Bonnie had never called her Mikki.

"*Just* Michelle?" said Jack.

Bonnie looked momentarily taken aback. When she spoke, her tone was less authoritative and more conciliatory. "This is hard on all of us. You know Fred and I had planned to move to Tempe next year after things were more settled with Lizzie and the kids. We were going this year, but then you got sick. And we stayed on, because that's what families do in those situations. We tried to do our best, for all of you."

"We couldn't have gotten on without you."

This remark seemed to please her, and she smiled and gripped his hand. "Thank you. That means a lot."

She continued, "We'll take Michelle with us. And because Jack Jr. will be in Portland with Becky and Cory in LA with Frances, they will all at least be on or near the West Coast. I'm sure they'll see each other fairly often. It's really the only workable solution that I can see."

"When?" Jack asked.

"The Christmas break is almost over, and we think we can get all the kids transitioned in the next month. We decided it was no good waiting until the fall, for a number of reasons. It'll be better all around for them."

"For you too," said Jack. As soon as he said it, he wished he hadn't.

Bonnie's conciliatory look faded. "Yes, us too. Jack, we're taking care of all the children. They'll all have homes with people they love and who love them. You can't have an issue with that."

Jack touched his chest. "And me?"

"Yes, well . . . I was getting to that, of course." She stood but didn't look at him. Instead, she stared at a spot right over his head. "Hospice. I'll arrange all the details." Now she looked at him, and Jack had to admit, she didn't look happy about this. "If we could take care of you, Jack, in the time that you have left, we would. But we're not young anymore, and taking in Michelle and all . . ."

Fred added, "And Lizzie dying."

Jack and Bonnie stared at him for an instant. Each seemed surprised the man was still there, much less that he had spoken. Bonnie said, "Yes, and Lizzie not . . . well, yes."

Jack drew a long breath and mustered his strength. He said, "*My* kids, *my* decision."

Fred looked at Jack and then over at his wife. Bonnie, though, had eyes only for Jack.

She said, "You can't care for the kids. You can't even take care of yourself. Lizzie did everything. And now she's gone." Her eyes glittered; her tone was harsh once more.

"Still my decision," he said defiantly. He had no idea where he was going with this, but the words had tumbled from his mouth.

"Who else will take three kids? If we do nothing, the matter is out of our hands and they'll go into foster care. They'll probably never see each other again. Is that what you want?" She sat down next to him, her face inches from his. "Is that really what you want?"

He sucked in some more air, his resolve weakening along with his energy. "Why can't I stay here?" he said. Another long inhalation. "Until the kids leave?"

"Hospice is much cheaper. I'm sorry if that sounds callous, but money is tight. Tough decisions have to be made."

"So I die alone?"

Bonnie looked at her husband. Clearly, from his expression, Fred sided with Jack on this point.

Fred said, "Doesn't seem right, Bonnie. Taking the family away like that. After all that's happened."

Jack shot his father-in-law an appreciative look.

Bonnie fidgeted. "I've been thinking about that, actually." She sighed. "Jack, I'm not trying to be heartless. I care about you. I don't want to do any of this." She paused. "But they just lost their mother." Bonnie paused but didn't continue.

It slowly dawned on Jack, what she was getting at.

"And to see me die too?"

Bonnie spread her hands. "But you're right. You are their father. So I'll leave it up to you. You tell me what to do, Jack, and I'll do it. We can keep the kids here until . . . until you pass. They can attend your funeral, and then we can make the move. They can be with you until the end." She looked at Fred, but he apparently had nothing to add.

Jack was surprised, then, when Fred said, "Anything you want, Jack, we'll take care of it. Okay?"

Jack was silent for so long that Bonnie finally rose, clutched her sweater more tightly around her shoulders and said, "Fine, we can have an in-home nursing service come. Lizzie had some life insurance. We can use those funds to—"

"Take the kids."

Fred and Bonnie looked at him. Jack said again, "Take the kids."

"Are you sure?" asked Bonnie. She seemed to be sincere, but Jack knew this way would take a lot of the pressure off her.

He struggled to say, "As soon as you can." *It won't be long,* Jack thought. *Not now. Not with Lizzie gone.*

When she turned to leave, Bonnie froze. Mikki and Cory were standing there.

Bonnie said nervously, "I thought you were upstairs."

"You don't think this concerns us?" Mikki said bluntly.

"I think the adults need to make the decisions for what's best for the children."

"I'm not a child!" Mikki snapped.

Bonnie said, "Michelle, this is hard on all of us. We're just trying to do the best we can under the circumstances." She paused and added, "You lost your mother and I lost my daughter." Bonnie's voice cracked as she added, "None of this is easy, honey."

Mikki gazed over at her father. He could feel the anger emanating from his oldest child. "You're all losers!" yelled Mikki. She turned and rushed from the house, slamming the door behind her.

Bonnie shook her head and rubbed at her eyes before looking back at Jack. "This is a big sacrifice, for all of us." She left the room, with Fred obediently trailing her. Cory just stood there staring at his dad.

"Cor," he began. But his son turned and ran back upstairs.

A minute went by as Jack lay there, feeling like a turtle toppled on its back.

"Jack?"

When he looked over, Bonnie was standing a few feet from his bed holding something in her hand.

"The police dropped this off yesterday." She held it up. It was the bag with Jack's prescription meds. "They found it in the van. It was very unfortunate that Lizzie had to go back out that night. If she hadn't, she'd obviously be alive today."

"I told her not to go."

"But she did. For you," she replied.

The tears started to slide down her cheeks as she hurried from the room.

8

The room was small but clean. That wasn't the problem. Jack had slept for months inside a shack with ten other infantrymen in the middle of a desert, where it was either too frigid or too hot. What Jack didn't like here were the sounds. Folks during their last days of life did not make pleasant noises. Coughs, gagging, painful cries—but mostly it was the moaning. It never ceased. Then there was the squeak of the gurney wheels as the body of someone who had passed was taken away, the room freshened up for the next terminal case on the waiting list.

Most patients here were elderly. Yet Jack wasn't the youngest person. There was a boy with final-stage leukemia two doors down. When Jack was being wheeled to his room he'd seen the little body in the bed: hairless head, vacant eyes, tubes all over him, barely breathing, just waiting for it to be over. His family would come every day; his mother was often here all the time. They would put on happy expressions when they were with him and then start bawling as soon as they left his side. Jack had witnessed this as they passed his doorway. All hunched over, weeping into their cupped hands. They were just waiting, too, for it to be over. And at the same time dreading when it would be.

Jack reached under his pillow and pulled out the calendar. January eleventh. He crossed it off. He had been here for five days. The average length of stay here, he'd heard, was three weeks. Without Lizzie, it would be three weeks too long.

He again reached under his pillow and pulled out the six now-crumpled envelopes with his letters to Lizzie inside them. He'd had Sammy bring them here from the house before it was listed for sale. He held them in his hands. The paper was splotched with his tears because he pulled them out and wept over them several times a day. What else did he have to do with his time? These letters now constituted a weight around his heart for a simple reason: Lizzie would never read them, never know what he was feeling in his last days of life. At the same time, it was the only thing allowing him to die with peace, with a measure of dignity. He put the letters away and just lay there, listening for the squeaks of the final gurney ride for another patient. They came with alarming regularity. Soon, he knew it would be his body on that stretcher.

He turned his head when the kids came in, followed by Fred. He was surprised to see Cecilia stroll in with her walker and portable oxygen tank resting in a burgundy sling. It was hard for her to go outside in the cold weather, yet she had done so for Jack. Jackie immediately climbed up on his dad's lap, while Cory sat on the bed. Arms folded defiantly over her chest, Mikki stood by the door, as far away from everyone as she could be. She had on faded jeans with the knees torn out, heavy boots, a sleeveless unzipped parka, and a black long-sleeve T-shirt that said, REMEMBER DARFUR. Her hair was now orange. The color contrasted sharply with the dark circles under her eyes.

Cory had been saying something that only now Jack focused on. His son said, "But, Dad, you'll be here and we'll be way out there."

"That's the way *Dad* apparently wants it," said Mikki sharply.

Jack turned to look at her. Father's and daughter's gazes locked until she finally looked away, with an eye roll tacked on.

Cory moved closer to him. "Look, I think the best thing we can do, Dad, is stay here with you. It just makes sense."

Jackie, who was struggling with potty training, slid to the side of the bed and got down holding his privates.

"Gramps," said Mikki, "Jackie has to go. And I'm not taking him this time."

Fred saw what Jackie was doing and scuttled him off to the bathroom down the hall.

As soon as he was gone, Jack said, "You have to go, Cor." He didn't look at Mikki when he added, "You all do."

"But we won't be together, Dad," said Cory. "We'll never see each other."

Cecilia, who'd been listening to all this, quietly spoke up. "I give you my word, Cory, that you will see your brother and sister early and often."

Mikki came forward. Her sullen look was gone, replaced with a defiant one. "Okay, but what about Dad? He just stays here alone? That's not fair."

Jack said, "I'll be with you. And your mom will too, in spirit," he added a little lamely.

"Mom is dead. She can't be with anyone," snapped Mikki.

"Mikki," said Cecilia reproachfully. "That's not necessary."

"Well, it's true. We don't need to be lied to. It's bad enough that I have to go and live with *them* in Arizona."

Tears filled Cory's eyes, and he started to sob quietly. Jack pulled him closer.

Jackie and Fred came back in, and the visit lasted another half hour. Cecilia was the last to leave. She looked back at Jack. "You'll never be alone, Jack. We all carry each other in our hearts."

Those words were nice, and heartfelt, he knew, but Jack Armstrong had never felt so alone as he did right now. He had a question, though.

"Cecilia?"

She turned back, perhaps surprised by the sudden urgency in his voice. "Yes, Jack?"

Jack gathered his breath and said, "Lizzie told me she wanted to take the kids to the Palace next summer."

Cecilia moved closer to him. "She told you that?" she asked. "The Palace? My God. After all this time."

"I know. But maybe . . . maybe the kids could go there sometime?"

Cecilia gripped his hand. "I'll see to it, Jack. I promise."

9

They all came in to visit Jack for the last time. They would be flying out later that day to their new homes. Bonnie was there, as was Fred. Cory and Jackie crowded around their father, hugging, kissing, and talking all at once to him.

Jack was lying in bed, dressed in a fresh gown. His face and body were gaunt; the machines keeping him comfortable until he passed were going full blast. He looked at each of his kids for what he knew would be the final time. He'd already instructed Bonnie to have him cremated. "No funeral," he'd told her. "I'm not putting the kids through that again."

"I'll call you as soon as I get there, Dad," said Cory, who wouldn't look away from his father.

"Me too!" chimed in Jackie.

Jack took several deep breaths as he prepared to do what had to be done. His kids would be gone forever in a few minutes, and he was determined to make these last moments as memorable and happy as possible.

"Got something for you," said Jack. He'd had Sammy

bring the three boxes to him. He slowly took them from the cabinet next to his bed and handed one to Cory and one to Jackie. He held the last one and gazed at Mikki. "For you."

"What is it?" she asked, trying to seem disinterested, though he could tell her curiosity was piqued.

"Come see."

She sighed, strolled over, and took the box from her father.

"Open them," said Jack.

Cory and Jackie opened the boxes and looked down at the piece of metal with the purple ribbon attached.

Mikki's was different.

Fred said to her, "That's a Bronze Star. That's for hero-ism in combat. Your dad was a real hero. The other ones are Purple Hearts for being . . . well, hurt in battle," he finished, looking awkwardly at Cory and Jackie.

Jack said, "Open the box and think of me. Always be with you that way."

Even Bonnie seemed genuinely moved by this gesture, and she dabbed at her eyes with a tissue. But Jack wasn't looking at her. He was watching his daughter. She touched the medal carefully, and her mouth started to tremble. When she looked up and saw her dad watching her, she closed the box and quickly stuck it in her bag.

Cecilia was the last to leave. She sat next to him and patted his hand with her wrinkled one.

"How do you feel, Jack, really?"

"About dying or saying good-bye to my kids for the last time?" he said weakly.

"I mean, do you feel like you want to let go?"

Jack turned to face her. The confusion, and even anger, seeping into his features was met by a radiant calm in hers.

"I'm in hospice, Cee. I'm dead."

"Not yet you're not."

Jack looked away, sucked down a tortured breath. "Matter of time. Hours."

"Do you want to let go?" she asked again.

"Yes. I do."

"Okay, honey, okay."

After Cecilia left, Jack lay there in the bed. His last ties to his family had been severed. It was over. He didn't need to pull out the calendar. There would be no more dates to cross off. His hand moved to the call button. It was time now. He had prearranged this with the doctor. The machines keeping him alive would be turned off. He was done. It was time to go. All he wanted now was to see Lizzie. He conjured her face up in his mind's eye. "It's time, Lizzie," he said. "It's time." The sense of relief was palpable.

However, his hand moved away from the button when Mikki came back into the room and held up the medal. "I just wanted to say that . . . that this was pretty cool."

Father and daughter gazed awkwardly at each other, as though they were two long-lost friends reunited by chance. There was something in her eyes that Jack had not seen there for a long time.

"Mikki?" he said, his voice cracking.

She ran across the room and hugged him. Her breath burned against his cold neck, warming him, sending packets of energy, of strength, to all corners of his body.

He squeezed back, as hard as his depleted energy would allow.

She said, "I love you so much. So much."

Her body shook with the pain, the trauma of a child soon to be orphaned.

When she stood, Mikki kept her gaze away from him. When she spoke, her voice was husky. "Good-bye, Daddy."

She turned and rushed from the room.

"Good-bye, Michelle," Jack mumbled to the empty room.

10

Jack lay there for hours, until day evaporated to night. The clock ticked, and he didn't move. His breathing was steady, buoyed by the machine that replenished his lungs, keeping him alive. Something was burning in his chest that he could not exactly identify or even precisely locate. His thoughts were focused on his last embrace with his daughter, her unspoken plea for him not to leave her. With the end of his life, with his last breath, the Armstrong children would be without parents. His finger had hovered over the nurse's call button all day, ready to summon the doctor, to let it be over. But he never pushed it.

As the clock ticked, the burn in Jack's chest continued to grow. It wasn't painful; indeed, it warmed his throat, his arms, his legs, his feet, his hands. His eyes became teary and then dried; became teary and then dried again. Sobs came and went. And still his mind focused only on his daughter. That last embrace. That last silent plea.

The nurses came and went. He was fed with liquid, shot like a bullet into his body. The clock ticked, the air continued to pour into him. At precisely midnight Jack started feeling odd. His lungs were straining, as they had been when Jackie had pulled the line out of the converter at home.

This might be it, Jack thought, button or no button; not even the machines could keep him alive any longer. He had wondered what the moment would actually feel like. Wedged in a mass of burning metal in Iraq after being blown up in his Humvee, he had wondered that too: whether his last moments on earth would be thousands of miles away from Lizzie and his kids. What it would feel like. What would be waiting for him.

Who would not be scared? Terrified even? The last journey. The one everyone took alone. Without the comfort of a companion. And, unless one had faith, without the reassurance that something awaited him at the end.

He took another deep breath, and then another. His lungs were definitely weakening. He could not drive enough oxygen into them to sustain life. He reached up and fiddled with the line in his nose. That's when he realized what the problem was. There was no airflow. He clicked on the bed light and turned to the wall. There was the problem; the line had come loose from the wall juncture. The pressure cuff had not come off, however, or he would've heard the air escaping into the room. He was about to press the call button but decided to see if he could push the line back in himself.

That's when it struck him.

How long have I been breathing on my own?

He glanced at the vitals monitor. The alarm hadn't gone off, though it should have. But as he gazed at the oxygen levels, he realized why the buzzer hadn't sounded. His oxygen levels hadn't dropped.

How was that possible?

He managed to push the line back in and took several deep breaths. Then he pulled the line out of his nose and breathed on his own for as long as he could. Ten minutes later, his lungs started to labor. Then he put the line back in.

What the hell is going on?

Over the next two hours, he kept pulling the line out and breathing on his own until he was up to fifteen minutes. His lungs normally felt like sacks of wet cement. Now they felt halfway normal.

At three a.m. he sat up in bed and then did the unthinkable. He released the side rail and swung around so his feet dangled over the sides of the bed. He inched forward until his toes touched the cold tile floor. Every part of him straining with the effort, little by little, Jack pushed himself up until most of his weight was supported by his legs. He could hold himself up for only a few seconds before collapsing back onto the sheets. Panting with the exertion, pain searing his weakened lungs, he repeated the movement twice more. Every muscle in his body was spasming from the strain.

Yet as the sweat cooled on his forehead, Jack smiled—for good reason.

He had just stood on his own power for the first time in months.

The next morning, after the hospice nurse had come through on her rounds, he edged to the side of the bed again, and his toes touched the floor. But then his hands slipped on the bedcovers and he crumpled to the floor. At first he panicked, his hand clawing for the call button, which was well out of reach. Then he calmed. The same methodical, practical nature that had carried him safely through Iraq and Afghanistan came back to him.

He grabbed the edge of the bed, tightened his grip, and pulled. His emaciated body slipped, slithered, and jerked until he was fully back on the bed. He lay there in quiet triumph, hard-earned sweat staining his hospice gown.

That night he half walked and half crawled to the bathroom and looked at himself in the mirror for the first time in months. It was not a pretty sight. He looked eighty-four instead of thirty-four. A sense of hopelessness settled over him. He was fooling himself. But as he continued to gaze in the mirror, a familiar voice sounded in his head.

You can do this, Jack.

He looked around frantically, but he was all alone.

You can do this, honey.

It was Lizzie. It couldn't be, of course, but it was.

He closed his eyes. "Can I?" he asked.

Yes, she said. *You have to, Jack. For the children.*

Jack crawled back to his bed and lay there. Had Lizzie really spoken to him? He didn't know. Part of him knew it was impossible. But what was happening to him seemed impossible too. He closed his eyes, conjured her image in his mind, and smiled.

The next night he heard the squeak of the gurney. The patient next door to him would suffer no longer. The person was in a better place. Jack had seen the minister walk down the hallway, Bible in hand. A better place. But Jack was no longer thinking about dying. For the first time since his death sentence had been pronounced, Jack was focused on living.

The next night as the clock hit midnight, Jack lifted himself off the bed and slowly walked around the room, supporting himself by putting one hand against the wall. He felt stronger, his lungs operating somewhat normally. It was as though his body was healing itself minute by minute. He heard a rumbling in his belly and realized that he was hungry. And he didn't want liquid pouring into a line. He wanted real food. Food that required teeth to consume.

Every so often he would smack his arm to make sure he wasn't dreaming. At last he convinced himself it was real. No, it wasn't just real.

This is a miracle.

11

Two weeks passed, and Jack celebrated the week of his thirty-fifth birthday by gaining four pounds and doing away with the oxygen altogether. Miracle or not, he still had a long way to go because his body had withered over the months. He had to rebuild his strength and put on weight. He sat up in his chair for several hours at a time. Using a walker, he regularly made his way to the bathroom all on his own. Another week passed, and four more pounds had appeared on his frame.

Things that Jack, along with most people, had always taken for granted represented small but significant victories in his improbable recovery. Holding a fork and using it to put solid food into his mouth. Washing his face and using a toilet instead of a bed pan. Touching his toes; breathing on his own.

The hospice staff had been remarkably supportive of Jack after it was clear that he was getting better. Perhaps it was because they were weary of people leaving this place solely on the gurney with a sheet thrown over their bodies.

Jack talked to his kids every chance he got, using his old

cell phone. Jackie was bubbly and mostly incoherent. But Jack could sense that the older kids were wondering what was going on.

Cory said, "Dad, can't you come live with us?"

"We'll see, buddy. Let's just take it slow."

With the help of the folks at the hospice, Jack was able to use Skype to see his kids on a laptop computer one of the medical techs brought in. Cory and Jackie were thrilled to see their dad looking better.

Mikki was more subdued and cautious than her brothers, but Jack could tell she was curious. And hopeful.

"You look stronger, Dad."

"I'm feeling better."

"Does this mean –?" She stopped. "I mean, will you . . . ?"

Jack's real fear, even though he did believe he was experiencing a true miracle, was that his recovery might be temporary. He did not want to put his kids through this nightmare again. But that didn't mean he couldn't talk to them. Or see them.

"I don't know, honey. I'm trying to figure that out. I'm doing my best."

"Well, keep doing what you're doing," she replied. And then she smiled at him. That one look seemed to make every muscle in Jack's body firm even more.

One time Bonnie had appeared on the computer screen after Mikki had left the room. Her approach was far more direct, as she stared at Jack sitting up in bed. "What is going on?"

"I'm still here."

"Your hospice doctor won't talk to me. Privacy laws, he said."

"I know," Jack said. "But I can fill you in. I'm feeling better. Getting stronger. How're things working out with Mikki?"

"Fine. She's settled in, but we need to address *your* situation."

"I *am* addressing it. Every day."

And so it had gone, day after day, week after week. Using Skype and the phone, and answering all the kids' questions. Jack could see that more and more even Mikki was coming to grips with what was happening. Every time he saw her smile or heard her laugh at some funny remark he made, it seemed to strengthen him even more.

It was on a cold, blustery Monday morning in February that Jack walked down the hall under his own power. He'd gained five more pounds, his face had filled out, and his hair was growing back. His appetite had returned with a vengeance. They had also stopped giving him pain meds because there was no more pain.

The hospice doctor sat down with him at the end of the week. "I'm not sure what's going on here, Jack, but I'm ordering up some new blood work and other tests to see what we have. I don't want you to get your hopes up, though."

Jack simply stared at him, a spoonful of soup poised near his lips.

The doctor went on. "Look, if this continues, that's terrific. No one will be happier than me—well, of course, except for you. All of my patients die, Jack, to put it bluntly. And we just try to help them pass with dignity."

"But," said Jack.

"But your disease is a complicated one. And always a fatal one. This might just be a false remission."

"Might be."

"Well, without dashing your hopes, it probably is."

"Have others in my condition had a remission?"

The doctor looked taken aback. "No, not to my knowledge."

"That's all I needed to know."

The doctor looked confused. "Needed to know about what?"

"I know I was dying, but now I'm not."

"How can you be so sure?"

"Sometimes you just know."

"Jack, I have to tell you that what's happening to you is medically impossible."

"Medicine is not everything."

The doctor looked him over and saw the new muscle, the fuller face, and the eyes that burned with a rigid intensity.

"Why do you think this is happening to you, Jack?" he finally asked.

"You're a doctor; you wouldn't understand."

"I'm also a human being, and I'd very much like to know."

Jack reached in his drawer and pulled out a photo. He passed it to the doctor.

It was a photo of Lizzie and the kids.

"Because of them," said Jack.

"But I thought your wife passed away."

Jack shook his head. "Doesn't matter."

"What?"

"When you love someone, you love them forever."

12

Two days later, Jack was in his room eating a full meal. He'd put on three more pounds. The doctor walked in and perched on the edge of the bed.

"Okay, I officially believe in miracles. Your blood work came back negative. No trace of the disease. It's like something came along and chased it away. Never seen anything like it. There's no way to explain it medically."

Jack swallowed a mouthful of mashed potatoes and smiled. "I'm glad you finally came around."

He saw his kids that night on the computer. He believed he actually made Jackie understand that he was getting better. At least his son's last words had been, "Daddy's boo-boo's gone."

Cory had blurted out, "When are you coming to see me?"

"I hope soon, big guy. I'll let you know. I've still got a ways to go. But I'm getting there."

Mikki's reaction surprised him, and not in a good way.

"Is this some kind of trick?" she asked.

Jack slowly sat up in his chair as he stared at her. "Trick?"

"When we left you, Dad, you were dying. That's what hospice is for. You said good-bye to all of us. You made me go live with Gramps and *her*!"

"Honey, it's no trick. I'm getting better."

She suddenly dissolved into tears. "Well then, will you be coming to take us home? Because I hate it here."

"I'm doing my best, sweetie. With a little more time I think—"

But Mikki hit a key and the computer screen went black.

Jack slowly sat back. He never heard the squeak of the gurney as the woman across the hall made her final journey from this place.

Day turned to night, and Jack hadn't moved. No food, no liquids, no words spoken to anyone who came to see him.

Finally, at around two a.m., he stirred. He rose from his bed and walked up and down the hall before persuading a nurse to scavenge in the kitchen for some food. He ate and watched his reflection in the window.

I'm coming, Mikki. Dad's coming for you.

A week later he weighed over one-sixty and was walking the halls for an hour at a time. Like an infant, he was relearning how to use his arms and legs. He would flex his fingers and toes, curl and uncurl his arms, bend his legs. The nursing staff watched him carefully, unaccustomed to this sort of thing. Families of other hospice patients observed him curiously. At first Jack was afraid they would be devastated by his progress when their loved ones still lay dying. At least he thought that, until one woman approached him. She was in her sixties and was here every day. Jack knew that her husband had terminal cancer. He'd passed by the man's door and seen the shriveled body under the sheets. He was waiting to die, like everyone else here.

Everyone except me.

She slipped her arm through his and said, "God bless you."

He looked at her questioningly.

"You give us all hope."

Jack felt slightly panicked. "I don't know why this is happening to me," he said frankly. "But it's an awfully long shot."

"That's not what I meant. I know my husband is going to die. But you still give us all hope, honey."

Jack went back to his room and stared at himself in the mirror. He looked more like himself now. The jawline was firming, the hair fuller. He walked slowly to the window and looked outside at a landscape that was still more in the grips of winter than spring, though that season was not too far off. He'd spent several winters apart from his family while he carried a rifle for his country. Lying in his quarters outside of Baghdad or Kabul he had closed his eyes and visualized Christmas with his family. The laughter of Mikki and Cory as they opened presents on Christmas morning.

And then there was the memory of Lizzie's smile as she looked at the small gifts that Jack had bought her before he was deployed for the first time. It had been the summer, so he had gotten her sunblock, a bikini, and a book on grilling. She'd later sent him a photo by e-mail of her wearing the bikini while cooking hot dogs on the Hibachi with mounds of snow behind her. That image had carried him through one hellish battle after another. His wife. Her smile. Wanting so badly to come back to her. That all seemed so long ago, and in some important ways it was.

He went to his nightstand and pulled out the bundle of letters. Each had a number on the envelope. He selected the envelope with the number one on it and slid the paper out. The letter was dated December eighteenth and represented the first one he'd written to Lizzie. He gazed down at the handwriting that was his but that also wasn't because the disease had made him so weak. Sometimes while writing he'd had to put down the pen because he just couldn't hold it any longer. But still it was readable. It said what he had wanted to say. It was the accomplishment of a man who was doing this as his final act in life.

Dear Lizzie,

There are things I want to say to you that I just don't have the breath for anymore. That's why I've decided to write you these letters. I want you to have them after I'm gone. They're not meant to be sad, just my chance to talk to you one more time. When I was healthy you made me happier than any person has a right to be. When I was half a world away, I knew that I was looking at the same sky you were, thinking of the same things you were, wanting to be with you and looking forward to when I could be. You gave me three beautiful children, which is a greater gift than I deserved. I tell you this, though you already know it, because sometimes people don't talk about these things enough. I want you to know that if I could've stayed

with you I would have. I fought as hard as I could.
I will never understand why I had to be taken from
you so soon, but I have accepted it. Yet I want you to
know that there is nothing more important to me than
you. I loved you from the moment I saw you. And the
happiest day of my life was when you agreed to share
your life with mine. I promised that I would always be
there for you. And my love for you is so strong that even
though I won't be there physically, I will be there in
every other way. I will watch over you. I will be there if
you need to talk. I will never stop loving you. Not even
death is powerful enough to overcome my feelings for
you. My love for you, Lizzie, is stronger than anything.
Love,
Jack

He put the letter back in the envelope and replaced
the packet in the drawer. He slipped the photo from the
pocket of his robe and looked at it. From the depths of the
color print, his family smiled back at him. He thought of
all the others in this place who would never leave it alive.
He had been spared.

Why me?

Jack had no ready answer. But he did know one thing.
He was not going to waste a second chance at living.

13

A few days later, Jack Armstrong was discharged from hospice and sent to a rehab facility. He rode over in a shuttle van. The driver was an older guy with a soft felt cap and a trim white beard. Jack was his only passenger.

As they drove along, Jack stared out in childlike wonder at things he never thought he would experience again. Seeing a bird in flight. A mailman delivering letters and packages. A kid running for the school bus. He promised himself he would never again take anything for granted.

As they pulled up in front of the rehab building, the man said, "Never brought anybody from that place to this place."

"I guess not," said Jack. He held his small duffel. Inside were a few clothes, a pair of tennis shoes, and the letters he'd written to Lizzie. When he got to his room, he looked around at the simple furnishings and single window that had a view of the interior outdoor courtyard, which was covered in snow. Jack sat on the bed after putting his few belongings away.

He looked up when a familiar person walked into the room.

"Sammy? What are you doing here?"

Sammy Duvall was dressed in gray sweats and had on a checkered bandanna. "Why the hell do you think I'm here? To get your sorry butt in shape. Look at you; you've obviously been dogging it. And they told me you were getting better. You look like crap."

"I don't understand. You didn't come by the hospice. And I left you phone messages."

The mirth left Sammy's eyes, and he sat down next to Jack on the bed. "I let you down."

"What are you talking about? You've done everything for me."

"No, I haven't. I told you at the cemetery that I'd always be there for you, but I wasn't." He paused. Jack had never seen Sammy nervous before. That emotion just never squared with a man like him. Nothing rattled Sammy Duvall.

Sammy's voice trembled as he said, "I should've come to visit you. But . . . seeing you in that place, just waiting to . . ."

Jack put a hand on the older man's shoulder. "It's okay, Sammy. I understand."

Sammy wiped his eyes and said, "Anyway, I'm here now. And you're probably gonna wish I wasn't."

"Why?"

"I'm your drill instructor."

"What?"

"Worked a deal with the folks here."

"How'd you do that?"

"Told 'em you were a special case. And you need special treatment. And if you're okay with it, so are they."

"I'm definitely okay with it. That was one reason I called you. To have you help me get back in shape."

"Famous last words, boy, because I'm gonna kick your butt."

The weeks went by swiftly. And with pain. Much pain.

The sweat streaming off him during one particularly arduous workout, Jack told Sammy, "I can't do one more damn push-up. I can't!"

"Can't or won't? 'Cause that's all the difference in the world, son."

Jack did one more push-up and then another and then a third, until he could no longer feel his arms. Jack had gone on to pump thousands of pounds of weights, run on the treadmill until he couldn't stand the stink of his own sweat, perform more push-ups until his arms nearly fell off, jump rope until his knees failed.

He cursed at Sammy, who laughed at him and goaded him into doing more, and more.

"You call yourself an army ranger? Sam Jr. can work harder than you, and he's a big, fat baby."

And Sammy didn't just instruct. He got down on the floor and did the exercises with Jack. "If an old man like me can do this, you sure as hell can," was his usual taunt.

On and on it went. Sammy screaming in his face and Jack gnashing his teeth, furrowing his brow, and doing one more pull-up, one more push-up, one more mile on the treadmill, one more set of curls, a hundred more pounds on the squat bar. But the thing was, Jack was growing stronger with every rep.

He talked to his kids every day. They knew he was in rehab. They knew he was getting stronger.

On one joint Skype session, Jack showed Cory and Jackie his muscles.

"You're ripped, Dad," said Cory.

"Whipped," crowed Jackie.

Later that night he saw Mikki. She hadn't agreed to do a Skype session with him in a while, but repeated phone calls from him and finally Sammy had convinced her.

"You look great, Dad," she said slowly. "You really do."

"You look thin," he replied.

"Yeah, well, Grandma is watching her weight, which means we all eat like birds."

"Cheeseburger's on me."

"When?" she said quickly.

"Sooner than you think, sweetie. I know I probably should have come out to see you before now. And I miss you more than anything. But . . . but I want to do this right. When I was in the army and we'd go on patrol, I always analyzed everything that might come up. Some of the other guys liked to wing it. Just turn on the fly. And sometimes in combat you have to do that. But being prepared for everything because you've done your homework is the best way to survive, Mikki. I hope you understand. I want to do this right. For all of you."

"I get it, Dad." She added playfully, "And Skype will get you ready for when I go to college and you really miss me."

Finally, the day came on a surprisingly warm spring morning. Jack's bag was packed and he was sitting on his bed when Sammy came into the room. "It's time."

"I know it is," said Sammy.

"I couldn't have done this without you."

"Sure you could, but it wouldn't have been nearly as much fun."

While his discharge papers were being finalized, Jack sat in a chair outside the rehab office. The months had been a blur. He drew a long, measured breath, trying to collect his thoughts. He looked out the window, where winter had passed and spring had arrived. Crocuses were pushing through the earth and trees were starting to bud out. *The world is waking up from a long winter's nap, and so am I.* He opened his duffel and pulled out an envelope with the number two on it. He slid out the letter.

Dear Lizzie,

  Christmas will be here in five days, and I promise that I will make it. I've never broken a promise to you, and I never will. It's hard to say good-bye, but sometimes you have to do things you don't want to. Jackie came to see me a little while ago, and we talked. Well, he talked in Jackie language and I listened. I like to listen to him because I know one day very soon I won't be able to. He's growing up so fast, and I know he probably won't remember his dad, but I know I will live on in your memories. Tell him his dad loved him and wanted the best for him. And I wish I could have thrown the football to him and watched him play baseball. I know he will have a great life.

  Cory is a special little boy. He has your sensitivity, your compassion. I know what's happening to me is probably affecting him the most of all the kids. He

came and got into bed with me last night. He asked
me if it hurt very much. I told him it didn't. He
told me to say hello to God when I saw him. And I
promised that I would.
　　And Mikki.

At this point Jack's hand trembled a bit. He remembered stopping at this point too as he was writing the letter. There was an old teardrop that had made the ink blotch. He started to read again.

　　Mikki is the most complicated of all. Not a little
girl anymore but not yet an adult either. She is a good
kid, though I know you've had your moments with her.
She is smart and caring and she loves her brothers.
She loves you, though she sometimes doesn't like to show
it. My greatest regret with my daughter is letting her
grow away from me. It was my fault, not hers. I see
that clearly now. I only wish I had seen it that clearly
while I still had a chance to do something about it.
After I'm gone, please tell her the first time I ever
saw her, when I got back from Afghanistan and was
still in uniform, there was no prouder father who ever
lived. Looking down at her tiny face, I felt the purest
joy a human could possibly feel. And I wanted to
protect her and never let anything bad ever happen to
her. Life doesn't work that way, of course. But tell her
that her dad was her biggest fan. And that whatever
she does in life, I will always be her biggest fan.
　　Love,
　　Jack

14

After being discharged, Jack rode with Sammy to his house. Along the way, he asked his friend to pass by his old home. Jack was surprised to see his pickup truck in the carport.

Sammy explained, "Went with the house sale, so I heard."

"Bonnie and the Realtor handled all that. Is that my tool bin in the back?"

"Yep. Guess that went too. All happened pretty fast." He eyed Jack. "Knew you'd beat that damn thing. Still got the tickets to Disney World?"

"Yeah," said Jack, staring glumly out the window.

Five of them.

Later, Jack drove to his bank. They had kept the account open to pay for expenses. It had a few thousand dollars left in it. That was a starting point. He had his wallet, and his credit cards were still valid. Driver's license was still good. Contractor's license intact. He drove to his old house and offered the owner eight hundred bucks on the spot for the truck and tools. After some negotiation back and forth, he got them for eight-fifty, the owner apparently glad to get the heap out of his driveway. Jack raced to the bank and got a cashier's check; the title was signed over, and he drove off in his old ride the same day.

He called the kids and told them he was out of rehab and getting a place for them all to live in. He next talked to Bonnie and explained things to her.

"That's wonderful, Jack," she'd said. But her words rang hollow. She asked him what his next step would be.

"Like I said, getting my family back. I'll be coming out there really soon."

"Do you think that's wise?"

"Bonnie, I'm their father. They belong with me."

That night he treated Sammy to dinner. While Sammy had a medium-rare burger, fries, and black coffee, Jack made three trips to the salad bar before settling down to devour his heaping plate of surf and turf.

"So what's the plan, chief?"

"Get my kids back pronto. But I need a place for us to stay."

"You're welcome to stay at my place, long as you want."

Sammy's place had one bedroom and a bathroom attached to the back with only an outside entrance; Sammy's massive Harley was parked in what he referred to as "the parlor." Besides that, his "puppy," Sam Jr., had the bulk of a Honda.

"That's fine for me, but with three kids, I'll need something a little bigger."

Late that night he slowly pulled his truck down the narrow roads of the cemetery. He'd been here only once, on a bitterly cold day, the ground flash-wrapped in ice and snow. And yet even though he'd been sick, he'd memorized every detail of the place. He could never forget where his wife was buried any more than he could ever fail to recall his own name.

He walked between the plots until he reached hers, represented by a simple bronze plate in the grass. He knelt down, brushed a couple of dead leaves off it. There was a skinny metal vase bolted to the plate where one could put flowers. There were roses in there, but they were brown. Jack cleaned them all out and placed in the vase a bunch of fresh flowers he'd brought with him. He sat down on his haunches and read the writing on the plate.

"Elizabeth 'Lizzie' Armstrong, loving wife, mother, and daughter. You will always be missed. You will always be loved."

He traced the letters with his fingers, even as his eyes filled with tears.

"I'm going to get the kids, Lizzie. I'm going to bring them home, and we're going to be a family again." He choked back a sob and tried to ignore the dull pain in his chest. "I wish you could be here with me, Lizzie. More than anything I wish that. But you were there for me in the hospital when I needed you. And I promise I will take good care of the children. I will make them proud. And I will raise them right. Just like you did."

The words finally failed him, and he lay down in the soft grass and wept. He finally became so exhausted, he fell asleep. When he woke he didn't know where he was for a few seconds, before he looked over and saw the grave. The dawn was breaking, the air chilly. As he looked overhead, he could see flocks of birds arriving for the start of spring.

Jack's clothes were damp from the dew. He coughed to clear his throat. His eyes and face were raw. In the distance he could hear the sounds of early morning traffic on the roads that fronted the cemetery. He walked silently back to his truck and drove off without the one person he needed more than anyone else.

15

One day later, Jack found it, a house owned by an elderly couple who had moved to an assisted-living facility. They couldn't sell their home because it needed a lot of repairs. And with dozens of homes in default on their street, it was difficult to sell anyway. Jack called the Realtor and offered his labor for free to fix up the place in exchange for staying there at no cost. Since the couple wasn't making any money off the house anyway, they quickly agreed. It wasn't perfect, but he didn't need perfect. He just needed his kids under the same roof as him. Jack moved his few possessions in the next day, after signing a one-page agreement. He made some quick cosmetic changes and bought some secondhand furniture.

Now it was time.

Using his credit card, he booked his plane tickets, packed his bag, and left for the airport. He went to collect Mikki first, because he knew if he went to the sisters' homes first, they would be on the phone to their mother before he'd even left their driveways.

He landed in Phoenix, rented a car, and drove to

Tempe. He reached Fred and Bonnie's house but then drove past it. He parked a little down from the house and waited. An hour later a car pulled into the driveway, and Fred and Mikki got out. She was carrying her schoolbag. His heart ached when he saw her. She'd grown even taller, Jack noted, and her face had changed too. She was wearing a school uniform, white polo shirt and checked skirt. Her hair was in a ponytail and had nary a strand of pink or purple in it. She looked utterly miserable.

They went into the house. Jack parked in their driveway, took a deep breath, climbed out of the car, and walked up to the door.

"Dad?"

Mikki stared at him openmouthed. When he held out his arms for a hug, she tentatively reached out to him. He stroked her hair and kissed the top of her head.

"Dad, is it really you?"

"It's me, sweetie. It's really me."

Bonnie and Fred came around the corner, saw him, and stopped.

"Jack?" said Fred. "My God."

Bonnie just stood there, disbelief on her features.

Jack moved into the house with Mikki. He held out his hand, and Fred shook it. He looked at Bonnie. She still seemed in a daze.

"My God," she said, echoing her husband's words. "It's true. It's really true. Even with all the phone calls and seeing you on that computer. It's not the same."

"What is all the commotion?" Cecilia came into the room, skimming along on her walker, her oxygen line trailing behind her. When she saw Jack, she didn't freeze like Fred and Bonnie had done.

She cackled. "I knew it." She came forward as fast as she could and gave him a prolonged squeeze. "I knew it, Jack, honey," she said again, staring up at him and blinking back tears of joy.

They all sat at the kitchen table sipping glasses of iced tea. Jack eyed Bonnie. "Docs gave me a clean bill of health."

Bonnie just kept shaking her head, but Fred clapped him on the shoulder. "Jack, we're so happy for you, son."

Later, when they were alone, Bonnie asked, "How long will you be staying?"

"From here I'm heading to LA and then on to Portland."

"To see the kids?"

"No, to take them back with me, Bonnie. I've already told Mikki to start packing her things."

"But the school year will be done in less than two months."

"She can go to school in Cleveland as easily as she can here."

"But the house was sold."

"I'm renting another one."

"How will you support them?"

"I've started my business back up."

"Okay, but who will watch them when you're working?"

"Mikki and Cory are in school the whole day. And they're old enough now to come home and be okay by themselves for a few hours. Jackie will be in extended day care. And if unexpected things come up, we'll deal with them. Just like every other family does."

Bonnie pursed her lips. "Michelle has settled into her new life here."

Jack said nothing about how miserable the girl had been here. He simply said, "I don't think she'll mind."

"You could have called before you came."

"Yeah, I could have. And maybe I should have. But I don't see what harm it did."

"What harm? You just expect us to give her back to you, with no notice, no preparation? After all we've done."

"I've been in constant contact over the last few months. I kept you updated on my progress. Hell, you've *seen* me on the computer getting better. And I told you I would be coming to take the kids back. Soon. So this shouldn't come as a shock to you. And it's not like you're never going to see them again." He paused, and his tone changed. "Even though you did leave me by myself."

"You said it was all right. You told us to do it. And we thought you were dying."

"Come on, Bonnie, what else could I tell you under the circumstances? But for the record, dying alone is a real bitch."

As soon as Jack finished speaking, he regretted it. Bonnie stood, her face red with anger. "Don't you dare talk to me about dying alone. My Lizzie is lying dead and buried. There was no one with her at the end. No one! Certainly not you."

Jack eyed her. "Why don't you just say it, Bonnie, because I know you want to."

"*You* should be dead, not her." Bonnie seemed stunned

by her own words. "I'm sorry, I didn't mean that." Her face flushed. "I'm very sorry."

"I *would* give my life to have Lizzie back. But I can't. I've got three kids who need me. Nothing takes priority over that. I hope you can understand."

"What I understand is that you're taking your children from a safe, healthy environment into something totally unknown."

"I'm their father," said Jack heatedly.

"You're a single parent. Lizzie isn't here to take care of the kids."

"I can take care of them."

"Can you? Because I don't think you have any idea what's in store for you."

Jack started to say something but stopped.

Could she be right?

16

"Mr. Armstrong?"

Jack stared down from the ladder he was standing on while repairing some siding on a job site. The sun was high overhead, the air warm, and the sweat on his skin thick. He had on a white tank top, dirty dark blue cargo shorts, white crew socks, and worn steel-toed work boots. The woman down below was pretty, with light brown curly hair cut short, and she wore a pair of black slacks and a white blouse; her heels were sunk in the wet grass.

"What can I do for you, ma'am?"

"I'm Janice Kaplan. I'm a newspaper reporter. I'd like to talk to you."

Jack clambered down the ladder and rubbed his hands off on the back of his shorts. "Talk to me about what?"

"Being the miracle man."

Jack squinted at her. "Come again?"

"You are the Jack Armstrong who was diagnosed with a terminal illness?"

"Well, yeah, I was."

"You don't look terminal anymore."

"I'm not. I got better."

"So a miracle. At least that's what the doctor I talked to said."

Jack looked annoyed. "You talked to my doctor? I thought that was private."

"Actually, he's a friend of mine. He mentioned your case in passing. It was all very positive. I became interested, did a little digging, and here I am."

"Here for what?" Jack said, puzzled.

"To do a story on you. People with death sentences rarely get a second chance. I'd like to talk to you about the experience. And I know my readers would want to know."

Jack and the kids had been back for nearly four weeks now. With parenting and financial support resting solely on his shoulders, Jack barely had time to eat or sleep. Bonnie had been right in her prediction. He didn't have any idea what was in store for him. Mikki had really stepped up and had taken the laboring oar with the cooking and cleaning, the shopping, and looking after the boys. He had never had greater appreciation for Lizzie. She'd done it all, from school to meals to laundry to shopping to keeping the house clean. Jack had worked hard, but he realized now that he hadn't come close to working as hard as his wife had, because she did all that and worked full-time too. At midnight he lay in his bed, numb and exhausted— and humbled by the knowledge that Lizzie would have still been going strong.

"A story?" Jack shook his head as he dug a hole in the mulch bed with the toe of his boot. "Look, it's really not that special."

"Don't be modest. And I also understand that you

turned your life around, built your business back, got a house, and went to retrieve your children, who'd been placed with family after your wife tragically died." She added, "I was very sorry to hear about that. On Christmas Eve too, of all days."

Jack's annoyance turned to anger. "You didn't learn all that from my doctor. That really is an invasion of privacy."

"Please don't be upset, Mr. Armstrong. I'm a reporter; it's my job to find out these things. And I'm probably not explaining myself very well." She drew a deep breath while Jack stared at her, his hands clenching into fists with his anxiety. "It's strictly a feel-good piece. One man's triumph against the odds, a family reunited. These are hard times for folks, especially around here. All we hear is bad news. War, crime, people losing their jobs and their homes. I write about that stuff all the time, and while it is news, it's also very, very depressing. But this is different. This is a great story that will make people smile. That's all I'm shooting for. To make people feel good, for once."

His anger quickly disappearing, Jack looked around while he considered her request. He saw Sammy up on another ladder watching him intently. He waved to show him things were okay. Jack turned back to the woman.

"So what exactly do I have to do?"

"Just sit down with me and tell your story. I'll take notes, do a draft, get back to you, polish it, and then it'll be published in the paper and on our Web site."

"And that's it?"

"That's all. I really believe it will be positive for lots of people. There are many folks out there with what seem like insurmountable obstacles in front of them. Reading about how you overcame yours could do a lot of good. It really could."

"I think I just got lucky."

"Maybe, but maybe not. From the research I've done on your condition, the odds were zero that you would recover. No one else ever has."

"Well, I'm just happy I was the first. How about tomorrow after dinner?"

"Great. About eight?"

Jack gave her his address. She glanced at his exposed upper right arm and then his scarred calves. "I understand you were in the military. Is that where you got those?" She indicated the ragged bullet wound on his arm and the network of scars on his legs.

"Arm in Afghanistan and legs in Iraq."

"Two Purples then?"

"Yeah. Were you in the military?"

"My son just got back from the Middle East in one piece, thank God."

"I guess we both have a lot to be thankful for."

"I'll see you tomorrow."

The story ran, and a few days later Janice Kaplan called.

"The AP picked up my article, Jack."

Jack had just finished cleaning up after dinner.

"What does that mean?" he asked.

"AP. Associated Press. That means my story about you and your family is running in newspapers across the country. My editor still can't believe it."

"Congratulations, Janice."

"No, thank *you*. It wasn't the writing; it was the story.

And it was a great picture of you and the kids. And I think lots of families will be inspired by your struggle and triumph. I just thought I'd give you a heads-up. You're famous now. So be prepared."

17

Janice Kaplan's words proved prophetic. Letters came pouring in, including offers to appear on TV and to tell his story to major magazines; one publisher even wanted Jack to write a book. Overwhelmed by the blitzkrieg and wanting a normal life with his kids, he declined them all. He figured with the passage of time other stories would emerge and take the focus away from him. His fifteen minutes of fame couldn't be over soon enough for him. He was no miracle man, he knew, but simply a guy who got lucky.

A week after Kaplan's call, Jack was lying in bed when he heard voices downstairs. He slipped on his pants and crept down to the main level.

"Stop it, Chris!"

Jack took the last three steps in one bound. Mikki was at the door, and a teenage boy had his hands all over her as she struggled against him. It took only two seconds for Jack to lift the young man off his feet and slam him against the wall. Jack said, "What part of *no* don't you get, jerk?" He looked over at Mikki. "What the hell is going on?"

"We . . . he just came over to work on some . . . Dad, just let him down."

Jack snapped, "Get upstairs."

"Dad!"

"Now."

"I can handle this. I'm not a child."

"Yeah, I can see that. Upstairs."

She stalked up to her room. Jack turned back to the young man.

"I ever catch you with one finger on her again, they won't be able to find all the pieces to put you back together, got it?"

The terrified teen merely nodded.

Jack threw him outside and slammed the door. He stood there, letting his anger cool. Then he marched up the stairs and knocked on his daughter's door.

"Leave me alone."

Instead he threw open the door and went in. Mikki was sitting on the floor, her guitar across her lap.

"We need to get a few rules straight around here," Jack said.

She stared up at him icily. "Which rules? The ones where you're ruining my life?"

"What was I supposed to do, let that little creep paw you?"

"I told you I could handle it."

"You can't handle everything. That's why there are people called parents."

"Oh, is that what you're pretending to be?"

Jack looked stunned. "Pretend? I brought all of you

back home so we could be together. Do you think I did that just for the hell of it?"

"I don't have a clue why you did it. And you didn't even ask me if I wanted to come back. You just told me to pack, like I was a child."

"I thought you hated it out there. You told me that a dozen times."

"Well, I hate it here too."

"What do you want from me? I'm doing the best I can."

"You were gone a long time."

"I explained that. Remember? I told you that story about being in the army? About taking your time and being prepared for every eventuality."

"That's crap!"

"What?"

"In case you hadn't figured it out, this isn't the army, Dad. This is about family."

"I did all that to make sure we *could* be a family," he shot back.

"A family? You don't have a clue what to do with us. Admit it. You're not Mom."

"I know I'm not, believe me. But you two were always arguing."

"That doesn't mean I didn't appreciate what she did for us. Now I do most of the cooking and cleaning and the laundry, and looking after Jackie. And your grocery-shopping skills are a joke."

Jack felt his anger continue to rise. "Look, I know I'm not in your mom's league, but I'm trying to make this work. I love you guys."

"Really? Well, Cory's being bullied at school. Did you

know that? His grades are going down even though he's a really smart kid. The teachers have sent home tons of notes in his bag, but you never check that, do you? And Jackie's birthday is in two weeks. Have you planned anything? Bought him a present? Planned a party for his friends or even thought about a cake?"

Jack's face grew pale. "Two weeks?"

"Two weeks, *Dad*. So you might want to try harder."

"Mik, I—"

"Can you please just leave me alone?"

When he left her room, Cory was standing in the hall in his underwear.

Jack looked embarrassed. "Cor, *are* you being bullied at school?"

Cory closed the door, leaving his dad alone in the hall.

18

Jack and Sammy were unloading Jack's truck in his driveway after a long day at work. Jack nearly dropped a sledgehammer on his foot. Sammy looked over at him.

"You okay? Haven't been yourself the last couple of days."

Jack slowly picked up the tool and threw it back in the truck bed. "What do you think Jackie would like for his birthday? It's just around the corner, and I wanted to get him something nice."

Sammy shrugged. "Uh, toy gun?"

Jack looked doubtful. "I don't think Lizzie liked to encourage that. And where can I get a cake and some birthday things? You know like hats and . . . stuff?"

"The grocery store up the street has a bakery."

"How do you know that?"

"It's right across from the beer aisle."

Jack drove to the store and got some items for Jackie's birthday. He was standing at the checkout aisle when he saw it. He had never been more stunned in his life. He was looking at *his* photo on the cover of one of the tabloid magazines that were kept as impulse buys at the checkout. He slowly reached out his hand and picked up a copy.

The headline ran, "Miracle Man Muddied."

What the hell?

Jack turned to the next page and read the story. With each word he read, his anger increased. Now he could understand the headline. The writer had twisted everything. He'd made it seem that Jack had forced Lizzie to go out on an icy, treacherous night to get his pain meds. And then, even worse, the writer had suggested that Jack thought his wife was having an affair with a neighbor. An obviously distraught Lizzie had run a red light and been killed. None of it was true, but now probably millions of people thought he was some kind of monster.

He left his items on the conveyor belt and rushed home.

On the drive there, it didn't take him long to figure out what had happened.

Bonnie had been the writer's source. But how could she have known? Then it struck him. Lizzie must've called her on the drive over to the pharmacy and told her what she was doing. Maybe she mentioned something about Bill Miller, and Bonnie had misconstrued what Jack's reaction had been, although it would have been pretty difficult to do that. More likely, Bonnie might've just altered what Lizzie had told her to suit her own purposes.

Jack could imagine Bonnie seething. Here he was getting all this notoriety, adulation, and sympathy, and Lizzie was in a grave because of him. At least Bonnie probably believed that. A part of Jack couldn't blame her for feeling that way. But now she had opened a Pandora's box that Jack would find difficult to close. And what worried him the most was what would happen when his kids found out. He wanted to be the first to talk to them about it, especially Mikki. He gunned the truck.

Unfortunately, he was too late.

19

Mikki was waiting for him on the front porch with a copy of another gossip paper with a similar headline. She was trembling and attacked him as soon as he got out of the truck. "This is all over school. How could you make Mom go out that night? And how could you even think that she would cheat on you?"

Jack exploded, "That story is full of lies. I never accused your mom of anything. I saw her slap Bill Miller. She and I had a laugh about it because he was drunk. And I didn't insist she go out that night. In fact, I told her not to."

"I don't believe you."

"Mikki, it's the truth. I swear. Tabloids make stuff up all the time. You know that."

"This never would have happened if you hadn't agreed to do that stupid Miracle Man story in the first place. That *was* your fault."

"Okay, you're right about that. I wish I hadn't but—"

"So now everybody thinks Mom was a slut and you're a jerk. And I'll spend the rest of the school year having people talking behind my back."

"Will you just listen to me for a sec—"

Before he could finish, she'd fled inside, slamming the door behind her. When he started to go in the house after her, he heard the lock click. Staring through the side window at him was Cory. He gave his father a furious scowl and ran off.

Jack ended up taking Cory and Jackie to Chuck E. Cheese's for Jackie's third birthday. Jack wore a ball cap and glasses so people wouldn't recognize him during his fifteen minutes of "infamy." On the table in front of him were a half-eaten cheese pizza and a mass-produced birthday cake. While Jackie jumped into mounds of balls along with a zillion other kids, Cory sat slumped in a corner looking like he would rather be attacked by sharks than be here. Jack didn't even know where Mikki was. The only moment in his life worse than this was when the cop told him Lizzie was dead.

Later, after they returned home, Jackie played with the monster truck that Jack had rushed out to buy him the night before. Cory had escaped into the backyard.

"You like the truck?" Jack asked quietly.

Jackie made guttural truck noises and rolled it across his dad's shoulder.

At least I've still got one kid who doesn't hate me.

Carrying his youngest son, Jack walked up the stairs and peered inside Mikki's bedroom. It was small, lighted by a single overhead fixture that gave out meager illumination, and her clothes were all over the floor. A half-empty jar of Nutella sat on a storage box. Her guitar and keyboard were in one corner. A device to mix musical tracks was on the floor. Sheet music was stacked everywhere. There was an old beat-up microphone on a metal fold-up table that she used as a desk.

Jack put his son down and then walked over and picked up some of the music. It was actually blank sheets with pencil notes written in, obviously by his daughter. Jack couldn't read music and didn't know what the markings represented, but they looked complicated. She could create this but couldn't even manage a B in math or science? Then again, he hadn't been a great student either, except in the subjects that interested him.

He took Jackie's hand and walked into the bedroom the boys shared. It was far more cluttered than Mikki's because it was smaller and housed two people instead of one. The beds were nearly touching. There was a small built-in shelf crammed with toys, books, and junk that boys tended to collect. Cory had stacked his clothes neatly in the small bureau Jack had gotten thirdhand. Jackie's clothes were on top of the bureau.

Jack noticed a box crammed with papers on the floor next to Cory's bed. He looked inside. When he saw the top page, he started going through the rest. It was printed information about his disease. He saw, in Cory's handwriting, notes on the pages.

"He thought maybe he could find a cure."

Jack spun around to see Mikki standing there.

She came forward. "He wanted to save you. Dumb, huh? He's only a kid. But he meant well."

Jack slowly rose. "I didn't know."

"Well, to be fair, you were pretty out of it at the time."

She sat down on one of the beds, while Jackie rushed toward her and held out his truck for her to see. "That's really cool, Jackie." She hugged her brother and said, "Happy birthday, big guy."

"Big guy," repeated Jackie with a huge smile.

She glanced at her dad. "It's a nice gift."

"Thanks." He stared back at her. "So where does that leave us?"

"This is not where we say stupid stuff and hug and then bawl our eyes out and everything is okay, cue the dumb music. It's one day at a time. That's life. Some days will be good and some days will suck. Some days I'll look at you and feel mad; some days I'll feel crappy about being mad at you. Some days I'll feel nothing. But you're still my dad."

"The thing is, I was supposed to be gone, not your mom. I'd accepted that. But then your mother was gone. And somehow I got better. It just wasn't supposed to happen that way."

"But it did happen exactly that way. You *are* here. Mom isn't."

"So where do we all go from here?"

"You're really asking me?"

"You obviously know a lot more about this family than I do."

His cell phone rang. He looked at the caller ID. It was Bonnie's number. Now what? Hadn't she done enough damage?

"Hello?" he said, bracing for a fight.

It was Fred. He sounded tired, and there was something else in his voice that made Jack stiffen.

He said, "Fred, is everything okay?"

"Not really, Jack, no."

"What is it? Not Bonnie?"

"No." He paused. "It's Cecilia. She died about two hours ago."

20

Though she'd lived the last ten years in Ohio with her daughter and son-in-law, except for her short stint in Arizona, Cecilia Pinckney was a southerner through and through. She'd requested to be buried in Charleston, South Carolina, in the family crypt. So Jack bundled the kids into a pale blue 1964 VW van with white top that Sammy had lovingly restored, and headed south. A large crowd gathered under a very hot sun and high humidity for the funeral. Bonnie looked older by ten years, shrunken and bowed. Seeing this, Jack couldn't bring himself to offer anything other than brief condolences. As she looked up at him, Jack thought he could see some affection for him underneath all the sorrow.

"Thank you for coming," she said.

"Cecilia was a great lady."

"Yes, she was."

"When some time has passed, we need to talk."

She slowly nodded. "All right. We probably should."

After the service was over, Jack and the kids drove back to the hotel, where they were crammed into one room.

Jack had just taken off his tie and jacket when the hotel phone rang. He answered, thinking it might be Fred, but it was a strange voice.

"Mr. Armstrong, I'm Royce Baxter."

"Okay, what can I do for you?"

"I had the pleasure of being Mrs. Cecilia Pinckney's attorney for the past twenty years."

"Her attorney?"

"That's right. I was wondering if I could meet with you for a little bit. My office is only a block over from your hotel. Fred O'Toole told me where you were staying. I assumed you'd be heading back to Ohio soon, and I thought I would catch you before you left. I know the timing is bad, but it is important and it won't take long."

Jack looked around at the kids. Jackie was passed out in a chair, and Cory and Mikki were watching TV.

"Give me the address."

Five minutes later he was sitting across from the very prim and proper Royce Baxter, who was dressed in a dark suit. He was in his sixties, about five-ten, with a bit of a paunch and a good-natured face.

"Let me get down to business." Baxter drew a document out of a file. "This is Ms. Cecilia's last will and testament."

"Look, if she left me anything, I really don't feel that I should accept it."

Baxter peered at him over the document. "And why is that?"

"It's sort of complicated."

"Well, she made this change to her will very recently.

She told me that even if you never used it, it would always be there for you."

"Well, what is it exactly?" Jack said curiously.

"The old Pinckney house on the South Carolina coast in a town called Channing."

"The Palace, you mean?"

"That's right. So you know about it?"

"Lizzie told me about it. But I've never been there. Once she moved to Ohio she never went back."

"Now, let me warn you that while it's right on the beach, it's not in good condition. It's a big, old, rambling place that has never been truly modernized. But it's in a lovely location. The coastal low country is uniquely beautiful. And I say that with all the bias of a proud South Carolinian. Ms. Cecilia told me that you're very good with your hands. I believe she thought you were the perfect person to take care of it."

"Beachfront? I couldn't afford the real estate taxes."

"There are none. Years ago Ms. Cecilia placed the property into a conservancy so it could never be sold and developed. She and her descendants can use the property but can never sell it. In return the taxes were basically waived."

"But we've got a home in Cleveland. The kids are in school."

"Ms. Cecilia thought that you might have some trepidation. But since most of the summer is still ahead of us, the issue of school does not come into play."

Jack sat back. "Okay. I see that. But I still don't think—"

Baxter interrupted. "And Cecilia said that you told her that Lizzie was thinking of taking the kids there this summer."

"That's right, Lizzie was. She told me that. I thought it was a good idea but . . ." Jack's voice trailed off. He'd made Lizzie promise him that she would take the kids to the Palace. Now she couldn't.

Baxter fingered the will and studied him. "Would you like to see it before you make up your mind?"

"Yes, I would," Jack said quickly.

21

Less than two hours after leaving Royce Baxter's office, Jack and the kids pulled down a sandy drive between overgrown bushes after following the directions the lawyer had given him. He surveyed the landscape. There were marshes nearby, and the smell of the salt water was strong, intoxicating.

"Wow!" said Cory as the old house finally came into view.

Jack pulled the VW to a stop, and they all climbed out. Jack took Jackie's hand as they walked up to the front of the house, which was shaded by two large palmetto trees. It was an elongated rambling wood-sided structure, with a broad, covered front porch that ran down three-quarters of the home's face. A double door of solid wood invited visitors to the entrance. The wood siding was faded and weathered but looked strong and reliable to Jack's expert eye. The hurricane shutters were painted black, but most of the paint was gone, leaving the underlying wood exposed to the elements. Five partially rotted steps carried them up to the front entrance.

The furniture on the porch was covered. When Jack and the kids looked underneath, they found quite the mess, along with animal nests. One squirrel jumped out and raced up a support post and onto the roof, which had many missing shingles, Jack had already noted. A snake slid out from under a pile of wood, causing the older kids to scream and run. Jackie approached the serpent and attempted to pick it up before Jack snatched him away. He looked at the other kids, who were cowering by the VW.

"It's a black snake. Not poisonous, but it will bite, so stay clear of it." He watched as the snake slowly made its way down the steps and into the underbrush around the house.

"They don't have giant snakes in Cleveland," said a breathless Cory.

"It was only a three-footer, son. And there *are* snakes in Ohio."

That information did not seem to make Cory feel any better.

"Come on," said Jack. "Let's at least check it out while we're here."

Using the key Baxter had given him, he opened the front door and went inside with Jackie. He turned to check on the other two kids. They hadn't budged from next to the VW. "Remember, guys, that snake is out there with *you*, not in here with us."

A moment later, the two kids flew up the front steps and past their dad into the house, with Cory screaming and looking behind him for the "giant freaking snake."

Jackie and his father exchanged a glance.

Jackie pointed at his brother and said, "Corwee funny."

"Yeah, he's a riot," said Jack, shaking his head.

Inside, the spaces were open and large, with high, sloped ceilings where old fans hung motionless. The kitchen was spacious but poorly lighted by tiny windows, and the bathrooms were few in number and small. There was an enormous stone fireplace that reached to the ceiling in the main living area, a big table for dining that showed a lot of wear and tear, and several other rooms that served various purposes, including a laundry room and a small library. On the lower level were an old billiards table, its green felt surface worn smooth with use, and a Ping-Pong table with a tattered net. Water toys, flippers, flattened beach balls, and the like were stacked in a storage room.

The furniture was old but mostly in good shape. The floors were random width plank, the walls solid plaster. Jack knocked on one section and came away impressed with the craftsmanship. Yet when he stepped toward the back of the house, he drew in a breath. The rear of the house was mostly windows and glass doors; there was also a second-floor screened-in porch with stairs leading down to the ground. The view out was of the wide breadth of the Atlantic, maybe two hundred feet away, the sandy beach less than half that distance.

Jack breathed in the sea air and pointed out to the ocean. "There's really not a drop of land between here and Europe or Africa," he said. "Just water."

As the kids stared out at the views, Jack looked down at the backyard. It was sandy, with dunes covered in vegetation. He stepped back inside and smelled the burned wood of fires from long ago.

They clumped upstairs and looked through the

shotgun line of bedrooms there, none of them remarkable, but all functional. Where others might have seen
limitations, builder Jack saw potential. All the bedrooms
had views of the ocean, and the largest one had a small
outdoor balcony as well.

"What do you think is up there?" This came from Mikki,
who was pointing to a set of stairs at the end of the hall
going up another half flight.

"Attic, I suppose," he said.

Jack eased open the door and fumbled for a light switch.
Nothing happened when he flicked it, and it occurred to
him that the power had been turned off when the place
became uninhabited. The room was under the eaves of
the house, and the ceiling slanted upward to a peak. It
was large, with two windows that threw in good morning light, though now the sun had passed over the house
and was going down. There was a bed, an old wrought-
iron four-poster, a large wooden desk, a shelf filled with
books, and an old trunk set in one corner. A door led to
a closet that was empty. Jack stepped cautiously over the
floor planks to test their safety.

"Okay," he said after his inspection was complete.
"Explore."

Cory made a beeline for the trunk, while Jack led his
youngest over to the desk and helped him open drawers.
He glanced back at Mikki, who hadn't budged from the
doorway.

"You going to look around?"

"Why? You're not thinking about moving here, are
you?"

"Maybe."

Her face flushed with anger. "I already had to move to Arizona. And all my friends are in Cleveland. My band, everything."

"I'm just looking around, okay?" But in his mind, Jack was already drawing up plans for repairs and improvements.

In his mind's eye, there was Lizzie seated next to him on the bed, on what would turn out to be her last day of life.

You never know, Jack, you might enjoy it too. You could really fix the place up. Even make the lighthouse work again.

"So Grand left you this place?" asked Mikki.

Jack broke free from his thoughts. "Yeah, she did."

"Well, why don't you sell it, then? We could certainly use the money."

"I can't. It's a legal thing. And I wouldn't have felt right selling it even if I could."

Mikki shrugged and leaned against the doorway, adopting a clearly bored look.

Jack glanced over at Cory, who'd nearly tumbled into the large trunk he'd opened in his eagerness. He came up wearing on old-fashioned top hat, black cloak, and a half mask covering the upper part of his face.

"Moo-ha-ha-ha," he said in a dramatically deep voice.

"That Corwee?" said Jackie, uncertainly, hugging his father tighter.

"That's Cory acting funny," said Jack encouragingly as he gently pried his youngest son's frantic fingers from around a patch of his hair.

Jack picked up a book and opened it, and his jaw dropped.

"What is it?" asked Cory, who had seen his reaction.

Jack held up the book. There was a bookplate on the inside cover.

"Property of Lizzie O'Toole," read Jack. "This was your mother's book," he said. "Maybe they all were." He looked excitedly around. "I bet this was your mom's room growing up."

Now Mikki stepped into the room and joined them. "Mom's room?"

Jack nodded and pointed eagerly to the desktop. "Look at that."

Carved into the wood were the initials *EPO*. Mikki looked at her dad questioningly.

He said animatedly, "Elizabeth Pinckney O'Toole. That was you mom's full name. Pinckney was Grand's maiden name. She kept her last name even after she married."

"Why did Mom leave her books behind?" she asked.

"Maybe she thought she would come back," replied Jack uncertainly.

"I remember her telling me about a beach house she grew up in, but she never really said anything else about it. Did you know much about it?"

"She told me about it. But I'd never been here before."

"Why'd she never bring us here?" Mikki asked.

"I know that she wanted to. In fact, she was planning to bring all of you here this summer after I . . . Anyway, that was her plan."

"Is that why we're here, then? Fulfilling Mom's wishes?"

"Maybe that's part of it."

Jackie tugged on his dad's ear.

"Corwee?" asked Jackie.

Jackie was pointing at his brother, who was now wearing a pink boa, long white gloves, and a tiara.

"Still Cory," said Jack, smiling broadly. "And obviously completely secure in his masculinity."

He glanced at Mikki, who was running her fingers over her mom's initials.

Jack looked out the window. "Hey, guys. Check this out."

The kids hurried to the window and stared up in awe at the lighthouse that rose into the air out on a rocky point next to the house.

"It's really close to the house," said Mikki.

Cory added, "Do you think it belongs to us too?"

Jack said, "I know it does. Your mom told me about it. It was one of her favorite places to go."

They rushed outside and over to the rocky point. The lighthouse was painted with black and white stripes and was about forty feet tall. He tried the door. It was locked, but he peered through the glass in the upper part of the door. He saw a spiral wooden staircase. There were boxes stacked against one wall, and everything was covered in dust.

"What a mess," said Mikki, who was looking through another pane of glass.

On the exterior wall of the lighthouse was an old, weathered sign. He scraped off some of the gunk and read, "Lizzie's Lighthouse." Jack stepped back and stared up at the tall structure with reverence.

Cory looked at the hand-painted sign. "How could this be Mom's lighthouse?"

"Well, it was one of her favorite places, like I said,"

answered his father, who was now circling the structure to see if there was another way to get in. "Isn't it cool?"

"It's just an old lighthouse, Dad," Mikki said.

He turned to look at her. "No, it was your *mom's* lighthouse. She loved it."

Jackie pulled on his dad's pants leg again. He pointed at the lighthouse.

"What dat?"

Cory said, "It's a lighthouse, Jackie. Big light."

"Big wight," repeated Jackie.

Jack gazed around at the property. "I'm sold."

"What?" exclaimed Mikki.

"This will be a great place to spend the summer."

"But, Dad," protested Mikki. "It's a dump. And my friends—"

"It's *not* a dump. This is where your mother grew up," he snapped. "And we're moving here." He paused and added in a calmer tone, "At least for one summer."

22

Back in Cleveland, they moved out of the rental and parked their few pieces of furniture at Sammy's place, because he'd decided to come with them to South Carolina.

"What am I gonna do by myself all summer?" he'd said when told of the family's plans. "And Sam Jr. expects the kids to be around now. Whines all the time when they're not here. I mean, I can get by without you folks, but it's the damn dog that troubles me."

They closed up Sammy's garage house and pushed Sam Jr.'s big butt into the VW, and off they went. Sammy drove the VW, and Jack followed in his pickup truck with Sammy's Harley tied down in the cargo bed. They made one stop, though, to Lizzie's grave. Jack knew it would be hard on everyone, but he also didn't want the kids to leave without going there to visit their mom.

They put fresh flowers in the vase, and each of the kids said something to their mother, though Mikki's remarks were inaudible. Jack stood behind them, trying to hold the tears back. When Jackie wanted to know where his mom was, Mikki told him that she was sleeping. Jackie lay down next to his mom's grave and started whispering things as though he didn't want to wake her. At that point Jack disappeared behind some bushes and cried into his hands.

They split the trip up into two days, spending the night in adjoining rooms at a motel outside of Winston-Salem, North Carolina. They left Sam Jr. in the van with the windows down and a big pan of water; he was too big to climb through the opening. But around midnight he started howling so mournfully that Jack and Sammy had to run out and bundle him into their room before anyone could see them. That night, Sam Jr. slept curled up around Jackie on a blanket on the floor.

Jack woke up early in the morning and went outside to get some fresh air. He found Mikki already fully dressed and leaning against the VW.

"What's up?" he asked, stretching out his back.

"Why are we doing this?" she said in a surly tone.

"Doing what?"

"You know what!"

He walked over to her. "What is your problem?"

"I don't have a problem. Do you?"

"What's that supposed to mean?"

"We just settled back in Cleveland, Dad. And now you're moving us down to South Carolina."

"Yeah, to the home where your mom grew up."

"Okay, Dad, but in case you didn't realize it, Mom's not there."

She turned and walked back to her room.

Jack stared after her, shook his head, and headed off to get ready for the rest of the trip.

They got an early start and arrived in Channing, South Carolina, before lunch. Jack had had the electricity and water turned back on at the beach house before they got there. He'd also found a cable TV provider, so when they hooked up the TV they'd brought, it actually worked. Huge TV watchers Jackie and Cory were immensely relieved by this development.

It didn't take them long to unload. They put the Harley under a side deck. As they were carrying things in, Jack found an envelope on the knotty pine kitchen table. It was addressed to him with a Post-it note on the outside from the lawyer, Royce Baxter. It read,

> *This is a letter that Ms. Cecilia left for you, with instructions to deliver it to you when you moved into the beach house.*

"Man," said Sammy, dumping his old army duffel bag on the floor and looking around. "This place is something else."

"This 'something else' needs a lot of work," said Jack. "But it's got great bones. I made a list when I was down here before. We'll need materials and a lot of sweat. There's a hardware store the lawyer recommended that's not too far from here."

Sammy looked at him curiously. "Fixing it up? You said you couldn't sell it."

"That's right, I can't."

"So why are you planning to fix it up?"

"Because Lizzie—I mean, because we might be staying down here."

"Staying down here? For how long?"

Jack didn't answer but pointed out the window.

Sammy exclaimed, "Is that a lighthouse?"

"Yep."

"Does it work?"

"No. But it used to. That's Lizzie's Lighthouse."

"Lizzie's Lighthouse?"

"Yeah. It was kind of her place."

Sammy eyed the letter that Jack was holding. "What's that?"

"Just something from Cecilia's lawyer." Jack stuffed the letter into his pocket, and they all spent the next several hours putting things away, cleaning up, and exploring. After that they changed into bathing suits. The kids sprinted toward the water, with Mikki in the lead, Cory second, and Jackie bringing up the rear. Sam Jr. stayed back with him, keeping pace with the chubby-legged three-year-old, who ran on his tiptoes. Sammy and Jack carried towels, a cooler, beach chairs, and an umbrella to stick into the sand. They'd found the chairs and umbrella in the lower level of the Palace.

After playing in the water for a while, Cory went up to the house and returned with a tattered old football.

"Hey, Dad," he called out. "Can you throw with me?"

Jack didn't look thrilled by the request; he was tired. However, right before he was about to decline, a memory struck him.

It had been a basketball, not a football. In his driveway. His father had driven up after work, and six-year-old Jack was bouncing his new ball. He'd asked his dad to play with him. He wasn't sure if his dad had even answered. All he'd remembered was the side door closing with a thud. And if that memory had stuck with him all these years?

He got up from his chair. "You're on, Cor."

Sammy said, "Okay, big guy, show your old man some moves."

They threw for more than an hour. Jack hadn't lost his touch from high school. And Cory, after a few dropped balls, started catching everything that came his way. Jack could see the athleticism showing through his son's chubby, prepubescent frame. Jackie, and even Mikki, finally joined them, and Jack ran them through some old high school football plays he remembered.

After everyone was sufficiently exhausted, Cory said, "Thanks, Dad, that was great."

Jack rubbed his son's head. "Nice soft pair of hands you got. Wish I had you on my football team in high school."

Cory beamed and Jackie squealed, "Me too?"

Jack snatched Jackie up, held him upside down, and ran to the water. "You too."

Hours later, the sun started to set while the kids were still running around in knee-deep water, building castles, chasing wide-butted Sam Jr., and throwing a Frisbee that they'd also found in the house. Sammy and Jack sat back in the tattered beach chairs, Jack with a Coke and Sammy with a Corona.

Sammy finally tipped his baseball cap over his eyes and leaned back, settling himself so deeply in the chair that his butt touched the sand. Jack drew the letter out of his pocket and opened it. In spidery handwriting, Cecilia sent her love and hope that Jack and the kids would find as much fun and contentment from the house as she and Lizzie had. As Jack read the letter it was as though Cecilia was talking to him in her richly soothing, southern cadence.

She wrote:

My life on earth is over of course, or else you wouldn't be reading this letter. But I had a fine, old run, did everything I wanted to do, and, hell, the things that might've got left out I didn't need anyway.

I'd never seen a little girl who loved the ocean and sand more than Lizzie. And she loved this old house, even though, as you know, it carries some bad memories. And Lizzie's Lighthouse, as she called it. That child was always up there. I think Mikki, Cory, and dear Jackie will love this place too; at least that's my hope. And I feel sure that you, Jack, will find some comfort and peace in the place where Lizzie grew up.

I know it has been a most difficult and heartbreaking time for you. I know that you loved Lizzie more than anyone could. And she loved you just as much back. Fate dealt you a terrible hand by separating you two long before you should have been. But remember that every day you wake up to those three darling children, you are waking up to the most precious things that you and Lizzie ever made together. Because of that, you will never be apart from the woman you love. That may not seem like nearly enough right now, when you want to be with her so badly. But as time goes by, you will realize that it will actually make all the difference in the world. It's not so much that time heals all wounds, honey, as it is that the passage of the years lets us make peace with our grief in our way.

I know they called you the miracle man after you got better. But just so you know, I considered you a miracle from the moment you came into Lizzie's life. And I know she felt the same way. You got a second chance of sorts, son, so you live your life good and well. And Lizzie will be waiting for you when your time has run too. And I'll probably come by for a cup of coffee myself. Until then, keep hugging those precious children and take care of yourself.

Love,
Cecilia

Jack slid the letter back in his pocket, drew a long breath, and wiped his eyes. Even though he had never been to this place before, he felt like he'd just come home. He rose, took off his shoes, and jogged out toward the water to be with his kids. When they were tired out and headed inside for a late dinner, Jack stayed behind, walking along the beach as the sun dropped into the horizon, burning the sky down to fat mounds of pinks and reds. The warm waters of the Atlantic washed over his feet. He stared out to sea, one of his hands absently feeling for the letter in his pocket. It had been a good first day.

"Hey, Dad!"

He turned to see Cory frantically waving to him from the rear screen porch.

He waved back. "Yeah, bud?"

"Jackie turned the hose on."

"Uhhh . . . okay?"

"After he dragged the other end in the house."

Jack started to walk fast to the Palace. "In the house? Where's Sammy?"

"In the bathroom with a magazine."

Jack started to jog. "Where's Mikki?"

Cory shook his head helplessly. "Dunno."

Jack started to run faster as he yelled, "Well, can't you turn the hose off or pull it out of the house?"

"I would, but the little knobby thing came off in my hand and Jackie won't let go of the end of the hose. He's a lot stronger than he looks." Cory's eyes grew a little wider. "Is it bad that stuff's starting to float, Dad?"

Oh, crap.

Jack started to sprint, rooster tails of sand thrown up behind him. "Jackie!"

My three precious children. This one's for you, Cecilia.

23

The next day, while Sammy stayed with the other kids, Jack and Mikki drove in the pickup truck to the hardware store in downtown Channing, about three miles from the beach house. Along the way, they reached a stretch of oceanfront that was lined with magnificent homes, estates really, thought Jack. There was serious money down here. If he could catch some work from some of these wealthy folks, it might really be good.

Mikki said, "Are those like condo buildings?"

"They're mansions. This is prime beachfront property here. Those places are worth millions each."

"What a waste. I mean, who needs that much room?" she said derisively.

He glanced at her. "Are you feeling better about things?"

"No."

As they passed one house that was even larger than the others, a teenage girl came out into the cobblestone driveway dressed in a bikini top and tiny shorts with the words HUG 'EM printed on the backside. She was blond and tanned and had the elegant bone structure of a model. She climbed into a Mercedes convertible about the same time a tall, lean, tousled-haired young man came hustling up the drive. He had on wakeboard shorts and a tank top. He hopped in the passenger seat, and the car roared off, pulling in front of their old truck and causing Jack to nearly run off the road.

Mikki rolled down the window and yelled, "Jerks!"

The girl made an obscene gesture.

"Catch up to them, Dad; I want to kick her butt."

"Since when did you develop such anger issues, my little miss sunshine?"

"What are—" She stopped when she saw him smiling.

She muttered, "Shut up."

They reached Channing and climbed out of the truck. Jack had on jeans and a white T-shirt and sneakers. Mikki was dressed in knee-length cotton shorts and a black T-shirt. Her skin was pale, and her hair was now partially green and purple. His daughter's supply of hair colors seemed endless.

Mikki looked around as Jack checked his list of supplies.

"Looks like something right out of Nick at Nite," she said. "Pretty old-fashioned place."

Jack looked around and had to admit, it was a little like stepping back in time. The streets were wide and clean and the storefronts well maintained. The shops were mostly mom-and-pops. No big-box retailers here, it seemed. A bank, grocery, large hardware store, barber's shop with a striped pole, restaurants, an ice cream parlor, and a sheriff's station with one police cruiser parked in front were all in his line of sight. They also saw a public library with a sign out front that advertised free Wi-Fi service inside.

Mikki said, "Well, at least we can get online here."

People walked by in shorts and sandals; some of the older ladies had scarves around their heads. One elderly gent had on seersucker shorts, white socks, and white sandals. Others rode bikes with wicker baskets attached to the fronts. A few people had dogs on leashes, and some kids ran up and down the street. Everyone was very tanned. There was also a sense of prosperity here. Most of the cars parked along the street were late-model luxury sedans or high-dollar convertibles. Some had out-of-state license plates, but most were from South Carolina. But then Jack noted dented and dirty pickup trucks and old Fords and Dodges rolling down the street. The people in those vehicles looked more like he did, Jack thought. Working stiffs.

They passed a shabby-looking building with a marquee out front that read, CHANNING PLAY HOUSE. An old man was sweeping the pavement in front of the double-door entrance. Next to the entrance was a glass ticket window. The man stopped sweeping and greeted them.

"What's the Channing Play House?" Jack asked.

"Back in its day it was one of the finest regional theater houses in the low country," said the man, who introduced himself as Ned Parker.

"Regional theater?" said Jack.

Parker nodded. "We had shows come all the way down from New York City to perform. Singers, dancers, actors; we had it all."

"And now?" Jack said.

"Well, we still have the occasional performance, but it's

nowhere near what it used to be. Too many video games and big-budget movies." He pointed at Mikki. "From your generation, missy."

Mikki pointed to the marquee, which read, CHANNING TALENT COMPETITION. "What's that?"

"Hold it every year in August. Folks compete. Any age and any act. Baton, dancing, fiddling, singing. Lot of fun. It's a hundred-dollar prize and your picture in the *Channing Gazette*."

They continued on, and Jack and Mikki went to the local, well-stocked hardware store and purchased what they needed. A young man who worked at the store helped Jack load the items. Jack noticed that the boy was giving Mikki far more attention than he was Jack. He stepped between the young man and his daughter. "Some of this stuff won't fit in my truck bed," Jack pointed out.

Before the helper could answer, a stocky man in his seventies with snow-white hair strolled out. He was dressed in pleated khaki pants and a dark blue polo shirt with the hardware store's name and logo on it.

He said, "That's no problem; we deliver. Can have it out there today. You're in the Pinckney place, right?"

Jack studied him. "That's right; how'd you know?"

He put out his hand and smiled. "You beat me to it. I was coming out to see you later today and formally introduce myself. I'm Charles Pinckney, Cecilia's 'little' brother." He turned to Mikki and extended his hand. "And this must be the celebrated Mikki. Cee wrote me often about you. Let me see, she said you could play a guitar better than anyone she'd ever heard and were as pretty as your mother. I haven't heard you play, but Cee was spot-on with her assessment of your beauty."

In spite of herself, Mikki blushed. "Thanks," she mumbled.

Pinckney looked at the young helper. "Billy, take the rest of these materials and set it up for delivery."

"Yes, sir, Mr. Pinckney." He hurried off.

Jack said, "Now I remember. You were at the funeral, but we didn't get a chance to talk."

Pinckney nodded slowly. "I'm the only one left now. Thought for sure Cee would outlive me, even though she was a lot older."

"There were ten kids? At least that's what Lizzie told me."

"That's right. Mother and Dad certainly did their duty. I was the closest with Cee. We talked just about every day. Feel like I lost my best friend."

"She was a fine lady. Really helped me out."

"She was one of a kind," agreed Pinckney. "She was duly proud of her heritage. Not many ladies of her generation kept their maiden name, but it wasn't a question for her. In fact, she told her husband he could change his surname to Pinckney if he wanted, but she wasn't switching." He chuckled at the memory.

"Sounds like Cecilia."

"She thought a lot of you. I suppose that's why she left you the Palace. She loved that place. Wouldn't have left it to just anyone."

"I appreciate that. But it came as a total shock. I knew about the place and all, but I'd never been here."

"Cee actually talked to me about it. I know she wanted

you to have it, and I was all for it. Especially after Lizzie died. She loved the place too, maybe more even than Cee."

Mikki, who'd been listening closely, added, "If she loved the place so much, why did they move to Cleveland?"

Pinckney said, "I think it had to do with Fred's work."

"People don't buy cars down here?"

"Mikki, knock it off," said her father.

"So why do you call it the Palace?" asked Mikki.

Pinckney grinned. "It was our mother's doing. Her mother and father, my grandparents, were quite the Bible thumpers, but she wasn't. Naming it the Palace made it seem like it was a casino or a saloon or something. It worked. Her parents never visited there, far as I know," he added with a smile.

"Sounds like my kind of woman," Mikki said tartly.

Pinckney looked at the materials in Jack's truck. "So, fixing the place up?"

"Yeah."

"Cee said you were great with your hands."

"If you hear of anyone who needs work done, let me know. I'm not in a position where I can just take the summer off. I've got a lot of mouths to feed."

"I'll put the word out. Good luck with the Palace. Love to see the old place like it used to be."

"Thanks," Jack said. "It has great bones, just needs some TLC."

"Don't we all," said Pinckney. "Don't we all."

24

"Friendly people," remarked Mikki grudgingly as they continued down the street.

"Southern hospitality, they call it. Hey, how about some lunch before we head back?"

"Dad, you don't have to—"

"It's just lunch, Mik. Work with me here, will you?"

"Fine," she said dully.

As they rounded the corner, the Mercedes sports car that had almost caused them to wreck earlier flew around the same corner. The girl's head was swaying to the music blasting from the car's radio. The same young man was in the front seat next to her.

Mikki yelled, "Hey!"

"Mik," said her dad warningly.

But she was already in the street flagging the car down. The girl hit her brakes and snapped, "What the hell do you think you're doing?"

"First, turn off that crap you think is music," said Mikki. The girl made an ugly face, but the guy hit the button and the sounds died.

"*You* cut us off earlier and almost made my dad roll his truck."

The girl laughed. "Is your hair naturally that color, or did someone throw up on it?"

The guy grimaced. "Tiff, knock it off."

The girl gave Mikki a condescending look and then laughed derisively. "Okay, whatever. Hey, sweetie-pie, now, why don't you go on off and play somewhere." She hit the gas, and they sped off.

"Creeps," Mikki screamed after them. She glared over at her dad. "Wow. So much for Southern hospitality."

When she saw the sign a few moments later, her face brightened. "Okay, *that* is the place for lunch."

Jack looked where she was pointing.

"Little Bit of Love Bar and Grill?" Jack read. "Why is that the place?"

"Come on, Dad, I have to see if this is what I think it is."

She hurried inside, and Jack followed. There were twenty retro tables with red vinyl covers on them and chairs with yellow vinyl covers. The floor was a crazy pattern of black-and-white square tiles. The walls were covered with posters of famous rock-and-roll bands. Behind the bar, which took up one entire wall, were acoustic, bass, and electric guitars along with various costumes actually worn by band members, all behind Plexiglas. Stenciled on another wall were lyrics from famous rock songs.

Mikki looked like she'd just discovered gold in a tiny coastal town in South Carolina. "I knew it. So cool."

Most of the tables were occupied, and the bar was doing a brisk business. Waiters and waitresses dressed in jeans and T-shirts were moving trays of food and drink from the kitchen to the patrons. Along another wall were old-fashioned pinball machines, all with a musical theme.

A woman about Jack's age headed toward them.

"Two for lunch?" the woman said.

Jack caught himself staring at her. She was tall and slim and had dark hair that curved around her long neck. Her eyes were a light blue, and when she smiled Jack felt his own mouth tug upward in response.

"Um, yeah," said Jack quickly. "Thanks."

They followed her to a table, and she handed them menus.

"I can take your drink order."

They told her what they wanted. She wrote it down and said, "Haven't seen you before."

Jack introduced himself and Mikki.

"I'm Jenna Fontaine," she said. "I own this pile of bricks."

"As soon as I saw the name, I just knew," said Mikki.

Jack looked at her. "What do you mean?"

Jenna and Mikki exchanged smiles. Mikki said, "Def Leppard, am I right?"

"You know your rock-and-roll lyrics." When Jack still looked puzzled, Jenna said, " 'Little Bit of Love' is a Def Leppard song."

"So you're into music?" said Jack.

"Yes, but not nearly as much as that guy."

She pointed to a tall, lanky teenager with long black hair who was setting plates full of food down at the next table.

"That's Liam, my son. Now, he's the musical madman in the family. When I decided to chuck the life of a big-city lawyer and move here and open a restaurant, the theme and décor were his idea."

Mikki eyed Liam and then turned back to her. "Does he play?"

"Just about any instrument there is. But drums are his specialty."

Mikki's eyes glittered with excitement for the first time since stepping foot in South Carolina.

"I take it you're into music too," said Jenna.

"You could say that," said Mikki modestly.

"So where y'all staying?"

"My great-grandma left us a house."

"Wow. That's pretty impressive. Well, enjoy your lunch."

She walked off, and Jack looked down at the menu but wasn't really seeing it.

Mikki finally touched his hand, and he jumped.

"Dad?"

"Yeah?"

"She's really pretty."

"Is she? I didn't notice."

"Dad, it's—"

"Mik, let's just get something to eat and get back, okay? I've got a lot of work to do."

After Mikki took refuge behind her menu, Jack snatched a glance at Jenna as she seated another party. Then he looked away.

25

It took several days of backbreaking work to thoroughly clean the house, and all the kids pitched in, although Mikki did so grudgingly and with a good deal of complaining. "Is this how the summer's going to go?" she said to her dad as she scrubbed down the kitchen sinks. "Me being a slave laborer?"

"If you think this is tough, join the army. There you clean the floor with a toothbrush, and it only takes about twelve hours, until they tell you to do it again," Jack told her. She glared at him darkly as he walked off with a load of trash.

They next attacked the outside, cleaning out flower beds, pruning bushes, clearing away dead plants, and power washing the decks and the outdoor furniture. The rest of the acreage was beyond their capability—and Jack's wallet.

With much tugging and cursing, Jack and Sammy were finally able to get the door to the lighthouse open. As Jack stepped into the small foyer, dust and disturbed spiderwebs floated through the air. He coughed and looked around.

The rickety steps looked in jeopardy of falling down. He looked through some of the boxes stacked against the wall. There was mostly junk in them, though he did find a pair of tiny pink sneakers that had the name "Lizzie" written on the sides in faded Magic Marker. He held them reverently and imagined his wife as a little girl prancing around in them on the beach. He looked through some other boxes and found a few things of interest. He carried them up to his bedroom.

They all trooped down to the beach that afternoon and ate lunch, letting the sun and wind wash over them. After the meal was over, Jack looked at Mikki, grinned, and said, "Let me show you something."

"What?"

"Stand up."

She did so.

"Okay, grab me."

"What?"

"Just come at me and grab me."

Mikki looked around, embarrassed, at the others. "Dad, what are you doing?"

"Just grab me."

"Fine." She rushed forward and grabbed him, or tried to. The next instant she was facedown on the sand.

She lay there for a second, stunned, then rolled over and scowled up at him. "Gee, Dad, thanks. That was really a great closer after a picnic on the beach."

He helped her up. "Let's do it again, and I'll show you exactly what I did."

"Why?" she asked. "Is this like National Kick Your Daughter's Butt Day and nobody told me?"

Sammy interjected. "He's showing you some basic self-defense maneuvers, Mik."

Mikki looked up at her dad. He said, "So you can handle yourself in certain situations. Without me helping," he added.

"Oh," she said, a look of understanding appearing on her face.

They went through the moves a dozen more times, until Mikki had first her dad, then Sammy, and even Cory lying facedown in the sand. Jackie begged until she did it to him too, and then started crying because he got sand in his eyes.

"Hello!"

They all turned to see Jenna Fontaine walking down the beach. She had on shorts and a tank top and a broad-brimmed sun hat. She was waving and holding up a picnic basket. "I brought you some things from the café."

Jack came forward. "There was no need to do that."

"No trouble. I know how it is coming to a new place." She showed him what was in the basket, and then Jack introduced her to Cory, Sammy, and Jackie. His youngest son hid behind his dad. She smiled and squatted down. "Well, hello, little man. You look just like your daddy."

"Daddy," said Jackie shyly, hiding his face.

Mikki asked, "So where do you live, Jenna?"

Jenna pointed to the south. "About a half mile that way. We have a rocky point too. So when you hit the rocks, our house is the pile of blue shingles with the vibrating roof."

"Vibrating roof?" said Mikki curiously.

Jenna looked at Jack. "It's another reason I stopped by. Charles Pinckney said you were a whiz at building things. He was the one who told me you were staying here. What I really need—to stop myself from either killing my son or committing myself to a mental institution—is a sound-proof room for his music studio."

"He has a music studio?" exclaimed Mikki.

"Well, he calls it that. Most of the equipment is second-hand, but he's got a lot of stuff. I don't understand most of what it does, but what I do know is it's killing my ears." She looked at Jack again. "Want to come by and give me an estimate?"

Jack looked uncertain for a moment but then said, "Sure, I'd be glad to."

"You want to stop by tomorrow evening? Liam will be there, and he can sort of tell you what he needs."

"It might be a little expensive," said Jack. "But we've done soundproofing before. You'll notice a big differ-ence."

"I think saving my hearing and my sanity is worth any price. Say about eight?"

"That'll be fine," said Jack.

Jenna told them her address, waved, and headed off.

Jack watched her go. When he turned back, he saw Mikki and Sammy staring at him. Jack said nervously, "Uh, I've got some stuff to do."

He handed the picnic basket to Mikki and trudged back to the Palace.

Sammy looked at Mikki. "Is he okay?"

Mikki glanced in Jenna's direction, then up to her

dad, who was just entering the house. "I don't know," she said.

Jack fell asleep that night with the tiny pair of pink sneakers on his chest.

26

Mikki had insisted on coming along with Jack to the Fontaines' house, so Sammy stayed behind to watch the boys. They drove there in Jack's pickup truck.

Jenna met them at the door and ushered them in. The house was old but well maintained, and the interior was surprising. Instead of a typical beach look, it was decorated in a Southwestern style, with solid, dark, and what looked to be handcrafted furniture. There were textured walls faux painted in salmon and burnt orange, oil paintings depicting both snowcapped mountains and smooth deserts, and brightly colored woven rugs with geometric patterns.

Jenna sat across from him. Jack ran his gaze over her and then looked away. She was wearing white capri pants and a pale blue pullover, and her feet were bare.

"Nice place," said Jack.

"Thanks. We tried to make it feel like home."

"Where's that?" asked Mikki as she looked around. "Arizona? I was just there recently."

Jenna laughed. "I've never been to Arizona or the

Southwest in general. That's why I decorated the house this way. Probably as close as I'll ever get, and I love the look and feel of it. We originally came from Virginia. I went to college and law school up there. Ended up in D.C., though."

"You look pretty young to have a teenager," said Mikki.

"Mik!" her father began crossly, but Jenna laughed.

"I'll take that as a huge compliment. Truth is, I had Liam while I was in high school." She pursed her lips but then smiled. "The best thing that came out of that marriage was Liam."

"So how did you end up down here?" asked Jack.

"Got tired of the rat race in D.C. I'd made really good money and invested it well. We came down to Charleston one summer, took a drive, happened on Channing, and fell in love with it." She glanced keenly at Jack. "When I talked to Charles Pinckney, he told me about his sister leaving you the Palace. It's a great old place. Never been inside, but I've always loved that lighthouse."

"Yeah, it's pretty cool," said Mikki, looking at her dad.

"My wife grew up in that house," said Jack.

"Charles told me about that too." She paused and added solemnly, "And I'm very sorry for your loss."

"Thanks," said Jack quietly.

Jenna stood and reassumed a cheery air. "Well, do you want to see the mad musician's space?"

Mikki jumped up. "Absolutely."

Mikki could see at a glance that it was set up as a recording studio, albeit on a tight budget. To her expert eye, the soundboard, mixing devices, mikes, and the like were old and looked jury-rigged. She knew because she and her band had done the very same thing. New equipment was far too expensive. A piano keyboard was against one wall; a bass guitar sat in a stand in a corner. A banjo and a fiddle hung on hooks on the wall.

And yet there were no sheets of music. No songbooks.

"Where's Liam?" Mikki asked. "I thought you said he'd be here."

"He's on his way. He was taking some inventory at the restaurant. What will you be next year, a junior?"

"Yeah."

"Liam too. He goes to Channing High. Only high school in town."

"He's a big kid," said Jack. "Does he play ball?"

Jenna smiled and shook her head. "He's a good athlete, but this"—she pointed at the room—"this is where his heart is."

Mikki slid over to the bass guitar. "Do you think he'd mind?"

"Go for it."

Mikki strapped the guitar on, placed her fingers, and started to play.

"Wow," said Jenna. "That's really good."

She started to take off the guitar, but a voice said, "Play those last two chords again."

They all turned to see Liam standing in the doorway. He had on wire-rimmed glasses and a T-shirt that said SAVE THE PLANET, CUZ I STILL LIVE HERE.

"Liam, I didn't hear you come in," said his mother. "Everything okay at the Little Bit?"

"A place for everything, and everything in its place."

He looked at Mikki again. "So knock those last two chords out."

Surprised, but pleased at his request, she did so. The sound rocked the room again.

He walked over to her and placed her index finger on the guitar neck in a slightly different spot. "Try that; it'll give the sound more depth," he said.

Her grin disappeared, and she flushed angrily. "I know how to place my fingers. I've been playing since I was eight."

He seemed unfazed by her hostility. "So let me hear it now."

"Fine, whatever." She checked the new position of her index finger and played the chord. Her eyes displayed her amazement. The sound was far richer. She looked at him with new respect. "How did you figure that one out?"

He held up his hand. His fingers were amazingly long and the tips heavily calloused. "Anatomical."

"What?"

"The fingertip has different strength points on the surface. Once you understand where they are and place your fingers accordingly, the tightness on the strings is increased. Gives a fuller sound because there's less vibration coming off the neck."

"You worked that out on your own?"

"Nope. I'm not that smart. Read about it in a article in *Rolling Stone*," he said. "So what's your name?"

"Mikki Armstrong. That's my dad."

Jack and Liam shook hands.

"Mr. Armstrong is here to see if he can save my hearing," said Jenna.

Jack said, "Just call me Jack."

Liam grinned. "Think you can help Mom out? I don't want her going deaf on me. But then again, that might have its advantages."

Jenna smacked him lightly on the arm. "Don't make me put you over my knee at your age."

Jack surveyed the room and then went around the space knocking on the walls. "Drywall on two-by-four studs set at standard width." He reached up and tapped the low ceiling at regular intervals. "Same here. Yeah, I can handle it if the hardware store has what I need."

Jenna looked impressed. "When can you start?"

"Soon as I get materials. I'll work up an estimate so you know how big a hit your pocketbook will take."

Mikki blurted out, "My dad is great at this stuff. He can build anything."

Jenna smiled. "I believe it."

Mikki eyed the room. "Liam, where's your music?"

He tapped his head. "All up here."

"But what about new pieces? You need sheet music to learn them."

"I can't read music. I play by ear."

"Are you kidding?"

He grinned. "Want to test me?"

She looked down at the bass guitar she was still holding. When she saw what it was, she exclaimed, "This is a Gibson EB-3 from the late sixties. Jack Bruce from Cream played one. It's vintage. How'd you score it?"

"EBay. Saved up two summers for it. Got a great deal. Its box is so smooth, and the sound is so pure. I think it's the best four-string ever made."

Jenna looked at Jack. "I don't know about you, but I don't speak this language. You want some coffee while our kids talk shop?"

Jack hesitated, but after a pleading look from Mikki he said, "Sure."

After they left, Mikki said, "Okay, Mr. Play-by-Ear, here's your test." She played a minute-long piece of a song she'd recently composed. She handed him the Gibson.

"Okay, go for it."

He strapped on the bass, set his fingers, and played back her song, note for perfect note.

Mikki exclaimed, "You're like Mozart only on percussion and bass. Ever been in a band?"

He scoffed. "There are no bands in Channing."

"Who're your favs?"

"Hendrix, AC/DC, Zeppelin, Plant, Aerosmith, to name a few."

"Omigod, they're like my top five of all time."

Liam picked up his drumsticks. "Want to score a few sets?"

She strapped the bass back on. "I'm dying to try out my new fingertip strength points."

27

Jenna and Jack were sitting out on her rear deck with their mugs of coffee when the music started up. The deck flooring really did appear to vibrate.

"Now do you see why I need the soundproofing?" she asked, covering her ears.

Jack nodded and laughed. "Yeah. I get it. We finally had to get Mikki to start practicing at another kid's house back in Cleveland. Even with that I'm not sure I can hear out of my right ear."

"The long-suffering parents of musical prodigies. Want to carry our coffee down to the beach? My head is already hurting."

They strolled along the sand together. It was well after eight but still light outside. A jogger passed them heading in the opposite direction, and an elderly couple were throwing tennis balls to a chubby black Lab. As the dog ran after a ball, the man and woman held hands and walked along.

Jenna eyed them and said, "That's how it's supposed to turn out."

Jack glanced at her. "What?"

She pointed at the couple. "Life. Marriage. Growing old together. Someone to hold hands with." She smiled. "A fat dog to throw balls to."

Jack watched the old couple. "You're right, it is supposed to turn out that way."

"So your wife grew up here?"

"Yeah."

"Is that why you came down here? Memories?"

"I guess so," Jack said slowly. He stopped and turned to her. "And my wife planned to bring the kids down here this summer. So I thought I'd do it for her. And I wanted to see the place too."

"You'd never been here before?"

Jack shook his head. "My wife had a twin sister who died of meningitis. They lived here for a while longer. But then I guess it just wasn't that . . . um . . . good," he finished, a bit awkwardly.

"I'm so sorry."

They started walking again. She said, "So how're the kids dealing with the move and all?"

"With three kids, they all sort of handle things differently."

"Makes my job seem simple. I've only got one."

"Well, Mikki is pretty independent. Just like her mom."

"She seems fantastic. Liam is not easily impressed when it comes to music."

"She and I butt heads a lot. Teenage girls. They need . . . stuff that dads just aren't good at."

"I feel that deficiency with Liam too, just on the flip side."

"He looks like he's doing fine."

"Maybe in spite of me."

"So you're divorced now?"

"Long time. Right after Liam was born. My ex moved to Seattle and has nothing to do with him. I just have to put it down to my poor choice in men."

"How'd you manage college and law school with a kid?"

"My parents were a huge help. But sometimes I'd take Liam to class with me. You do what you have to do."

Jack stopped, picked up a pebble off the beach, and threw it into the oncoming breakers. "Yeah, you do."

Jenna sipped her coffee and watched him. "So are y'all just down here for the summer?"

"That's the plan. Look, I'll write up that estimate and get it to you tomorrow."

"I tell you what. Why don't I just give you a check tonight to help cover the materials and you can get started."

"You don't want an estimate?" he said in surprise.

"No."

"Why not?"

"I trust you."

"But you don't know me."

"I know enough."

"Okay, thanks for the coffee." He smiled. "And the trust."

"Stop by the Little Bit again. Have to try the killer onion rings."

As they walked back, she said, "I really am sorry about your wife."

"Me too." Jack glanced back at the old couple still walking slowly hand in hand. "Me too."

28

Mikki awoke the next morning in her attic bedroom. She stretched, yawned, and sat back, bunching her pillows around her. Then she rose, picked up her guitar, and started playing a new song she'd been working on, using the new technique Liam had taught her. The long fingers of her left hand worked the neck of the instrument, while her right hand did the strumming. She put down the guitar, went to her desk, picked up some blank music sheets, and started making notations and jotting down some lyrics. Then she started singing while she played the guitar.

A minute later, someone knocked on her door.

Startled, she stopped singing and said, "Yeah?"

"Are you decent?" Jack called through the door.

"Yes."

He opened the door and came in. He had a breakfast tray in hand. Bacon, eggs, an English muffin smeared with Nutella, and a glass of milk. He set it down in front of her. Mikki put the guitar aside.

"How'd you know I like Nutella?"

"Did some good old-fashioned reconnaissance." He pulled a rickety ladder-back chair up next to the bed.

"What?"

"Okay, I looked in your room back in Cleveland. Dig in before it gets cold."

Mikki began to eat. "Where's everybody else?" she asked.

"Still sleeping. It's early yet. Did you have fun last night with Liam?"

Mikki swallowed a piece of bacon and exclaimed, "Omigod, Dad, he is, like, so awesome. That thing he showed me with the fingers, the pressure points? It works. We played some sets together, and he likes the bands I like, and he's funny, and—"

"So is that a yes?"

"What?"

"You did have a good time last night?"

She grinned sheepishly. "Yeah, I did. How did things go with Jenna?"

"I agreed to do the job. She gave me a check to start. Sammy and I will get the materials and go from there."

"She seems really cool. Don't you think?"

"She's very nice." Jack slipped something from his pocket and handed it to her. "I found this in a box in the lighthouse this morning."

"The lighthouse? Pretty early to have already been out there."

"Look at the picture."

Mikki held it tightly by the edges, her brow furrowing. "Is this Mom?"

"Yep. There's a date on the back. Your mom was right

about your age in that photo. It was taken down here at the beach. It must've been the summer before she moved to Cleveland. The lighthouse is in the background." He paused. "You see, don't you?"

"See what?"

"That you look just like her."

Mikki squinted at the image of her mom. "I do?"

"Absolutely you do. Well, except for the weird hair color and goth clothes. Your mom was more into pony-tails and pastels."

"Ha-ha, real funny. And my clothes are not goth, which is, like, so last century anyway."

"Sorry. Why don't you finish your breakfast and we can go for a walk on the beach before things get going."

"Is this part of you being a dad thing?" she asked bluntly.

"Partly, yeah."

"And the other part?"

"I had a long time to be alone after you guys left, and I hated it. I never want to be alone again."

As they hit the sand, the sun was slowly coming up and the sky was a sheet of pink and rose with the darkened mass of the ocean just below it. There was a wind that had dispelled most of the night's heat. Gulls swooped and soared over the water before diving, hitting the surface and sometimes coming away with breakfast in the form of a wriggling fish.

"It's really different down here," said Mikki, finally breaking the silence.

"Ocean, sand, hotter."

"Not just that."

"I guess no matter where we'd be right now, it would be different," he replied.

"I wake up sometimes and think she's still here."

Jack stopped walking and looked out to the ocean. "I wake up every morning expecting to see her. It's only when she's not there that I realize . . ." He started to walk again. "But down here, it's different. I feel . . . I feel closer to her somehow."

Mikki gazed worriedly at her dad but said nothing.

They threw pebbles into the water and let the fingers of the tides chase them up and down the sand. Mikki found a shell that she pocketed to later show her brothers.

"You've got a great voice," he said. "I was listening outside the door this morning."

"It's okay," she said modestly, although it was clear his praise had pleased her.

"Do you want to study music in college?"

"I'm not sure I want to go to college. You didn't."

"That's true."

"I'm not sure the sort of stuff I want to play would be popular in college curriculums or in the mainstream music industry."

"What kind is it?"

"Are you asking just to be polite, or do you really want to know?"

"Look, do you have to make everything so complicated? I just want to know."

"Okay, okay. It's very alternative, edgy beats, non-traditional mix of instrumentals. No blow-you-out-of-the-house cheap synthesizer tricks. And no lollipop lyrics. Words that actually mean something."

Jack was impressed. "Sounds like you've given this a lot of thought."

"It's a big part of my life, Dad; of course I've thought about it."

"It's nice to have something you're so passionate about."

"Were you ever passionate about anything?"

"Not until I met your mother; then she sort of took up all the passion I had."

Mikki made a face. "That is, like, so gross to tell your own daughter."

"I didn't mean it like that. Before your mom came along, I was just drifting. I had my sports and all that. But not much else. And my dad was dying of cancer."

"But you still had your mom."

"Yeah, but we had our issues."

"Didn't get along? Like you and me?" she added, poking him in the side.

"Let's just say I spent a lot more time at the O'Tooles' instead of my house."

"What was the issue?"

His expression turned serious. "I've never really talked about this with anyone, except your mother. There were no secrets between us."

"Fine, I was just curious. You don't have to tell me."

Jack stopped walking, and she pulled up too.

"Okay, full confessional. It got to the point where I really wondered if my mom actually loved me."

Mikki looked shocked. "She had to love you. She was your mother."

"You'd think so, wouldn't you?"

"Why did you think she didn't?"

"Probably because she left when I was seventeen. Right after my dad died."

"What? Nobody ever told me that."

"Well, it's not the sort of thing you announce to the world."

"What happened?"

"She met some guy and moved to Florida. She kept the house in Cleveland, and I lived there until I married your mom and enlisted. She died in a boating accident when you were still a baby and I was still in the army."

Mikki looked at him in amazement. "You lived there, what, by yourself?"

"Didn't have any other relatives, so yeah."

"But you weren't even out of high school yet."

"But I was over sixteen. It wasn't like foster care was an option. I got part-time jobs to pay for expenses."

"My God, Dad. I mean, you were all by yourself."

"*You* like to spend time alone."

"Yeah, but I could come downstairs and everybody would be there."

"Well, I had your mom. She was my best friend. She helped me through some really tough times."

When they got back to the Palace, Mikki said, "Thanks for the walk and talk."

"Hope it's one of many this summer."

As she ran up the deck steps ahead of her father, Sammy appeared from around the side of the house. "You got an early start." He glanced at Mikki as she went into the house. "Little father-daughter time?"

"She's a pretty amazing kid, Sammy. Half her life I was

carrying a gun for my country. The other half I was driving nails. I've got a lot to learn about her."

"Probably why I never got married," said Sammy. "Too complicated."

"You ever regret it? No kids, no wife?"

"I didn't, until I started hanging out with you Armstrongs."

29

Later that week, before her dad left for work and she had to watch the kids, Mikki pulled on some shorts, tennis shoes, and a tank top, stretched her legs, and headed to the beach to run. She was naturally athletic, taking after her dad, but she'd never gone out for any school sports teams. The jocks at her school were obnoxious, she thought. And she disliked the competitiveness of sports. She simply liked to run, not try to beat someone running next to her.

She headed down the beach, listening to tunes on her iTouch. She'd put on lots of sunblock because her skin was still pale from the bleak Ohio winter and cold spring. The sun felt great; the views were breathtaking. Her arms pumped, and her long legs ate up ground at a rapid pace. People were fishing from the shore; kids were playing in the sand; teenagers were body surfing in the rough breakers. Though it was still early, a few people were already lying out on beach blankets, reading and talking.

"What the—" she gasped.

The guy had run right up beside her.

"Hey," he said, grinning.

Mikki saw that it was the boy from the Mercedes convertible. He had on board shorts, no shirt. He was lean and muscled. Up close he looked like a Ralph Lauren model, which meant she instantly despised him.

She took out her earbuds, though she kept running.

"The beach is pretty wide," she said back, trying to look indifferent, "so pick another spot."

"I'm Blake Saunders." As they ran, he put out his hand to shake.

She ignored it. "Good for you."

"Can we stop running for a sec?"

"Why?"

"It's important."

She stopped, and he did too.

"Okay, what?" she demanded.

"I wanted to apologize for what happened the other day. Tiff can be a real piece of work."

"Tiff?"

"Tiffany, Tiffany Murdoch."

Mikki snorted. "She looks like a Tiffany."

"Yeah, she's pretty spoiled. Her dad was some big-shot investment guy in New York before they moved down here and built the biggest house on the beach."

"So why do you hang out with her?"

"She can be fun."

Mikki gave him a scathing look. "Oh yeah, I'm sure she can be fun." She slapped her behind. *"Hug 'em?"*

"No, I didn't mean it that way."

Mikki said, "I'm going to finish my run."

"Mind if I jog along with you? I'm the quarterback on

the high school football team and I'm trying to keep in shape."

"Suit yourself, QB."

"And your name?"

She hesitated but then said, "Mikki. Mikki Armstrong."

They ran on.

"So what grade are you in?"

"Junior next year."

"I'll be a senior. So you guys just moved down here?" said Blake.

"Yeah, from Cleveland."

"Wow, Cleveland."

She looked to see if he was making fun of her. "Yeah, Cleveland. Got a problem with that?"

"No, I meant that was cool. You have a pro football team. Although no more LeBron James."

"Yeah, but we have the Rock and Roll Hall of Fame."

"That's cool. You play music?"

"Some, yeah. Mostly guitar. And bass."

"I'd like to hear it sometime."

"Why?"

"You're hard to get to know."

"Yes, I am."

"Maybe we can hang out sometime."

"Again, why? If Tiffany is your type, it would be a waste of time. Because I'm not a *Tiffany* by any stretch of the imagination."

"Because it's nice to meet some people who aren't from around here. Small towns can be pretty boring."

"Well, I plan to run on the beach about this time every day."

"Great. Maybe next time I won't get the evil eye as much."

He playfully punched her in the arm, and Mikki let slip a tiny smile.

"Finally, a crack in the armor," he kidded.

"Do you know Liam Fontaine?" she asked.

"Yeah, he's cool but a little odd."

"Odd? Why?"

"No sports, though I know he's a good athlete."

"Well, he works at the restaurant and he has his music. Not much time for anything else."

"Sounds like you already know him."

"I met him. He's an amazing musician."

Blake grinned. "Maybe you should ask him out."

"Please. I don't really know him."

"That's all I'm asking for. A chance to get to know you."

Later, they finished their run. Blake said, "See you tomorrow?"

"Okay."

"You're a good runner."

"So are you," she conceded.

"Have a good one."

He took off at a full sprint, and she caught herself admiring his tanned, muscled back and legs. Then she headed on to the Palace.

30

At the Channing hardware store, Jack and Sammy loaded up the truck with the materials for the work at Jenna Fontaine's house. Charles Pinckney came outside to see them, and Jack introduced him to Sammy.

"Appreciate the referral, Charles," said Jack, as he hoisted another box into the truck bed. "And thanks for putting a rush on these materials for me. I know it's not stuff you'd normally keep in stock."

"Glad to do it. And Jenna is a fine person. She runs the most popular restaurant in town, so she can be a great lead for other work."

"And gorgeous to boot," said Sammy.

Both men were wearing cargo shorts, tank tops, and work boots. It was still morning, but the temperature was already in the eighties.

"Charles, I had a question," said Jack. "I was wondering about the lighthouse. Its history."

"My father built it along with the house. It was originally listed on the official navigational charts. But one day it just stopped working."

"Anybody ever try to get it running again?"

Pinckney looked surprised. "Why, no. What would be the point? By the time it broke, they didn't use it for a navigational aid anymore."

"Just asking," said Jack.

He and Sammy left Pinckney and drove on to Jenna's house. She'd already left for the restaurant, but she'd pinned a note to the front door telling them that the entrance on the lower level was unlocked. They hauled the materials in, and after covering all of Liam's musical instruments and the furniture with drop cloths, they began to tear out the existing drywall. The plan was to backfill the wall and ceiling spaces with soundproofing materials and then replace the original drywall with specialized denser material that would also act as a sound block.

Around one o'clock they heard someone upstairs.

"Hello?" It was Jenna's voice.

"Down here," called out Jack.

She came down the steps carrying a large white bag.

She held up the bag. "Well, I hope you boys haven't eaten yet."

"You didn't have to do that," said Jack.

"Well, I'm glad you did. I'm hungry," exclaimed Sammy.

Jenna smiled and unpacked two large turkey and cheese sandwiches, chips, pickles, cookies, and sodas on a table against a wall. While she did this, she gazed around the room. "Boy, you two have been busy."

Jack nodded. "It's going better than I thought it would. That means it'll be less expensive for you."

Sammy put down his tools, wiped off his hands on a clean rag, walked over, and examined the food she'd brought. He bowed formally and said, "You are a goddess sent from above for two weary travelers."

Jenna laughed. "It's so nice to meet a real gentleman."

Jack rinsed off his hands using a bottle of water and a rag and sat down across from Sammy. He looked at Jenna. "You didn't bring yourself anything?"

"I always eat early before the lunch crowd gets in. Place is packed. Always is during the summer."

"Looks like you have a gold mine there," Jack noted.

She sat on a small hassock, crossed her legs, and said, "We do fine. But the profit margins are small and the hours are long."

"Buddy of mine ran a restaurant," said Sammy after he swallowed a bite of his sandwich. "Said it was the hardest work he'd ever done."

Jack munched on a chip and said, "So why do you do it, then, Jenna?"

Jenna had on a black skirt and a white blouse. She'd slipped her heels off and was rubbing her feet. Jack's gaze dipped to her long legs before quickly retreating. If she noticed, she didn't react.

"I'm my own boss. I'm a people person. I admit I get a kick out of walking into the Little Bit and knowing it's mine. And it's something I can leave for Liam, if he wants it, that is. He'll probably be off touring with a band. But it'll be there for him."

"Nice legacy for your kid," said Sammy.

"I know about Jack, but do you have any children, Sammy?"

"No, ma'am. Uncle Sam was my family. That was enough."

"Uncle Sam? You mean?"

Jack answered. "Sammy was in the army. 'Nam. After that, Delta Force."

Jenna looked at Sammy in awe. "That's pretty impressive."

Sammy wiped his mouth with a napkin. "Well, Jack won't tell you about himself because he's too damn modest. So I'll do the honors."

"Sammy," Jack said in a warning tone. "Don't."

"Two Purple Hearts and a Bronze Star," Sammy said, giving Jack a defiant look. He pointed to Jack's bullet wound on his arm. "Purple for that." He pointed to Jack's scarred calves. "And a Purple for that. And the Bronze for saving a bunch of his buddies from an ambush that almost cost him his life."

Jenna gazed at Jack, her lips slightly parted, her eyes wide. "That's amazing."

"What it was, was a long time ago." Jack finished his meal and balled up the paper, putting it in the white bag she'd brought. "Really appreciate the lunch, Jenna." He rose. "We need to get back to work, Sammy."

Jack started cutting out more of the walls.

Jenna eyed Sammy.

In a low voice, he said, "He's a complicated guy."

As Jenna watched Jack attack the walls, she said, "I'm beginning to see that."

31

Later that night, after the kids were asleep, Jack grabbed a flashlight and headed out to the lighthouse. He opened the door and shone his light around. He'd already gone through the boxes lining the walls, but now he walked up the rickety stairs carefully, testing each step before continuing on.

He heard scurrying feet and flashed his light in time to see a mouse rush past his foot. He kept going as the old wooden stairs creaked under his weight. He finally reached the top platform, directly under the access door that led into the space where the light mechanism was located.

As Jack moved his light around, it picked out things in the darkness; the images flew by like a reel of black-and-white film on an old projector. He stopped at one point and drew closer. It was an old mattress. He knelt down and touched it. Sitting on the mattress with its back against the wall of the lighthouse was an old doll. Jack reached down and picked it up. The doll's hair was grimy and moldy, its face stained with dirt and water. Still, he looked at it as though it were a bar of gold. He *knew* this had been

Lizzie's. He'd seen her holding it in an old photo of her as a child.

He stood and moved the light around some more. His beam froze on a picture that had been drawn with what looked to be black Magic Marker on the wall. It was a little girl with pigtails and a huge smile. Under the figure was the name "Lizzie." Next to the picture of the girl was a drawing of the lighthouse with the beam on. Above that was written the word "Heaven." Jack noted that the lighthouse beam had been extended out to encompass the word.

He was about to move on when his light caught on something else. He knelt down and held the flashlight close to the wall. The image had been partially rubbed out, but Jack could still tell what it was. It was another drawing of a little girl, with pigtails. At first Jack thought it was merely a second drawing of Lizzie. But as he eyed the faded image more closely, he saw there was a major difference. In the drawing the little girl wasn't smiling. Her mouth pointed downward.

"Not a happy girl," whispered Jack. His gaze shot lower. He edged closer to read what was written there on the wall. Three letters: "T-i-l."

It had to refer to Tillie, Lizzie's twin sister, who'd died of meningitis. He sat back on his haunches and viewed the drawing in its entirety. The remaining letters had faded too badly to be read.

The drawing of the beam of light from the lighthouse extended outward but fell short of encompassing the image of Tillie. She remained firmly in the dark.

"You never found Heaven, Lizzie. And you never found Tillie."

Jack felt tears creep to his eyes, and his lungs suddenly couldn't get enough air.

Holding the doll under one arm, he pushed open the door that led to the catwalk encircling the top exterior of the lighthouse. Jack stared up at the dark sky. Heaven *was* up there somewhere. And, of course, so was Tillie.

And now Lizzie too.

He held up his hand and waved to her. And then, feeling slightly foolish, he let his hand drop but continued to stare up. Right this minute his wife seemed so close to him. He shut his eyes and conjured her face. It couldn't possibly be more than six months since he'd heard her voice and her laugh, felt her skin or watched her smile.

It can't possibly be that long, Lizzie.

He reached up. His finger covered a star that was probably a trillion light-years away and the size of the sun. But his finger covered it all. How close Lizzie must be to him, if he could cover up an entire star with his finger.

Heaven must be right up there.

He carefully set the doll down and slipped the envelope from his pocket. It had the number three written on the outside. The letter was dated December twentieth. He already knew what it said. He'd memorized every word of every letter. But if Lizzie could not read them, he would do it for her.

Dear Lizzie,

Christmas is five days away and it's a good time to reflect on life. Your life. This will be hard. Hard for me to write and hard for you to read, but it needs to be said. You're young and you have many years ahead of you. Cory and Jackie will be with you for many more years. And even Mikki will benefit. I'm talking about you finding someone else, Lizzie.

I know you won't want to at first. You'll even feel guilty about thinking about another man in your life, but, Lizzie, it has to be that way. I cannot allow you to go through the rest of your life alone. It's not fair to you, and it has nothing to do with the love we have for each other. It will not change that at all. It can't. Our love is too strong. It will last forever. But there are many kinds of love, and people have the capacity to love many different people. You are a wonderful person, Lizzie, and you can make someone else's life wonderful. Love is to be shared, not hidden, not hoarded.

Jack paused for a moment as a solitary tear plunked down on the paper.

And you have much love to share. It doesn't mean you love me any less. And I certainly could never love you more than I already do. But in your heart you will find more love for someone else. And you will make him happy. And he will make you happy. And Jackie especially will have a father to help him grow into a good man. Our son deserves that. Believe me, Lizzie, if it could be any other way, I would make it so. But you have to deal with life as it comes. And I'm trying my best to do just that. I love you too much to accept anything less than your complete and total happiness.

 Love,
 Jack

Jack slipped the letter into the envelope and put it back in his pocket. He picked up the doll and stared out over the ocean for a long time. He finally walked back down the stairs and out into the humid night air. He stared up at the lighthouse.

Lizzie's Lighthouse.

He walked back to the house, his heart full of thoughts of what should have been.

32

Mikki rolled over in her bed. Outside she could hear the breakers. The physics of waves crashing on sand had been completely foreign to her a short while ago. Now she'd grown so accustomed to their presence that she wasn't sure she ever wanted to be without the sound.

She yawned, sat up, and did a prolonged cat stretch. Glancing at her clock, she saw it was six thirty a.m. She liked to take her run around now so she could get back before her dad and Sammy left for work.

She slipped off the long-sleeve T-shirt she normally slept in and pulled on running shorts, a tank shirt, ankle socks, and sneakers. She made a pit stop at the bathroom and tied her hair back in a ponytail. On the way out she looked in on both her brothers, who shared a room at the end of the hall next to her dad's bedroom. They were both still asleep. Cory was sprawled on his stomach, while Jackie was on his back, but with both legs bent so his covers made a tent.

She smiled as she listened to her brothers' gentle snores.

As Mikki passed her dad's room, she could hear him stirring.

She rapped on the door. "Dad, I'm going running. I'll put the coffee on. Be back in about an hour."

"Okay. Thanks," came his sleepy response.

She put on the coffee and laid out two mugs for her dad and Sammy. The men got their own breakfast, but Mikki had been making her brothers' meals. Sometimes it was just cereal. But other times she'd pull out the black skillet and whip up eggs, bacon, and something called grits, apparently a Southern thing, which her brothers had instantly loved but she couldn't stand.

She bounced down the steps and passed through the dunes to the flat beach. She did a more thorough stretch and started her run. She kept to the hard, compacted sand, and her long strides carried her down the beach at a rapid clip. About a half mile into her run, Blake joined her. They talked as they ran. All normal subjects that teens gabbed about. She found herself liking him more, in spite of his association with someone like Tiffany Murdoch. He made her laugh.

He said his good-byes a few miles later and jogged back up to the street.

Mikki made her turn to head back toward the Palace when she saw someone out in the surf.

"Liam?"

She jogged down closer to the edge of the water as he stood up and waved.

"Early-morning swim?" she asked.

He high-stepped through the surf to stand next to her.

"Musicians and short-order cooks come here to keep in shape. And I'm not into running."

She smiled and looked out at the water.

"My mom taught me to swim in a wading pool in our backyard," she said.

"Always a good skill to have." He brushed sand out of his hair. "You look like you're working out. Don't let me interrupt you."

"Just a few more miles to go."

"Miles! I'd be puking."

"Come on! You look like you're in awesome shape."

"If I keep eating at the Little Bit, they'll have to start wheeling me out of the kitchen."

"My dad says the soundproofing is coming along."

"Then we can really jam. And my mom won't kill me."

"Looking forward to it."

Back at the Palace, Mikki showered and changed her clothes. Her dad had surprised her by making breakfast for everyone. Pancakes and ham.

"I help," announced Jackie. He proceeded to pour about a gallon of syrup on his dad's pancakes.

Before her dad and Sammy left, Mikki ran back up to her closet to get some things to take down to the beach later with the boys. Her bag spilled over, though, and when she started crawling around the floor picking things up, she noticed a loose floorboard near the rear of the closet. When she pressed the board up, she saw the edge of the photo. She pulled it out and studied the images. She went downstairs and showed her dad, who was finishing up his breakfast.

Jack looked at the picture of Lizzie as a young girl. She was surrounded by her family. A much younger Fred and Bonnie. And her siblings.

"See, Dad," said Mikki. She pointed to one of the people in the photo.

"Yeah, honey, I see."

"That was mom's twin, right? The one who died?"

"Yes. Her name was Tillie."

"Is that why they left here? Not because of Gramps' job? But because it was so sad with her dying and all?"

"Yeah," admitted Jack. "I guess that was part of it."

"I don't know what I'd do if something happened to Cory or Jackie. And to lose a twin. It's like you lost a part of yourself in a way."

"I think you're right."

He held out his hand for the photo, but Mikki drew it back.

"Do you mind if I keep this?"

"No, sweetie, I don't mind at all."

33

"Bonnie?"

When Jack had opened the door in answer to the knock, his mother-in-law was the last person he expected to see.

She was dressed casually in slacks and a turquoise blouse, with sandals on her feet. She slid off her sunglasses and said, "Can I come in?"

"Of course." He moved aside and looked behind her.

"Fred didn't come with me," she said.

"When did you get in?"

"A couple of days ago. We're renting a house on the marsh."

"Here?"

"Yes. This *is* my hometown."

"Of course. I was just surprised."

They sat on the couch in the front room.

"I have to say, I was surprised that Mother left the place to you," she began.

"No more than I was."

"Yes," she said absently. "I suppose not."

Jack hesitated and then just decided to say it. "I heard Lizzie tell you she wanted to bring the kids here after I died."

Bonnie shot him a glance but said nothing.

"That stunned you, didn't it? Her wanting to come back here?"

"Where are the kids?" she asked, ignoring his question.

"On the beach. I can call them up."

"No, let's talk first." She looked around. "I noticed the new boards on the porch and steps, and the yard looks good."

"Sammy and I have been doing a little work to it. Electrical, plumbing, roofing, some landscaping."

"Probably more than a little." She stared at him. "I suppose that's why she left you the place. You could fix it up."

"Like I said, it came as a total shock."

"She left me a letter that explained things."

"She left me one too."

"Mother always did think of everything," Bonnie noted dryly.

"I've been thinking about fixing up the lighthouse too. Lizzie's Lighthouse."

"Please don't do that. Do you know she became obsessed with that damn thing?"

"She told me about it," said Jack. "But she was a little kid."

"No, it lasted for years. She would go up in that lighthouse every night. She would make us turn on the light and shine it over the sky looking for Tillie."

"Heaven," said Jack.

"What?"

"Lizzie said she was looking for Tillie in Heaven."

"Yes, well, it was very stressful for all of us. And then the light stopped working and she became very depressed. When Fred got the job offer in Cleveland, we jumped at it to get away from here. And to answer your question, I *was* stunned when she told me she was thinking of coming back here."

"But she was a grown woman with three kids. She wasn't going to be searching the sky for Heaven and her dead sister."

"Can you be sure of that?"

"Yeah, I can."

"How?"

"Because I know Lizzie."

Bonnie looked away but did not appear to be convinced.

Jack decided to change the subject. "You and Fred are welcome to use the place anytime you want. It's certainly more your home than mine."

"That's very nice of you, but I really couldn't. It took everything I had just to come here today." She stood and went over to one doorjamb that had horizontal cuts in the wood. "I measured the kids' heights here. Lizzie grew faster than her older sisters. Drove them crazy."

"We saw that," said Jack. "I was going to start doing that for Cory and Jackie."

Bonnie went over to the window and gazed up at the lighthouse, and then shuddered again. "I can't believe the damn thing is still standing."

She sat back down. "I'd like to see the kids while Fred and I are here."

"Of course. Anytime you want."

Jack started to say something else but then caught himself. They were having such an unusually pleasant time together that he didn't want to shatter it. However, Bonnie seemed to sense his conflict.

"What is it?"

"The tabloid story about the Miracle Man?" he said.

"Disgusting. If I could have found that reporter I would have strangled him."

Jack looked confused. "If you could have found him?"

She stared at him, and then what he was thinking apparently dawned on her. Her face flushed angrily. "Do you really think I would have spoken to a trashy gossip paper about my own daughter?"

"But the things in the story. Who else would have known about them?"

"I don't know. But I can assure you it wasn't me. They made Lizzie out to be . . . well, someone she very clearly wasn't."

"But you never called about it."

"Why would I? I knew none of it was true. Lizzie cheating on you? As preposterous as you cheating on her. I knew you never would have suspected that about her."

"And her going back out that night for the meds? You brought me the bag of pills. You seemed really angry about it."

Bonnie looked embarrassed. "I *was* angry about it. But I knew it wasn't your doing. I called Lizzie thinking she was home. She was at the pharmacy. She told me you hadn't wanted her to go out, that you could do without them. I only acted that way toward you because . . . well, I'd just buried my daughter, and I was hardly thinking clearly. I'm sorry."

"Okay, I completely understand that."

"I care about the children. I want the best for them."

"I know; so do I."

She drew an elongated breath. "Jack, this is hard, but hear me out."

Okay, here it comes, thought Jack. *The real reason she's here.*

"I've spoken with numerous doctors since your recovery."

"Why would you do that?" he said sharply.

"Because they are only one parent from becoming orphans; that's why."

"I'm alive, Bonnie, in case you hadn't noticed."

"Every doctor I talked to said it's not possible. The disease you have is fatal, without exception. I'm sorry, but that's just what they said."

"Had. I *had* the disease. I don't have it any longer. I was given a clean bill of health."

"Which these same doctors—and one of them was from the Mayo Clinic—said was also impossible. It does not go away. It may go dormant, but it always comes back. And when it does, the consensus is that you won't have more than a few weeks."

"Bonnie, why are we having this discussion? Look at me. I'm not sick anymore."

"Those three children have been through so much. You on your deathbed. Lizzie dying. Having to be uprooted and moved around the country."

"That was your doing, not mine."

"And what choice did I have exactly? Tell me that."

Jack looked away. "Okay, maybe you didn't have a choice. But I don't see your point now."

"What if you get sick again? What if it comes back? And you die? Do you have any idea what it will do to them? A person can only take so much misery, so much sorrow. They're only children; it will destroy them."

"What do you want me to do? Give them back to you? Go crawl off in a corner and wait and see if I get sick again?"

"No, but you could come and live with us in Arizona. You and the kids. That way they can get into a stable routine. And if something does happen to you, we'll be there to help you, and the kids will be used to living with us."

Jack looked askance at her. "Are you telling me that you're willing to take me and all three kids?"

"Yes. Even though Mother left you the Palace, she also left me quite a bit of money. We're in a position to purchase a larger house and have the resources to support all of you."

"I appreciate that, but I can support my own family," he said firmly.

"I didn't mean it that way."

"Okay."

"I'm just looking to help you."

"I appreciate that."

"So you won't consider my offer?"

"No, I'm afraid not."

Bonnie stood. "Well, I guess that's that. Can I go and see the children now?"

"Absolutely. I can take you down there. And I want you involved in the kids' lives."

"I want that too."

34

On Sunday, while Sammy took his motorcycle for a spin, Jack piled all the kids into the VW and drove into Channing. He'd been working hard at Jenna's house and a few other jobs, and the kids needed a break from the Palace. Jack had gotten hold of Ned Parker, and he'd agreed to give the family a behind-the-scenes tour of the playhouse.

Parker met them outside the theater, and over the next hour he took them through the darkened spaces. He showed Cory how to manipulate the house lights, lift and lower scenery, move equipment on stage dollies, and work the trapdoor in the middle of the stage that would allow people to seem to vanish. Jackie in particular thought that was very cool.

They left the theater and walked along, looking at various restaurants. Someone called out to Jack from across the street. He looked over and saw Charles Pinckney hurrying over to them. He was dressed casually in khaki shorts and a short-sleeve button-down oxford shirt with a T-shirt underneath it; leather sandals were on his feet.

"Taking the Sabbath off to enjoy some sunshine and the pleasures of Channing?"

Jack nodded. "Get away from the house for a bit. See the town."

"You hungry?"

Jack said, "We're deciding where to go."

Charles's eyes twinkled. "Then there's only one real option."

"A Little Bit of Love," said Mikki immediately.

Jack said, "We've already been there. How about another place? There're three right here on this block."

"But Jackie and Cory haven't seen it." She turned to her brothers. "It's full of musical stuff; it's so cool."

"Cool," chimed in Jackie.

She smiled. "You want a bit of love, Jackie, huh?"

He jumped up and down. "Bitalove. Bitalove." He grabbed his dad's leg. "Bitalove. Bitalove."

Cory said, "That was, like, such a cheap trick, Mikki."

"Jenna does the best Sunday brunch in town, actually," advised Charles. "I was just heading there myself."

"Okay," Jack said in a resigned tone.

Jenna smiled when she saw them come in. The place was crowded, but she said, "I've got a nice window table. Catch some of the breeze from outside. Follow me."

She seated them at the table, handed out menus, and took their drink orders.

"Is Liam around today?" asked Mikki.

"In the kitchen, grilling. He's turned into quite the short-order cook."

"We'd arranged that I could come by tonight to do a few sets."

Jack looked at her. "You did?"

She stared back at him and said sharply, "Yeah, I did. Sitting home all day watching Cory and Jackie isn't exactly how I planned to spend my summer."

"You don't need to watch me," said Cory.

"Yeah," said Jackie. "Not me."

Jenna looked at Jack and, sensing his distress, said, "Well, your dad is working really hard on the soundproofing, but it's not done yet. And while you guys sound great together, I do like a little peace and quiet in the evening. But I tell you what: Come by around eight. Liam will be home by then, and that's when I take my walk on the beach. I'll be gone about an hour or so. Does that work?"

"That's cool, Jenna, thanks."

Jenna looked at Jack. "And is that cool with Dad?"

"Yeah," Jack said slowly.

"So where's your Delta buddy?" she asked.

"Out riding his Harley," answered Cory.

"Ah. Well he better watch himself. I know a few single ladies of a certain age in this town who will snap him up."

"Snap!" cried out Jackie.

After Jenna left, Jack leaned over and whispered to his daughter, "This is strictly music between you and Liam, right?"

"Dad, please."

"Just asking." He turned to Charles. "Bonnie came by to see me."

"She told me she was."

"Did she tell you what about?"

"Yes. I saw her afterward too. She told me what you two talked about. She told me what you said. And I told her I agreed with you. I don't think that's what she wanted to hear, but so be it."

Mikki, who'd been listening, said, "What didn't she want to hear?"

"Another time, Mik; not now," said her father, shooting a glance at the boys. Then he added, "Did you have a good visit with her, Mik?"

"She was more laid-back than in Arizona," Mikki replied. "There she was like a control freak. Drove me nuts."

Jack turned to Charles. "I checked out the lighthouse the other night."

"Did you? And how is it looking?"

"Not great, actually."

"It really was something in its day."

"I bet it was," said Jack. "I bet it was."

35

After lunch they were walking back to the van when Charles pointed across the street and said, "Speak of the devil."

Jack saw where he was pointing. Bonnie and Fred were just entering a gift shop. Mikki walked up beside him and said in a low voice, "Okay, Dad, what is going on with Grandma? Why is she really here?"

"She just came by to make an offer." Mikki waited expectantly. "For us all to go and live with her in Arizona."

"No way. You're not thinking of doing that, are you?"

"No, I'm not."

Mikki was about to say something else when she saw Blake Saunders coming down the street with two beefy young men. They were all wearing mesh football jerseys with CHANNING HIGH printed on the front.

"Hi," said Mikki. Jack looked at her questioningly. "Blake and I met on the beach when I was going for a run," she explained. "And we've run a few more times together since then."

"Thanks for telling me." He eyed Blake. "You look familiar."

Blake looked embarrassed. "I was in the car that almost ran you off the road that day."

"The girl's name is Tiffany," said Mikki. "And she's super-rich. What a shock."

Blake said, "I told her to slow down, but she doesn't listen to anyone."

"Yeah, I bet," said Mikki.

Blake turned to her. "Hey, we're having a little party on the beach next Saturday. I was wondering if you'd like to come out and hang with us. There's food, a bonfire, and we play some tunes."

"And no alcohol, of course," interjected Jack.

"No, sir," said Blake right away, though his friends gave goofy grins.

"*Right*. She'll have to get back to you on that, sport," said Jack, while Mikki scowled at her father.

"Nine o'clock. About the midpoint of our run, near where the big yellow house is," he added.

"Right."

"Okay, hope to see you there."

The young men walked off.

"What was that all about?" demanded Jack.

"Do you have a boyfriend?" a grinning Cory wanted to know. "I thought you liked this Liam guy."

Mikki's face reddened. "Will you two just knock it off?"

"That guy doesn't even have an earring, and his hair is perfectly normal," said Jack. "He's not your type. He's a football player, for God's sake. You hate football players."

"Who told you that?"

"Your mom. She made a big joke out of it because she *married* a football player."

"I think I can decide for myself what my type is," Mikki said hotly.

"Well, I'm still your dad and I don't like the idea of—"

"Hey, Miracle Man!"

Jack jerked around to see where the voice had come from.

"Over here, Miracle."

Jack turned to see two large men sitting in the cab of a pickup truck staring at him. One man stuck his head out of the truck. "I need me a miracle. You want'a come over here and sprinkle some water on my head?" He waved a five-dollar bill. "I ain't expecting miracles for free. I'll pay good money for it." Both men burst out laughing. They got out of the truck and leaned against it, their big arms folded over their thick chests. They were dressed in jeans and dirty T-shirts, with greasy ball caps on their heads. Their bare arms were covered in tattoos.

Cory said fearfully, "Dad?"

"It's okay, son. We'll just keep on walking."

They passed by the men.

One of them said, "Hey, Miracle, you too good to stop for us poor folk?"

Mikki whirled around and said, "Grow up, you creeps!"

"Mikki," Jack snapped. "Just keep walking."

"Yeah, Mikki," mimicked one of the men. "Just keep walking, sugah."

Jack stiffened at this remark. He almost turned around, but his kids were with him, and he knew nothing good would come out of a confrontation. Jack said to the kids, "We'll go on down to the beach when we get back, and—"

"Hey, Miracle, was it true your slutty wife was cheating on you with your best bud?"

Jack moved so quickly, Cory's hand was still up in the air where it had been clutching his dad's. When Jack rushed at them, the first man threw a punch. Jack ducked it, grabbed the man's hand, ripped it back and then over his shoulder, swung him around, and slammed him head-first into the truck. When the bloodied man turned back around and charged at Jack, he sidestepped the attack and leveled the guy with a crushing blow to the jaw. The second man slammed into Jack's back, propelling him forward and face-first into a lamppost. In the next instant he'd spun out of the man's grasp, laid a fist into his diaphragm, doubling him over, and then kicked his legs out from under him. Jack's elbow strike to the back of the man's neck sent him down to the pavement, where he stayed, groaning loudly.

Jack was bent over, his breaths coming in gasps and blood pouring down his face from where he'd hit the post. As he straightened up and looked around, it seemed like the entire town of Channing was staring back at him. No one moved; no one seemed even to be breathing. As he glanced across the street, he saw Jenna and Liam staring at him from the door to the Little Bit. When he looked to his left, he saw Bonnie and Fred gawping at him in shock from the entrance to the gift shop. Bonnie looked at Jack, then to the unconscious men, and then back at her bleeding son-in-law.

"Daddy!"

Jack looked over his shoulder. Jackie was standing on the sidewalk bawling. Cory stood there looking in amazement at his dad, while Mikki glowered contemptuously at the two men lying on the pavement. "Idiots," she said. Jack quickly piled his kids into the VW and drove off.

36

Jack sat at the kitchen table with ice wrapped in a paper towel and held over his left cheek. Dried blood was stuck to his forehead from the impact with the street lamp. When someone knocked on the door, Jack half expected it to be the police.

"Old man and wady," squealed Jackie after he managed to open the door.

Jenna and Charles strode in. She was carrying a small bag and sat down next to Jack. She started pulling things out: sterilized wipes, Band-Aids, an ice pack, and antibiotic cream.

"What are you two doing here?" asked Jack.

Jenna moved Jack's hand away from his battered face and cleaned up the cuts, applied the ointment, and covered it all with a large Band-Aid.

Charles said, "We thought you might need a little assistance."

"Those two idiots," said Jenna. "Going off half-cocked like that. Probably drunk."

"You know them?" asked Jack.

"They come into the bar every once in a while. But I can't really say I know them."

"They're from Sweat Town," added Charles.

Jenna frowned. "I despise that term."

"Well, it's not very nice, but I think the residents actually coined it," said Charles.

"What exactly is Sweat Town?" asked Mikki.

"Other side of the tracks," replied Charles. "Poor side of town. Every coastal area has them. Most of the people who do the actual work around here live there."

Jenna said, "Here's an ice pack. It'll work faster on that swelling."

"Thanks."

She closed up her bag, sat back, and studied Jack's face. "Okay, you should be good to go."

"You're pretty slick at that," said Mikki.

"Just your mom-standard-procedure stuff."

Jackie jumped up and down trying to get to her bag of medical supplies. Jenna finally placed a Band-Aid on his finger and kissed it. "Now your boo-boo is all gone too." She straightened back up and gazed steadily at Jack. "Looks like you didn't forget your army training. Those weren't small guys, and you put 'em down pretty fast."

Jack grimaced. "It was stupid. Never should've happened."

The door opened, and Sammy walked in carrying his motorcycle helmet. "Had a nice little ride—" When he saw Jack, he exclaimed, "What the hell happened? You fall off a ladder?"

Jackie yelled, "Daddy pighting." The little boy did a kick and then swung his fist so hard he fell over.

"Fighting? Who with?" demanded Sammy.

Mikki and Cory both started telling Sammy what had happened. The older man's features turned dark as he listened to them. When they got to the slur that the one man had called Lizzie, Sammy went over to his toolbox and pulled out a crowbar. "You tell me what they look like and where I can find these maggots."

"No, Sammy," said Jack.

"I'm not letting them get away with this crap," barked Sammy.

"I'll handle it."

"What, you think I'm too old to take care of myself?"

"That's not the point. You beat them up, your butt will land right in jail."

Charles said, "He's right, Sammy. That's not the way to go about it."

"Uh-oh," said Jackie. He was peering out the window into the front yard.

"What is it, Jackie?" asked his sister.

Jackie pointed to the door, his eyes so big they appeared to touch. *"Cop dude,"* he said in a very un-Jackie-like whisper. Then he sped into the next room to hide.

Jack looked sternly at his older kids. "Cop dude? Where did he learn that?"

Mikki looked uncomfortably at the floor. Cory studied the ceiling, his teeth clenched over his bottom lip.

"Great," said Jack stiffly as he rose to answer the door.

The sheriff identified himself as Nathan Tammie. He was a big man with a bluff, serious face and dark curly hair. He took Jack's statement and scratched his chin. "That pretty much matches up with what other people said happened. But you *did* go after them."

"He was provoked. They were saying nasty things about our mom," exclaimed Mikki. "What did you expect him to do?"

Jenna said, "Sheriff, Charles and I saw the whole thing. It's exactly as Mikki said. He was provoked. Anybody would've done what Jack did."

"I'm not saying I wouldn't have done the same thing, Jenna, but I also can't let things like this happen in town without consequences. I've already told those two boys to back off. And I expect you to hold on to your temper, Mr. Armstrong. If something happens again, you come tell me, and I'll handle it. Do we understand each other? 'Cause if there's a next time, people are gonna end up in jail."

"I understand."

After the sheriff left, Charles said, "He's a good man, but he also means what he says." He looked at Jenna. "I can drive you back to town."

"Can you give me a minute, Charles?"

A sulking Sammy had gone into another room, and the kids had disappeared.

Jenna said to Jack, "Miracle Man?"

Jack stared at her, the ice pack held to his face. "It's a long story."

"I'm a good listener."

"I appreciate that, Jenna. It's just that . . ."

"I can tell you're the sort of man who doesn't open up easily. Keeps it all inside."

"Maybe we can talk about it. Just not right now."

"Well, you need anything else, just let me know." She rose to go.

"Jenna?"

She turned back to see him watching her. "Yes?"

He touched the Band-Aid on his face. "Thanks for coming over. Means a lot."

She smiled. "Only next time I hope I don't have to bring my first-aid kit."

37

The sound woke all of them. Lights burst on. Jack and Sammy made sure the kids were okay before checking the rest of the house.

"Sounded like a bomb going off," said Sammy. "Or a building collapsed."

Jack looked at him quizzically and then said, "Oh, damn!"

He ran toward the rear of the house.

"Jack! What is it?"

Sammy raced after him.

Jack sprinted across the backyard and over to the rocks. He ripped open the door of the lighthouse and stopped. The stairs had collapsed. He shone his light upward. Forty vertical feet of wood had tumbled down.

Sammy ran up next to him and saw what he was looking at. "Hell. Weren't you just up there?"

Jack nodded, his gaze still on the fallen structure. Now he couldn't get to the top.

"Close call, boy."

Jack turned to him. "I need to rebuild the stairs."

"What?"

"We can go get the materials tomorrow."

"But we still have to finish some other jobs. And Charles has got some more referrals for us. Lady named Anne Bethune has a big house on the beach. She wants a screen porch enclosed and some other stuff done. Good money."

"I'll do this on my own time."

"Yeah, all your spare time."

"I *have* to do it, Sammy."

Sammy looked at the jumble of splintered wood. "Gonna be expensive."

"Take it out of my share. And I don't expect you to help."

Sammy frowned. "Since when do we have shares and don't help each other?"

"But this is different, Sammy. I can't expect you to do this too."

Sammy looked at the hand-painted sign next to the door and said quietly, "We'll take some measurements in the morning. Get the materials. We'll do the paying stuff during the day and this after hours. Okay?"

"Okay," said Jack. As Sammy turned to go back in the house, he added, "Thanks, Sammy."

He turned around. "Never been married, Jack. But I understand losing somebody. Especially someone like Lizzie."

He continued on into the house, and Jack turned to look back at the lighthouse he was now going to rebuild.

"What's all this for?" Charles asked as Jack and Sammy finished loading the truck to capacity. He eyed the items in the truck bed. "Scaffolding, and you've ordered enough wood to build another Noah's ark?"

"Had a little accident at the Palace," said Sammy when it appeared Jack was not going to answer the man's question.

Charles looked alarmed. "Accident? Was anyone hurt?"

"Stairs in the lighthouse fell down," said Jack. "No one was hurt."

"So you're going to rebuild the stairs?" he asked, looking perplexed.

"Yes," said Jack tersely.

Sammy eyed Charles and shrugged.

"But the light doesn't even work."

"He plans on fixing that too," replied Sammy.

"But why? It's not registered as a navigational aid anymore."

Jack finished strapping everything down before he looked at Charles and pulled out a sheet of paper and handed it to him. "I found a schematic on the lighting system. I'd appreciate it if you could see if these pieces of equipment could be ordered."

Charles glanced down at the list. "Might take some time. And it won't be cheap."

Jack started to climb into the truck. "Thanks."

Sammy gave Charles a helpless look and got in the truck.

As they were driving out of town, Sammy said, "Isn't that Bonnie?"

Jack looked where he was pointing. It was indeed Bonnie. And she was sitting in a car with a younger man dressed in a suit.

"Who's the guy?" asked Sammy.

"Never seen him before."

"She's a strange bird."

"Yeah." Jack glanced back at the woman and then drove on.

They unloaded the materials at the Palace. Then Sammy took the VW and drove off to meet with Anne Bethune about what she needed done, while Jack continued on to Jenna's house in the truck.

Jenna met him at the door. She was still dressed in a robe and slippers.

"Sorry about my appearance. The restaurant business isn't nine to five; it's more like ten a.m. to midnight. You want some coffee?"

Jack hesitated.

"No extra charge," she said, smiling.

"Okay, thanks."

She poured out a cup and brought it down to him in the music room. She watched him work hanging new drywall.

"You really know what you're doing," she said.

"It's just drywall. Once you know what to do, it's pretty easy."

"Right. I can't even hang a picture."

"I doubt being a lawyer in D.C. was easy."

"Just a bunch of words, legal gobbledygook."

"If you say so."

Jenna sipped her coffee and continued to watch. "Our kids have really hit it off playing music together."

"Yeah, Mikki told me."

"First time I've seen Liam really take an interest in anyone down here."

"He seems like a fine young man. And Mikki's mood is a lot better. That's worth its weight in gold."

He put down his tool and took a sip of coffee. "Mind if I ask you a personal question?"

She eyed him with mock caution. "Should I be scared?"

"No."

"Then shoot."

"Ever think about getting married again?"

"I've thought about it, sure."

"I mean, from what you've said, you've been divorced a while. You're young, well-off, smart, and educated. And . . . really pretty."

"Can I hire you as my publicist?"

"I'm serious, Jenna."

She put her cup down, sat, and covered her bare knees with her robe. "There have been some men interested in a permanent relationship with me. Some right here in Channing."

"But?"

"But they weren't the right ones. And I'm a woman who's willing to wait for the real Mr. Right. Especially considering how *wrong* I got it the first time."

Jack picked up his tool again. "Lizzie and I met in high school. We would've celebrated our seventeenth wedding anniversary this year."

"Sounds like you found Mrs. Right on your first try."

"I did," he said frankly.

"I suppose that makes the loss that much harder."

"It does. But I've got our kids to raise. And I have to do it right. For Lizzie."

"And you, Jack. You're part of the equation too."

"And me," he said. "I hope you find Mr. Right."

"Me too," said Jenna wistfully, as she stared at him.

38

Sammy turned to Jack and said, "I think it's time to knock off. It's almost midnight."

"You go on. I'm just going to finish up a few things."

They were in the lighthouse. After working most of the last three days at Anne Bethune's house, Sammy and Jack had eaten a hasty dinner and worked another four hours on the lighthouse. They had cleared out all the wood from the collapsed stairs and assembled the scaffolding up to the top platform, which also needed repair. Fresh lumber delivered from Charles Pinckney's hardware store was neatly stacked outside in preparation for the rebuilding process.

"Jack, you've put in sixteen hours today. You need to get some rest."

"I will, Sammy. Just another thirty minutes."

Sammy shook his head, dropped his tool belt on the lower level of the scaffolding, stretched out his aching back, and walked slowly to the Palace.

Jack tightened down some of the scaffolding supports and then climbed up to the top and stepped out onto the catwalk. What he was trying to imagine was how Lizzie the little girl would have thought of the view from up here.

"Were you scared at first, Lizzie? Did you think you might fall? Or did you love it the first time you saw it?" He stared out at the dark ocean and let the breeze wash over his face. He eyed the sky, looking for the exact spot where little Lizzie had imagined Heaven to be perched. And also where her twin sister had gone.

And now where you are, Lizzie.

Farther out to sea he could see ship lights as they slowly made their way across the water. He closed his eyes, and his thoughts carried back to that frozen cemetery four days after Christmas, when they'd laid Lizzie into the ground. She was there right now, alone, in the dark.

"Don't, Jack," he said. "Don't. Nothing good will come from dwelling on that. Remember Lizzie in life. Not like that."

He looked to his right and was surprised to see someone walking along the beach. As the person drew closer, Jack could see that it was Jenna. She was holding her sandals in one hand, slowly swinging them as she walked close to the waterline. He looked at his watch. It was nearly one in the morning. What was she doing out here?

She suddenly looked up and under the arc of moonlight saw him. She waved and started toward the rocks.

She called up to him. "Working late?"

He said, "Just finishing up a few things. Surprised to see you out."

"I sometimes take a walk on the beach after closing down the Little Bit. Helps to relax me." She gazed at the lighthouse. "Heard you were fixing it up."

"Trying." He added, "Guess it seems pretty crazy."

"I think it's a good idea," she said, surprising him.

"Why?"

"I just think it's a good idea. That's all." He didn't say anything. "By the way, you did a great job on the sound-proofing. Can't hear a thing. It's raised the quality of my life a thousand percent. And I won't have to kill my only child."

"I'm glad I could help."

"Well, I guess I better head back."

Jack looked down the dark beach from where she had come. "Do you want me to walk back with you? It's pretty dark out there."

"No, I'll be fine. It's a safe place. And you look like you have some thinking to do still."

Before he could say anything, she'd turned and walked off. He slowly climbed back down the scaffolding. When he touched bottom, he passed through the doorway and then turned and looked at the hand-painted sign.

"I'm going to get it working," he said. "Lizzie, I promise that this light will work again. And then you can look down from Heaven and see it."

And maybe see me.

39

"Oh, great," said Mikki. It was Saturday night and she was at the beach party Blake Saunders had invited her to. There were lots of people already there, and one of them was Tiffany Murdoch, holding court by the large bonfire that spewed streams of embers skyward. There were quite a few large young men in football jerseys and teenage girls in short shorts, tight skirts, and tighter tops. A catering truck was parked on the road near the beach. Mikki, who'd brought a blanket and a bag of marshmallows, looked on in shock as men and women in white jackets carried trays of food and drinks around to the teens partying on the sand.

Blake spotted her and strolled over, a bottle in his hand.

"Hey, glad you could make it."

"Never been to a beach party that was catered before," she said in a disapproving tone.

"I know. But Tiffany's dad is a big football booster, and he pays for the party every year."

"So I guess that's why Tiff's here?"

"Oh, yeah. The center of attention as always. A real queen bee."

"Bees sting," Mikki shot back.

"What's in the bag?" he said.

"Nothing," she said quickly, hiding the bag of marshmallows behind her.

He held up the bottle. "Want a taste?"

"Thanks, but I'll pass."

"It's not alcohol."

"I'll take your word for it."

A little put off, he said, "Well, there's plenty of food and drink. Help yourself and then come join us."

He left, and Mikki went to the tables manned by other adults in white jackets. She asked for a Coke. The woman, weathered looking with stringy gray hair, poured it out for her.

"Thank you," said Mikki.

The woman looked surprised.

"What?" asked Mikki. She looked down at her jeans and T-shirt. "Something wrong?"

"You're not with that group, are you?" said the woman quietly.

"No, we just came down from Ohio for the summer. Why?"

"You said thank you."

"And that's, like, unusual?"

The woman eyed the partygoers. "With some folks it's apparently impossible. Ohio? Are you Cee Pinckney's folks?"

"She was my great-grandmother. I'm Mikki."

"Nice to meet you, Mikki. Ms. Pinckney was a fine lady. Sorry she's gone."

"I take it you live in Channing?"

"All my life, but just not the postcard part."

"What?"

"You know the part you see on postcards? I live in the area tourists never see. We can't afford the pretty ocean views."

"Would that be Sweat Town?"

"So you've heard of it?"

"Somebody told me. Sounds like where we lived in Cleveland. What's your name?"

"Folks call me Fran."

"It was nice talking to you, Fran."

"Same here, honey."

She turned away to serve someone else.

Troubled by what Fran had told her, Mikki strolled around the pockets of people, many of whom were already wasted. The boys looked at her with lust, the girls with hostility.

Why did I come?

"Well, look who we have here."

Inwardly groaning, Mikki closed her eyes and then opened them. Things were about to get worse.

Tiffany stood in front of her, swaying slightly, plastic cup filled with beer in hand. She had on a string-bikini bottom with a mesh cutoff jersey that barely covered her chest. "What's your name again?"

Between gritted teeth she said, "Mikki."

"Oh, like Mickey Mouse." Tiffany giggled and looked around at the others and made an exaggerated bow. "Mickey Mouse, people." Laughter swept through the ranks of the partiers. A nervous-looking Blake ran up and put his arm around Tiffany's bare waist. "Hey, Tiff, let's go get something to eat."

"Not hungry," said Tiffany with a pout. Mikki could sense this was her method of getting what she wanted. Putting her thick lips together and acting like a two-year-old.

Mikki looked at the beer and then eyed Tiffany's red convertible parked by the catering truck. "Hope you're not the designated driver."

"I can be anything I want," Tiffany replied, a coy smile on her face.

Blake pulled on her arm. "Come on, Tiff, let's get some food. You don't want to piss off your dad again, remember?"

"Shut up!" snapped Tiffany. She looked at Mikki. "I hear you and Blake have been running together on the beach."

"Yeah, so?"

"I was just surprised."

"Why's that?" Mikki asked, a hard edge to her voice.

"I didn't think he liked hanging out with freaks."

Mikki eyed the other girl's scant clothing. "You know, next time you might want to consider something that actually comes close to covering your big butt."

"Shut up!"

"Okay, I'm leaving now." Mikki turned to walk away.

"Hey, I'm talking to you."

Tiffany grabbed her shoulder. Mikki's arms and legs seemed to move of their own accord. Her hand clamped like a vise on the other girl's wrist. Mikki spun the arm behind Tiffany's back, jerked upward, angled one of her feet in front of Tiffany's legs, and gave a hard shove from behind. The next moment Tiffany was lying facedown in the sand, her mesh top up around her head.

Blake looked at her in amazement. "How'd you do that?" he asked Mikki.

Mikki looked down at her hands as if they belonged to someone else. "My . . . my dad taught me."

They both looked down at Tiffany, who was spitting out sand and crying. Other people were walking toward them.

"I'm outta here," said a panicked Mikki.

She turned, pushed past some folks, and raced off. As she passed by Fran, the woman winked at Mikki and raised a serving spoon in silent salute.

40

Hurrying down the beach, Mikki collided with someone who appeared, ghostlike, out of the darkness.

"Liam?"

The tall, gangly Liam had on a hoodie and sweatpants.

"What are you doing here?" she asked breathlessly.

"Walking. What about you?" He looked over her shoulder in the direction of the party Mikki had just left. "Tiffany's party? Don't tell me you've gone over to the dark side?" he said with a grin.

"It was stupid," admitted Mikki.

"Well, if you want to come with me, I'll show you a much better party."

"What?"

"But I have to warn you, they don't have caterers."

"How'd you know Tiffany's party was catered?"

"Because my mom did it for a couple years until little Tiffany demanded alcohol be served. Then my mom told old man Murdoch where to stick it."

"Good for her."

"Yeah, funny, for some reason, after that, I never got

invited to her little shindig. Well, enough about the rich and the spoiled. Let's get going."

He started to walk off, and Mikki hurried after him. "Where to?"

"Like I said, a better party."

The breakers crashed on the beach, providing a slow, melodious chorus to their footsteps slapping against the hard, wet sand. The sounds and the lights reached them about a quarter of a mile down the beach.

"Is that the better party?" she asked.

"Yep."

As they drew closer, the scene became clearer. The bonfire was full and the flames high. Girls and guys sat around the fire holding out sticks with hot dogs and marshmallows riding on their points. Mikki could hear a guitar strumming and sticks popping on a drum pad. Laughter and whoops amid the crash of waves. There were a few couples making out, but most were just hanging out, talking and dancing.

"Hey, Liam," said one guy as he approached them. "Everyone was hoping you'd make it." He handed them each a long stick. "Dogs are cooking." They joined the crowd. Mikki could see a few football jerseys, but most were dressed in jeans and T-shirts. There were no designer labels in sight. Everyone greeted Liam with high fives, chest bumps, and knuckle smacks.

"Pretty popular guy," Mikki remarked.

"Nah, the guys think my mom is hot, and the girls want jobs at the Little Bit. They're just looking to use me."

Mikki laughed. "So do all of you go to high school together?"

"Yeah. But most of these kids are from Sweat Town, which I find a lot more palatable than Tiffany's mansion crowd." Liam eyed the two guys playing the guitar and the drum pad. He looked at Mikki. "Want to really get this party cooking?"

She instantly got his meaning. "Oh, let's *so* do it."

They played for nearly thirty minutes while the crowd whooped and cheered.

Mikki sang parts of a song she was working on and that the crowd really got into, even chanting back parts of the lyrics. Then Mikki grabbed the drumsticks and showed herself to be nearly as adept at drums as she was at guitar. Even Liam looked at her in amazement when she finished her set. She explained, "When I formed my band, I learned every instrument. I'm sort of a control freak."

Afterward they roasted some hot dogs. When someone started playing tunes off a portable CD player, Liam said, "Hey, you want to do some sand dancing?"

"What's that?"

"Uh, it's really complicated. It's dancing in the sand in your bare feet."

She smiled. "I think I can manage that."

He put both arms around her waist, and she put her hands on his shoulders. They moved slowly over the beach.

"Feels sort of cool," Mikki said. "On the feet," she added quickly.

"Me too," he said, grinning. "Okay, now it's time for the old tradition of sand angels. Now, that's—"

"Let me guess." She plopped down on her back in the sand and moved her arms and legs up and down.

Liam joined her. "Wow, brains and beauty."

As the music played on, they danced and grew closer.

"This is really nice, Liam."

"Yeah, it is."

She cupped his chin with her hand.

"Mikki?" he said questioningly.

She kissed him and then stepped back. "I had a great time, Liam. Thanks for bringing me."

"Any time. I'm working the late shift this coming week at the Little Bit. Come on down, and I can get you anything you want for free."

"How can you do that?"

"I'm the cook. Ain't nothing happening without me."

Mikki laughed.

"You need a way home?" he asked.

"I actually rode a bike I found at the house. Left it up on the street. It's not that far."

"I've got a bike too. I'll ride with you. It's on my way."

"You don't have to do that."

"I know. I want to." He paused, looking embarrassed. "I mean . . ."

"I know what you mean," she said softly.

He saw her safely to her house, waved, and rode off.

When she walked in the house, her dad called out to her from the darkened front room.

"So?" he said.

She came forward, squinting in the poor light to see him. He was on the couch looking at her.

"So what?"

"Have fun?"

"Yeah, just at a different party."

She told her dad about the evening.

"Sounds like you made the right choice."

She sat down next to him. "So how's the lighthouse coming? You've really been spending a lot of time on it."

He looked down. "I know it must seem strange."

"Dad, it doesn't seem strange. Okay, maybe a little," she amended with a smile. "But you said the reason we came down here was so you could spend more time with us. Remember? But you and Sammy work all the time, and I'm stuck watching Cory and Jackie."

Jack's head dropped lower with this comment. "It's just . . . I don't know. It's complicated, Mikki. Really complicated."

Mikki rose. In a disappointed tone she said, "Yeah, I guess it is."

"But I'll try to get better. Maybe we can do something next weekend?"

She brightened. "Like what?"

Jack said lamely, "Um, I haven't thought of it yet."

Her face fell. "Right. Sure. Good night."

As she headed up the stairs to bed, Jack started to call after her, but then he stopped and just sat there in the dark.

Neither one of them noticed Sammy standing at his bedroom door listening to their exchange. The former Delta Force member went into his room, picked up his cell phone, and made a call.

41

As Mikki was running on the beach a few days later, Blake joined her.

He said immediately, "Look, I'm sorry about what happened at the party. Tiff was wasted."

"Gee, really?"

"She's usually not that obnoxious."

"Give me a break. She's a fricking nightmare in a G-string."

"Okay, maybe she is. Where'd you end up?"

"Another party on the beach."

"What party?"

"One Liam Fontaine took me to. And most of the people there were from Sweat Town. Heard of it?"

"Mikki, I live in Sweat Town."

This stunned her so much she stopped running. "What?"

"My mom works as the housekeeper for the Murdochs."

"Then why do you hang out with Tiffany?"

"Like I said, my mom works for them."

"And what, that obligates you to do her bidding?"

Blake laughed nervously. "I don't do her bidding. I just hang out with her sometimes."

They started running again. "Well, good for you. Who you hang out with says a lot about a person."

"Hey, what's wrong with me being friends with her? Are you saying poor people can only hang out with other poor people?"

"No, of course I'm not saying that."

"I have a lot of friends in Sweat Town. I play football with a bunch of them. And I go to Tiffany's and she has cool stuff and I have fun with her. So what?"

"Look, do what you want."

"Well, what I want is to go out with you." This time Blake stopped running, forcing Mikki to do the same. "So how about it? Will you go out with me?"

"Why?"

"Why? Because I like you."

"You don't really know me."

"Which is a perfect reason to go out. To get to know each other better. But hey, if you're not interested, forget it. Have a good one, and I'm sorry I don't fit your idea of a perfect person. Maybe Liam does." He started to jog off in the other direction.

"Wait a minute."

He stopped as she walked over to him. "What exactly do you want to do on this date?"

"What?"

"The plan, Blake. I need to know the parameters of what you're talking about. I'm not looking to run into a crowd of rich people again and have to kick somebody's butt." She added, "Unless it's Tiffany's. I actually enjoyed that."

"It's nothing like that. There's a coffee bar in town. They play music at night. Nothing live, but they have a DJ who's really good. I thought we could go and listen to some tunes, dance, and chill out. That's all."

She considered this. "That sounds okay. But just dancing and listening to tunes."

He eyed her closely. "Why? You got something else going?"

"No, I just—"

"Liam?"

"That's none of your business," she said hotly.

"Okay, okay. You're right. Look, I've got my license. I can pick you up tomorrow night around seven?"

"I'll check with my dad, but I think that'll be okay."

"Good," said Blake. "Glad we got that settled. Want to finish the run?"

She grinned and pushed him backward over a bump in the sand. He fell sprawling on his backside. "Catch me if you can," she called out as she sprinted off laughing.

He jumped up and raced after her.

42

"I'm hungry, Jack, so let's go."

They were parked on the street in Channing. Sammy was eyeing Jenna's restaurant, but Jack didn't seem to want to budge.

"It's not like this is the only place to eat in town, Sammy."

Sammy opened his door. "You just need to get over it."

"Over what?"

Sammy snapped, "She's just a nice lady who's trying to be friends with you, and you won't give her the time of day because you feel guilty about Lizzie."

"I don't know what the hell you're talking about! I'm nice to her."

"Great. If that's the way you want it. I'm going to eat. Stay here if you want."

Sammy slammed the truck door and went inside A Little Bit of Love.

Jack sat there brooding, his fingers tapping against the steering wheel. Finally, he climbed out of the truck and followed Sammy inside. His friend was tucked in a corner, already studying his menu. Jenna wasn't at the hostess stand, so Jack wandered back and sat down across from Sammy. The older man handed him a menu. "Figured your empty belly would bring you to your senses."

Jack took the menu, glanced at it, and then dropped it on the table. "I don't know what you expect from me."

"I don't expect anything from you."

"Well, something's clearly bugging the crap out of you."

Sammy dropped his menu too. "Okay, man, let's hash this out. When's the last time you played with Jackie? Or Cory? Or said two words to Mikki?"

"I talked to Mikki about stuff just the other night."

"I know you did because I was there listening. But what exactly has changed? You work all day, and then you work on that damn lighthouse all night. It's not healthy, Jack. You planning on having any fun ever again?"

Jack stared hard at his friend. "What makes you think I deserve to have any fun ever again?"

"You half killed yourself clawing your way back from a death sentence. And for what? To be miserable the rest of your life?"

Jack picked up the menu. "You're making it way too simple."

"And you're making it way too complicated. You got kids, Jack. They need you."

"I'm busting my ass to support them."

"Is that all?"

"What do you mean?"

"The only reason you're busting your ass? Because of them?"

"I know I haven't exactly been the perfect father. My daughter has already reminded me of that."

"She does that because she cares about you. And, hell, she's damn near sixteen. She probably wants to spend her time down here doing something other than watching her two kid brothers all day."

"She went to a party on the beach. She plays music with that Liam kid."

"Okay, fine, excuse me for giving a damn."

Jack's anger evaporated with this last comment. "You're right. It's not enough to support my kids. I have to be there for them."

Sammy looked surprised and relieved. "Well, hallelujah. Maybe after all that work on the lighthouse, you're finally seeing it."

"What?"

"The damn light."

But Jack wasn't listening to him anymore. He was thinking about something else Sammy had said.

She's damn near sixteen.

The date popped into Jack's head. Her birthday. Coming up fast. And it was a big one.

"You guys ready to order?"

Jack looked up to see a waitress standing next to their table. "What?"

The woman smiled and tapped the menu. "This is a restaurant. And that's a menu. I just took it on faith that you might want to order some food."

"I'll take care of these two, Sally," said a voice. Jenna walked up. "They could be trouble," she added with a coy smile.

"Okay, boss." Sally walked off.

Sammy looked at her and grinned. "So tell me the specials."

"Now, Mr. Duvall, you know that everything on the menu is special, and you've eaten most of it."

Jack looked at Sammy in surprise. "You have?"

Sammy said defensively, "I get hungry. Just because you don't eat doesn't mean I have to do the same."

"How about our famous pork barbecue sandwich with fried onion rings and slaw on top? It's hell on the arteries, but you're guaranteed to die with a smile on your face."

"Sounds good," said Sammy. He stared at Jack. "Make it two. And make sure you put a smiley face on his; might improve the man's mood." He winked at Jenna.

She said, "Well, I wanted to talk to you about something anyway, Jack. Let me put your order in, and I'll be right back."

She walked off and returned a minute later, drawing up a chair.

"I'll get to the point. Your daughter would like to waitress here. And I want to hire her."

"What?" said Jack. "She didn't tell me about it."

Sammy said testily, "She wanted to, but it's not like you've been around."

Jack ignored this and looked at Jenna. "Waitress?"

"It's an honest profession, and I pay a fair wage."

Jack glanced at Sammy. "I'll have to get someone to watch the boys."

Jenna said, "I actually thought of that. The lady you're doing work for, Anne Bethune? She runs a summer camp at her place. It's right on the beach. The boys could go there. They'd have a great time."

Sammy said, "I've gotten to know Anne, and I saw how the camp was set up. They'll love it."

"But *I* don't really know the woman."

"She's the principal at the local elementary school, Jack," said Jenna. "She has two kids of her own. In fact, when I first moved here, I put Liam in the camp and he had a blast. She has qualified people helping her too."

Sammy added, "So that way Mikki can work here during the day. Earn some money, get out of the house. Have a life."

Jenna added, "And she gets her meals free. I think it'll be good for her."

"How much does the camp cost?"

"Now, that's the interesting thing," said Sammy. "I'm doing some extra work for her on the side, and Anne agreed to let the boys come there in exchange for it."

"Sammy, you didn't have to do that."

"Like hell I didn't. They need to have some fun too."

Jack looked between Jenna and Sammy. "Why do I sense this was all planned out?"

Sammy snapped, "You got a good reason not to do it?"

"Well, no. It actually sounds like a great idea."

"Okay, then. So what's the problem?"

Jack locked gazes with Sammy for a long moment before finally looking away. "Okay, fine."

Sammy slapped the table. "There you go. That wasn't too hard, was it? Now, Jenna, can you add two beers to our order? I feel the need to celebrate."

Jenna went off to do this while Jack pretended to go to

the restroom. Instead he followed Jenna. "Can I talk to you about something?"

She looked at him in surprise. "Is everything okay?"

"Yeah," he said quickly. "I just need to ask you about something."

"Look, Jack, I know it seemed like we ganged up on you about the camp and Mikki working here, but—"

He smiled. "I actually really appreciate what you're doing."

"Thank Sammy. It was his idea. You got a good friend in that man."

"You're right. I do." He looked at her. "And a good friend in you too."

This comment seemed to catch Jenna off-guard.

"I'm just . . . It's not that . . ."

She stopped in midsentence and looked away, flustered.

Jack said, "I know I've been a little unfriendly with you, and I'm sorry."

She quickly looked back at him. "You don't have to apologize, Jack. In my book you've done nothing wrong. So what did you want to ask me?"

"I don't want to do it now. What time would be good later?"

"I can get away from here around nine."

"I can pick you up here. Drive you home."

"That's fine. Liam has his license. He can drive the car back."

"I'll see you then."

43

The café was crowded, and Blake and Mikki got as close to the DJ as possible. The tunes were already blasting, and people were dancing. Blake and Mikki got Cokes from the bar and settled into a corner to watch and listen.

"You look really good," Blake said.

Mikki had on jean shorts, flip-flops, a white sleeveless blouse, and a pair of earrings her mother had given her for her fourteenth birthday. Her hair was tied back in a pony-tail, and she'd washed the latest color out of the strands. Her skin had tanned, and her face glowed.

Blake had on jeans and a long-sleeve shirt worn out with the sleeves rolled up. She eyed him. "You don't look so bad either."

He laughed. "Thanks a lot. Want'a dance?"

"Okay."

They hit the dance floor and spent a half hour getting sweaty and out of breath, as they jostled next to kids doing the same thing. After another couple hours of listening to the music, things started to wind down. Blake said, "How about a walk on the beach? Nice night."

"Okay, but remember what I did to Tiffany." She held up her hands in a pseudo-martial arts pose.

Blake laughed. "I'm not messing with you. Or your dad."

They strolled along the sand. Mikki took her flip-flops off and carried them in one hand. Her free hand touched Blake's, and he wrapped one of his fingers around one of hers. At first she pulled back, but a moment later they were holding hands.

They reached an isolated section of beach where tall dunes were covered with lush, tangled vegetation.

Blake said, "I guess we better head on back."

"Okay."

He turned to her. She faced him.

"This was nice," she said.

"Not just saying that?"

"No, I'm not."

"Most girls are easy to read. But not you."

"I get that a lot."

He grinned, cupped her chin with his hand. He dipped his head to hers.

She pulled back.

He looked annoyed. "What's wrong? You've kissed before, right?"

"Of course I have," she said heatedly. "I'm almost six-teen."

"So what's the problem?"

"There's no problem." She grabbed him by the neck and planted a kiss on him. When they pulled apart, he exclaimed, "Wow. Okay, that was cool."

However, from Mikki's look, the kiss had not had the same effect on her. In fact, she looked a little guilty.

"Let's get back," she said hurriedly.

They'd only walked a few feet when Blake said, "What was that?" He turned around and stared at the dunes.

"What was what?" said Mikki.

Then the sound came again. Something was moving through the dunes.

"What is it?" Mikki asked, her fingers closing around Blake's wrist.

"I don't know. But something's up there."

"Maybe a dog or a cat?"

Another sound.

Mikki said, "That's not a dog or cat. That was someone talking. Blake, let's just get out of here."

"Hold on, there's something weird going on here. I think I recognize that voice." He called out, "Dukie? Dukie, is that you?"

"Who's Dukie?"

"Left tackle on the football team. Big and dumb. I don't know what he'd be doing here." He looked around. "Look, just hang here a sec; I'll be right back."

"Blake, don't go up there."

"Just hang on; I'll be right back."

He scooted toward the mounds of sand and quickly disappeared into the darkness. Mikki stood there looking anxiously around. There was no moon tonight, and it was hard to tell where the water ended and the land began.

"Blake?" she whispered harshly, but there was no answer. She moved closer to the dunes. "Blake?"

Hands came out of nowhere and grabbed her. She tried to scream, but something clamped over her mouth. As she looked frantically around, she saw that all the people around her were wearing Halloween masks, dark, gruesome ones.

Somebody put duct tape across her mouth. Another bound her hands behind her back. She jerked and pulled and fell down. Hands held her against the sand. Something was poured over her hair. Someone covered her eyes, and she felt something being sprayed on her clothes. She kept jerking and trying to scream. Tears poured down her face.

Someone yelled, and then there was a loud grunt.

Suddenly, whoever was holding her down fell over hard. The crowd abruptly moved away from her. Mikki sat up and struggled to see what was going on. As her eyes focused, she saw Liam hitting one of the masked people, and the person crumpled. Someone jumped on Liam's back, but he whirled around and threw the attacker off. As the person hit the sand, the mask popped off and Mikki saw Tiffany Murdoch staring at her. Mikki managed to get the rope off her hands and tore the duct tape off her mouth as another, larger person in a mask hit Liam and knocked him down. Two others jumped on top of him. Then another guy roughly pulled those two off and straddled Liam. Mikki leapt up, raced across the sand, and jumped on top of the guy, pulling his head backward, her nails raking his face.

He yelled something and pushed her off as he twisted away and fell down. Then he jumped to his feet, his mask askew. Sitting on her butt in the sand, Mikki looked up in disbelief.

"Blake?"

He rubbed the scratch marks on his face, turned, and

ran. Mikki saw him grab Tiffany's hand, and they raced off toward the dunes. Mikki tore her gaze away from them in time to see the remaining guy drive his foot into Liam's stomach. She scooped up some sand, jumped up, ripped off the guy's mask, and threw the sand in his eyes. He yelled and started jumping around, clawing at his eyes. She pushed him backward, and he fell, then picked himself up and staggered after the others.

Mikki raced over to Liam, who lay facedown in the sand holding his stomach.

"Oh my God, Liam, are you okay?"

He slowly sat up, breathing hard. She wiped the sand off his face and clothes.

"Wow, you really know how to party," he said, grinning weakly.

"What are you doing here?" she asked.

"Just got off work. Was taking a stroll to wind down before I drove home. Then I heard some weird stuff and saw some people behind that dune. Then you two came walking by. When they jumped you I came flying in."

"You . . . you were watching us? Then you saw . . . ?"

"Hey, no big deal. I'm just glad you're okay." He rose gingerly. "Come on. I'll drive you home."

Mikki didn't move. "I'm sorry, Liam."

"Sorry for what?"

"It wasn't nearly as cool as when you and I kissed."

He looked down, his fingers clenching as though looking for the comfort of his drumsticks. "Really?"

"Absolutely, really."

She stood. "You were really brave to do that. You saved me."

"Jerks." He looked at her and drew in a quick breath. "Damn."

"What?"

"Your hair and your clothes."

She looked down at her clothes. They were spray painted red along with her exposed skin. She touched her hair; it was sticky and clumped and smelled like rotten eggs.

"Jerks," she said. She looked in the direction of the dunes. "Blake was part of it. I can't believe I was that stupid."

"So were you on a date with him? I mean, that's cool. He's the quarterback, not a bad-looking guy either."

"It was a mistake," she said, gripping his arm. "For a lot of reasons. And he set me up. I bet it had to do with me beating up Tiffany at the beach party."

Liam looked shocked. "You beat up Tiffany? You didn't tell me that."

"Well, she had it coming."

He laughed and then grabbed his ribs.

"Are you sure you're okay?" she said worriedly as she put a hand around his waist to support him.

As their bodies touched, they looked at each other.

She said, "I'm really gross right now, Liam."

"No, you're not; you're beautiful."

Mikki went up on her tiptoes even as the tall Liam bent down to her. They kissed, this time far longer than they had the first time.

As they drew apart and opened their eyes, she said, "You're my knight in"—she looked at his dark clothes and smiled—"black shining armor and hiking boots."

He touched her cheek and grinned. "And you're my fair maiden in flaming red with stinky stuff in her hair."

"Liam, we can't tell our parents. My dad will go after all of them and probably end up in jail."

"But what about your clothes and hair?"

"I'll clean up before I sneak in the house."

Liam said, "So we're not going to get back at Tiffany and her friends?"

"Oh, I didn't say that. We're going to get back at them, but we're going to do it the right way, not the stupid way they tried to do it."

"So how, then?"

"You'll see."

She plopped down in the ocean water and started to scrub.

44

Jack was waiting outside the restaurant when Jenna came out promptly at nine. She climbed in the VW van, and he pulled off.

"This looks like a vintage ride," she said.

"Sammy's. He likes to tinker with cars."

"That's not all he likes to tinker with."

He glanced at her. "Meaning what?"

"Meaning he and Anne Bethune are seeing each other."

"What? Why am I always the last to know?"

She squeezed his shoulder. "You just need to get out more, honey."

"When did it start?"

"Oh, about the time they laid eyes on each other; at least that was how Anne described it. In fact, that's where he was the day you beat up those guys. They went for a ride on his Harley." Jenna bent down and took off her shoes and started rubbing her feet. "Sorry, after ten hours these puppies are screaming." She rolled down the window and breathed in the crisp evening air. "God, I remember in college, a guy I dated had a Harley. One time when Liam was staying with my mom we rode it all over the Blue Ridge Parkway. It was so much fun."

"Were you away from Liam a lot back then?"

She rolled the window back up. "Hardly ever, actually. I went to college close to home so I could stay there. My mom was divorced and ran a business out of her house. She would watch Liam for me when I was at class or working."

"Working?"

"Only way to pay for school. No silver spoons in my neighborhood. I knew I wanted to go to college, and then law school. And then work at a big firm in a big city."

"Sounds like you had it all mapped out."

"Well, I didn't have Liam mapped out. He just happened. Two stupid teenagers." Her features grew solemn. "But I don't know what I'd do without him in my life. He's a great kid. And he and Mikki really seem to have hit it off. When I told him she was going to be working at the Little Bit, he was really psyched."

"Well, that's actually the reason I wanted to talk to you. About Liam."

"What about him?"

Jack told her his plan.

She was smiling and nodding as he finished. "Okay, that sounds terrific. In fact, I'm real proud of you, *Dad*. But in return you have to do one thing for me."

He looked at her warily. "What?"

"Can you take me for a ride on the Harley?"

Jack drove to the Palace, got Sammy's permission, and

fired up the Harley. Jenna got on back, and they drove off, paralleling the ocean on the long, winding road. As the wind whipped across their faces, Jenna said, "Boy does this bring back memories."

"Having fun, then?"

"You know it." She squeezed his middle as they leaned into turn after turn. After thirty minutes he drove her home.

"Liam's not here yet. Would you like to come in for some tea or coffee, or something stronger?"

They sat out on the rear deck sipping glasses of Chardonnay Jenna had poured them. After going over the details of Jack's plan in more depth, Jenna said, "How's the lighthouse coming?"

He put down his glass. "Good. Stairs are coming along, and Charles found the parts to repair the light."

"I bet it'll be something to see it fired up again."

"Yeah, I think it will," Jack said absently.

"And why do I think that's not why you're really doing it?"

He glanced up at her. "I fix things. That's what I do."

"Some things can't be fixed with a hammer and a set of plans."

He drained the rest of his glass. "I better get going." He rose.

"Jack?"

"Yeah?" His voice seemed defensive.

"Let me know when you get the lighthouse working. I'd really love to see it."

Taken aback by her obvious sincerity, he said, "I will, Jenna."

"And thanks for the ride. Most fun I've had in a long time."

Before he realized, Jack had already said it.

"Me too."

45

The next morning at the breakfast table Jack said, "I didn't hear you come in last night, Mik."

"I actually got in early," Mikki lied as she poured out a glass of OJ.

"So how was the date?"

"It was okay. But we're just not that compatible."

"It happens."

"Yeah, it does. Hey, Dad, I'm going into town today."

"Why?"

"Just an errand to run. Liam's going with me. I won't be long. Sammy said he'd watch Jackie for me."

"When do you start working at the restaurant?"

"Tomorrow. That's when Cory and Jackie start camp."

"You know, you could have come to me with all that."

She put a hand on her hip and said, "Could I have, Dad? Really?"

He looked away. "So how are you getting to town? Want a lift?"

"Liam's picking me up."

"Look, Mikki, I want you to be able to talk to me about

stuff. If we can't do that, then we've got no shot at this father-daughter thing."

"You really mean that?"

"Yeah, I do."

"Well, it would be a nice start if you didn't work all day and then go to the lighthouse all night."

"But I've almost got it finished."

"Okay, Dad, whatever. We can talk when you're done with it."

Mikki walked out to the street, where Liam was waiting for her in his car.

Liam grinned. "When you called this morning with your plan, I have to admit I was really intrigued. Now I'm downright fired up."

"Good, because so am I."

They arrived in downtown Channing and parked in front of the Play House. There were a number of cars sitting at the curb, including Tiffany's red convertible. The marquee read, CHANNING TALENT COMPETITION APPLICATIONS TODAY.

Mikki grinned. "When I saw that sign last night, I really didn't think anything of it. You know, who cares? But now—now the timing couldn't be more perfect."

"Let's do it," said Liam.

They walked inside the lobby and joined a line of people standing in front of a long table behind which sat a number of ladies with hair styled to the max and wearing clothes that probably cost more than some automobiles. One of them, an attractive blond woman in a formfitting dress, seemed to be in charge.

"Let me guess," Mikki whispered to Liam as she pointed at the woman. "Tiffany's mom?"

Liam nodded. "How'd you know?"

"I just flash-forwarded Tiffany twenty-five years."

"Chelsea Murdoch. I heard my mom once say she was even worse than her daughter."

"Wow, now, that's a lady I have got to tangle with."

When Liam and Mikki reached the table, Chelsea Murdoch looked up at them with such a haughty expression that Mikki just wanted to slap her. "Yes?"

"We'd like to enter the competition," said Mikki politely.

Murdoch glanced at Liam and looked confused. "Both of you?"

"That's right. Together."

"Liam Fontaine, right?" she said.

"The one and only."

The woman smirked, and then her gaze swiveled to Mikki. "And you are?"

"Michelle Armstrong. We're down here from Cleveland for the summer."

The woman looked amused. "Cleveland?"

"Yes, it's the largest city in Ohio. Did you know that?" Mikki said innocently.

"No, I never saw a good reason to find out," she replied dryly and then bumped elbows with the woman sitting next to her, who chuckled. Mrs. Murdoch pushed a paper toward them. "Fill this out. And there's a ten-dollar processing fee. What are you going to do for your act?"

"Music," said Mikki. "Drums, keyboard, and guitar."

Murdoch looked at her coolly. "Pretty ambitious."

"I'd like to think so," Mikki replied sweetly. "I'm sure the competition is pretty tough."

"It is. In fact, one young lady has won it three years in a row and is looking to make it four."

"Would that be Tiffany?"

"Yes. She's my daughter."

"Of course. But I already knew she'd won it three times in a row."

"How?"

Mikki pointed to the mammoth banner on the wall behind them, which had a large picture of Tiffany holding up three trophies with the words TRIPLE CROWN stenciled over her head. "That was, like, sort of the first clue."

Mikki returned Murdoch's scowl with a smile.

"Just put the form in the box over there and give your money to the lady in the blue dress," she snapped.

"Great. Thanks for all your help, Mrs. Murdoch," Mikki said in her most polite schoolgirl voice.

Mikki could feel the woman firing laser eye darts at her as they walked off. She filled out the form and gave it and their entry fee to the woman in the blue dress.

"Okay, step one is done," Liam said.

"And here comes step two."

Tiffany and some of her friends had just walked into the lobby of the theater.

When Mikki marched up to them, Tiffany stiffened.

"Hey, Tiff."

Tiffany looked puzzled, and then glanced at her friends and back at Mikki. "Hi," Tiffany said coolly.

"I wanted to thank you for the great time on the beach. It was really memorable."

Tiffany snorted, and the other girls laughed. "Uh, okay," said a grinning Tiffany.

Mikki leaned closer. "And just so we're straight, we're, like, so going to kick your ass in the talent competition."

The smile vanished from Tiffany's face, and her friends stopped laughing.

Mikki drew even closer. "Oh, one more thing. You ever lay another finger on me, they won't be able to find all the pieces to put you back together again, sweetie." She'd unconsciously used the same threat she'd overheard her dad invoke back in Cleveland.

Tiffany blinked and took a step back. "You think you're so tough?"

Mikki put her face an inch from the other girl's. "I'm from Cleveland. It's sort of a requirement."

Outside, as they passed Tiffany's red convertible, Liam glanced around to make sure no one was watching, then reached in his pocket and pulled out a white tube. Pretending to be picking up something, he squirted the clear liquid from the tube onto the convertible's driver's seat. It was invisible against the leather.

"What's that?" Mikki asked.

"After what they did to you, I think Super Glue is in order."

"Liam, I'm so liking your style, dude."

46

"Okay, so what's the conspiracy?"

Jenna had come into the kitchen at the Little Bit to find Liam and Mikki using their break to huddle in one corner.

"Nothing, Mom," Liam said a little too innocently.

"Son, you forget I was a lawyer. My lie detector is well oiled."

He looked sheepish and glanced at Mikki. "You want to tell her?"

Mikki said, "We entered the talent competition as a musical act."

"Well, that's great. Why keep it a secret?"

Liam answered. "We'll be going up against Tiffany, and I know her family is an important player in town. We beat her out of winning for the fourth year in a row, the Murdochs might mess with you."

"They can try and mess with me, but I don't think it'll do much good. The Little Bit is pretty much here to stay." She looked at both of them curiously. "So why this sudden interest in beating Tiffany Murdoch?"

The two teens looked at each other.

Sensing they were holding something significant back, Jenna said, "Okay, both of you, I happen to be the boss. And I want the truth. Right now."

Between them, Mikki and Liam told her what had happened on the beach.

When they'd finished, the look on Jenna's features was very dark. "That was a criminal assault on you, Mikki. And you too, Liam. You two could have been really hurt."

"It was no big deal, Mom," said Liam.

"It was a very big deal. Those kids need to be held accountable for what they did. Otherwise, they might do it again."

"Mom, please don't do anything. We want to handle this in our own way."

Mikki added, "And if my dad finds out, he'll beat them all up and probably end up in jail. I know my dad. He's really overprotective. They were just teenagers, and he's an ex–army ranger. You saw what he did to those two big guys. He can be like a SWAT team all by himself when he needs to be. They'd throw the book at him. So please don't say anything, Jenna. Please."

Jenna's features finally lightened. "Okay, I see your logic. But does your dad know you're entering the talent competition?"

"Not yet."

"Well, I think the sooner he knows, the better."

Mikki gazed at her. "Would you mind telling him?"

"Me? Why?"

"It might be better coming from another parent. I don't think he'll mind, but he's been a little preoccupied lately. And we've already entered. I can't pull out now."

Jenna thought about this for a few seconds. "Okay, I'll talk to him." She checked her watch and smiled. "Break time's over. We run a real sweatshop here. So get to it."

Mikki gave her a quick hug. "Thanks. You're a lifesaver. So when do you think you'll talk to him?"

"I think I know where to find him at the right time."

At a little past midnight, Jack stood on the catwalk of the lighthouse, staring out at a clear sky. After his conversation with Mikki and the disappointment so evident on her face, he had really tried not to come out here, but something made his legs move, and here he was.

He'd worked all day with Sammy on Anne Bethune's project, which had also given him time to see her camp. He had to admit that Jackie and Cory were having a wonderful time, and they were learning things too. Anne had an instructor who took the kids down to the water and showed them about marine life and other science subjects appropriate for younger kids. Cory was in his element with painting and acting out scenes that he had written in a performance art workshop the camp also offered. It was exactly the sort of experience Jack had hoped for when they came down here for the summer. However, Jack was trying not to focus on the fact that he wasn't an integral part of that experience, that it was being done through what amounted to surrogates.

If I can just finish the lighthouse.

He walked back inside the structure and gazed down at the new stairs. He'd just driven in the last nail a few minutes ago. Work still needed to be done on them, mostly finishing items, but they were safe to walk on and would last a long time. He planned to start disassembling the scaffolding tomorrow night and return it to the hardware store. He picked up Lizzie's doll and went back out on the catwalk. Sweaty from all the hard work in the confines of the lighthouse, he took off his shirt and let the cool breeze flow over him.

He looked at the doll and then gazed up at the sky. Heaven was somewhere up there. He'd been thinking about where a precocious little girl would have thought it was located. He looked at discrete grids of the sky, much like he'd compartmentalized and studied the desert in the Middle East when he was fighting in a war there. Which spot was most likely to hold an IED or a sniper?

Only now he was looking for angels and saints.

And Lizzie.

He set the doll down and took the letter from his shirt pocket. Now that he'd finished the stairs, he told himself it was time to read the next one. The envelope had the number four written on it. He slipped the letter out. It was dated December twenty-first. He leaned against the railing and read it.

Dear Lizzie,

Christmas is almost here, and I promise that I will make it. It will be a great day. Seeing the kids' faces when they open their presents will be better for me than all the medications in the world. I know this has been hard on everyone, especially you and the kids. But I know that your mom and dad have really been a tremendous help to you. I've never gotten to know them as well as I would have liked. Sometimes I feel that your mom thinks you might have married someone better suited to you, more successful. But I know deep down that she cares about me, and I know she loves you and the kids with all her heart. It is a blessing to have someone like that to support you. My father died, as you know, when I was still just a kid. And you know about my mom. But your parents have always been there for me, especially Bonnie, and in many ways, I see her as more of a mom to me than my own mother. It's action, not words, that really counts. That's what it really means to love someone. Please tell them that I always had the greatest respect for her and Fred. They are good people. And I hope that one day she will feel that I was a good father who tried to do the right thing. And that maybe I was worthy of you.

Love,
Jack

47

"Am I interrupting something?"

Jack turned to see Jenna standing there on the catwalk, a bottle of wine and two glasses in hand. She saw the letter in his hand but said nothing as he thrust it in his jeans pocket and quickly pulled his shirt on, his fingers struggling to button it up as fast as possible.

"What are you doing here?" he said a little harshly.

She took a step back. "I'm sorry if I snuck up on you."

"Well, you did."

"Look, I'll just leave."

She turned to go when he said, "No, it's okay. I'm sorry. I didn't mean to snap at you. I just wasn't expecting anyone."

She smiled. "I wonder why? It's after midnight and you're standing on your own property at the top of a lighthouse. I would've thought there'd have been hundreds of people through here by now."

His anger faded, and a grin crept across Jack's face. "Dozens maybe, but not hundreds." He eyed the wine. "Coming from a party?"

She looked around and set the glasses on an old crate while she uncorked the wine. "No, hoping I was coming *to* one."

"What?"

She poured out the wine and handed him a glass, then clinked hers against his. "Cheers." She took a sip and let it go down slowly as she gazed out over the broad view. "God, it's beautiful up here."

"Yeah, it is."

"So you finished the stairs, I see."

"Still need to do some work, but the heavy lifting's done."

"I guess you're wondering what the heck I'm doing here?"

"Honestly? Yeah, I am."

She told him about Liam and Mikki entering the talent competition but withheld the reason why.

"Hey, that's great. I bet they have a good chance to win."

"They do, actually. I'm no expert, but I'd pay money to hear them."

Jack swallowed some of his wine. "But why didn't Mikki just come and tell me?"

"I'm not really sure. She asked me to, and I agreed. Maybe you should ask her."

Jack slowly nodded. "I know I've gotten my priorities screwed up."

"Well, realizing the problem is a good first step to fixing it. And like you said, you fix things."

"Yeah, well, lighthouses are easier than relationships."

"I would imagine anything is easier than that. But that doesn't mean you can ignore it."

"I'm starting to see that."

"I know what you told me before, but why is this so important to you, Jack?"

He put his wineglass down. "This feels like the place I can be closest to her," he said slowly. He glanced over to find Jenna staring at him with a concerned expression. "Look, I'm not losing touch with reality."

"I didn't think you were," she said quickly.

"But it's still crazy, right?"

"If you feel it, it's not crazy, Jack. You've been through a lot."

"The Miracle Man," he said softly.

Jenna gazed at him but said nothing, waiting for him to speak.

"I wasn't supposed to be here, Jenna. I mean living. I was just hanging on 'til Christmas, for the kids. For Lizzie."

She touched his shoulder. "I shouldn't have asked. You don't owe me an explanation about anything."

"No, it's okay. I need to get this out." He paused, drawing a long breath, seeming to marshal his thoughts. "I spent half our marriage in the army, most of it away from home." He stopped, glanced at the dark sky. "I was crazy in love with my wife. I mean, they say absence makes the heart grow fonder? I could be in the next room and miss Lizzie, much less halfway around the world."

A tear trickled from Jack's right eye, and Jenna's mouth quivered. She swallowed with difficulty.

"I always saw Lizzie and me as one person whose halves

got separated somehow, but they found each other again. That's how lucky I was."

Jenna said quietly, "Most people never have that, Jack. You were truly blessed."

"The last night we were together she told me she wanted to come back here for the summer. I could tell she wanted to believe that I would be alive to come with her. She even talked about me fixing up the place. This light-house. I never thought I'd have the chance."

"So you're fulfilling Lizzie's last wish?"

"I guess." He turned to look back out to sea. "Because she never got the chance to come back."

Jenna said, "And then you got better?"

He glanced at her, his eyes red. "But do you know why I got better? Because Lizzie was right there with me every step of the way. She wouldn't let me die."

"Why are you telling me all this?"

"Because if I don't tell someone, I think I'm going to . . . to . . . I don't know. And you seemed like someone who would understand."

A gentle rain began to fall as they stood there. Jenna put down her glass, gripped Jack's shoulders, turned him to her, and put her arms around him.

As the rain continued to come down, they stood there in the darkness slowly swaying from side to side.

"I do understand, Jack. I really do."

48

"Jenna, you really don't have to do this," said Mikki.

They were at a women's clothing store in downtown Channing during a break from working at the restaurant.

She continued, "It's no big deal. I mean it's only dinner out with my family. Dad and Sammy and certainly Cory and Jackie aren't going to care what I have on."

"But it's also your sixteenth birthday, honey, and that only happens once in your life."

Together, they'd selected a half dozen outfits, and Mikki was trying them on. After Mikki decided on a dark sleeveless dress, Jenna helped her pick out shoes, a purse, and other accessories.

"Thanks, Jenna. I can't exactly go bra shopping with my dad."

"No, I guess you really can't." She smiled mischievously. "Though it might be kind of fun if you did. Just to see the former tough-as-nails army ranger squirm over cup sizes."

Mikki was looking down at all the items and mentally calculating the prices. Her face turned red. "Uh, I'm going to have to put some of these things back."

"Why?"

"I . . . I don't have enough money."

"Sure you do; I just gave you an advance on your salary."

"What?"

"I do it with all my new employees, or at least the ones turning sixteen who want something new to wear."

"I'm not looking for a freebie."

"And I'm not giving it. This will be deducted from your pay-check in equal installments over the next sixty years, young lady."

Mikki laughed. "Are you sure?"

"Absolutely. Seriously, you're a really good waitress and a hard worker. That should be rewarded."

After they left the shop, Jenna said, "How about an ice cream? I've got something I want to talk to you about."

They sat outside on a street bench with their cones.

"First things first. I spoke with your dad about the talent competition, and he's completely fine with you entering."

"Wow, that's great."

"Although he did wonder why you didn't just come and ask him directly about it."

"And what did you tell him?"

"I played dumb and basically dodged the question." She licked her cone and seemed to be choosing her next words carefully. "The lighthouse?"

Mikki sighed. "What about it?"

"Your dad spends a lot of time out there."

"How did you know that?"

"Well, aside from your miserable expression, I just

know; let's leave it at that. Now, have you ever been out there with him?"

"No."

"Why?"

"I just don't; no reason."

"You resent it?"

"Resent a stupid building? That's a dumb question," she said irritably.

"Is it?"

Mikki finished her ice cream, wiped off her fingers, and threw the trash in a bin next to the bench. "Look, if he chooses to be out there instead of with his family, who am I to rock the boat?"

"I think you just answered my question. You know that was your mom's lighthouse?"

Mikki scowled. "Yeah, my mom when she was a little girl."

"So you think it's odd he seems so . . ."

"Obsessed? Yeah, a little. What would you think?"

"Hard to say. Now, tell me about what those jerks were yelling at your dad on the street that day. Miracle Man?"

Mikki looked uncomfortable and drew a long breath. "I don't really want to talk about that."

"Please, Mikki. I really do want to help. But I need to know."

Mikki took the next few minutes to fill her in.

Jenna looked thoughtful. "So basically the tabloid made everything up?"

"Well, that's what my dad says."

"And you believe a newspaper that makes millions selling lies over your father? How does that make sense?"

Mikki refused to look at her. She said, "Where there's smoke, there's fire."

"That makes even less sense."

"Easy for you to say. It wasn't your family getting destroyed."

"No, but let me put on my lawyer hat for a minute and analyze this." She paused, but only for a moment. "Your dad loses the woman he loves in a tragedy that was really no one's fault. Then he loses the rest of his family and is left to die alone. Instead, he somehow finds the strength to beat a certain death sentence, brings his family back together, and tries to make a go of it as a single parent. And then a bunch of gut-wrenching lies get spread all over the news and people are calling him terrible things based on those lies, and he has to just stand there and take it." She stopped. "What an evil guy your dad is."

Jenna looked over to find Mikki staring down at her feet, a stunned expression on her face.

"I guess I never looked at it that way," she said after a long silence. "I can see why you were a lawyer."

"It's the hardest thing in the world to put yourself in someone else's place, try to really feel what they feel, figure out why they do the things they do. Especially when it's easier to stick a label on something. Or someone."

"And the lighthouse?"

"Lizzie loved it at some point in her life. It was important to her. She wanted to see it work again. That's good enough for your father. He'll work himself to the bone to try and fix it."

"For her?"

"Your dad isn't crazy. He knows she's gone, Mikki.

He's doing this for her memory. At least partly. This is all part of the healing process; that's all. Everyone does it differently, but this is just your father's way."

"So what do you think I should do?"

"At some point, find the courage to talk to him."

"About what?"

"I think you'll figure it out."

Mikki laid her hand on Jenna's arm. "Thanks for the ice cream. And the advice."

"You're very welcome to both, sweetie."

49

On Saturday night Jenna helped Mikki get dressed in her new clothes and did her hair. She pinned most of it back but let a few strands trickle down Mikki's long, slender neck.

Cory and Jackie were sitting on the couch together watching TV. They both stared wide-eyed at their sister when she came down the stairs followed by a proud looking Jenna.

"Mikki bootiful," said Jackie.

Cory didn't say anything; he just kept staring, like this was the first time he'd realized his sister was a girl.

Sammy came out of the kitchen, saw her, and said, "Wow. Okay, people, heartbreaker coming through, make room. Make room."

Mikki blushed deeply and said, "Sammy, knock it off!"

"Honey, take the compliments from the men when you can," advised Jenna.

Sammy yelled, "Jack, get your butt in here. There's big trouble."

Jack walked in from the kitchen and froze when he saw her.

Mikki took in all the males staring at her and finally said, "What?"

"Nothing, sweetie," said Jack. "You look terrific."

"Jenna helped me."

Jack flashed her an appreciative look. "Good thing. I'm not really all that great with hair and makeup."

Jenna chuckled. "Gee, don't they teach that in the army?"

"So where are we going?" asked Mikki.

"Like I said, dinner with the family. To celebrate your sweet sixteen."

She looked at Cory and Jackie watching cartoons and munching on cheese curls. Jackie's face and hands were totally orange and sticky. Cory let out a loud belch. "Great," she said, trying to sound enthusiastic.

Sammy looked at Jack. "Hold on a sec. You said we had to finish that job tonight. Promised the lady. Remember?"

"Oh, damn, that's right. What was I thinking?" Jack slapped his forehead in frustration.

Mikki scowled, "Tonight? What job?"

Jack looked stricken. "A big one. I forgot, honey."

Mikki's face flushed and her eyes glistened. "Dad, it's my *sixteenth* birthday."

"I know, sweetie, I know. Thank goodness I had a backup plan."

"What?"

He opened the front door, and Mikki gasped.

Liam was standing there dressed in pressed chinos and a white button-down shirt. His face was scrubbed pink, and he'd even combed his long hair. In his hand was a bouquet of flowers.

Mikki looked from him to her dad. "Uh, what is going on?"

Jack grinned. "Like you really wanted to go out on your sixteenth birthday with your old man and two little brothers? Give me a break."

"That would've been fine," she said, trying to keep a straight face.

"Yeah, right," scoffed Sammy. He turned to Liam, who hadn't budged an inch. "Well, get in here, son, and deliver the flowers to the lady." He grabbed Liam's arm and propelled him into the room.

Liam handed the bouquet to Mikki. "You really look great," he said shyly.

"Pretty slick yourself." She eyed her dad. "How did you possibly manage this without Cory or Jackie squealing?"

"That's easy. I didn't tell them. But Jenna was a major co-conspirator."

Jenna did a mock curtsy. "Guilty as charged."

"So, what's the plan?" Mikki asked.

"Like I said, dinner. For two. Reservations have already been made."

Jenna amended, "Not the Little Bit. At the fancy restaurant in town. I know the owners really well. They've got a great table picked out for you and a special menu."

"Wow, I can't believe this is happening. I feel like Cinderella."

Jack put his arm around his daughter. "Nice to know I can still surprise you."

"Thanks, Dad. Well, I guess we better go," she said.

"Wait a sec," Jack said. "Close your eyes."

"Dad!"

"Please, just do it."

Sighing heavily, she closed her eyes. Jack slipped the necklace from his pocket and affixed it around her neck. "Okay."

She looked down and gasped. She rushed to a mirror hanging on the wall.

"This was Mom's necklace," she said in a hushed tone.

Jack nodded. "I gave it to her on our first wedding anniversary."

Mikki turned to look at him, tears glimmering in her eyes.

"Happy birthday, baby."

Father and daughter shared a lingering hug.

After Liam and Mikki had gone off on their date, Jack stood on the front porch staring at the sandy yard. Jenna joined him there. Jack's eyes were moist, and he wouldn't look at her.

"You okay, *Dad*?" she asked.

"They grow up fast, Jenna."

"Yes, they do. But growing up is okay. What we don't want them to do is grow *away* from us."

"You're pretty good at this parenting thing."

"You do something solo long enough, I guess you either get good at it or you crash."

"So there's hope for me?"

"I'd say definitely." She slid her arm through his. "She's a great kid, Jack."

"Because of Lizzie."

"Give yourself some of the credit. You did good tonight, Jack Armstrong."

"You really think so?"

"Yeah, I really do."

50

Mikki and Liam had just finished dinner when he excused himself to go to the restroom. A few seconds later, Mikki was stunned to see Blake Saunders walk up to her table.

"What are you doing here, you weasel?" she snarled.

"I work here."

"You work here?"

"Busing tables. Sweat Town, like I said."

"Gee, doesn't sweet little Tiffany give you an allowance?"

"Look, I know you're upset, and you have every right to be."

"You're wrong, Blake. If I were upset, that would mean I cared, and I don't. You had your stupid fun, but Liam could have really gotten hurt."

"I pulled those two idiots off him, in case you didn't notice. I was on top of him to protect him. Nobody was supposed to get hurt. But then you jumped on my back and basically scratched my face off."

"Hey, let's not forget that none of it would've happened if you hadn't set me up. And why exactly did you do that?"

Blake looked down. "Because of what you did to Tiff. She was upset. She wanted to get back at you."

"And you do whatever Tiff tells you to? That's beyond pathetic."

"Yeah, I guess it is," Blake admitted.

"Look, you're not going to fool me with your 'I'm all sorry' act. Okay? So just save your breath."

"Did you put the glue in her car seat?"

"Don't know what you're talking about."

"Well, in case you were wondering, she was pissed. She had to take off her pants to get out of the car. And she hadn't bothered to put on underwear. She had to run up the steps to her house. But she slipped and fell over into the bushes, scratched her rear end up good. At least that's what my mom said. Guess all the hired help got a good laugh about that later."

Hearing this, Mikki could not suppress a grin. "It's nice to know that bad things do happen to bad people."

"I heard you entered the talent competition."

"That's right. Me and Liam. I'm sure you'll be there to root on precious Tiff."

"Actually, I hope you kick her butt."

He turned and walked away.

After leaving the restaurant, Liam and Mikki drove to the beach, parked, took off their shoes, and walked along the sand.

"I never saw the ocean before coming here," said Mikki as she drew close enough to the water to let it cover her feet.

"Mom and I have always been close to the water. Well, pretty close."

"I really like it here. I didn't think I would after living in the city all my life, but I do."

"It took some adjustment on my part, but it can be cool."

"Blake Saunders came up to me at the restaurant while you were in the bathroom."

Liam did not seem annoyed by this, only curious. "Really? What did he want?"

"To apologize for helping Tiffany get the jump on me. He said he was trying to protect you, not hurt you."

"Yeah, I actually believe him."

"You do?"

"Blake is not your typical bully jock, Mikki. He's actually a nice guy. Okay, he runs around with Tiffany too much, but I've never had a problem with him. In school he's been cool with me. We even hang out and stuff sometimes."

"I didn't know that."

"Yeah."

It started to rain, and they ran toward an old lifeguard shack and took cover under the roof overhang.

"Your mom is really cool, Liam."

"I don't even remember my dad. He was gone right after I was born."

"That must've been hard."

"I guess it could've been. But my mom loves me enough for two parents," Liam said firmly.

"I really miss my mom."

Liam put an arm around her. "That's completely normal, Mikki. You should miss her. She was your mom. She helped raise you. She loved you, and you loved her."

"Pretty sensitive stuff coming from a guy."

He smiled. "I'm a musician. It's in our blood."

He put his arms around her, and they kissed as the rain and wind picked up and the breakers started to roll and crash with more intensity.

Mikki said, "Your mom talked to me the other day about my dad. It made me really start to think about things."

"What do you mean?"

"I didn't handle things really well when my dad was sick. In fact, I pretty much screwed it up."

"How?"

"When people are in trouble and they reach out, you can either reach out to them or pull back. I pulled back. I was a bitch to my mom. I was no help to my dad. In fact, I avoided him. I was rebellious, pushed the envelope, did all sorts of crap that made things harder for them." Tears trickled down her cheeks. "And do you know why I did all that?"

Liam looked at her. "Because you were scared?"

She stared back. "I was terrified watching my dad die. And instead of trying to make the time he had left pleasant, I just ran the other way. I couldn't deal with it. I didn't want to lose him, and a part of me hated him for leaving us. For leaving *me*." She let out a sob. "And it's just killing me now that my mom died and all I can think is that I made her life miserable at the end. Just *miserable*."

As she started to cry, Liam held her and then undid his cuff button and held his sleeve out for her to use as a handkerchief. When she finally stopped crying, she rubbed her eyes with his sleeve. "Thanks."

"It's okay, Mikki. This stuff is hard. No easy answers.

It's not like music. The notes are all there. You just play, have a good time. Families are really hard."

"Your mom said I needed to talk to him."

"I think she's right. You do."

The rain began to let up, and they made a run for the car. Liam drove her home. As she got out of the car, she said, "Thanks for a great sixteenth birthday."

"Hey, you made it easy."

"Right, crying on your shoulder, real easy."

"I always thought that was part of being a friend."

She leaned back in and kissed him. "It is. And you are."

51

Jack lay on his back in the room of the lighthouse that contained the lighting machinery. His hands were greasy, he was hot and sweaty, there was dust in his throat, and he was not making much progress. He'd followed the schematic detailing of the electrical and operational guts of the machinery to the letter, but still something was off. He angled his work light into a narrow gap between two metal plates.

"Dad?"

He jerked up and hit his head on a piece of metal. Rubbing the injured spot, he pulled himself out from the confined space and looked over at the opening to the area below. Mikki, her hair plastered back on her head, was staring back up at him.

"Mik, are you okay?"

"I'm fine, Dad."

He scrutinized her. "You're wet."

"It's raining."

He looked out the window. "Oh. I guess I came out here before it started."

"Can I come up?"

He gave her a hand and pulled her into the small space.

As she drew closer, he said, "It looks like you've been crying. Liam didn't—"

"No, Dad. It has nothing to do with him. Liam was great. We had an awesome date. I . . . I really like him. A lot."

Jack relaxed. "Okay, but then why . . .?"

She took her dad's hand and drew him over to a narrow ledge that ran the length of the room under the window. They sat.

"We need to talk."

"What about?" he said warily.

"What happened with Mom, you, me. Everything, basically."

"Now?"

"I think so, yeah."

Jack wiped his hands with a rag and tossed it down.

"Look, I know you guys think it's crazy what I'm doing out here. And hell, maybe it is."

She put a hand on his arm to forestall him. "No, Dad, I don't think it's crazy." She paused. "Jenna talked to me about some things."

"What things?" Jack said abruptly.

"Like how you've basically been through hell and we all need to cut you some slack and that everybody grieves in their own way."

"Oh." Jack looked over at the lighting apparatus and then back at her. "I'm trying to get through this, Mikki; I really am. It's just not easy. Some days I feel okay; some days I feel completely lost."

Mikki's face crumpled, and she began to sob as she poured her heart out. "Dad, I was just so scared when you were sick. I didn't know how to handle it. So I just thought if I ran away from it all, I wouldn't have to deal with it. It was selfish. I'm so sorry."

He put his arm around her heaving shoulders and let her cry. When she was done, he handed her a clean rag to wipe her eyes.

"Mikki, you are one smart kid, but you're also only sixteen. You're not supposed to have all the answers. I'm thirty-five and I don't have all the answers either. I think people need to cut you some slack too."

"But I still should have known," she said, another sob hiccuping out of her.

He stroked her hair. "Let me tell you something. When my dad was dying, I did pretty much the same thing. At first I was sad, and then I was scared. I would go to bed at night scared and wake up scared. I would see him walking around in his pajamas in the middle of the day. He was just waiting to die. No hope. And this was a big strong guy I'd always looked up to. And now he was all weak and helpless. And I didn't want to remember my dad like that. So I just pushed everything inside. And I tuned everyone out. Even him. I was selfish too. I was a coward. Maybe that's why I went into the military. To prove that I actually had some courage."

She looked at him with wide, dry eyes. "You did, honest?"

"Yeah."

"Life really sucks sometimes," Mikki said, as she sat back and wiped her nose.

"Yeah, sometimes it really does. But then sometimes it's wonderful and you forget all about the bad stuff."

She looked down, nervously twisting her fingers.

"Mik, is there something else you need to tell me?"

"Will you promise not to get mad?"

Jack sighed. "Is that a condition of you telling me?"

"I guess not, but I was only hoping."

"You can tell me anything."

She turned to face him and drew a long breath. "I was the one who talked to that gossip paper."

Jack gaped at her. "You?"

Fresh tears spilled down Mikki's cheeks. "I know it was so stupid. And it got completely out of hand. Most of the junk he wrote he just made up."

"But how did you know about any of it?"

"I overheard you and Mom talking the night she died. And I saw what that jerk Bill Miller did."

"But why would you talk to a tabloid? You know what those papers do. It made your mom look . . ."

"I know. I'm so sorry, Dad. It was so totally stupid. I . . . I don't know why I did it. I was confused and angry. And I know you probably hate me. And I don't blame you. I hate myself for doing it." All of this came out in a rush that left her so out of breath she nearly gagged.

Jack put his arms around her and drew her to him. "Just calm down. It doesn't matter anymore. You messed up. And you admitted to it. That took a lot of courage."

Mikki was shaking. "I don't feel brave. I feel like a shit. I know you hate me. Don't you?"

"It's actually against the law for a dad to hate his daughter."

"I'm just really, really sorry, Dad. Now that my head's on right about things, it just seems so stupid what I did."

"I don't think either of us was thinking too clearly for a while."

"Will you ever be able to forgive me? To trust me again?"

"I do, on both counts."

"Just like that?"

He touched her cheek. "Just like that."

"Why?"

"Something called unconditional love, honey."

52

Jenna looked up from the counter at the Little Bit to see Jack standing there.

She smiled. "I heard the kids had a fabulous time."

"Yeah, Mikki's still gushing about it."

"You want something to eat? Steak sandwich is the special."

"No, I'm good. Look, I was wondering if you had time tonight for some dinner."

Jenna came from behind the counter to stand next to him.

"Dinner? Sure. What did you have in mind? Not here. Even I get sick of the menu." She smiled and then turned serious. "Hey, I can cook for you."

"I don't want you to have to do that."

"I love to cook. It's actually therapeutic. But you'll have to be my sous chef."

"What does that mean?"

"Slicing and dicing mostly."

"I can do that. But can you get away from this place?"

"For one night, yes. Practically runs itself these days,

and my number one son will be here, along with your daughter. I don't think they even need me anymore. Say around seven-thirty?"

"Okay, great."

"Anything in particular you want to talk about?"

"A lot of things."

When Jack got to Jenna's house that night, music was on, wine was poured, and scented candles were lit.

"Don't be freaked out by any of this," she said as she ushered him in. "I just like to be comfortable. I'm not going all *Sex and the City* on you." She eyed him. "You look nice."

He looked down at his new pair of jeans, his pressed white collared shirt, and a pair of pristine loafers that were pinching his feet. Then he looked at her. She had on a yellow sundress with a scalloped front and was barefoot.

"Not as nice as you," he replied. "And can I go barefoot too? These new shoes are killing me."

When he looked at her feet, she smiled. "You go for it. When I was a kid, my mom had to force me to wear shoes. Loved the feel of the grass on my feet. I think one reason I moved to the Deep South is because not many people wear shoes down here."

She led him into the kitchen and pointed to a cutting board and a pile of vegetables and tomatoes next to it. "Your work awaits."

Jack chopped and sliced while Jenna moved around the kitchen preparing the rest of the meal.

"So you like to cook?"

"I actually wanted to do it professionally."

"But you became a lawyer instead?"

"Yep, it was one of those crazy zigzags that life takes. When Liam was older, I took culinary classes. Then when I was thinking about changing careers, running a restaurant seemed a nice fit. The Little Bit's menu is limited, but I've made every dish on it." She slid a pan of chicken into the oven. "And at home is where I really get to impress people."

"I'm looking forward to being impressed, then."

An hour later they sat down to eat. After a few bites, Jack raised his glass of wine in tribute to her skills in the kitchen. "I'm not exactly an expert, but this is great."

She clinked her glass against his. "I'm sure it was all due to how you sliced and diced the veggies."

"Yeah, right."

She put her glass down and eyed him. "Okay, do we talk about things now or with dessert and coffee?"

"How about *after* dessert and coffee?"

"Why?"

He looked sheepish. "Because I'm having a great time."

"And you think what you want to say will spoil that?" she said with a bit of alarm.

"No, nothing like that. But it will change it."

They walked on the beach after the cake and coffee were consumed. Jack ambled slowly, and Jenna matched his stride.

"Mikki said you and she talked."

"She's a really smart kid. She gets it, Jack. She really does."

"We talked after she came back from her date. She said

you had basically told her to see things from my perspective."

"I thought that was important."

"I can understand why she was upset." He stopped and kicked at the wet sand. "After I got the kids back, I fell into my old routine. And Mikki jumped on that."

"On what?"

"That I didn't have a clue how to run a family."

"Who does? We all just wing it."

"That's nice of you to say, Jenna. But it's giving me credit I don't really deserve."

"You really put a lot pressure on yourself. Bet you did that in the army too."

"Only way you survive. You practice perfection. You have a mission, you prep the crap out of it, and you execute that prep. Same with building stuff. You have a plan, you get your materials, and you build it according to the plans."

"Okay, but did every mission and every building project go according to plan?"

"Well, no. They never do."

"Then what did you do?"

"You improvise. Fly by the seat of your pants."

"I think you just defined parenting in a nutshell."

"You really believe that?"

"Belief isn't a strong enough word. I basically *live* that."

"You'd think I'd know that by now, having three kids."

"All kids are different. It's not like one size or model fits all. I only have Liam, but I have five siblings. We drove my parents nuts, all in different ways. It's not smooth, it doesn't make sense half the time, and it's the hardest, most exasperating job you can ever have. But the payoff is also the biggest."

"Does it get easier?"

"Truthfully, some parts of it do, only to be replaced by other parts that are actually harder." Jenna gripped his shoulder. "Time, Jack. Time. And little steps. You nearly died. You lost the woman you love. You've moved to a different town. That's a lot."

"Thanks, Jenna. I needed to hear all this."

"Always ready to give advice, even if most of it is wrong."

"I think most of it is right, at least for me."

She slowly pulled her hand away. "Things get complicated, Jack, awfully fast. I'm a big believer in taking your time."

"I think I'm beginning to see that. Thanks for dinner."

She pecked him on the cheek. "Thanks for asking. But why did you think this was going to change things between you and me? I think you just wanted some assurance, maybe some comfort."

"But those are big deals for me. I don't go to people with things like that. I'm more of a loner. When Lizzie was alive, I'd go to her."

"Your soul mate?"

"And my best friend. There was nothing we couldn't talk about."

Jenna sighed resignedly. "You just described my image— no, my *dream*—of the perfect relationship."

"It wasn't all perfect. We had our problems."

"But you worked them out together?"

"Well, yeah. That's what a marriage is, right?"

"It's supposed to be that way. But more and more I don't think it is. People seem to give up on each other way too easily. Grass is greener crap."

"I'm surprised you never got married again. I'm sure it wasn't for lack of offers."

"It wasn't," she admitted. "But like I said before, I guess the right offer never came along."

As they headed back to the house, she asked, "So how's the lighthouse coming?"

"Not great," he admitted. "I guess I'll die trying to get it to work again."

As he drove off later, Jenna watched from the front porch, a worried look on her face.

53

A week later Jack turned the wrench one more time, taped over an electrical connection, spun the operating dial to the appropriate setting, and stepped back. It had been a week since he'd had dinner with Jenna. And every night he'd been out here working until the wee hours of the morning on the lighthouse. He felt like a marathoner near the end of the run. Three times he thought he had it right. Three times he turned out to be wrong. And his anger and frustration had grown with each disappointment. He'd snapped at Sammy and at all three kids over the last few days. He'd even made Jackie cry one time and felt awful about it for days afterward. Yet still, here he was.

"Come on," he said, looking at the guts of the light. "Come on. Everything checks out. Down to the smallest detail. There is no good reason you won't work."

He stood back and reached for the switch that powered the system. He counted to three, made a wish, took a breath, held it, and hit the switch.

Nothing happened. The light remained as dark as it had been for years.

Instead of another intense sense of disappointment, something seemed to snap in Jack's head. All the misery, all the frustration, all the loss bottled up inside of him was suddenly released. He grabbed his wrench and threw it at the machinery. It struck the wall, ricocheted off, and cracked the window. Then he ran down the steps, grabbed a crate at the bottom of the lighthouse, carried it out to the rocks, and hurled it as far as he could. It crashed down, and the contents exploded over the wet rocks. With another cry of rage, he ran down to the beach, yelling and cursing, spinning around uncontrollably before he dropped down into the sand and sat there, rocking back and forth, his face in his hands, tears trickling between his clenched fingers.

"I'm sorry, Lizzie. I'm sorry. I tried. I really tried. I just can't make it *work*. I can't make it work," he said again in a quieter voice. "I can't accept that you're gone. I can't! You should be here, not me. Not me!"

His breathing slowed. His mind cleared. The longer he sat there, the greater his calm grew. He looked out to the darkened ocean. He saw the usual distant pinpoints of light representing far-off ships making their way up or down the Atlantic. They were like earthbound stars, thought Jack. So close, but so far away.

He looked skyward toward Lizzie's little patch of Heaven . . . somewhere. He'd never found it. *It just swallows you up. It's so big and we're so small,* thought Jack.

Now he could fully realize how a little girl could become obsessed over a lighthouse. He was a grown man and it had happened to him. The mind, it seemed, was a vastly unpredictable thing.

"Dad?"

Jack turned to see Mikki standing behind him. She was in pajama bottoms and a T-shirt, with a scared look on her face.

"Are you okay?" she said breathlessly. "I . . . I heard you yelling." She wrapped her arms around his burly shoulders. "Dad, are you okay?" she asked again.

He drew a long breath. "I'm just trying to understand things that I don't think there's any way to understand."

"Okay," she said in a halting voice.

He looked back at the Palace. "I moved all of us here for a really selfish reason. I wanted to be close to your mom again. She grew up here. Place was filled with stuff that belonged to her. Every day I'd find something else that she had touched."

"I can understand that. I didn't want to come here at first. But now I'm glad I did." She touched his arm. "I look at that photo of Mom you gave me every day. It makes me cry, but it also feels so good."

He pointed to the lighthouse. "Do you want to know why I've been busting my butt trying to get that damn thing to work?"

She sat down next to him. "Because Mom loved it?" she said cautiously. "And she wanted you to repair it?"

"At first I thought that too. But it finally just occurred to me when I saw you standing there. It was like a fog lifted from my brain." He paused and wiped his face with his sleeve. "I realized I just wanted to fix something, anything. I wanted to go down a list, do what I was supposed to do, and the end result would be, presto, it works. Then everything would be okay again."

"But it didn't happen?"

"No, it didn't. And you know why?"

Mikki shook her head.

"Because life doesn't work that way. You can do everything perfectly. Do everything that you think you're supposed to be doing. Fulfill every expectation that other people may have. And you still won't get the results you think you deserve. Life is crazy and maddening and often makes no sense." Jack paused and looked at his daughter. "People who shouldn't be here are, and someone who should be here isn't. And there's nothing you can do about it. You can't change it. No matter how much you may want to. It has nothing to do with desire, and everything to do with reality, which often makes no sense at all." He grew silent and looked out to the black ocean.

Mikki leaned against him and gripped his hand.

"We're here for you, Dad. *I'm* here for you. *I'm* part of your reality."

He smiled. And with that smile her look of fear finally was vanquished. "I know you are, baby." He hugged her. "You know I told you I was scared when my dad was dying, that I withdrew from everybody?"

"Yeah."

"Well, when my mom left me, I pulled back even more. If it wasn't for your mother, I think I would've just kept pulling back until I disappeared. I played sports and all, but I didn't have many friends, I guess because I didn't want them. Then we got married and I went off to the military. Then when I got home I picked a job that required a lot of hours and a lot of sweat."

"You had to support your family."

"Yeah, but in a way I think I was still retreating. Still trying to hide."

"Dad, you were there for us."

"I missed a lot of things I shouldn't have. I know it, and so do you."

She squeezed his arm. "There's still a lot more to see," Mikki said quietly.

He nodded. "There is a lot more to see, honey. A lifetime more."

She shivered. He put his arm around her. "Come on. Let's go in."

As they walked past the lighthouse, Mikki glanced at it and said, "Are you sure?"

Jack didn't even look at it. "I'm very sure, Mikki. Very sure."

54

After Jack got back to his room, he dropped, exhausted, onto the bed, but he didn't go to sleep. He lay there for a while, staring at the ceiling. Life was often unfair, insane, damaging. And yet the alternative to living in that world was not living in it. Jack had been given a miracle. He had already squandered large parts of it. That was going to stop. Now.

He opened his nightstand and pulled out the stack of letters. He selected the envelope with the number five on it, slid out the letter, and flicked on the light. What he'd just told Mikki, he firmly believed, because he'd once written down these same sentiments. He had just forgotten or, more likely, ignored them in his quest for the impossible. He began to read.

Dear Lizzie,
 As I've watched things from my bed, I have a
confession to make to you. And an apology. I haven't
been a very good husband or father. Half our
marriage I was fighting a war, and the other half

*I was working too hard. I heard once that no one
would like to have on their tombstone that they wished
they'd spent more time at work. I guess I fall into that
category, but it's too late for me to change now. I had
my chance. When I see the kids coming and going, I
realize how much I missed. Mikki already is grown
up with her own life. Cory is complex and quiet. Even
Jackie has his own personality. And I missed most of
it. My greatest regret in life will be leaving you long
before I should. My second greatest regret is not being
more involved in my children's lives. I guess I thought
I would have more time to make up for it, but that's
not really an excuse. It's sad when you realize the
most important things in life too late to do anything
about them. They say Christmas is the season of second
chances. My hope is to make these last few days my
second chance to do the right thing for the people that I
love the most.*

Love,
Jack

Jack slowly folded the letter and put it away. These letters, when he was writing them, were the only things he
had left, really. They represented the outpouring from his
heart, the sort of things you think about when the trivial
issues of life are no longer important because you have
precious little time left. If everyone could live as though
they were in jeopardy of shortly dying, Jack thought, the
world would be a much better place. But in the end they
were only letters. Lizzie would have read them, and perhaps they would have made her feel better, but they were

still just words. Now was the time for action. He knew what he had to do.

Be a father for my children. Repair that part of my life.

Jack rose and went from room to room, checking on his kids. He sat next to Jackie as the little boy slept peacefully, his hand curled around his monster truck. Cory slept on his stomach, his arms coiled under him. A tiny snore escaped his lips. Next, Jack stood in the doorway of Mikki's room, watching the rise and fall of her chest, the gentle sound of her breathing.

He closed her door and went downstairs and onto the rear screened porch. From here he could see the lighthouse soaring into the sky. He had built it into some mythical symbol, but it was only a pile of bricks and cinder blocks and metal guts. It wasn't Lizzie. It had no heart. Not like the trio beating in the bedrooms above. Three people who needed him to be their father.

In this last letter he had been lamenting that there were no second chances left to him. Yet that insane, unfair world that he had sometimes railed against had done something remarkable. It had given him another shot at life.

I'm done running.

Jack went back to bed and slept through the night for the first time in a long time.

55

Beginning the next day, Jack literally hung up his tool belt for the rest of the summer. Instead of going to work, he drove Jackie and Cory to Anne Bethune's camp. And he didn't just drop them off and leave. He stayed. He sat and drew pictures and built intricate Lego structures with Jackie, and then, laughing, helped his son knock them down. He instructed Jackie on how to tie his shoes and cut up his food. He helped construct the sets for a play that Cory was going to be in. He also helped his oldest son with his lines.

After camp they would go to the beach, swim, build sand castles, and throw the ball or the Frisbee. Jack got some kites and taught the boys how to make them do loops and twisters. They found some fishing tackle under the deck at the Palace and did some surf fishing. They never caught anything but had great fun in their abject failure to hook a single fish.

Jenna and Liam came by regularly. Sometimes Liam would bring his drums, and he and Mikki would practice for the talent competition. Since the Palace wasn't soundproofed, the pair would go up to the top of the lighthouse. That high up, their powerful sound was dissipated, although the seagulls were probably entertained.

At least the lighthouse was good for something, thought Jack.

He and Mikki took long walks on the beach, talking about things they had never talked about before. About Lizzie—and high school and boys and music and what she wanted to do with her life.

Mikki continued to waitress at the Little Bit. Jack and Sammy dropped in to eat frequently. And they also did some repairs for Jenna, but only because she refused to charge them for their meals. Charles Pinckney visited them at the Palace. He would tell them stories of the past, of when Lizzie was a little girl about Jackie's age. And all of them would sit and listen in rapt attention, especially Jack.

Jack took Jenna for rides on the Harley, and they were over at each other's homes for meals. They would take walks on the beach and talk. They laughed a lot and occasionally drew close, and arms and fingers touched and grazed, but that was all.

They were friends.

The summer was finally going as Jack had hoped it would. He would lie awake at night, listening to the sounds in the darkness, trying to differentiate among his children's breathing. He got pretty good at it. Sometimes Jackie would have a nightmare and would bump open his dad's door and climb into bed with him. The little boy would lay tight against his dad, and Jack would gently stroke his son's hair until he fell asleep again.

One evening he and Sammy were drinking beers out on

the screen porch. Mikki and Liam were at the top of the lighthouse having one last practice before the competition. The two boys were down on the beach building the last sand castle of the day. The sun had just begun its descent, flaming the sky red and burning parts of it orange.

Sammy looked over at his friend. "Life good?"

Jack nodded. "Life is definitely good."

"Summer's almost over."

"I know."

"Plans?"

"Still thinking about it." Jack gazed at him. "You?"

"Still thinking about it."

They both turned when someone knocked on the door to the porch. It was Jenna.

"I came to pick up Liam and all his drum stuff," she said, joining them. "Big day tomorrow. They need to get their rest."

Sammy said, "I'll go help him."

Before either of them could say anything, he headed on down, leaving Jack and Jenna alone.

"So what happened?" she asked.

Jack looked over at her. "What?"

"You're a changed man, Jack Armstrong. I was just wondering why."

He finished his beer. "This will sound really corny, but sometimes when a person opens their eyes, they can actually see," he said.

"I'm happy for you; I really am."

"You were a big part of it, Jenna."

She waved this off. "You would've figured it out on your own."

"I don't know about that. I hadn't figured it out for a long time." They both looked out to the ocean and then to the lighthouse.

"Never got it to work," he said.

"Sometimes things don't seem to work unless you really need them to."

He nodded slowly. "Going to the competition tomorrow?"

"Are you kidding? Of course."

"Why don't you drive over with us? Sammy's taking their stuff over in the truck, and we can all ride in the VW."

"Sounds like a plan."

Jenna left with Liam, and the Palace settled down for the night.

Jack knocked on Mikki's door and went in.

She was sitting on her bed going over the program she and Liam were going to perform. Jack perched on the edge of her bed.

"You know that stuff by heart," he said.

"Can never be too prepared."

"Now you're starting to sound like your old man."

"And is that a bad thing?"

He gave her a lopsided grin. "I hope not. Look, you're going to do great tomorrow. Win or not."

She stared at him over the top of her musical sheets. "Oh, Dad, we're, like, so going to win."

"Nothing wrong with confidence. But don't get cocky."

"It's not that. I've checked out all the other acts. I even saw a video of Tiffany's little baton twirl from last year. She's mediocre at best. I have no idea how she won three years in a row. Well, I do have an idea. Her mother runs the show. But nobody has worked as hard as Liam and I have."

"Well, whatever happens, I'll be out there in the audience cheering for you." He rose to go. "But you do need a good night's sleep. So not up too late, okay?"

He turned to the door.

"Dad?"

He turned back to her. "Yeah, Mik?"

She got off the bed, wrapped her arms around him, and squeezed.

"Thank you, Daddy."

Jack wrapped his arms around her. "For what, baby?"

She looked up at him. "For coming back to us."

56

"Okay, we're on next to last," said Mikki, coming backstage at the Play House.

Liam looked at her. "Who's last?"

Mikki made a face. "Who do you think? Ms. Reigning Champion. That way she gets a look at all the competition and her performance is the clearest in the judges' minds."

Liam shrugged. "I don't think it'll matter. I've seen the judges. They're all cronies of her mom's."

"Keep the faith. We've worked our butts off, and we've got a terrific act."

"How's the crowd?"

"Big. With our families smack in the middle."

When Mikki turned back around, Tiffany stood there wearing a short white robe.

Mikki eyed her. "Saving the debut of the skimpy for the crowd?"

"My daddy always said you don't give it away for free, sweetie." She looked Mikki up and down. "But then if you don't have anything somebody wants, I guess you *have* to give it away."

Mikki smirked. "Wow, that's really deep. So do you do flaming batons?"

Tiffany looked at her like she was insane. "No. Why would I? That stuff is dangerous."

"Well, to beat us you're going to have to get out of your comfort zone. 'Cause the level of competition just got stepped up, big-time. *Sweetie.*"

Tiffany laughed, but Mikki could tell by the sudden look of uncertainty in the girl's eye that she had done what she'd intended to do.

Freeze her opponent.

Before the competition began, she and Liam went out to the audience to see their families.

The Armstrongs, Sammy, Charles Pinckney, and Jenna were all sitting together.

Jenna smiled and gave Mikki and her son hugs. "I'm really proud of you two."

"Knock 'em dead," called out Cory.

"Yeah, dead," yelled Jackie.

Chelsea Murdoch walked by with her entourage. Her dress was too tight and too short and her heels too high for her age. She looked like what she was: her daughter, only a quarter century older.

She eyed Jenna. "Haven't seen you here before."

"Never had a reason to come before, Chelsea," said Jenna. "This is Liam's first time competing."

Murdoch smiled condescendingly. "Tiffany's going for four straight. Crowd always loves her routine. She's thinking of carrying on baton in college," she added loftily.

"Well, good for her," piped in Mikki. "It's always nice to have a career plan."

Before Murdoch could say anything, Mikki added, "Okay, we gotta go. Show's about to start."

"Good luck, Mik," said Jack.

Looking dead at Tiffany's mom, she said, "It won't be about luck, Dad. Like the sign says, it's a *talent* competition."

There were twenty-one acts, mostly younger people, but there was an older barbershop quartet that was pretty good. Mikki watched from the side of the stage, mentally calculating where the serious competition was. Liam just stayed backstage chilling and idly tapping his sticks together. She came back to him and strapped on her guitar.

"It's showtime, big guy."

"Cool. I was about to fall asleep."

"Now, that's exactly what I need: a drummer with ice in his veins."

Liam smiled. "Let's rock this sleepy little town."

"Oh, yeah," said Mikki.

57

At first the beat was mellow. Still, the crowd whooped and clapped. Sensing the rising energy, Mikki gave Liam the cue they'd practiced. She cranked her amp and stomped on her wah-wah pedal, and her hand started flying across the face of the Fender guitar. They dove right into a classic Queen roof blaster, with Liam moving so fast he appeared to be two people, alternating between drums and keyboard. The crowd was on its feet singing the lyrics.

Mikki knew that once you had the crowd right where you wanted them, and they thought you'd already given everything that was in your tank, you did something special.

You gave them more.

She unplugged her amp and pulled off her guitar. She actually pitched it across the stage. At the same moment, Liam tossed his stick in the other direction. She snagged the sticks, he caught the Fender, and they exchanged positions. Liam plugged in the amp and became the guitarist, his long fingers expertly traversing the Fender. Mikki perched on the stool and hammered away at the full array of the drum set.

The finale was a dual one, with a solo each. Mikki rocked the house with a six-minute broadside and finished up with a mighty crescendo, her hands moving so fast there appeared to be six pairs of them. And when the audience didn't have any breath left and their palms were raw from clapping, Liam performed a guitar solo that would have made Jimmy Page and Santana proud. He held the last chord for a full minute, the amp-powered beat shaking the Channing Play House like cannon fire.

And then there was silence. But only for a few seconds as the crowd caught its collective breath, and then the applause and screams and cheers came in waves. Mikki held hands with Liam and took bow after bow. They finally had to motion for the people to sit down and stop applauding.

As they went backstage, the other performers rushed up to congratulate them.

"You rock," said the fiftyish baritone in the barbershop quartet. "You took me back to my Three Dog Night days."

Breathless and wearing wide grins, Liam and Mikki moved off to the side. Tiffany passed by them, not saying a word. She loosened her robe and let it fall off. The outfit underneath did not leave much, if anything, to the imagination. She turned to them and, using her fingers, formed an *L* on her forehead.

Mikki pointed to the stage. "You're not a loser *yet*. That comes later, *sweetie*."

Other than stumbling twice and nearly dropping her baton, Tiffany did okay. The applause was polite except for the section led by her mother, which lasted so long that finally some people turned in their seats to see who was still applauding what had been a fairly mediocre performance.

A few minutes later, all the contestants were called to the stage in a single group.

Mikki found her dad in the crowd and gave a thumbs-up. Jack gave her two thumbs-up back while Sammy extended a crisp salute. Cory did an elaborate bow to his sister's dominance on the stage, and Jackie copied him.

Jenna caught Liam's eye and blew him a kiss.

The head judge stood and cleared her throat. "We have reached our decisions. But first I would like to thank all the contestants for their fine performances."

This statement was followed by polite applause.

"Now, in third place, Judy Ringer for her sterling dance performance of *The Nutcracker*."

Judy, a skinny fourteen-year-old, ran out to get her trophy and a bouquet of flowers.

"Thank you, Judy. Now, in second place, we have Dickie Dean and his Barbershop Four."

The man who had lauded Mikki and Liam's performance hustled out and received the award for his group as the crowd clapped.

"And now for the first-place champion."

The crowd held its collective breath.

The judge cleared her throat one more time. "For the fourth year in a row, Tiffany Murdoch and her fabulous baton routine."

Tiffany stepped forward, all smiles, and whisked over to get her trophy, hundred-dollar check, and flowers, while her mother beamed. Trophy and flowers in hand, Tiffany strode to the microphone. "I'm truly overwhelmed with gratitude. Four years in a row. Who would have thought it possible? Now I'd like to thank the judges and—"

"That's a load of crap," bellowed a voice.

All heads turned, including Jack's and Jenna's, to see Cory standing up on his seat and pointing an accusing finger at the head judge.

"This sucks!" roared Cory.

"This sucks!" repeated Jackie, who was standing on his chair and pointing his finger too.

"Cor," snapped Jack. "Jackie, get down and be quiet."

But Jenna put a hand on his arm. "No. You know what? They're right." She stood and yelled, "This stinks."

Jack shrugged, stood, and called out, "Are you telling me that Mikki and Liam didn't even make the top three? You people are nuts."

The head judge and Chelsea Murdoch scowled back at them.

Another chorus came from farther back in the theater.

Mikki craned her neck to see. It was Blake and some of the other people from Sweat Town, including Fran, the woman who'd worked as a caterer at Tiffany's party.

"Recount," demanded Blake. "Recount."

Mikki grinned at him.

"Recount! Recount!" chanted the crowd.

Tiffany stood in the center of the stage trying to pretend she was oblivious to all of the criticism. She held her trophy and posed for pictures for a photographer from the local paper.

Then the crowd started chanting, "Encore! Encore!"

Mikki looked at Liam. He said, "What the heck, let's give 'em the Purple."

She nodded, picked up her guitar, cranked her amp, poised her foot on top of her wah-wah pedal, and struck a chord so powerfully amplified that Tiffany screamed and almost fell off the stage. Mikki looked over at Liam and nodded. A moment later the heart-pumping sound of "Smoke on the Water" by Deep Purple roared across the theater.

Minutes later, as the last note of the song died away, Liam and Mikki, their arms around each other, took a bow together. This was a trigger for the ecstatic, cheering crowd to rush the stage. Tiffany had to run to get out of the way of the stampede. The news photographer and reporter joined the crowd, leaving the baton twirler all alone. Tiffany stormed off the stage and threw her trophy in the trash, while her mother followed her out of the theater, trying to soothe her furious daughter.

Later, on the drive home, Mikki and Liam sat in the back of the VW bus. The two teens glowed both with the sweat of their musical exertions and also with sheer excitement.

Liam said, "This is like the greatest day of my life. I mean I've *never* felt this good about losing before."

Jack looked in the rearview mirror at his daughter. "So what happened to alternative edgy beats with a non-traditional mix of instrumentals?"

She grinned. " Wow—you *were* listening. I'm impressed. Anyway, sometimes you just can't beat good old rock and roll, Dad."

"The best part," said Cory, "was watching Tiffany storming off."

Jenna looked in the back of the van and tapped Jack on the arm, motioning with her eyes. He gazed into the rearview mirror to see Liam and Mikki sneak a kiss.

She whispered, "I think, for them, that's the best part."

58

"Hey!" Jack yelled.

He and Sammy had just come out of the grocery store in downtown Channing when Jack saw a guy grab his tool belt out of the truck's cargo bay and run off. Jack and Sammy raced after him, Jack a few paces in front. He saw the guy duck down a side street. He turned the corner and accelerated, Sammy right behind him. The side street turned into an alley. Then they left the alley and entered a wider space. But it was a dead end; a blank brick wall faced them. They pulled up, puffing.

Jack realized what was going on about the same time Sammy did.

"Trap," Jack said.

"And we just ran into it like a couple of high school knuckleheads."

They looked behind them as five large men holding baseball bats came out of hiding behind a Dumpster. Jack could see that the man in the lead was the same one he'd thrown headfirst into the side of the pickup truck shortly after they'd arrived in Channing.

The men moved forward as Jack and Sammy fell back until they were against the brick wall. Jack slipped off his belt, coiled it partially around his hand, and stood ready. Sammy rolled up the sleeves of his work shirt and assumed a defensive stance. He beckoned them on with a wave of his hand.

"Okay, who wants to go to the hospital first?" he said.

With a yell, the biggest man ran forward and raised his bat. Jack whipped his belt, and the metal tip caught the man right on the arm, cutting it open. He screamed and dropped the bat. Sammy drilled a foot into his gut, sending him to his knees. Next, Sammy clamped an iron grip around the big man's neck.

"I don't waste my A game on the JV." Sammy crushed the man's jaw with a sledgehammer right hand that sent him to the asphalt. Sammy looked back up. "One down, four to go. Who's the next victim?"

Two more men, including the one whom Jack had beaten up before, yelled and ran forward. Jack grabbed the man's bat, pivoted his hips, and pulled hard. The man sailed past him and hit the wall, bouncing off. Groggy, he rose in time to be put back down by Jack's fist slamming into his face.

The other guy had his feet kicked out from under him by Sammy. He ripped the bat out of the guy's hands and bopped him on the head with it, knocking him out. When Jack and Sammy looked up, the other men had disappeared.

"Okay, that was fun," said Sammy.

His smile vanished a minute later when Sheriff Tammie hustled into the alley with a skinny deputy in tow. Tammie took one look at the men lying on the ground and Jack and Sammy holding bats, and he pulled his gun, his face dark and furious.

"Put those bats down now. You're both under arrest."

"They attacked us!" exclaimed Jack as he and Sammy dropped the bats.

"Then how come they're knocked out and you two had the bats?"

"Because they were crappy fighters," said Sammy. "Is that our fault?"

Jack pointed at one of the men on the pavement. "Look, he's the same one I fought with before. He and a bunch of his guys came after us to settle the score. We were just defending ourselves."

"That's for a court to decide."

"You're really charging us?" said Jack. "What about the other guys?"

"Their butts are going to jail too."

"Well, at least that's some justice," snapped Sammy.

"And we got to let the wheels of justice do their thing. Just the way it has to be," said Tammie.

Jack and Sammy were cuffed, loaded into the sheriff's cruiser, and transported to the jail. Jack slumped down on a bench at the back of the cell, but Sammy said, "Hey, we get a lawyer, right?"

"That's what I said when I read you the Miranda card," replied Tammie.

Tammie let Jack make a call.

He said, "Jenna, it's Jack. Uh, I'm in a little bit of trouble."

Ten minutes later, Jenna and Charles Pinckney hurried

into the sheriff's office and were escorted back to see the prisoners.

"My God, Jack, what happened?" she said.

He explained everything that had happened in the alley-way.

"I've talked the sheriff into releasing you on your own recognizance," she said.

"So we can go?"

"For now, yes, but it looks like the men are pressing charges, at least according to Tammie."

"But isn't it our word against theirs?" said Sammy.

"Still have to go to court."

"But we didn't do anything wrong."

"I'm sorry, Jack," said Jenna. "I'm doing the best I can."

His anger faded. "I know. And I appreciate you getting down here so fast. Didn't know anyone else to call."

"Well, for now, you're free to go. I'll get the sheriff."

Two days later, a man in a suit knocked on the door of the Palace.

Jack answered it.

"Jack Armstrong?"

"Yeah. Who are you?"

The man stuffed some papers into Jack's hand. "Consider yourself served."

The man walked off as Sammy joined Jack at the door.

"What is it?" he asked him. "Served with what? Those jerks from the alley really suing us?"

Jack read quickly through the legal documents.

When he looked up, his eyes held both anger and fear.

"No, it's a lot worse. Bonnie is suing for custody of the kids."

59

"I can't believe Grandma is doing this," said Mikki. "Why would she?"

The Armstrongs were arrayed on the couch and floor at the Palace. Sammy was there, and so were Liam and Jenna. Jack had shown Jenna the documents, and she had read them carefully with her lawyer's eye.

"I don't know," said Jack, though he actually had a pretty good idea.

Jenna looked up from the papers. "She's requested an expedited hearing to get temporary custody pending a full hearing. In non-legalese, that means she wants to get in front of a judge fast to get the kids now and then worry about the rest later."

"She can do that?" said Sammy.

"The courthouse is open to everyone. But she has to prove her case. It's difficult to have children taken away from a parent."

Jack asked, "Exactly when and where is all this going to happen?"

"In two days. In family court in Charleston."

"But we live in Ohio."

"But you have property in South Carolina and you're living here now, if only for the summer. However, I can argue that the South Carolina court lacks jurisdiction."

"*You* can argue?" said Jack.

"Do you have anyone else in mind to represent you? I've got a license to practice in South Carolina, and I've kept everything current."

"Did you practice family law?" asked Mikki.

"I've done some of it, yes. And I know my way around a courtroom." She held up the documents. "But we don't have much time to prepare."

"Jenna, you don't have time to do this. You've got a business to run."

Before she could respond, Liam said, "I can do that. Mom taught me everything about the business. It'll be fine."

Jenna smiled. "See?"

"Are you sure?"

"Heck, nice change of pace. You can only bake so many pies before you feel the need to punch somebody. Going to court gives me a chance to whack some idiots—not literally, of course, but you get the point."

"All right, but you're going to bill me for your time."

"We'll work something out."

Mikki said, "What exactly is she saying that would make a court take us from Dad?"

Jenna's face grew serious and she looked at Jack questioningly. He nodded, "You can tell them."

"Basically that your father is unfit to be your guardian. That he's a danger to himself and others."

"That's stupid," said Cory, jumping to his feet.

"Yeah, stupid," said Jackie, though, in an act of surprising independence from his brother, he remained seated, his arms folded defiantly over his little chest.

"I'm not agreeing with her, just telling you what she's alleging."

"Does she have any proof of that?" said Mikki heatedly. "Of course not, because it's not true."

"She'll be able to show any proof she has at the hearing," Jenna explained. She looked at Jack again. "And we have to show proof that you are fit."

"How do we do that?"

"You can testify. So can Mikki and Cory. Jackie's too young, of course. I can get Charles to be a character witness. And Sammy here. They can all attest to your fitness. I have no idea what angle she's using, but I can't imagine she'll be able to show the level of proof required to take children away from their surviving parent."

Later, Jack walked Jenna out to her car.

"Jack, there is one thing I didn't want to say in front of the kids."

"What?"

"I don't think the timing on Bonnie's action is coincidence. I think it's tied to your arrest for assault. She could've easily found out. And I can guarantee they'll use that to prove their case.

"But I'm innocent."

"Doesn't matter. It's all perception. And if they can convince the judge you're violent? Not good."

"Great. Guilty until proven innocent."

"Jack, if there's anything to tell me about this, now would be a good time."

"What do you mean?"

"I mean why you think your mother-in-law is doing this."

"She blames me for Lizzie's death. She came here pretending to want to reconcile, but I turned down her offer of moving in with her in Arizona. And she only came by *once* to see the kids this summer. Some grandparent she is."

"Uh, that's actually not right, Dad."

They turned to see Mikki standing behind them.

"What?" said Jack.

"Grandma came by like six times while you were out working."

"You never told me that."

"She asked us not to. Said you might get mad."

"I told her to come and visit. I wouldn't have gotten mad."

"Well, that's not what she said."

Jenna looked at her. "What did you talk about?"

Mikki shrugged. "Stuff."

"Did she ever ask about your dad?"

"Yeah," Mikki said nervously.

"Mikki, you need to tell us everything. We can't be surprised in court."

Mikki started to tear up. "It was when Dad was working so hard and he was out in the lighthouse all the time."

Jack said gently, "It's okay, sweetie; I understand. Just tell us what you told her."

Mikki calmed. "She asked what your mood was, if you

were doing anything strange. If you didn't seem to be feeling well."

"And you told her about the lighthouse and . . . things?" said Jack.

Mikki nodded, a miserable expression on her face. "I'm sorry, Daddy. I didn't know she was going to sue you."

"It's not your fault. It'll be okay."

"Are you sure?"

"Absolutely." He looked at Jenna. "I've got a great lawyer. Now, go back in the house, Mik. Jackie's probably attempting somersaults from one of the ceiling fans."

After she left, Jack looked at Jenna. "I lost the kids once. I can't lose them again."

She put her hand over his. "Listen to me, Jack. You're not going to lose them, okay? Now, I've got to go. Lots of stuff to prepare."

She drove off, leaving Jack standing in the front yard of the Palace, looking at the ground and wondering if his second chance was coming to a premature end.

60

The kids were scrubbed and dressed in their best clothes. Jack and Sammy had bought jackets and dress slacks for the courtroom appearance. Jenna was dressed in a black skirt and jacket, heels and hose. Liam had taken time off work to join them for moral support. He and Mikki sat holding hands in the front row.

The courtroom was surprisingly small, and Jack felt immediately claustrophobic as he stepped inside. And it was very quiet. Jack didn't like such quiet. He had sensed it on the battlefield many times. It usually heralded an ambush.

The judge was not on the bench yet, but the uniformed bailiff was standing ready. Bonnie's lawyer was already seated at his table. Jack jerked when he saw Bonnie and Fred sitting behind him. Fred was studying his hands, while Bonnie was actively engaged in discussion with her lawyer, and also with another man in a suit. Other than that, the courtroom was empty.

As Jack looked at the young man, he suddenly remembered where he'd seen him before. In a car with Bonnie parked on the streets of Channing.

Jenna walked over and spoke with the bailiff for a minute or so before approaching Bonnie's lawyer. They went off to a corner to speak in private, while Bonnie stayed sitting and talking to the other man, who was showing her something on a laptop computer.

Jack watched as Bonnie's lawyer handed Jenna a packet of documents. She frowned and asked him something, but he shook his head. She said something else to him that Jack couldn't hear, but it made the other man turn red and scowl. She whipped around and marched back over to Jack. She sat down and pulled her chair closer to him and the kids.

At that moment, Sammy walked in with Charles Pinckney. Pinckney greeted Jack, Jenna, and the kids. Then he eyed Bonnie. He surprised Jack by walking over to her.

"Fred," he said. "How are you?"

Fred O'Toole looked up and seemed surprised to see Pinckney standing there. He took the other man's extended hand. "Fine, Charles, you?"

"I've been better, actually, but thank you for asking." He turned to Bonnie, who was gazing steadily at him. "Hello, Bonnie."

She nodded curtly. "Charles."

"Let's just be thankful Lizzie and Cee aren't alive to see this god-awful spectacle," he said in a tight voice.

Bonnie looked like she had been slapped. But Charles had already turned away.

Jenna held up the stack of documents and whispered to Jack. "Opposing counsel just now gave me these documents. I asked him if he would not contest an extension on the hearing date, but he refused."

"What's in those documents?" Jack asked.

"I haven't had a chance to read them, but I've glanced at a few pages. Your mother-in-law apparently has had a private detective follow you this summer." She pointed to the other man holding the laptop. "That guy."

"What?" said a shocked Jack.

"That is, like, totally insane," added Mikki.

Jack gazed nervously at him. "What's he got on the laptop?"

"Apparently some video they intend to show the judge."

"Video? Of what?"

"I don't know."

"I didn't think they could do stuff like this," said Sammy. "Surprise the other side with crap."

"Normally they can't. But this is family court. The rules are different. Everything is supposed to be done with the best interests of the children in mind. That sometimes trumps official procedures. And they're alleging that the children are in an unsafe and even dangerous environment."

"That's poppycock," said Charles.

"And we'll show it," promised Jenna. She had previously gone over with them the questions she would ask and what questions to expect the other side to throw at them.

A moment later, the bailiff announced the entrance of the judge. He turned out to be a small, thin, balding man, with thick spectacles, named Leroy Grubbs.

They rose on his entrance and then took their seats. The case was called, and Bonnie's lawyer, Bob Paterson, rose. But Jenna cut him off and asked the court for an extension, citing the late delivery of crucial documents. This was denied by Grubbs almost before Jenna finished speaking.

Paterson made his opening statement.

"Fine. Call your witnesses," said Grubbs.

The lawyer said, "Bonnie O'Toole."

61

Bonnie was sworn in and sat down in the witness box.

"You're the children's grandmother?" asked Paterson.

"Yes."

"Can you lead us through the series of events leading up to your filing this legal action?"

Bonnie spoke about Jack's illness, her daughter's death, Jack being in hospice, the children living with relatives, and Jack's recovery and his taking the children back. And, finally, she described her offer to have them all live with her because of her concerns, after consulting with doctors, that Jack's illness would most assuredly come back with fatal results.

"And what was Mr. Armstrong's response to your offer?"

"He categorically refused it."

"And what specific event prompted you to have your son-in-law put under surveillance?"

"I saw Jack beating up two men on the street in Channing, South Carolina, in broad daylight while his children were with him. The youngest, Jackie, was bawling his eyes out. It was awful. It was like Jack had lost his mind. I don't know if it was a symptom of the disease coming back or not, but I was terrified and I could tell the children were too."

The lawyer finished with Bonnie, and Jenna rose.

"Mrs. O'Toole, do you love your grandchildren?"

"Of course I do."

"And yet you seek to separate them from their father?"

"For their own good."

"And not to punish Mr. Armstrong?"

"No, of course not."

"So you're not angry with your son-in-law? You don't blame him for your daughter's death?"

"I've never blamed him. I told him that I knew it was an accident."

"But did you really believe that? Didn't you tell Mr. Armstrong that you thought he should be dead and not your daughter?"

Bonnie pursed her lips and remained silent.

"Mrs. O'Toole?"

"I've tried to move past that."

"But you still harbor resentment toward him?"

"I don't think so, no."

"And that is partly the reason you're filing for custody, for revenge?"

"Objection," said Paterson. "The witness has said she harbors no resentment."

"Withdrawn," said Jenna. "No more questions."

"Next witness," said Grubbs.

Jack and the others were surprised to see Sheriff Nathan Tammie amble into the courtroom, not looking too happy about being there. He was sworn in, and Paterson took him through his paces as a witness.

"So you warned Mr. Armstrong on the occasion of the first assault he was involved in?"

"Yes, although I warned the other guys too. Apparently Mr. Armstrong was provoked."

"And there was a second, more recent, assault involving Mr. Armstrong, was there not?"

"Yes."

"Can you tell us the circumstances?"

Tammie sighed, glanced at Jack, and explained the altercation in the alley.

"So, to sum up your testimony, Mr. Armstrong and Mr. Duvall were holding baseball bats in an alley, and three unconscious men were lying at their feet?" The lawyer glanced at the judge, presumably to gauge the man's reaction. The judge was following the line of questioning very closely. "So you arrested Mr. Armstrong and his companion, Mr. Duvall?"

"Yes. But I arrested the other guys too."

"But Mr. Armstrong will be going to court on these charges?"

"Yes."

"Could he receive prison time?"

"I really doubt that—"

"Could he?"

"Well, yes."

"No further questions."

Jenna rose. "Sheriff Tammie, why didn't you charge Mr. Armstrong on the first altercation?"

"Well, from the witness statements it was clear that he was provoked."

Jenna glanced at Bonnie. "Provoked how?"

Tammie took out his notebook. "Three witnesses said that one of the guys Mr. Armstrong went after had yelled out something about him being the miracle man and they were willing to pay him five dollars to perform a miracle on him. And he said other stuff, trying to get Mr. Armstrong's goat, I guess."

"All directed at Mr. Armstrong personally?"

"Yes."

"Did Mr. Armstrong attack at that point, when he was the subject of these statements?"

"No. He just kept walking along with his kids."

"Go on."

Tammie looked at his notes. "Then the same guy said, "Hey, Miracle, was it true your slutty wife was cheating on you? That why you came back from the dead?"

Jenna turned to look at Bonnie in time to see her glance sharply at Jack.

"And is that when Mr. Armstrong went after them? Because they insulted his deceased wife?"

"Yes."

"So he exercised admirable restraint when the insults were only directed to him?"

"Probably more restraint than I would have exercised if it'd been me."

"And the alleged second assault? Is it true that one of the men engaged in this assault was also the same man who was involved in the first altercation?"

"Yes."

"So it could have been that these men attacked Mr. Armstrong in that alley and he was merely defending himself?"

"Objection," said Paterson. "Calls for a conclusion that the witness is not qualified to give."

"Sustained," said Grubbs, but he looked curiously at Tammie and then over at Jack.

Jenna said, "No further questions."

Paterson said, "I call Michelle Armstrong to the stand."

As Mikki rose and moved forward, she stopped next to her dad. He gave her a reassuring smile and gripped her hand. "Just tell the truth, sweetie," he said.

62

"Ms. Armstrong?" said Paterson politely. "You had a number of conversations with your grandmother this summer, didn't you?"

Mikki looked at her father, but the lawyer moved to block her view. "You must answer my questions truthfully and not look to your father for instruction."

Mikki took a deep breath. "Yes, I spoke with Grandma."

"And what did you tell her about your father's . . . um . . . actions during the summer?"

"I don't understand the question."

"All right. I mean with regards to the lighthouse, for instance."

"Lighthouse?" said the judge.

Paterson addressed him. "It was apparently Mr. Armstrong's deceased wife's favorite place as a child, and he was spending most of the nights there."

Jenna rose. "Objection. Mr. Paterson has not been sworn in as a witness, Your Honor, and has no personal knowledge of the situation."

"All right," said Grubbs. "Sustained."

Paterson turned back to Mikki. "Your statements about the lighthouse? Can you tell the court please?"

Mikki fidgeted. "I just told her that Dad was working on the lighthouse, that's all. It was no big deal."

"Would he work out there late at night?"

"Yes."

"With Mr. Duvall?"

"Yes."

"Leaving you three children alone in the house?"

Mikki's face grew hot. "I'm *not* a child. I'm sixteen."

"All right, leaving you and your younger brothers alone in the house?"

"Sometimes, but nothing happened."

"On the contrary, did you not tell your grandmother on at least three occasions that your younger brother, Jack Jr., got out of bed and once fell down the stairs?"

Jack looked shocked. He stared at Mikki. She swallowed hard. "But he was okay. Just a bruise on his back."

"And on another occasion Jack Jr. wandered out of the house and you couldn't find him for at least an hour? And he turned up walking down the street?"

Jack slumped back in his chair, totally flummoxed.

"Yes. But he was okay."

"And did you tell your father about these incidents?"

"No."

"Why not?"

"I . . . I didn't want him to get upset."

"Does he get upset often?"

"Well, I mean, no; no, he doesn't."

"Did you also tell your grandmother that your dad was obsessed with the house and the lighthouse because your deceased mother loved it so much there and he was trying to reconnect somehow with her?"

Mikki flushed a deep red and started breathing quickly. Tears trickled from her eyes. "I was mad at him; that's why I said those things."

"So they weren't true? Remember you are under oath."

Jenna rose. "Your Honor, counsel is badgering. I request a recess so the witness can compose herself."

Grubbs looked at Mikki. "Are you all right?"

Mikki drew in a deep breath, wiped her eyes, and nodded. "I'm okay."

"Proceed."

Paterson continued. "And did you also tell your grandmother that your father had no clue how to run a family and didn't seem to care about you and your brothers?"

Jack looked down.

Mikki teared up again. "That was before he changed."

"Changed?"

Obviously flustered, Mikki started speaking too fast. "Yes, I mean he was like that before. No, I mean, not bad. He did love us. I mean he *does* love us. He takes great care of us."

"But didn't you also tell your grandmother that you were worried about your dad's mental state?"

In a hushed voice Mikki said, "No, I don't remember saying that."

"So you've never seen your dad acting irrationally or even in a fit of rage?"

"No, never."

Paterson turned to the man in the suit sitting next to Bonnie. "Mr. Drake, if you would?" The man rose and wheeled forward a TV on a rolling stand and slid a DVD into a player underneath the TV.

Paterson said to the judge, "Your Honor, Mr. Drake is a licensed private investigator hired by Mrs. O'Toole to keep watch over the Armstrong children. The video you're about to see represents one of the results of this surveillance."

The TV screen came to life, and they all watched as Jack came running out of the lighthouse carrying the crate. He smashed it on the rocks and then raced down to the beach, twisting and turning in what looked unmistakably like a fit of insane rage. Then he dropped to the sand and wept. The next image was Mikki creeping up to her father.

On Paterson's cue the DVD was stopped, and he turned back to Mikki.

"You obviously saw your father that night?"

Mikki nodded.

"And you wouldn't describe that behavior as irrational or even a fit of rage?"

"He was upset, but he got better."

"So in your mind he was . . . sick?"

"No, that's not what I meant." She stood. "You're putting words in my mouth," she cried out.

Grubbs said, "Young lady, I understand that this is very stressful, but please try to keep your emotions under control. This is a court of law."

Mikki sniffled and settled back in her chair.

"If your father were to fall ill again while you were living with him, who would take care of the family?"

"I would."

Paterson smiled. "You may not be a child, but you're also not of legal age to live alone with your brothers."

Mikki looked furious. "And Sammy. He's my dad's best friend."

"Ah, Mr. Duvall. Yes." Paterson glanced at some notes. "Did you know that after he returned from Vietnam, Mr. Duvall underwent psychiatric counseling and that he also received two drunk-driving citations?"

Sammy erupted from his chair. "My whole damn unit was ordered to undergo that counseling because we'd done two tours in 'Nam and seen atrocities you never will, slick. And those DUIs were over thirty years ago. Never had a damn one since."

The judge smashed his gavel down. "Another outburst like that, sir, and you will be removed from this court-room."

Paterson turned back to Mikki. "So, Mr. Duvall will look after you?"

"Yes," Mikki said stubbornly.

He turned to Drake again and nodded. The TV screen came to life. They watched first as Sammy drove his Harley way too fast and without a helmet. The second scene was Sammy dozing on the beach with a couple of empty beer cans lying next to him as Jackie and Cory played very close to the water.

"Quite a responsible caretaker," said Paterson dryly. "Now, Ms. Armstrong, can you tell us what you think your mother's death did to your father?"

Jenna jumped to her feet. "Relevance?"

"We're trying to determine the conditions of the children's environment, Your Honor. The state of mind of the surviving parent is highly relevant."

"Go ahead."

"Ms. Armstrong, please answer the question."

"He was devastated. We all were."

"Is he still devastated?"

"What do you mean?"

"Your father has been involved in two fights and been arrested for an assault for which he could go to prison. You saw the video of him throwing things and jumping around in a state of fury, and of your two brothers being left in the care of Mr. Duvall while he was apparently either drunk or asleep. You've given testimony that he neglected his three children to work on a lighthouse, resulting in injury to your younger brother. Do you believe those to be the acts of a rational person?"

"But I told you he's better now."

"So he was worse at some point?"

"Look, I know what you're trying to do, but my dad is not crazy, okay? He's not."

"But you're not qualified to make that judgment, are you? It really is for this court to decide if your father is fit to have custody of his children."

Mikki stood again, tears streaming down her face. "My dad is not crazy. He loves us. He is a great dad."

Paterson gave her a weak smile. "I'm sure you love your dad."

"I do," Mikki said fiercely.

"And you'd say anything to protect him."

"Yes, I would. I . . ." Mikki realized her mistake too late.

"No further questions."

As Paterson walked away, Mikki looked at her dad. "I'm sorry, Dad. I'm really sorry."

Jack said quietly, "It's okay, sweetie." When Jenna rose to question Mikki, Jack put a hand on her arm and shook his head. "No, Jenna, she's been through enough."

"But Jack—"

"Enough," said Jack firmly.

Jenna turned to the judge. "No questions," she said reluctantly.

Grubbs looked at Paterson. "Any more witnesses?"

"Just one, Your Honor, before we rest our case." Paterson turned toward the table where Jenna was sitting. "We call Jack Armstrong."

63

Jack was sworn in and settled uncomfortably into the witness box, hitching his suit jacket around him.

Paterson approached. "Mr. Armstrong, did you know that your illness can cause severe depression and even mental instability?"

"I don't have an illness."

"Excuse me?"

"I was given a clean bill of health. Look at me. Does it seem to you like I'm dying?"

Paterson picked up some documents and handed them to the bailiff. "These are opinions from three doctors, all world-class physicians, who state categorically that there is no cure for your illness and that it is fatal one hundred percent of the time."

"Then they'll have to change that to 99.9 percent, won't they?"

"Do you blame yourself for your wife's death, Mr. Armstrong?"

"A person will always blame themselves, even if they could do nothing to prevent it. It's just the way we are."

"So is that a yes?"

"Yes."

"That must be emotionally devastating."

"It's not easy."

"Talk to me about your obsession with the lighthouse."

Jenna said, "Objection. Drawing a conclusion."

"Sustained."

"Tell us about your reasons for working so long and hard on the lighthouse, Mr. Armstrong."

Jack furrowed his brow and hunched forward. "It's complicated."

"Do your best," said Paterson politely.

"It was her special place," Jack said simply. "That's where she'd go when she was a kid. I found some of her things there—a doll, a sign that she'd made that said, 'Lizzie's Lighthouse,' and some other things. And when she was alive she said she wanted to come back to the Palace. I guess me going there instead and fixing it up was a way to show respect for her wishes."

"All right. What else?"

Jack smiled. "Lizzie thought she could see Heaven from the top of the lighthouse."

"Heaven?"

"Yes," Jack said. "She believed that when she was a little girl," he added quickly.

"But you're an adult. So you didn't believe that, or did you?"

Jack hesitated. Jenna glanced at the judge and saw his eyebrows rise higher the longer Jack waited to answer.

"No, I didn't. But . . ." Jack shook his head and stopped talking.

The lawyer let this silence linger for a bit as he and the judge exchanged a glance.

"So you wanted to fix up the place?"

"Yes. The stairs to the lighthouse fell in, and I wanted to repair them. And the light too."

"Fix the light? It's my understanding that the lighthouse in question is no longer registered as a navigational aid."

"It's not. But it stopped working while Lizzie was still there. So I decided to try and repair it."

"So let me get this straight, if I can," said Paterson in a skeptical tone. "You neglected your family so that you could repair a lighthouse that is no longer used as a navigational aid, solely because your wife as a child thought she could see Heaven from there? Let me ask the question again: Did you think you could see Heaven from there?" he asked in a chiding tone.

"No, I didn't," said Jack firmly.

"We have one more video to show, Your Honor."

"All right."

Paterson turned to Drake, who worked the controls, and the image appeared on the TV of Jack standing on the catwalk around the lighthouse reading one of his letters to Lizzie.

"Could you tell us what you're doing in that picture, Mr. Armstrong?"

"None of your business," snapped Jack, who was staring at the TV.

Jenna stood. "Your Honor, relevance?"

"Again, state of mind," replied Paterson.

"Answer the question," instructed the judge.

"It's a letter," said Jack.

"A letter? To whom?"

"My wife."

"But your wife is deceased."

"I wrote the letters to her before she . . . before she died. I wrote them when I was sick. I wanted her to have them after . . . I was gone."

"But she can't read them now. So why were you reading them? You obviously knew what was in them."

"There's nothing wrong with reading old letters. I'm pretty sure people do it all the time."

"Perhaps, but not in the middle of the night on top of a lighthouse while small children are alone in the house."

"Argumentative," snapped Jenna.

"Sustained," said Grubbs.

Jack looked at Paterson and said, "I know you're trying to make it look like I'm nuts. But I'm not. And I'm not unfit to care for my children."

"That's for this court to decide, *not* you."

Jack sat there for a few seconds. The walls of the courtroom seemed to be closing in on him, cutting off his oxygen. His anger, always near the surface ever since Bonnie had filed her lawsuit, now burst to the surface. He looked at Paterson. "Have you ever lost anyone you loved?"

Paterson looked taken aback but quickly recovered. "I'm asking the questions."

Jack now looked directly at Bonnie. "You know how much I loved Lizzie."

Paterson said, "Mr. Armstrong, you're not allowed to do that."

Jack ignored him. He stood, his eyes burning into his

mother-in-law's. "I would've gladly given my life so that she could have lived. You know that."

"Mr. Armstrong," cautioned the judge.

"She meant everything to me. But she died."

"Mr. Armstrong, sit down!" snapped Grubbs as he smacked his gavel.

Jack pointed a finger at Bonnie and cried out, "No one feels worse than I do about what happened. No one! It is a living hell for me every day. I lost the only woman I have ever loved. The only person I wanted to share my life with. The best friend I will ever have!" The tears were sliding down Jack's anguished face.

The judge barked, "Bailiff!"

Jack said, "The best things that Lizzie and I ever created were our kids. *Our* kids. So how dare you try to take away the only parent they have left just because you're mad at me. How *dare* you."

The bailiff forcibly removed Jack from the courtroom while Bonnie looked on, obviously shocked by his outburst.

Paterson said, "Nothing further, Your Honor." He walked back to his chair, barely able to conceal his smile.

The judge looked critically at Jenna. "Do you have anything to add, counselor?"

Jenna looked at the distraught kids and then at the judge. "No, Your Honor."

The judge said, "I'll render my judgment on the motion this afternoon."

Jack was released from the bailiff's custody a few minutes later. They didn't wait at the courthouse but drove back in silence to Channing. They waited in a small room at the back of the Little Bit. They all jumped when Jenna's cell phone buzzed. She answered the call and listened, and her expression told Jack all he needed to know.

"The judge granted the motion for temporary custody," she said.

And it's my fault, thought Jack. *I've lost my family. Again.*

64

Jack sat on his bed at the Palace holding letter number six in his hand. He hadn't read it yet. He was thinking about other things.

No matter what you do, no matter how hard you fight, life sometimes just doesn't make sense.

Bonnie and representatives from Social Services were coming this evening to take the kids away from Jack, perhaps forever. He looked down at the letter, then balled it up and threw it down on the bed next to the other five. As he looked out the window, three cars pulled into the driveway of the Palace, including Sheriff Tammie in his police cruiser. Though it was only seven in the evening, the sky was as dark as midnight. A tropical storm was just off the coast, and the wind was beginning to slam the low country with a fury. That was the major reason they were coming tonight. To move the kids farther inland. Jack had put up no fight, principally because he wanted his kids to be safe. The lights kept flickering on and off in the house.

Someone tapped on his door.

"Yeah?"

It was Jenna. "They're here, Jack," she said quietly.

"I know."

As Jack came downstairs, he stared at the three packed bags standing next to the front door. Then he looked over at the kids. Cory and Mikki were on the couch crying, and Jackie, not understanding what was going on, was crying too. He clutched his monster truck in one hand and hugged his siblings with the other, his little body quaking.

Liam simply stood by, not knowing what to do. His big hands clenched and unclenched in his anxiety. Jack went over to his kids and started whispering to them. "It's going to be okay, I promise. This is only temporary."

Jack and Jenna both answered the door. Bonnie, Fred, and the Social Services people stood there with umbrellas in hand.

"Are the children ready?" one of the Social Services folks asked Jack.

He nodded, his gaze squarely on Bonnie.

"Bonnie?" She looked at him, her face flushed. "Do we have to do it this way?"

"I'm only thinking of the children, Jack."

"Are you sure about that?"

"I'm very sure."

Sammy, Liam, Jackie, and Cory had joined them on the front porch.

Cory said, "Grandma, please don't do this. Please. We want to stay with Dad."

One of the Social Services people, a woman, stepped in and said, "This is not the time or place to discuss this. The judge has ruled." She looked at Jack. "We really want this to go smoothly. And I'm sure you do too, for the sake of the kids." The woman glanced over her shoulder at Sheriff Tammie, who stood outside his cruiser looking very uncomfortable.

Sammy eyed Jack, but it was Jenna who stepped forward and said, "We do." Sammy took a step back, and Jack looked at his two kids. "Okay, guys, you're going to be back here faster than you can say Jack Rabbit."

Cory nodded, but the tears still slid down his face. Jackie looked at Cory and started to tear up again. Jack hugged both of them. "It's going to be okay," he said. "We're a family. We'll always be a family, right?" They both nodded. "We'll get your bags. Liam, go get Mikki. I'm sure you want to say good-bye to her. They need to get on the road before the storm gets any worse."

Sammy and Jack carried the bags out to the car, and Jack strapped Jackie in while Cory buckled up next to him. When Jack looked back up at the porch, he knew something was wrong. Liam was standing there, his face pale and his expression wild.

Bonnie had seen this too. Despite the wind and rain, she got out of the car.

"What is it?" said Jack as he ran up to Liam.

"I can't find Mikki."

Jack and the others raced into the house. It took only ten minutes to search the place. His daughter was gone.

A quarter mile down the beach, Mikki was stumbling along, crying hard. The wind and rain battered her, but she kept going, leaning into the gusts swarming off the ocean. She kept weaving away from the waterline as the storm pushed the Atlantic farther landward. As upset as she was, Mikki didn't see the palmetto tree toppling over until it was almost too late. At the last possible instant, she lunged out of the way, but dodging the tree carried her too close to the waterline and in the path of a huge wave that crashed over her. Mikki didn't even have time to scream before the receding wave swept her out.

65

Jack stared out at the darkened sky from the front room of the Palace. The rain was coming down even harder. Liam had quickly driven home to see if Mikki had gone there, but he'd called to say she wasn't at his house.

Bonnie said, "Jack, what do we do? What do we do?" Her voice was hysterical.

Jack turned to her and said sharply, "The first thing we do is not panic."

One of the Social Services personnel said, "We should call the police. The sheriff drove off before this happened, but I'm sure we can get him back."

Jack shook his head and said in a crisp, take-charge manner, "There's only Tammie and one deputy, and they'll be preoccupied with the storm. We can call them, but we can't just sit around and wait for them to start looking for her. We have to start searching the area. We need to split up. Search by street and also the beach." He pointed to Fred. "Fred, you and Bonnie drive west in your car. Go slow, look for Mikki that way." He turned to the pair from Social Services. "You go east in your car and do the same thing. Let's exchange cell phone numbers. Whoever finds her calls the others. Sammy and I will take opposite directions on the beach." He turned to Cory. "Cor, can you be a real big guy for me and stay here with Jackie? Go to the lower level and stay away from the windows."

Cory swallowed and looked terrified at his dad. "Mikki's coming back, right?"

"She absolutely is. I bet she shows up here any minute. And we need someone to be here when she does, okay?"

"Okay, Dad."

Jack headed right on the beach while Sammy went left. The rain was being pushed nearly sideways by the wind, and most of the sand was underwater. Jack swung his flashlight in wide arcs, but it barely penetrated the darkness. It finally caught on one object, and when Jack saw what it was, his heart thudded in his chest and a cold dread settled over him.

It was Mikki's sneaker floating in a pool of shallow water. He looked in all directions for his daughter but could see nothing. He called out her name, but the only thing he heard in response was the scream of the wind. He raced on to check backyards and behind dunes, but found nothing.

"I can't see a damn thing," he said to himself. He stared out at the angry ocean, engorged and rendered infinitely more dangerous by the strength of the storm pushing it against the coast. He turned and jogged back, his gaze toggling between land and sea. He had to bend forward to keep from being blown back by the powerful winds. Every ten seconds he screamed out her name.

Near the Palace he met Sammy, who reported similar failure.

Jack showed him the sneaker.

"That is not good, Jack," said Sammy.

"We're running out of time. The storm is just about to really hit."

"What do you want to do?"

"We need to be able to see a big swath of land and water."

"No way you can get a chopper with a searchlight up in these conditions."

At this remark, Jack started and looked up at the lighthouse. He turned and ran toward it, Sammy on his heels. He kicked open the lower door and took the steps two at a time. He reached the top and hoisted himself through the access door. Sammy poked his head through a few seconds later, breathing hard.

"What the hell are you doing?"

"Getting a light."

"Jack, this damn thing doesn't work."

"It's going to work tonight! Because I'm going to find my daughter," Jack shouted back at him. He ripped open his toolbox, which he'd left in the corner, snatched some wrenches, grabbed the old schematic, and began to analyze it, his gaze flitting up and down its complex drawings. While Sammy held the paper, Jack worked on section after section of the mechanism, his ability to repair it having assumed a whole new level of urgency.

As Sammy watched him work, he said, "But we need a searchlight, not something that's going to—"

"There's a manual feature," Jack snapped as he squeezed his body into a narrow crevice to check the wiring there. "The light path can be manipulated by hand."

He pulled himself out of the space and hit the power switch.

"Damn it!" Jack flung his wrench down.

He peered out into the darkness, where his little girl was . . . somewhere.

He involuntarily shuddered.

No. I will not lose my daughter.

A burst of lightning that speared the water was followed by a boom of thunder as the storm reached its peak. Footsteps came from below, and first Jenna's and then Liam's faces appeared at the opening to the room. They were both soaked through.

"We've been searching the street and beach on our end, but there's no sign of Mikki," Jenna said to Sammy as she looked at Jack's back.

"We were trying to power up the light," Sammy explained, "but no luck."

Sammy said, "Bonnie called. And so did the other people. They found nothing either." He held up Mikki's soaked shoe. Jenna and Liam paled when they saw it. All three instinctively looked out to the frothing ocean.

Jack remained frozen against the glass, staring out into the darkness. The electricity to the lighthouse flickered, went out, and then sputtered back on. Jack was still staring at the darkness when he saw it. At first he thought it was another bolt of lightning lancing into the water, but there was no boom of thunder following it. Yet it had been a jagged edge of current; he'd seen it! Jack suddenly realized that in that second of darkness, what he'd seen had been reflected in the glass, only to become invisible when the power came back on and the lights were restored.

He whirled around and leapt toward the machinery. "Turn the light off, Sammy," he screamed.

"What?"

"Turn it off. Off!"

Sammy hit the switch, plunging them all into darkness.

Jack, his chest heaving with dread because he knew this was his last chance, stared at the machinery with an intensity he didn't know he even had. He could hear nothing, not the storm, not Sammy's or Jenna's or Liam's breathing, not even his own. There was nothing else in the world; only him and this metal beast that had confounded him all summer. And if he couldn't figure it out right now, his daughter was lost to him.

"Turn the lights back on."

Sammy hit the switch.

And Jack saw the beautiful arc of electrical current nearly buried between two pieces of metal in a gap so narrow he didn't even know it was there. *That* was what had been reflected in the window.

He dropped to his knees, scuttled forward, and hit the gap with his flashlight. Two wires were revealed. They were less than a centimeter apart, but not touching.

"Sammy, get me electrical tape and a wire nut and then turn the main power off."

Sammy grabbed the tape from the box, tossed the roll and red wire nut to Jack, and then turned off the power. While Jenna held the flashlight for him, he slid his hands in the gap, pieced the two wires together using the wire nut, and then wound tape around it.

Jack stood and called out, "Turn the power back on, and then hit the switch. Everyone look away from the light."

Sammy turned on the power and flicked the switch. At first nothing happened. Then, as if it was awakening from years of sleep, the light began to come on, building in energy until, with a burst of power, it came fully to life. If Jack hadn't told them to look away, they would have been blinded. The powerful beam illuminated the beach and ocean to an astonishing degree as it started to whirl around the top of the lighthouse.

Jack raced around to the back of the equipment, hit a button, and grabbed a slide lever. The light immediately stopped swirling across the landscape and became a focused beam that he could maneuver.

"Sammy, take control of this. Start from the north and move it slowly southward in three-second stages."

While Sammy guided the light, Liam, Jack, and Jenna stayed glued to the window, looking at the suddenly lightened nightscape.

Jenna spotted her first. "There! There!"

"Steady on the beam, Sammy," screamed Jack. "Hold right there."

Jack threw himself through the opening and took the steps three at a time. He nearly flattened Bonnie, who was coming up the stairs.

"What is—"

Jack didn't bother to answer.

He ran on.

The light had revealed Mikki's location. She was in deep water, clinging to a piece of driftwood as ten-foot-high waves pounded her. She looked to be caught in the seesaw grip of the storm. She might have only a few minutes left to live.

Then so do I, thought Jack.

66

Jack Armstrong ran that night like he had never run before. Not on the football field, and not even on the battlefield when his very life depended on sheer speed. He high-stepped through four-foot waves that were nearly up to the rocks the lighthouse was perched on. A towering breaker ripped out of the darkness and knocked him down. He struck his head on a piece of timber thrown up on the sand by the storm. Dazed, he struggled to his feet and kept slogging on. He saw the light, a pinpoint beam. But he couldn't see Mikki. Frantic, he ran toward the illumination.

"Mikki! Mikki!"

Another wave crushed him. He got back up, vomiting salt-water driven deeply down his throat. He ran on, fighting rain driven so hard by turbocharged wind that it felt like the sting of a million yellow jackets.

"Mikki!"

"Daddy!"

It was faint, but Jack saw the light shift to the left. And then he saw it: a head bobbing in even deeper water. Mikki was being pulled inexorably out to sea.

"Daddy. Help me."

Like a charging rhino, Jack ran headlong toward the brunt of the storm. An oncoming wave rose up far taller than he was, but he avoided most of its energy by diving under it at the last possible second. He emerged in water over his head. The normal riptide was multiplied tenfold by the power of the storm, but Jack fought through it, going under and coming up and yelling, "Mikki." Each time she called back, and Jack swam with all his might toward the sound of her voice.

The lightning and thunder blasted and boomed above them. A spear of lightning hit so close that Jack felt the hairs on his arms and neck stand. He snatched a breath and went under again as another foaming wave crashed down on him. He came up. "Mikki!"

This time there was no answer.

"Mikki!"

Nothing.

"Michelle!"

A second later he heard a faint "Daddy."

Jack redoubled his efforts. She was getting weak. It was a miracle she was still alive. If that piece of driftwood got ripped from her, it would all be over. And then he saw her. The sturdy beam of light was tethered to the teenager like a golden string. Mikki was managing to stay afloat by using the driftwood she'd snagged somehow, but there was no way she could keep that up much longer. Jack swam as hard as he could, fighting through wave after wave and cursing when one threw him off course, costing him precious seconds. But the whole time he kept his eyes on his daughter.

And yet he realized that as each second passed, she was moving farther from him. It was the storm, the riptide, the wind, everything. He swam harder. But now he was fifty feet away instead of forty. He took a deep breath and slid under the water to see if he could make better time. But it was pitch-dark even just below the surface, and the current was just as strong.

When he came back up, he couldn't see her and cursed himself for taking his eyes off his daughter. His limbs and lungs were so heavy. Jack looked to the shore and then at the angry sky. He was being pulled out too now. And he wasn't sure he had the strength to get back in. It didn't matter.

I'm not going back without her.

Jack treaded water, looking in all directions as the storm bore down with all its weight on the South Carolina coast.

He shook with anger and fear and . . . loss.

I'm sorry, Lizzie. I'm so sorry.

What if I just stop swimming? What if I just stop?

He would sink to the bottom. He looked at the shore. He could see the lights. His family—what was left of it— was there. Bonnie would raise the boys. He and Mikki would go to join Lizzie.

He looked to the sky again. When a bolt of lightning speared down and lighted the sky, he thought he could see Lizzie's face, her hand reaching out, beckoning to him. He could just stop swimming right now. Right now.

"Daddy!"

Jack turned in the water.

Mikki was barely twenty feet from him. This time the movement of the water had carried him toward her.

Finding a reserve of strength he didn't think he had, Jack exploded through the water. The ocean pushed back at him, throwing up wall after wall of frothing sea to keep him from her. He swam harder and harder, his arms slicing through the water as he fought every counterattack the storm threw at him.

A yard. A foot. Six inches. Every muscle Jack had was screaming in exhaustion, but he fought through the pain.

"Daddy!" She reached out to him.

"Mikki!"

He lunged so hard he nearly came fully out of the water. His hand closed like a vise around her wrist, and he pulled his daughter to him.

She hugged him. "I'm sorry, Daddy, I'm so sorry."

"It's okay, baby. I've got you. Just lie on your back."

She did so, and he put his arms under hers and kicked off toward land.

Now all I've got to do is get us back, thought Jack.

The problem was that when Jack tried to ride a wave in, the undertow snatched him back before he could gain traction on the shore. Then a huge wave forced them both underwater, before Jack brought them back, coughing and half-strangled. Jack was very strong, and as a ranger he'd swum miles in all sorts of awful conditions. But not in the middle of what was now likely a category 1 hurricane with someone else hanging on to him. He was caught in a pendulum, and he couldn't keep it up much longer. He might be able to get to shore by himself, but he was prepared to die with his daughter.

"Jack!"

He looked toward the beach. Liam and Sammy were

standing there with a long coil of rope and screaming at him. Tied to the end of the rope was a red buoy. He nodded to show he understood. Sammy wound up and tossed the rope. It fell far short. He pulled it back and tried again. Closer, but still not close enough.

"Sammy," he screamed. "Wait until the waves push us toward the beach, and then toss it."

Sammy nodded, timed it, and threw the rope. Just a few feet short now. One more time. Jack lunged for the buoy and snagged it. But a monster wave crashed down on them, and Mikki was ripped from him.

He caught a mouthful of water and spit it out. As he looked down, he felt Mikki sliding past him and away from shore, out to sea. Everything was moving in slow motion, reduced to milliseconds of passing time.

"No!" screamed Jack.

He shot his hand down and grabbed his daughter's hair an instant before she was past him and gone forever. Sammy and Liam pulled with all their strength on the rope. Slowly, father and daughter were pulled to shore.

As soon as he hit solid earth, Jack carried Mikki well away from the pounding waves. His daughter was completely limp, her eyes closed.

As Jack bent down, he could see that Mikki was also not breathing. He immediately began to perform mouth-to-mouth resuscitation. He pinched Mikki's nose and blew air into her lungs. He flipped her over and pushed against her back, trying to expand her lungs, forcing the water out.

Sammy called 911 while Jack continued to frantically work on his daughter and was now doing CPR.

A minute later, Jack sat up, his breaths coming in jerks. He looked down at Mikki. She wasn't moving; her skin was instead turning blue. His daughter was dead.

He'd lost her. Failed her.

A crack of lightning pierced the night sky, and Jack looked up, perhaps to that solitary spot his wife had tried to find all those years ago. With a sob he screamed, "Help me, Lizzie, help me. Please."

He looked down. No more miracles left. He'd used the only one he would ever have on himself.

Liam knelt next to Mikki, tears streaming down his face. He touched Mikki's hair and then put his face in his hands and sobbed.

Suddenly Jack felt a force at the back of his neck. At first he thought that Sammy was trying to pull him away from his dead child. But the force wasn't pulling; it was *pushing* him back to her. Jack bent down, took an enormous breath, held it, put his mouth over Mikki's, and blew with all the strength he had left in his body.

As the air fell away from him and into Mikki, everything for Jack stopped, and the storm was gone. It was like he had envisioned dying to be. Quiet, peaceful, isolated, alone. As that breath rushed from him, the events of the last year also raced through his mind.

And now, this; Mikki. Gone.

Jack felt himself drifting away, as though over calm water, propelled to another place, he had no idea where. But he was alone. Lizzie and now Mikki were gone. He no longer wanted to live. It didn't matter anymore. There was peace. But there was also nothing else because he was alone.

The water hitting him in his face brought him back. The thoughts of the past retreated, and he was once more in the present. It was still raining. But that's not what had struck him.

He looked down as Mikki gave another shudder and coughed up the water that had been buried deeply in her lungs. Her eyes opened, fluttered, opened again, and stayed that way. Her pupils focused, and she saw her dad hovering above her. Mikki put out her arms, gripped her father's neck tightly.

"Daddy?" she said in a tiny voice.

Jack sank down and held her. "I'm here, baby. I'm here."

67

The ambulance took Mikki and Jack to the hospital to be checked out. Sammy followed in his van with Liam, while Jenna stayed with the boys at the Palace. Jenna had made hot tea for Bonnie, who had watched Jack's heroic rescue of his daughter from the top of the lighthouse. Now she just sat small and stooped on the edge of the couch, a sob escaping her lips every few seconds.

Jenna had tried to comfort her, while Fred just sat in another chair and stared at his hands. When Sammy called from the hospital and told them they would be home shortly and that everyone was okay, Jenna had finally broken down and wept.

Afterward, Jenna had ventured into Jack's room; she wasn't sure why. As her gaze swept the space, it settled on the letters, which were still lying on the bed. She went over, sat down, picked them up, and started reading.

She emerged from the room ten minutes later, her eyes red with fresh tears. She walked over to Bonnie and tapped her gently on the shoulder. When Bonnie looked up, Jenna said, "I think you need to read these, Mrs. O'Toole."

Bonnie looked confused, but she accepted the letters from Jenna, slipped on her reading glasses, and unfolded the first one.

The storm, its fury rapidly spent after fully hitting land, had largely passed by the time they returned from the hospital. An exhausted Mikki was laid in her bed with Cory and Liam watching over her like guardian angels, counting each one of her breaths.

Jack told everyone that Mikki had suffered no permanent damage and should be as good as new.

"The doctor said she was one strong lady," added Sammy.

"Like her mother," said Jack as he looked at Bonnie.

He passed through the house and went outside and up to the top of the lighthouse. He stared out now at the clearing sky, the sun coming up in the east. He bent down and saw the wires he had spliced the night before. It was a miracle that he had finally spotted the trouble that had befuddled him for so long. Yet a miracle, thought Jack, was somehow what he, however irrationally, had been counting on.

He leaned against the wall of glass and stared out at what looked to be the start of a beautiful late-summer day.

He turned when he heard her.

Bonnie, wheezing slightly, appeared at the opening for the room. He helped her through, and they stood side by side looking at each other.

"Thank God for what you did last night, Jack."

Jack turned and looked back out the window. "It was Lizzie, you know."

"What?" Bonnie moved even closer to him.

Jack said, "I'd given up. Mikki was dead. I didn't have any breath left. She was dead, Bonnie. And I asked Lizzie to help me." He turned to her. "I looked up to the sky and I asked Lizzie to help me." A sob broke from his throat. "And she did. She did. She saved Mikki, not me."

Bonnie nodded slowly. "It was both of you, Jack. You and Lizzie. The match made in Heaven. Two people meant for each other if ever there was."

He stared at her, surprised by the woman's blunt words.

From her pocket she drew out the letters. "I think these belong to you." She handed them back to him and reached out and touched his face. "Sometimes people can't see what's right in front of them, Jack. It's strange how that works. How often it happens. And how often it hurts people we're supposed to love." She paused. "I do love you, son. I guess I always have. And one thing I know for certain is that you loved my daughter. And she loved you. That should have been enough for me." She paused again. "And now, it is."

They exchanged a hug, and she turned to go.

"Bonnie?"

She looked back.

"The kids?" he said in a small voice.

"They're right where they should be, Jack. With their father."

68

When Mikki opened her eyes, the first thing she saw was her dad. Right after that she saw Liam, peering anxiously over Jack's shoulder.

"I'm really okay, guys," she said a little groggily.

Jack smiled and looked at Liam. "Give us a minute, will you?"

Liam nodded, flashed Mikki a reassuring grin, and left the room.

Jack gripped her hand, and she squeezed back. Mikki said, "Sorry for all the excitement I caused. It was really dumb."

"Yes, it was," he agreed. "But we were all under a lot of pressure."

"So the lighthouse finally worked?"

He let out a long breath. "Yeah. If it hadn't . . ." His voice trailed off, and father and daughter started to weep together, each clutching the other, their bodies shaking with the strain.

"I can't believe how close I came to losing you, baby."

"I know, Dad, I know," she said in a hushed voice.

They finally drew apart.

"So what now? We still go with Grandma?"

"No, you're staying right here with me."

Mikki screamed with joy and hugged him again.

"Does Liam know?" she said excitedly.

"No, I thought I'd leave that to you." He rose. "I'll go get him."

As he turned she said, "Dad?"

"Yeah?"

"No matter what happens in my life, you'll always be my hero."

He bent down and touched her cheek. "Thanks . . . Michelle."

Later, as he stood by the doorway watching the two teens excitedly talking and hugging, Jack first smiled, then teared up, and then smiled again. She was clearly not a little girl anymore. And Jack could easily see how fast her life, and his, would change in the next few years.

Later, as Jack walked along the beach, a voice called out, "I'm going to miss you Armstrongs when you go back to Ohio." He turned to see Jenna walking toward him.

"No, you won't," said Jack, "because we're staying right here."

She drew next to him. "Are you sure?"

He smiled. "No, but we're still staying."

She slipped an arm around him. "I'm glad things have worked out."

"I couldn't have done it without you."

"You're way too generous with your praise."

"Seriously, Jenna, you helped in a lot of ways. A lot."

"So what are we going to do about the budding romance?"

"What?" he said in a startled voice.

"Between our kids."

"Oh."

She laughed, and he grinned sheepishly.

"I think we take it one day at a time." He looked directly at her. "Does that sound okay, Jenna?"

"That sounds very okay, Jack."

Epilogue

A little over two years later, Jack sat on the beach in almost the exact spot he and Mikki had occupied the night he'd realized he had so much to live for. The house was quieter now. Mikki and Liam had just left for college. She'd aced her last two years in high school and gone out to Berkeley on a scholarship. Liam the drummer had cut off his hair and was at West Point. Though they were a continent apart, the two remained the best of friends.

Cory was working part-time at the Play House and learning the ropes of theater management from Ned Parker. Jackie had started talking full-blast one morning about a year ago and had never stopped since. Although, Jack noted with some measure of fatherly pride, his favorite toy was still the monster truck.

He got up and made his way to the top of the lighthouse. He hadn't been up here since the morning after almost losing Mikki. He stepped out onto the catwalk and looked toward the sea. His eyes gravitated to the spot where father and daughter had fought so hard for their lives. Then he looked away and up to a clear, blue summer sky.

Lizzie's Lighthouse. It worked when I needed it to.

Jack had two very important things to do today. And the first one was waiting for him down the beach. He left the lighthouse and set off along the sand. His hands rode in his pockets; the words he would say slipped through his mind. As he drew closer, Jack realized that he had just traveled over a half mile by beach and a lifetime by every other measure.

She was there waiting for him by prearrangement. He slipped his arms around Jenna and kissed her. And much like he had done two decades before, Jack knelt down and asked a woman he loved if she would do him the honor of becoming his wife.

Jenna cried and allowed him to slip the ring over her shaky finger. After that they held each other for a long time on that South Carolina beach as a gentle breeze rippled across them.

"Sammy's going to be the best man," Jack said.

"And Liam will be giving me away," Jenna replied. "I love you, Jack."

"I love you too, Jenna."

They kissed again and visited for a while, discussing plans. Then Jack walked back to the Palace. His pace this way was not quite as brisk. The distance seemed a lot longer going back. There was a reason for this.

The first trek had been to create a bridge for his future.

This trip involved him making a painful separation from the past.

He reached the beach in front of his house and sat down in the sand. He pulled out a photo of Lizzie and held it in front of him. It was still nearly impossible for him to believe that she had been gone nearly three years. It just couldn't be. But it was.

He traced the curve of her smile with his finger while he stared into those beautiful green eyes that he always believed would be the last thing he would see in life before passing on. While Jack had just asked another woman to marry him, and this seemed fitting and right in so many ways, he knew that a significant part of him would always love Lizzie. And that this too was fitting and right in so many ways.

Bonnie had been correct about that. Lizzie and Jack had been meant to be together forever if ever two people were. Only sometimes life doesn't match what should be. It just is. And people have to accept it, no matter how hard it may be.

You should respect the past. You should never forget the past. But you can't live there.

And now he had something else to finish. Something very important.

From his windbreaker he pulled out a single piece of paper and a pen. His hand shaking slightly and the tears already sliding down his face, Jack Armstrong touched the pen to the paper and began to write.

> *Dear Lizzie,*
> *A lot has happened that I need to tell you about.*

An hour later he finished the letter with, as always,

> *Love,*
> *Jack*

He sat there for a while, allowing the sun and breeze to dry his tears because for some reason he did not want to wipe them away by hand. He folded the letter carefully and placed it in an envelope marked with the number seven. He put the envelope and the photo of Lizzie in his pocket and walked toward the house.

When he reached the grass, he turned and looked upward. His mouth eased to a smile when he realized what he was looking at. Today, he'd finally found it, after all this time searching.

Right there was the little piece of the sky that contained Heaven. He somehow knew this for certain. Ironically, like so many complexities in life, the answer had been right in front of him the whole time.

"Pop-pop!"

He turned to see Jackie flying toward him. The boy gave a leap, and Jack caught him in midair.

"Hey, buddy."

"What are you doing?"

Jack started to say something and then stopped. He turned so they were both looking out toward the ocean. He pointed to the sky. "Mommy's up there watching us, Jackie."

Jackie looked awestruck. "Mommy?" Jack nodded. Jackie waved to the sky. "Hi, Mom." He blew her a kiss.

Then Jack turned back around and carried his son toward the house. Right before he got there, he slowly looked back at that little patch of blue sky.

Good-bye, Lizzie.
For now.

JACK'S LETTERS

Dear Lizzie,

There are things I want to say to you that I just don't have the breath for anymore. That's why I've decided to write you these letters. I want you to have them after I'm gone. They're not meant to be sad, just my chance to talk to you one more time. When I was healthy you made me happier than any person has a right to be. When I was half a world away, I knew that I was looking at the same sky you were, thinking of the same things you were, wanting to be with you and looking forward to when I could be. You gave me three beautiful children, which is a greater gift than I deserved. I tell you this, though you already know it, because sometimes people don't talk about these things enough. I want you to know that if I could've stayed with you I would have. I fought as hard as I could. I will never understand why I had to be taken from you so soon, but I have accepted it. Yet I want you to know that there is nothing more important to me than you. I loved you from the moment I saw you. And the happiest day of my life was when you agreed to share your life with mine. I promised that I would always be there for you. And my love for you is so strong that even though I won't be there physically, I will be there in every other way. I will watch over you. I will be there if you need to talk. I will never stop loving you. Not even death is powerful enough to overcome my feelings for you. My love for you, Lizzie, is stronger than anything.

Love,
Jack

Dear Lizzie,

Christmas will be here in five days, and I promise that I will make it. I've never broken a promise to you, and I never will. It's hard to say good-bye, but sometimes you have to do things you don't want to. Jackie came to see me a little while ago, and we talked. Well, he talked in Jackie language and I listened. I like to listen to him because I know one day very soon I won't be able to. He's growing up so fast, and I know he probably won't remember his dad, but I know I will live on in your memories. Tell him his dad loved him and wanted the best for him. And I wish I could have thrown the football to him and watched him play baseball. I know he will have a great life.

Cory is a special little boy. He has your sensitivity, your compassion. I know what's happening to me is probably affecting him the most of all the kids. He came and got into bed with me last night. He asked me if it hurt very much. I told him it didn't. He told me to say hello to God when I saw him. And I promised that I would.

And Mikki.

Mikki is the most complicated of all. Not a little girl anymore but not yet an adult either. She is a good kid, though I know you've had your moments with her. She is smart and caring and she loves her brothers. She loves you, though she sometimes doesn't like to show it. My greatest regret with my daughter is letting her grow away from me. It was my fault, not hers. I see that clearly now. I only wish I had seen it that clearly while I still had a chance to do something about it. After I'm gone, please tell her the first time I ever saw her, when I got back from Afghanistan and was still in uniform, there was no prouder father who ever lived. Looking down at her tiny face, I felt the purest joy a human could possibly feel. And I wanted to protect her and never let anything bad ever happen to her. Life doesn't work that way, of course. But tell her that her dad was her biggest fan. And that whatever she does in life, I will always be her biggest fan.

    Love,
    Jack

Dear Lizzie,

Christmas is five days away and it's a good time to reflect on life. Your life. This will be hard. Hard for me to write and hard for you to read, but it needs to be said. You're young and you have many years ahead of you. Cory and Jackie will be with you for many more years. And even Mikki will benefit. I'm talking about you finding someone else, Lizzie.

I know you won't want to at first. You'll even feel guilty about thinking about another man in your life, but, Lizzie, it has to be that way. I cannot allow you to go through the rest of your life alone. It's not fair to you, and it has nothing to do with the love we have for each other. It will not change that at all. It can't. Our love is too strong. It will last forever. But there are many kinds of love, and people have the capacity to love many different people. You are a wonderful person, Lizzie, and you can make someone else's life wonderful. Love is to be shared, not hidden, not hoarded.

And you have much love to share. It doesn't mean you love me any less. And I certainly could never love you more than I already do. But in your heart you will find more love for someone else. And you will make him happy. And he will make you happy. And Jackie especially will have a father to help him grow into a good man. Our son deserves that. Believe me, Lizzie, if it could be any other way, I would make it so. But you have to deal with life as it comes. And I'm trying my best to do just that. I love you too much to accept anything less than your complete and total happiness.

Love,
Jack

Dear Lizzie,

Christmas is almost here, and I promise that I will make it. It will be a great day. Seeing the kids' faces when they open their presents will be better for me than all the medications in the world. I know this has been hard on everyone, especially you and the kids. But I know that your mom and dad have really been a tremendous help to you. I've never gotten to know them as well as I would have liked. Sometimes I feel that your mom thinks you might have married someone better suited to you, more successful. But I know deep down that she cares about me, and I know she loves you and the kids with all her heart. It is a blessing to have someone like that to support you. My father died, as you know, when I was still just a kid. And you know about my mom. But your parents have always been there for me, especially Bonnie, and in many ways, I see her as more of a mom to me than my own mother. It's action, not words, that really counts. That's what it really means to love someone. Please tell them that I always had the greatest respect for her and Fred. They are good people. And I hope that one day she will feel that I was a good father who tried to do the right thing. And that maybe I was worthy of you.

Love,
Jack

Dear Lizzie,

As I've watched things from my bed, I have a confession to make to you. And an apology. I haven't been a very good husband or father. Half our marriage I was fighting a war, and the other half I was working too hard. I heard once that no one would like to have on their tombstone that they wished they'd spent more time at work. I guess I fall into that category, but it's too late for me to change now. I had my chance. When I see the kids coming and going, I realize how much I missed. Mikki already is grown up with her own life. Cory is complex and quiet. Even Jackie has his own personality. And I missed most of it. My greatest regret in life will be leaving you long before I should. My second greatest regret is not being more involved in my children's lives. I guess I thought I would have more time to make up for it, but that's not really an excuse. It's sad when you realize the most important things in life too late to do anything about them. They say Christmas is the season of second chances. My hope is to make these last few days my second chance to do the right thing for the people that I love the most.

Love,
Jack

Acknowledgements

To Michelle, for taking the journey with me.

To Mitch Hoffman, for readily jumping in with both feet on something so different.

To David Young and Jamie Raab, for allowing me to stretch.

To Emi Battaglia, Jennifer Romanello, Chris Barba, Karen Torres, Tom Maciag, Maja Thomas, Martha Otis, Anthony Goff, Michele McGonigle and Kim Hoffman, and all others at Grand Central, for their unparalleled support.

To Aaron and Arleen Priest, Lucy Child, Lisa Erbach Vance, Nicole James, Frances Jalet-Miller, and John Richmond, for carrying the laboring oar so much.

To Maria Rejt, Trisha Jackson, and Katie James at Pan Macmillan, for so successfully building my career across the waters.

To Eileen Chetti, for a superb copyediting job.

To Grace MyQuade and Lynn Goldberg, for doing what you do so damn well.

To Lynette and Natasha, for keeping the home fires well lit and burning robustly.

extracts reading groups

competitions books new

discounts extracts extracts events

competitions discounts

books extracts reading groups

new extracts events reading groups

events books

extracts new titles reading groups

interviews

events extracts extracts books

discounts events

new books events

events new events

discounts extracts discounts

www.panmacmillan.com

extracts events reading groups

competitions books extracts new